'A rambunctious storyline with cleverly integrated meditations on racism, miscegenation, self-loathing, and the construction of identity. Riveting' *Village Voice*

'Hugely impressive . . . there is writing here of real power and originality' *Evening Standard*

'A laugh-out-loud satire, a bawdy romp that wears its intellectual vigour and sheer perceptiveness almost casually' *Mirror*

'Fantastic, beautifully written. Kunzru has created a wonderfully flowing novel which makes you chuckle in recognition' *Sentinel Sunday*

'Witty, engrossing . . . brilliantly succeeds' *Los Angeles Times*

'A smart novel about an identity crisis . . . a lot of fun' *The Times Literary Supplement*

'Utterly fresh and invigorating . . . I roared through this story and many times burst into hysterical laughter. Epic' *Punch*

'An impressive, highly enjoyable debut, sparkling with tragi-comic wit' *Economist*

'A rich, imaginative story. Kunzru writes with the elegance and sure-footedness of someone born to tell stories' *Arizona Republic*

'Expert, ambitious, excellent, intriguing. A remarkable book' *New York Magazine*

'An uproarious quest of identity. You'll be picking yourself off the floor where you've been rolling around laughing, giving vent to a glory hallelujah for a novelist like Kunzru' *Business Standard*, India

'Witty, profound and beautifully written. Kunzru has created one of the most engaging characters of recent fiction [and] produced one of the great books of the year' *Metro*

'Exhilarating' *India Today*

'An epic on a grand scale' *Wallpaper*

ABOUT THE AUTHOR

Hari Kunzru was born in 1969 and lives in south-east London. He was an associate editor at *Wired* and was named the *Observer* Young Travel Writer of the Year in 1999. He is a contributing editor of *Mute* magazine and music editor at *Wallpaper*. *The Impressionist* was the winner of the Betty Trask Prize 2002 and the Pendleton May First Novel Award, and shortlisted for the *Guardian* First Book Award and the Whitbread First Novel Award. Hari Kunzru was named one of *Granta*'s 20 Best of Young British Novelists, 2003. This is his first novel.

The Impressionist

HARI KUNZRU

PENGUIN BOOKS

PENGUIN BOOKS

Published by the Penguin Group
Penguin Books Ltd, 80 Strand, London WC2R 0RL, England
Penguin Putnam Inc., 375 Hudson Street, New York, New York 10014, USA
Penguin Books Australia Ltd, 250 Camberwell Road,
Camberwell, Victoria 3124, Australia
Penguin Books Canada Ltd, 10 Alcorn Avenue, Toronto, Ontario, Canada M4V 3B2
Penguin Books India (P) Ltd, 11 Community Centre,
Panchsheel Park, New Delhi – 110 017, India
Penguin Books (NZ) Ltd, Cnr Rosedale and Airborne Roads,
Albany, Auckland, New Zealand
Penguin Books (South Africa) (Pty) Ltd, 24 Sturdee Avenue,
Rosebank 2196, South Africa

Penguin Books Ltd, Registered Offices: 80 Strand, London WC2R 0RL, England

www.penguin.com

First published by Hamish Hamilton 2002
Published in Penguin Books 2003
17

Set in Monotype Dante
Printed in England by Clays Ltd, St Ives plc

'Remember, I can change swiftly. It will all be as it was when I first spoke to thee under Zam-Zammah the great gun –'

'As a boy in the dress of white men – when I first went to the Wonder House. And a second time thou wast a Hindu. What shall the third incarnation be?'

Rudyard Kipling, *Kim*

Contents

Pran Nath

One afternoon, three years after the beginning of the new century, red dust which was once rich mountain soil quivers in the air. It falls on a rider who is making slow progress through the ravines which score the plains south of the mountains, drying his throat, filming his clothes, clogging the pores of his pink perspiring English face.

His name is Ronald Forrester, and dust is his speciality. Or rather, his speciality is fighting dust. In the European club at Simla they never tire of the joke: *Forrester the forester*. Once or twice, he tried to explain it to his Indian subordinates in the department, but they failed to see the humour. They assumed the name came with the job. Forester Sahib. Like Engineer Sahib, or Mr Judge.

Forrester Sahib fights the dust with trees. He has spent seven years up in the mountains, riding around eroded hillsides, planting sheltering belts of saplings, educating his peasants about soil conservation and enforcing ordinances banning logging and unlicensed grazing. Thus he is the first to appreciate the irony of his current situation. Even now, on leave, his work is following him around.

He takes a gulp from a flask of brackish water and strains in the saddle as his horse slips and rights itself, sending stones bouncing down a steep, dry slope. It is late afternoon, so at least the heat is easing off. Above him the sky is smudged by blue-black clouds, pregnant with the monsoon which will break any day. He wills it to come soon.

Forrester came down to this country precisely because it has no trees. Back at his station, sitting on the veranda of the Government Bungalow, he had the perverse idea that tree-lessness might make for a restful tour. Now he is here he does not like it. This is desolate country. Even the shooting is desultory. Save for the villagers' sparse crops, painstakingly watered by a network of dykes and canals, the only plants are tufts of sharp yellow grass and stunted thorn bushes. Amid all this desiccation he feels uncomfortable, dislocated.

As the sun heats up his tent in the mornings, Forrester has accelerated military-march-time dreams. Dreams of trees. Regiments of deodars, striding up hill and down dale like coniferous redcoats. Neem, sal and rosewood. Banyans that spawn roots like tentacles, black foliage blotting out the blue of the sky. Even English trees make an appearance, trees he has not seen for years. Oddly shaped oaks and drooping willows mutate in lock-step as he tosses and turns. The dreams eject him sweating and unrested, irritated that his forests have been twisted into something agitated, silly. A sideshow. A musical comedy of trees. Before he has had time to shave, red rivulets of sweat and dust will be running off his forehead. He has, he knows, only himself to blame. Everyone said it was a stupid time of year to come south.

If asked, Forrester would find it difficult to say what he is doing here. Perhaps he came out of perversity, because it is the season when everyone else travels north to the cool of the hills. He has spent three weeks riding around, looking for something. He is not sure what. Something to fill a gap. Until recently, his life in the hills had seemed enough. Lonely, certainly. Unlike some, Forrester talks to his staff, and is genuinely interested in the details of their lives. But differences of race are hard to overcome, and even at the university he was never the social type. There was always a distance.

More conventional men would have identified the gap as

woman-shaped, and spent their leave wife-hunting at tea parties and polo matches in Simla. Instead Forrester, difficult, taciturn, decided to see what life was like without trees. He has found he does not care for it. This is progress, of a sort. To Forrester, the trick of living lies principally in sorting out what one likes from what one does not. His difficulty is that he has always found so little to put on the plus side of the balance sheet. And so he rides through the ravines, a khaki-clad vacancy, dreaming of trees and waiting for something, anything, to fill him up.

That something is no more than a mile off as the crow flies, though with the undulations of the dirt track, the distance is probably doubled. As the sun sinks lower, Forrester makes out a glint of light on metal and a flash of pink against the dun-coloured earth. He halts and watches, feeling his jaw become inexplicably tight, stiffening in the saddle like a cavalryman on parade. He has seen no one for the last day and a half. Gradually he discerns a party of men, Rajput villagers by the looks of them, leading camels and escorting a curtained palanquin, bumpily carried at shoulder height by four of their number.

By the time the party is within hailing distance, the sun has dipped almost to the horizon. Bands of angry red show against a wall of thick grey cloud. Forrester waits, his horse stamping its hoofs on one bank of a dried-up stream bed. The palanquin-bearers stop a little way off and put down their load. Heads swathed in enormous pink turbans, moustaches teased out to extravagant length, they appraise the sweating Englishman like buyers eyeing up a bullock. Eight sets of black eyes, curious and impassive. Forrester's hand flutters involuntarily up to his neck.

From the rear pops up a lean middle-aged man, clad in a dhoti and a grubby white shirt, a black umbrella under his arm. He looks like a railway clerk or a personal tutor, his appearance strange and jarring against the waste land. He is clearly in charge, and just as clearly irked that his servants have not waited for

instructions to halt. Shouldering his way forward, he salaams
Forrester, who touches the brim of his topi in response. Forrester
is about to speak to him in Hindi, when the man salutes him in
English.

'Looks like rain, what?'

They both peer up at the sky. As if in response, a fat drop of
water lands on Forrester's face.

Fire and water. Earth and air. Meditate on these oppositions and
reconcile them. Collapse them in on themselves, send them
spiralling down a tunnel of blackness to re-emerge whole, one
with the all, mere aspects of the great unity of things whose
name is God. Thought can travel on in this manner, from part
to whole, smooth as the touch of the masseur's oiled hands in
the hammam. Amrita wishes she could carry on thinking for
ever. That would be true sweetness! But she is only a woman,
and for ever will not be granted her. In the absence of infinity,
she will settle for spinning out what time she has, teasing it into
a fine thread.

Inside the palanquin it is hot and close, the smells of food and
stale sweat and rosewater mingling with another smell, sharp
and bitter. Once again Amrita's hand reaches out for the little
sandalwood box of pills. She watches the hand as she would a
snake sliding across a flagstone floor, with detachment and an
edge of revulsion. Yes, it is her hand, but only for now, only for
a while. Amrita knows that she is not her body. This crab-like
object, fiddling with box and key and pellets of sticky black resin,
belongs to her only as does a shawl or a piece of jewellery.

A bump. They have stopped. Outside there are voices. Amrita
rejoices. At nineteen years old, this is will be her last journey,
and any delay is cause for celebration. She swallows another
opium pellet, tasting the bitter resin on her tongue.

*

As it does every year, the wind has blown steadily out of the south-west, rolling its cargo of doughy air across the plain to slap hard against the mountains. For days, weeks, the air has funnelled upwards, cooling as it rises, spinning vast towers of condensation over the peaks. Now these hanging gardens of cloud have ripened to the point where they can no longer maintain themselves.

So, the rain.

It falls first over the mountains, an unimaginable shock of water. Caught in the open, herdsmen and woodcutters pull their shawls over their heads and run for shelter. Then in a chain reaction, cloud speaking to cloud, the rain rolls over the foothills, dousing fires, battering on roofs, bringing smiles to the faces of the people who run outside to greet it, the water for which they have been waiting so long.

Finally it comes to the desert. As it starts to fall, Forrester listens to the grubby brahmin's chit-chat, and hears himself tetchily agreeing that now would be a good time and here a good place to camp. Perhaps this Moti Lal is offended by his brusqueness, but Forrester can't worry about that. His eyes are fixed on the palanquin, the grumpy maid fussing around its embroidered curtain. Its occupant has not even ventured a peek outside. He wonders if she is ill, or very old.

Soon the rain is falling steadily, swollen droplets splashing into the dust like little bombs. Camels fidget and grumble as they are hobbled. Servants run around unpacking bags. Moti Lal keeps up a steady stream of conversation as Forrester dismounts and unsaddles his horse. Moti Lal is not the master here, oh no, just a trusted family retainer. It has fallen to him, the duty of escorting the young mistress to her uncle's house in Agra. Most unusual, of course, but there are extenuating circumstances.

Extenuating circumstances? What is the bloody fool on about? Forrester asks where they have come from, and the man names a small town at least two hundred miles west of where they stand.

'And you have walked all the way?'

'Yes, sir. The young mistress says walk only.'

'Why on earth didn't you go by rail? Agra is hundreds of miles from here.'

'Unfortunately train is out of the question. Such are extenuating circumstances, you see.'

Forrester does not see, but at the moment he is far more concerned with erecting his tent before the rain worsens. It seems to be getting stronger by the second. Moti Lal puts up his umbrella and stands over the Englishman as he bashes in pegs, just close enough to get in his way without actually offering any shelter. Forrester curses under his breath, while all the time the thought circulates in his head: so she is a young woman.

Rain drips through the ceiling and lands in her lap, darkening red silk with circles of black. Amrita turns her face upwards and sticks out her tongue. The rain sounds heavy. Outside it is dark, and perhaps, though she is not sure, she feels cold. To ward off the feeling she imagines heat, calling up memories of walking on the roof of her father's haveli in summertime. Vividly she senses the burning air on her arms and face. She hears the thud of carpets being beaten and the swish of brooms as the maids sweep sand from the floors. But heat leads on to thoughts of her father, of walking round the pyre as the priest throws on ghee to make it flame, and she recoils back to the dark and cold. Drops of water land on her forehead, on one cheek, on her tongue. Soon the rain is pouring through in a constant stream. The soaked curtains start to flap limply against her side. The wind is rising, and still no one has come for her. No one has even told her what is happening. With no mother or father she is mistress now. If only she could gather the energy to assert herself.

Amrita unlocks her box, shielding it from the water. She is to be delivered to her uncle, and that will be an end. He writes that he has already found her a husband. At least, said the old women, she will arrive with a good dowry. So much better off than other girls. She should thank God.

Within half an hour the dust has turned to mud. Despite his tent, Forrester is drenched. He clambers to the top of a hill and looks out over the desert, scored by a fingerprint whorl of valleys and ridges. There is no shelter. As the wind tugs at his topi and forked lightning divides the sky into fleeting segments, he is struck by the thought that perhaps he has been a fool. His red-brown world has turned grey, solid curtains of water obscuring the horizon. Here he is, out in the middle of it, not a tree in sight. He is the tallest thing in this barren landscape, and he feels exposed. Looking back down at his tent, set at the bottom of a deep gully, he wonders how long the storm will last. The Indians are still struggling to put up their own shelters, fumbling with rope and pegs. Amazingly, the palanquin is still where they discarded it. If he had not been told otherwise, he would have sworn the thing must be empty.

Before long, a trickle of muddy water is flowing through the gully, separating Forrester's army tent from the Indians' contraptions of tarpaulin and bamboo. A fire is out of the question, and so the bearers are huddled together forlornly, squatting on their haunches like a gaggle of bidi-smoking birds. Moti Lal climbs the ridge to engage Forrester in another pointless conversation, then follows him back down the hill and crouches at the door of the tent. Finally Forrester is forced to give in and talk.

'So who exactly is your mistress?'

Moti Lal's face darkens.

She was always ungovernable, even before her mother died. Her father took no notice of her, whether she was good or bad, too busy weighing out coin to bother about the world outside his cloth-bound ledgers. The servants would come and report to him in the counting house, saying that the girl had thrown a cup at the porter, that she refused food, that she had been seen speaking to Bikaneri tribeswomen by the Cremation Gate. In the mornings her maid would find sand when she was combing her hair, as if she had spent the night out in the desert.

She was bringing shame on the family, and if the master chose to ignore it, the job of curbing her fell to his head clerk. At first Moti Lal used words. Then, when he found a cake of sticky black resin in her jewellery box, he dragged her into the courtyard and beat her with a carved stick kept for scaring away monkeys. She was locked in her room for three days. Distracted, as he was finalizing a land deal, the master asked who was weeping in his house. Told it was Amrita, he seemed surprised. Does she want for something, he asked.

As soon as the bolt was drawn, she disappeared, returning with a wild look in her eye and garbled talk of trees and rushing water. Moti Lal could never find who brought the drug to her, and gradually she lost interest in everything else. She took to her bed, and stopped speaking. It was as if she had withdrawn to another world. He had to shake her and slap her face before she understood the news about her father.

His killer had left a length of wire wrapped tightly around his neck. The body had been found lying on a rubbish heap outside the town walls, the soles of its feet turned up at the sky like two pale fish. No one seemed surprised. Moneylenders are not popular people. Do you understand, Moti Lal shouted at her. Now you are completely alone.

Now the flood is coming. The earth will be drowned, but, like Manu the first man, Amrita will float on the ocean and be saved.

She cups her hands and sees a little fish flip and curl in the rainwater. She will show it compassion because it is the Lord come to her as a sign, and though she is cold to the bone, the little horned fish means that she will survive.

They do not come to get her. The water saturates the palanquin, soaking the curtains and the cushions, running over the wooden frame in a constant stream. Amrita has no shawl, and the thin sari plastered over her skin offers no protection. She does not expect them to come. Moti Lal hates her and wants her dead. Why should he help her? She should move, but it will make no difference. The flood is imminent, and when it comes it will lift her up and sweep all of them away.

When it was time for the journey, Moti Lal had the haveli closed and the valuables packed into trunks which went on ahead with one of the servants. In the street, carts waited outside to take them to the railhead, three days' journey by road. Shopkeepers sat by their scales and spat betel-juice into the gutter, pointing out to each other the possessions of the murdered Kashmiri broker: his carpets, his scales. The bullocks swished their tails and the drivers scratched themselves. Everything was ready. And the girl would not go.

Moti Lal beat her and she lay on the floor and said she would kill herself. Moti Lal beat her again, and told her he did not care if she lived or died, but he had given his word to her uncle that he would bring her to Agra to be married. She said she had no uncle in Agra and marriage meant nothing to her because soon she would be dead. Moti Lal beat her until his arm was sore. When her face had puffed up and a tooth had loosened in her jaw she said she would go, but not by train. Finally, he gave in.

Moti Lal gave in and now he has been walking for weeks across country, the sweat running off his balding pate, while inside her palanquin Amrita lies still and has visions. Every day as he slips his feet into his dusty chappals, he finds it more absurd. He is a trusted man, a man with a position and a certificate, and he is trudging across country like a beggar. Every day as he squats for his morning evacuation, a thought bubbles up in his mind – that her will is stronger than his. The girl does not care if she dies. It is as if she is taunting him.

So maybe she deserves to be left here, in the rain and the cold. If she dies of exposure, it will be God's work. Then he can board the train and read a pamphlet and drink station chai out of a glass, knowing all this is behind him. He marvels that the slut, for all her stubbornness, will not even drag her carcass under-cover where it is dry. The water is pouring down with a strength he has not seen before, tearing out of the sky like blood from an open wound.

All the world is in the past. Now there is nothing but a torrent of white water rushing down a mountain, and the future is contained in that water, suspended in it like the tree trunks and thick red mud it has swept off the hillside. The water moves at an extraordinary pace, propelled downwards as if by a great hand, and it rushes over the desert like an army, forced through narrow clefts in the earth until it arrives in the gully where Forrester kneels, wrestling a loose tent peg back into the slack wet ground. He looks up, and it appears in front of him, a huge white wall.

'Oh God –' he begins, giving it a name. Then he is engulfed.

The palanquin smashes like a child's toy, and Amrita smiles as the night explodes into a vast rush, the force she has longed for since she can first remember. Camels bray and strain at their hobbles, turning end over end in the water as they try desperately to free themselves. Men and bags are sucked down, barrelling along in the flood. For an instant Moti Lal keeps hold of his umbrella, standing bolt upright in roiling foam with a looks-like-rain expression on his face. Then he is swept under, and the umbrella goes skating off across the swell. As his lungs fill with water, he thinks with irritation about the expense of replacing it. Then, one more bead flicked across the abacus, one more column of figures completed with a stroke of the pen, he drowns. All the world is in the past.

This should be everything. Yet small miracles are woven into the pattern of every large event. Forrester finds himself snagged on something. White water screams round his chest but leaves his head clear, his mouth and nose free to breathe. When small hands clasp his wrists and help him up out of the flood, he ceases to understand what is happening to him. His consciousness is entirely adrift.

He scrambles up a slope and falls to his hands and knees, still reflexively gulping for breath. Gradually he realizes that he is somewhere dry and dark, and stands up. The mouth of a cave. Again, the touch of fingers. He recoils, then collects himself and allows his wrist to be grasped. The hand guides him further in. He kneels down a second time, not entirely trusting his legs to follow orders. He tries to breathe more slowly. It is no good. When a fire flickers into existence, he is convinced that he has died.

The native mother goddess stands before him in the firelight, elemental and ferocious. Her body is smeared with mud. A wild tangle of hair hangs over her face. She is entirely naked. Kneeling, he flushes and averts his eyes, awed by the black-tipped breasts, the curve of the belly, the small tight mat of pubic hair. So much more real than the girls who populate his wakeful nights in the mountains. Those are picture-postcard girls, flimsy as lace. They peep back over parasols, milk white and rosy-cheeked, asking oh will you not come into the garden my dear.

Forrester realizes he is in the presence of a spirit. He died in the flood and this is some kind of phenomenon, the sort of thing one tries to conjure up with table rapping and Ouija boards. But she seems real, this goddess. Shaped out of the raw clay by the flood. He wonders if he has created her, sculpted her with his sleepless nights and his meanderings through the desert. Perhaps, he reasons, if you lack something enough you can force it into being.

Then she steps towards him and starts to unbutton his shirt, and as she does so he feels the tug of fingers on button and wet hair against his cheek and smells her clean rich smell of woman and mud and hair oil. His hands brush over her skin and they touch real skin cut and scratched by stones and branches and he knows he has not created her at all. She clears her hair out of her eyes and looks directly at him, and with a start Forrester realizes that it is the other way around. He has not created her. She has created him. He has not, never will have, any other purpose than the one she gives him.

As the fire crackles and dries his skin, she strips him of his clothing, and he does not even wonder that he is in a warm dusty place with brass water pots and a stack of brushwood piled neatly against one wall. Outside the storm is raging and inside the cave her small hands are curling round his penis and tugging him down in a tumble of limbs on to the floor.

The flood comes and the whole world is swept away except Amrita. The water shakes and paws her, unwrapping her from her sari, batting her around like a huge rough dog. Then it sets her down and she slips out of it, shivering at the sear of the wind on her bare skin. Objects stream past her in the dim light, men and beasts and valuables, the things of the defunct world being swept off into oblivion.

That is the old world and she is the mother of the new. She peers into the watery darkness and pulls a pearl-skinned man out of the flood. He is panting like a baby. The raw heavy sound of his breathing excites her.

Amrita drags the pearl man backwards and a roof closes over them. He falls on the floor. She looks around. Everything is there, everything they could need. So the mother of the world squats with flint and tinder and lights a fire and looks at her find. He has no colour at all, face and hair washed clean and pure as milk. He is wearing wet feringhi clothes, which she takes off. He seems very helpless, lifting up his arms to assist her with his shirt, putting a hand on her shoulder as he steps out of his khaki shorts.

Then he is naked, and although he is helpless he is very beautiful. Amrita traces the line of his hip, the arrow of hair leading down from his navel. In small extraordinary stages, his hands start to return her touch, and soon she does something she has only imagined, and pulls him downwards.

Their sex is inexpert and violent, more fight than sex as they roll and claw across the packed earth floor. It happens quickly and then for a long time they lie tangled together and breathing hard. The unprecedented sensations of each other's bodies make them start again and they do this twice more, roll and claw, then lie exquisitely, drunkenly still. By the last time the fire has guttered, and sweat and dust has turned their skins to an identical red-brown colour. The colour of the earth.

They lie until the fire has died out completely. Then, in an instant, something tiny sparks in Forrester's brain. This small thing cascades into something larger and potentially threatening and he takes a shot at giving it a name and fails, though he thinks it may be something to do with duty and India Office ordinances, and this thing which now seems enormous and important and panic-inducing makes him leap to his feet and stagger backwards, turning round to try to confront it or at least have some idea of its shape and meaning. Perhaps it is unnameable, the unnameable thing which strikes a lost man whose sole short purpose has just been achieved, but, whether or not it can be named, it makes Forrester look at the girl wildly and understand nothing about why and where he is, except to know that he has changed everything about his life and cannot see where it will lead.

So Forrester wheels round and steps out of the cave and down to the edge of the water, which has formed itself into a fast-flowing red river. As he rubs his eyes and straightens his back and tries to control his panic, he sees, with a surge of joy, something coming towards him that he knows. A young deodar tree, snapped off at the trunk, is sailing towards him down the flooded gully, its branches quivering like the beginning of speech. The tree seems so freighted with wisdom and routine that it might as well be playing the National Anthem, and Forrester lets out an incoherent cry and hails it like a cab and jumps on and is swept away. The last Amrita sees of him is a mud-streaked torso heading downstream, continuing the journey she interrupted a few hours before.

In 1918 Agra is a city of three hundred thousand people clenched fist-tight round a bend in the River Jamuna. Wide and lazy, the river flows to the south and east where eventually it will join with the Ganges and spill out into the Bay of Bengal. This, one of countless towns fastened to its banks, is an anthill of traders and craftsmen which rose out of obscurity around five hundred years before, when the Mughals, arriving from the north, settled on it as a place to build tombs, paint miniatures and dream up new and bloodier modes of war.

If, like the flying ace Indra Lal Roy, you could break free of gravity and view the world from up above, you would see Agra as a dense, whirling movement of earth, a vortex of mud-bricks and sandstone. To the south this tumble of mazy streets slams into the military grid of the British Cantonment. The Cantonment (gruffly contracted to Cantt. in all official correspondence) is made up of geometric elements like a child's wooden blocks; rational avenues and parade grounds, barracks for the soldiers who enforce the law of His Britannic Majesty George. To the north this military space has a mirror in the Civil Lines, rows of whitewashed bungalows inhabited by administrators and their wives. The hardness of this second grid has faded and softened with time, past planning wilting gently in the Indian heat.

Agra's navel is the Fort, a mile-long circuit of brutal red sandstone walls enclosing a confusion of palaces, mosques, water tanks and meeting halls. A railway bridge runs beside it, carrying passengers into the city from every part of India. The bustling crowd at Fort Station never thins, even in the small hours of the morning. The crowd is part of the grand project of the railway, the dream of unification its imperial designers have engineered into reality. The trails of boiler-smoke which rise over heat-hazy fields and converge on the station's packed platforms are part of a continent-wide piece of theatre. Like the 103 tunnels blasted through the mountains up to Simla, the two-mile span of the Ganges Bridge in Bihar and the 140-foot piles driven into the mud of Surat, the press of people at the station proclaims the power of the British, the technologists who have all India under their control.

For such a lively city, Agra is heavily marked by death. This is largely the fault of the Mughals, who, in contrast to the current mechanically minded set of masters, thought hard about the next life and the things which get lost in the transition from this one. Everywhere they have left cavernous mosques, chilly monuments to absence. Round the curve of the river from the Fort is the Taj Mahal. For all its massive marble beauty, for all the relief its cold floor and dark interior afford on a scorching day, it is a melancholy place, forty million rupees and who knows how many lives' worth of autocratic mourning. The Emperor Shah Jahan loved Mumtaz-i-Mahal. Now the pain of his loss rises up at the edge of town, clothed in the work of countless hands, surrounded by a formal garden still used as a meeting place by steam-age lovers. Despite all this effort love still refuses to conquer, and the trysting couples have a subdued, pensive look about them.

Now, as it does every so often, death has come to hang over the city. This time the killer is not siege or famine but the influenza epidemic, making its way eastwards across the world from its mystical birth in a pile of dung behind an American army camp. By the time it leaves it will have taken with it a third of Agra's people: a third of all the shoemakers, potters, silk weavers and metalworkers in the bazaars; a third of the women pounding their washing against flat stones by the river bank; a third of the six hundred hands at John's ginning mill; a third of the convicts making rugs in the city gaol; a third of all the farmers bringing produce in to market; a third of the porters sleeping on the station platform between shifts; a third of the little boys playing shin-shattering games of cricket, bowling yorkers off the baked mud of their tenement courtyards. Rajputs, Brahmins, Chamars, Jats, Baniyas, Muslims, Catholics, members of the Arya Samaj and communicants of the Church of England will all succumb to the same sequence of fatigue, sweating, fever and darkness.

Across the world, the scale of this killing is even greater than the slaughter that is finally playing itself out in Europe. Here, it hangs like a miasma over the knot of streets near Drummond Road, the quarter of the city called Johri Bazaar where the jewellers have their shops. Now, like the pilot Roy, trailing black smoke over faraway London, plummet down into the middle of all this death, to a large, impressive house cut off from the street noise by high brick walls. Swoop down over the parapet topped with shards of broken glass to a low flat roof, a place where a boy reclines on a charpai, one hand working steadily inside his pyjamas.

Pran Nath Razdan is not thinking about death. Quite the opposite. The bazaars may be empty and the corridors of the Thomason Hospital clogged with corpses, but none of it has anything to do with him. At the age of fifteen, his world is comfortably circumscribed by the walls of his family house. The only son of the distinguished court pleader Pandit Amar Nath Razdan, he is heir to a fortune of many lakhs of rupees and future owner of the roof he lies on, along with all the courtyards and gardens, the cool high-ceilinged rooms, the servants' quarters and the innovative European-style toilet block. Further afield there are other houses, a brace of villages, a boot-blacking business in Lucknow and a share in a silk-weaving concern. When he glimpses his future, it seems full of promise.

With a sigh, he looks down at the tent in his raw-silk pyjamas. Full of promise. Money is the least of it. Clearly he is loved by everyone. His father will not hear a word spoken against him. The servants smile as they struggle upstairs with his bath water. When his aunties come to visit, they pinch his cheeks and coo like excited doves. Pran Nath, so beautiful! So pale! Such a perfect Kashmiri!

Pran Nath is undeniably good-looking. His hair has a hint of copper to it which catches in the sunlight and reminds people of the hills. His eyes contain just a touch of green. His cheekbones are high and prominent, and across them, like an expensive drumhead, is stretched a covering of skin that is not brown or even wheaten-coloured, but *white*. Pran Nath's skin is a source of pride to everyone. Its whiteness is not the nasty blue-blotched colour of a fresh-off-the-boat Angrezi or the greyish pallor of a dying person, but a perfect milky hue, like that of the marble the craftsmen chip into ornate screens down by the Tajganj. Kashmiris come from the mountains and are always fair, but Pran Nath's colour is exceptional. It is proof, cluck the aunties, of the family's superior blood.

Blood is important. As Kashmiri Pandits, the Razdans belong to one of the highest and most exclusive castes in all Hindustan. Across the land (as any of them will be happy to remind you) the Pandits are known for their intelligence and culture. Princes often call on them to serve as ministers of state, and it is said that a Kashmiri Pandit was the first to write down the Vedas. The Razdan family guru can recite their lineage back hundreds of years, back to the time before the valley was overrun by Muslims, and they had to leave to make a new life on the plains. The blood stiffening the bulge in Pran Nath's pyjamas is of the highest quality, guaranteed.

Pran Nath is not alone on the roof. The servant girl's choli has ridden up her back, exposing a swathe of smooth dark flesh and a ridge of spine. She is sweating, this girl, her skin glistening in the sunshine, her broom held loosely in one hand as she sniffs the air, catching the strong smell of raw onions wafting up from the master's bedchamber. Beneath her many-times-washed cotton sari he can make out the curve of her buttocks, which was the original stimulus for unlacing his pyjamas. Somehow looking is no longer enough. She is not far away. He could grab her, and pull her down on the bolsters. There would be a fuss, of course, but his father could smooth it over. She is only a servant, after all.

Gita the servant girl has no idea of her peril. Her eye has been caught by a monkey, and she is thinking how nice it would be if it spoke. Perhaps the monkey has been sent by her prince to watch over her, and perhaps it will grow to an enormous size and put her on its furry shoulder and carry her off to a palace where there will be a wedding with singers and dancing – or if not a prince then at least the monkey could turn into the pretty boy who cleans for the fat Baniya druggist, or if not a shape-changing monkey then a talking monkey which could tell her fortune, and if not a fortune telling monkey then one which would do something more to distract her from her aching back than just sitting there, scratching its lurid red bottom and rolling its lips backwards and forwards over its nasty teeth. She straightens up and wipes a hand over her forehead. As usual there is more work to do.

For its part, the monkey has no intention of changing shape. Lacking royal connections or powers of augury, its primary interest is the strong onion smell wafting under its nostrils. Onions are edible. It sits on a crumbling section of wall and cocks its head at a shape it has spotted moving about in an open doorway, unable to decide whether it too is edible, or perhaps dangerous.

The shape is Anjali the maid, and she is trying to stay out of sight. It is lucky she came. Something told her, a tightness at her temples, that she should keep a close eye on her daughter today. Look at the filthy boy! If he touches so much as a hair on little Gita's head, he will pay for it. This is not an idle threat. Anjali the maid knows things about Pran Nath Razdan. In fact she knows rather more than he does himself. One touch, and she will tell.

Anjali was brought up in the moneylender's house at the edge of the desert. Some years older than the moneylender's daughter, she had been placed with the family as a maid as soon as she was old enough to plait hair and wield a flat iron. She watched her young mistress withdraw from the world, and tended to her as she lay inert on her bed, transfixed by the invisible objects of her imagination. Among the servants, Amrita's madness was said to be of that very holy type which reveals the illusory nature of the world. Some of the women would even contrive to touch her clothing when they brought her tea. Anjali was not one of them. She found the girl frightening. Trying to get Amrita to take a sip of water or a mouthful of dal, she would stretch her arm out straight, keeping herself as far from the bed as she could, on guard against evil spirits which might jump from the afflicted body to hers. When she was told she would be accompanying her on the journey to Agra, the first thing she did was consult a palmist, who told her to beware of water.

Perhaps it was this advice which saved her. After the flash-flood, she and two of the porters were the only ones still left alive, or so they thought. Searching for other survivors, they waded down a gully until they found a dacoits' cave, with Amrita sitting outside it, dressed in a khaki shirt and a pair of shorts. They pulled the Englishman's naked body out of the mud a few miles further south. It was not hard to imagine what had happened.

Amrita mumbled poetry-words about trees, and about the water. Anjali dressed her in a sari and made her decent, repeating charms to ward off the evil eye. Inside the shirt pocket was an illegible document, with a photograph of the dead Englishman. She slipped the picture discreetly into her skirts. Once they finally reached Agra, pulling into Fort Station on the third-class carriage of the train, she lost no time in breaking the shocking news to the servants of her new household. The girl had polluted herself. Surely she would have to be sent away.

In the uncle's house, Anjali was locked in an upstairs room, while the uncle held meetings with brothers and cousins. Then one of them summoned the girl and gave her a silver bangle, a nose stud and a pair of heavy earrings. She understood that she was to keep her mouth shut. They had found a husband for Amrita, a Razdan, and they would not tolerate any impediment to the marriage. Had anyone asked her opinion, Anjali would have said she thought it was an ill-fated match. She had often seen the girl naked. She had examined her closely, and she had a mole on her stomach, right at the very centre just under her breasts. The meaning, as she whispered to the mali, was clear. The new bride would die young.

The unlucky bridegroom was a very serious young man by the name of Amar Nath, who had recently started practising law and was a member of societies for the promotion of hygiene, tradition, cultural purity, cow protection and correct religious observance. He had recently published an article in *The Pioneer* on the question of loss of caste through foreign travel, coming down firmly against the notion of leaving Indian soil.

Amar Nath's studies had left him little time to acquire social graces. On first meeting his betrothed, he stuttered a few words, then stared at his shoes until the chaperones got bored and called the tea party to a halt. Amrita, of course, said nothing at all, a ghost of a smile playing over her face. She was beautiful, which helped. She gave no immediate sign of insanity. Amar Nath was a dutiful son, and his elderly parents were worried that he showed no interest in anything except books and moral rectitude. So they accepted her uncle's assurances, and pressed their son to do their bidding. The wedding went ahead.

It passed off smoothly. An auspicious hour was determined, and the ceremony duly performed. The priest spoke the mantras correctly, and the bride's smile was coy and demure as she was decked with jewellery by the young women of her new family. Sweets were distributed to an improbable number of relatives, and the groom looked more or less dashing as he arrived at the head of the wedding procession. There was, however, one thing of which Anjali strongly disapproved: the sapphire set into the bride's necklace. Sapphires are tricky gems, and though they can deflect Saturn's harmful rays, they can also focus them.

Amar Nath was obviously taken aback by his wife's eagerness in the marriage bed. Anjali, who had joined the household with her mistress, sat up late and listened to his gasps of surprise, little kittenish sounds that carried out of the window and up to the roof where she lay. As she would later remark to the paan-vendor, it was a fair bet that this serious boy was not expecting his silent bride to take charge in such a manner. Lucky for her he was so unworldly. Anyone else would have become suspicious. But although rumours of the bride's adventures had already reached as far as the hijras who came to mock the wedding guests, Amar Nath and his family were too lofty to listen to the prattle of eunuchs or servants. With his new wife installed safely in his house, the bridegroom returned to his ruminations about disputed land boundaries and the value of Persian in the education of young gentlemen. So nine months passed, or perhaps a little less, while the young husband attended public meetings, the young wife grew big and Anjali surrounded herself with a delicious web of speculation and rumour. Then one afternoon, a shriek echoed around the courtyard. Amrita had gone into labour. The baneful influences of the sapphire and the mole started to take effect.

The astrologer was called well before Pran Nath made his entry into the world. The family installed the man under a fan on a shady veranda, where he sat drinking sweet tea and clutching his case of charts.

He waited for a very long time.

He finished his tea. He put his case neatly on the table in front of him. He ate some fruit, peeling it carefully with a sharp knife. He declined more tea. He stood up and stretched, feeling his vertebrae click satisfyingly into place. He declined lime soda. The screams of the labouring mother echoed around the garden.

Later the astrologer took a short walk, smelling the jasmine and enjoying the shade of the trees. The gardener was watering a bed of delicate white lilies, and the astrologer stopped to praise him for his work. The mali beamed with pride. Then the two of them fell silent, listening as the gasps and sobs from the mother's apartment became more anguished.

As the sun dipped low over the roofs, he was offered a bed on which to relax. He accepted, but found it difficult to doze. Though his business was birth and its meanings, he always found the actual event distressing. The blood and pain. It was a woman's thing, beyond the fathoming of a man, even one educated in the science of Jyotish, to whom most common mysteries are transparent. He preferred to think of birth as a mathematical event, the stately progression of planets and constellations through clearly defined houses, gridded sections of airless space. This agony, the scurrying of maids, the scene of mess and horror that was no doubt unfolding in the upstairs

room, all of it was most unpleasant. It was not nice to think of
the planets tugging so hard at this unfortunate woman's womb.
The astrologer always imagined stellar influence as something
ethereal, light to the touch.

Then everything fell ominously silent. He strained his ears
into the gathering darkness, hearing the immense noise of insects,
the rasp of parrots arguing in the trees. Nothing else. Nothing
human. Soon a maid came, carrying an oil lamp which she set
on the table in front of him. At once, moths started beating
against its glass sides.

'The baby is born,' said the maid, with an odd, triumphant
expression on her face. 'It is a boy. The mother is dead.'

He nodded resignedly. Then he looked at his watch, opened
his case, took out pen and paper, and set to work.

The chart was strange and frightening. The stars had contorted
themselves, wrung themselves into a frightening shape. Their
pattern of influences had no equilibrium. It was skewed towards
passion and change. To the astrologer this distribution looked
impossible. Forces tugged in all directions, the malefic qualities
of the moon and Saturn auguring transmutations of every kind.
It was a shape-shifting chart. A chart full of lies. He kept going
back to the almanac to check his results, covering his brown-
flecked paper in calculations.

The boy's future was obscure. The astrologer could predict
none of the usual things – length of life, marital prospects, wealth.
Patterns emerged, only to fade when another aspect of the
conjunction was considered. Planets seemed to flit through
houses, hovering between benign and malevolent positions.
Clusters of possibilities formed, then fell apart. He had never
been so confused by a reading.

Perhaps (though he would not have liked to bet on it) there
was a route through the chaos. If so, then it was certainly a
bizarre one. How could so many delusions lead to their opposite,

to the dissolution of delusion? He glanced up at the square of light in the upstairs window. The child would have to endure suffering and loss. Could he really tell the father this? The man was grieving for his wife. On the table, a mandala of crisped moth corpses lay around the lamp. The astrologer thought of the dead woman, and shuddered.

When the maid came back, she found him sitting in front of a fresh, neat chart depicting a bland future of long life, many sons and business success. The torn-up pieces of the first attempt had been stuffed, out of sight, into his case.

When the astrologer brought the master his new son's chart, Pandit Razdan seemed satisfied, but everyone knows that astrologers say what their clients want to hear. If a man's beard is on fire there is always someone who will warm their hands on it, but then again who gives a tip to the bearer of bad news? As soon as Anjali saw the white skinned baby, she knew it was ill starred.

The baby cooed and gurgled, and a boy ran down to the cremation ghats for a priest, and the midwives burned bloody sheets in the garden. No one, it seemed, had a thought for the dead mother beyond disposing of her body as quickly as possible. The girl had been an anomaly, an irritant against the skin of a smooth-running household. Now there was a silent agreement to treat her as a vision, a temporary phenomenon which had simply evaporated.

Anjali too thought it was for the best that Amrita had died. It was a wonder she had lasted so long. The family seemed overjoyed by their son. So big! So healthy! Yet she could not look at the child without thinking of his true parentage, of a Brahmin woman defiled by the pale man in the photograph. Still, she might have been able to hold her tongue – if the child had not become such a monster.

*

It was obvious even when Pran Nath was small. He spat, kicked shins, and then threw tantrums when anyone dared to punish him. He was given fine clothes, which he tore to shreds, and a roomful of toys, which he pounded to splinters. The presents were a substitute for speaking to the boy, which his father did rarely, and then only in the form of clipped admonishments, like excerpts from a book of household hints. *Keep your hair clean as a precaution against infestation. Memorize the various ways of starting a letter.*

When Pran reached the age of six, a tutor was employed to administer the tripartite programme of moral, intellectual and physical education which Amar Nath Razdan had outlined in his article 'Towards an Uplifting Hindu Pedagogy'. He left after a week, nursing a broken ankle that had been caused, he claimed, by his charge tripping him down a steep flight of stairs. He was followed by a series of others, none of whom lasted more than a few months. After the injured man came an ex-army sergeant who had a breakdown when he found his cherished cache of love-letters burnt to cinders, a Bengali with a squint, an alcoholic Sindhi with a fondness for Keats, two or three terrified university students and even an Englishman, who left after one lesson, saying that he would never set foot in the house again.

Anjali put these failures down to bad blood, and was prepared to argue her case against all comers. Though at first Pran Nath had his defenders, one by one they slipped away, alienated by his arrogance or his unappealing practical jokes. There were those who pointed out that the boy was actually quite bright, but they found his cleverness was mostly directed towards destroying their possessions, or finding some new and disgusting thing to secrete in their food, hair or bedclothes. His talent for mimicry, another potential saving grace, was employed in cruel parodies of the chowkidar's limp, or the way the dirzi's hare-lipped son ate dal. People tried to explain to him, but it was like feeding salt to a monkey. One by one they came to agree with the cook: the boy was a curse.

Still, officially he was the only son. Everything he said or did was, by definition, perfect. With his father shut in his study, and no mother, brother or even a consolation-prize sister to turn to, he was also more or less alone. The household bit its collective lip. Pran Nath was oblivious to their dislike, supremely convinced of his central position in the cosmos. This was based on the admiration of his extended family, but after a few years even they had started to turn away. One by one the proud aunties died or ceased visiting. His paternal uncle suffered a stroke, brought on, it was whispered, by Pran Nath imitating the sound of a wild animal outside his window one night.

So as Pran reaches out a hand towards Anjali's daughter, his world is more precarious than he thinks. Huge forces are tensed, ready to uncoil. If his fingers connect, things will move fast, but the moment has a certain frozen grace to it, a fake stillness which approaches the true stillness of synchronicity. Time out of time, mysteriously pervaded by the smell of raw onions.

By the end of the Great War, the distinguished court pleader Pandit Amar Nath Razdan has become the proud author of no less than 276 published articles, which have appeared in organs ranging from Kashmiri Youth Society pamphlets to national newspapers. His interests are wide ranging. Politically he favours a cautious nationalism, based on the maintenance of the separate identities of all communities. On matters of religion he belongs to the conservative wing of the Kashmiri Pandit community, equating social with moral status, and sternly disapproving of all relaxations of caste restriction. On the important issue of individual health he is a staunch and prolific advocate of rigorous personal hygiene, which he believes should be reinforced by local government ordinances, or perhaps even a salaried inspectorate paid for out of the coffers of the Department of Health. On etiquette he mourns the decline of the formal canons of traditional politeness. On language he is a fierce opponent of debased or impure usage, impropriety, profanity and slang. In literature he favours the Ancient writers over the Moderns. In the pictorial and plastic arts, likewise. Food, he has opined, should be prepared plainly and nutritiously, taking care to avoid faddishness, innovation or undue richness of sauce. On matters of dress, personal modesty and avoidance of overbold patterning are the watchwords, especially when considering the reckless combination of checks and stripes.

On the whole, Pandit Razdan's opinions are received politely and attentively by those to whom he offers them. If, in court, rival pleaders and members of the audience are occasionally to be observed with heads lolling or eyes shut during one of his famously meticulous summings-up, this is usually put down to the hot weather, heaviness of diet or some otherwise unrelated cause.

The acute observer, a man perhaps who has followed Pandit Razdan's publications over a period of years, might observe a thread of argument which runs through them all. The same thread is rather more obvious to those who wash his clothes, sweep his floors and cook his food nutritiously and without undue saucing. He is terrified of pollution. It is his main enemy, an adversary he battles daily through every aspect of his life. The maintenance of impermeable boundaries between himself and the world's filth has gradually come to take up most of his energy, time and love.

By 1918, aged forty, Pandit Razdan's morning routine is fixed in the pattern that it has followed for almost ten years. He awakes from his bed cautiously, having scanned the room for any new obstacles or dangers that might have manifested themselves during the night. When he is certain the coast is clear, he stands, says a short prayer and makes his way to the latrine. There he squats for a minimum of ten minutes, easing out the contents of his colon and examining the results. Assuming nothing untoward detains his attention, he can then proceed to the bathroom.

There he first makes sure the floor is free of dirt, with special reference to the drain in the far corner. He checks that no insects or small animals are lurking in or near any of the water vessels or furniture, then stands on the low wooden platform by the tub and pours seven lotas of water on his head, then a further seven over his body. Next he squats to pour a lota-full very carefully over his genitals, assisting with his fingers in areas of folding or supplementary hair. A fresh cake of soap is always placed, still in its paper wrapper, within reach of the platform. He discards the wrapper neatly to one side and soaps and sluices his body in a series of moves as precise and as solemn as the progress of a military funeral.

Shaving requires the arrival of hot water at precisely the right moment, and his servant considers this his most important duty of the day. The razor is stropped for no less than two minutes and the lather whipped for another two as the master, naked, bends and stretches his body into a series of post-bath postures which are fully described in his seminal 'Next to Cleanliness and Godliness Third Let Us Put Correct Circulation of the Blood'.

This duty attended to, the razor is handed over, handle first, and shaving can commence. The operation is very delicate, and requires no small nerve on Pandit Razdan's part. There are no circumstances in which he will trust the servant to shave him. The blade is so sharp, his ear so close, the floor always potentially treacherous despite his care to move to an area away from the tub. He feels he can barely trust himself to do the job. Sometimes he fantasizes that he has lost control of his hand, that it is swiping uncontrollably at his throat. Once the thought is broached, it takes an iron effort of will to carry on shaving.

Just before the outbreak of the war he solved the worst of this problem by growing a beard. Nevertheless, trimming is still required, and even this is fraught with danger. Each morning the difficulty of shaving nearly reduces him to tears, but each morning he accomplishes it. It is only one of a hundred such tiny battles he fights during an average day.

Dressing involves shaking shoes to dislodge scorpions and calling for fresh linen should a garment fall on the floor or get contaminated by a drop of hair oil, interspersed by attempts to control his breathing and quell his racing heart. At intervals during this routine, he may detect some trace of illness in his body, and order his servant to call a doctor. The servant will rush convincingly out of the room and spend a few minutes smoking a bidi on the steps outside. Pandit Razdan never questions the doctor's non-appearance, and the symptoms invariably subside as soon as his attention is diverted elsewhere.

At the courts, Pandit Razdan makes sure a supply of soap, water and towels is always available. He also takes care to provide himself with a spare set of clothes. Mealtimes are conducted with immense formality, and should the pleader be unfortunate enough to find himself travelling, he makes stern inquiries about the caste status of any potential cook. 'In this debased age,' he writes in his well-received commentary on 'The Perils of the Modern Kitchen', 'it is sadly necessary to don the hat of a policeman in ascertaining the fitness of a cook, should one wish not to jeopardize one's spiritual welfare.'

Pandit Razdan avoids shaking hands with the English Circuit Judge, and has thus acquired a reputation as something of a radical. However, the real reason has nothing to do with politics and everything to do with his horror of touching a casteless beefeater with suspect personal habits. Once an eager young English lawyer strode forward and clasped Razdan's hand in his, before he could do anything to prevent it. Proceedings were held up by almost three quarters of an hour while the shocked pandit, who had locked himself in the men's cloakroom, obsessively washed his hands to get rid of the taint.

When the influenza epidemic comes, it is as if the universe has personally challenged Amar Nath Razdan to a duel. No greater terror could have been devised. The first victim he sees is a street-dweller, laid out by the side of the road, surrounded by weeping relatives. The corpse's face is distorted, blue-black and swollen. Later, when ordinary systems of propriety have broken down, he sees a dying Englishwoman being carried out of one of the houses in the Civil Lines. Her face is the same blue-black colour, all distinction of race erased by the disease. The collapse of categories appals him almost as much as the fact of death itself.

Within a week of the first cases of 'Spanish Flu' being reported in the city, thousands are ill or dying. In America and Europe millions have already succumbed, and it is known that little can be done for the afflicted. It is rumoured that troopships crossing the Atlantic have been arriving half empty, their human cargo decimated by the disease. Panic sets in and the bazaars empty of people. Stories filter in from remote districts about ghost villages and bullock trains found by the roadside with all the drivers dead in their seats. When the hospitals and zenanas can no longer cope, rich families start opening their houses as temporary wards. Despite his membership of various benevolent societies, Pandit Razdan refuses to do this. He starts to pen an article provisionally entitled 'Twenty Prophylactic Measures in the Struggle Against Airborne Maladies' but before a first draft is complete, his confidence has evaporated. He no longer believes that 'superhuman acts of cleanliness', well-ventilated rooms or the wearing of a cotton face mask will be enough to protect him.

It is generally held that the influenza is a ground-dwelling organism, so for a while the pandit takes to conducting all his business on horseback. He has his borrowed mare saddled in the front courtyard of the house, so that when he goes out on to the street he is already out of harm's way. Unable actually to ride into the law courts, he writes down his pleas and sends them in by hand, his servant running up and down the steps while he sits in splendour outside, watched by children and an unamused British police sergeant. Forced by a fire to visit tenants in a slum quarter of the city, Pandit Razdan refuses to enter their low-roofed houses, and conducts meetings from his saddle, a handkerchief pressed to his face. This lasts a week, until an urchin hits the horse with a stone, and it bucks its rider into a muddy puddle, a body of water almost certainly teeming with disease of every kind. After marathon washing, Pandit Razdan decides to rely on other measures, like taking regular mustard foot baths and gargling with a variety of foul-smelling tonics based, for the most part, on chlorinated soda water, bhang and boric acid. He determines that his house should be fumigated, and instructs the servants to sprinkle sulphur and molasses on hot coals, which creates a thick blue-green smoke that makes everyone choke and leaves a disgusting smell in the rooms.

At night he dreams about the contagion. Bloated faces and the sound of coughing follow him through streets where the very houses and shops seem to melt into one another, losing their integrity, invaded by their own unstoppable architectural diseases. The dream people are horrific and indistinct. At a look or a touch they blur into one another – woman into man, black into white, low into high. It seems the epidemic will obliterate all conceivable distinctions, hybridizing his whole world into one awful undifferentiated mass.

From his locked bedroom, Pandit Razdan calls for the doctor, and keeps calling until one is brought. The man wears a face mask and will come no further than the threshold. He sells the pandit some expensive medicine, and advises him to stay clear of foul air and crowded spaces. The warning is unnecessary. Most public meetings and processions have been banned. The work of the law courts is suspended by general order of the District Health Officer. A junior clerk is dispatched to inform the pandit, but Razdan refuses to admit him into the house.

One morning, during the hour-long extended bath routine he has adopted to combat the crisis, Pandit Razdan feels light-headed. He tries to fight the tide of panic which grips his chest, but the more he fights the worse it gets. Eventually he is obliged to return to bed and wait for the feeling to subside. It worsens. After an hour he has a headache, painful and unmistakable, a throbbing between his eyes which seems to rap out news of his imminent death in a skeletal tattoo. After two hours, despite drinking several glasses of water, he feels hot and feverish. When he draws a finger across his top lip, it comes away wet.

His terror deepens as the morning wears on. The ache in his head spreads out to envelop his arms and legs, and he feels the beginnings of a new drum-throb of pain at the base of his spine. The whitewashed walls and open shutters of his bedroom seem to reflect the crisis, shifting tauntingly at the threshold of his perception as if they too are animated by the fever. Around midday he begins to scream for his servants.

Pandit Razdan has one final anti-flu remedy, a measure he has been saving in case things came to this sort of head. An hour or so later he admits a line of people with baskets of onions and an enamelled tin bath. Heedless of modesty, the master strips off and jumps in. One of the younger girls runs outside and has to be coaxed back in to do her work. The onions are chopped and poured into the bathtub. Every onion available in the sabzi mandi is here, and nearly the whole household is employed in dicing them. Gradually Pandit Razdan's thin limbs are covered over, until only his head and the tops of his knees remain exposed. The onions are packed down firmly, so that his entire body is slathered in flesh and juice. Finally white cloths are wrapped tightly around the bath and folded under his head, making him into a kind of onion-mummy, swaddled tight and sweating. Eyes streaming, the servants file out and shut the door, leaving the cure to work its magic.

The theoretical basis of the onion cure is straightforward. Onions are a notoriously hot and fiery vegetable, which induce the body to cry and sweat to counteract their influence. The power of a single raw onion is enough to repel unwanted inter-locutors and clean the eater's insides of all manner of damp or bilious humours. Spanish flu is one of the dampest diseases ever known, which makes the onion a potent weapon. Pandit Razdan hopes to draw the illness out of his body, immolating the parasite in the vegetable's cleansing fire. For good measure, he munches handfuls of his remedy as he lies, desperately fighting the panic building up inside his shivery frame.

This is how Amar Nath chooses to face his illness. For it is real: this particular hypochondriac is facing the skull-necklaced embodiment of his worst fears. He picks at his chest, imagining in his increasingly disordered mind that he can pluck flu organisms off his body like mites. He sweats and the walls shimmer and the fever vibrates his body like a hammer hitting a metal string.

Distantly he hears screaming, the sound of a bedstead being turned over. His son's voice, Anjali's voice, cursing each other roundly. He turns his head, trying to make out what they are saying to each other. But it comes from the other side of the world. In his bath of onions, Pandit Amar Nath Razdan is pleading the ultimate case.

Gita runs crying down the stairs to the courtyard, as her mother (personifying fate, doom, justice, karma and all manner of other vast impersonal forces given to crushing ant-like mortals underfoot) jabs Pran in the kidneys with a monkey stick. He doubles up, and she brings her weapon smartly down on his knees and elbow joints, each well-aimed blow producing sudden and excruciating pain.

Anjali's victory is swift and total. Hampered by his pyjamas, which are twisted around his ankles, Pran is unable to resist. As he tries to crawl underneath the protective frame of the charpai, she sprinkles his squirming body with a few choice curses, pincers his ear between fingers made vice-like by years of pea-shelling and okra-chopping, and drags him off to see his father.

She raps on the door. An ominous squelching sound comes from the other side.

'Master? Master, are you there?'

There is no response. Impatiently, she tries the catch, and the door swings open into an onion stench of such ferocity that her eyes begin to stream. Pandit Razdan is in the thirtieth hour of his bath. Now he is definitely, conclusively ill, sweating and shivering like a man having a fit. His head protrudes over the white swaddling like that of a premature baby, his eyes red-raw, his skin flushed and unpleasantly puckered. He looks as if he has been pickled, which is more or less the case.

'I am dying,' he says in a tiny voice.

'Maybe so,' raps Anjali brutally, gathering the palla of her sari over her face. 'However, I think I know the reason.' Pandit

Razdan's expression becomes urgent, and he wags his head, indicating that she should continue. Filled with the gravity of the moment, she raises a hand in the direction of the heavens. 'This household,' she intones, 'is under a curse.'

The master succumbs to a violent fit of coughing.

How does one tell a sick man that his only son, the son he has cherished for fifteen long years, is in fact the bastard child of a casteless, filth-eating, left-and-right-hand-confusing Englishman? The gifts of tact and sensitivity are given to very few, and Anjali is not among the blessed. She spares nothing; no surmise is left unfloated, no nasty insinuation unslithered into the long grass of the master's mind. She besmirches Amrita's memory with delicate indirectness, avoiding anything which might tempt the cuckolded husband to defend his dead wife. Then she paints a lurid (though admittedly not too far exaggerated) picture of Pran's faults, drawing the incontrovertible conclusion that the boy exhibits all the signs of tainted blood.

This would be enough for most people, but Anjali is only beginning. She expounds on the theme of miscegenation, and all its terrible consequences. Impurities, blendings, pollutions, smearings and muckings-up of all kinds are bound to flow from such a blend of blood, which offends against every tenet of orthodox religion. Small wonder the city of Agra is suffering a plague. She, for one, would not be surprised to discover that the entire influenza epidemic, all twenty million global deaths of it, was down to Pran. The boy is bad through and through. Finally she produces her trump card: the battered photograph. *Ronald Forrester, IFS*.

'Now tell me who he looks like.'

Razdan turns the snapshot over in his onion-encrusted hands. Forrester's sepia face stares back at him. The nose, the fine lines of the mouth. But for the skin it could be an Indian face. The photograph-man seems to smile at him, a distant, water-damaged smile which cuts through his fever like acid etching a metal plate. For the first time since Anjali dragged him into the room, he turns to look at Pran Nath.

The boy is kneeling on the floor, blood flowing from a wound on his temple. Dishevelled and snivelling, he looks faintly revolting. At last Razdan realizes why he avoids him. He always thought it was because of the mother. She would whisper to herself. When he entered a room he would feel he was interrupting. Yet despite his public campaigns for purity, since her death he has made secret visits to the lamplit rooms upstairs in the bazaar. There he tells the women to behave in a certain way, to touch him in places he finds embarrassing to name. The son has always been an unwelcome reminder of the mother who planted that guilty seed in his consciousness, a sign of his enslavement to carnality.

No. It is simpler than that.

With a feeling like drowning, he realizes that the servant-woman is telling the truth. Pran Nath and the photograph are two versions of the same image. *This is not his son.* With that, something snaps. His orderly life scatters like an up-ended wooden tray of letters at a printing press. His breath leaves his body in a drawn-out sigh of disappointment.

'Father?' asks Pran Nath plaintively. There is no response.

They do not even wait for the corpse to cool before they throw him out. The servants drag him straight to the front door and sling him into the street.

Pran lies in the dust, smelling the onion-stink on his clothes. A crowd gathers, fascinated by the unprecedented events unfolding before their fortunate eyes. The chowkidar brandishes a lathi and Anjali gives a reprise of her miscegenation speech, adding that the evil boy has, to cap it all, just caused Pandit Razdan's untimely death. Then the door is slammed shut, the bolt drawing across it with a heavy metallic rasp.

Pran gets up and hammers on the door, the familiar door with its iron studs and hinges, its scuffed blue paint. The crowd scrutinizes him eagerly for signs of Englishness, pointing out to each other the alien features which suddenly seem so obvious.

'Please!' he begs. 'Let me in!'

From the other side, the chowkidar growls at him to clear off.

'Please! Open up!' There is no response. 'My uncle,' he shouts tremulously, 'will come and flog you. Then you'll be sorry.'

To his delight, the bolt scrapes back, and the blue door opens a chink. A hand appears briefly and drops a little sepia square in the dust. Then the door slams shut again. Pran picks up the photograph and carries on pounding with his fists, crying and pleading. In his confusion he turns to the crowd, only to be faced with a ring of people who have no reason to like him. The sweet-seller, the old woman from next door, the man who sells dry goods, the druggist's boy – all are smiling the same wolfish, unsympathetic smile. He starts to wish he had not played quite so many practical jokes.

Out of the crowd arcs a lump of dung, which hits him, hot and wet, on the back of the neck. As he scrapes it off, another missile splats into his face. He lunges forward, and a gaggle of little boys scatter, howling with mock alarm. The adults laugh indulgently. Then he goes sprawling on to the ground, tripped by an unseen foot.

He spends the afternoon skulking around outside his house, his mind as blank as one of his school notebooks. A string of people knock at the blue door, members of the community who have heard about Pandit Razdan's tragic death, and have come to pay their respects. They all seem to know about Pran's disgrace. Though he rushes up to them, begging for help, most will not even make eye contact. One by one they are admitted, the door thudding behind them. He cannot understand it. He is Pran Nath Razdan: the beautiful, the son and heir. It is like a bad dream.

As night falls, stallholders hang oil lamps over their wares and the woodsmoke smell of cooking begins to lace the air. Pran starts to feel hungry and asks for some pakoras. Digging in his pocket, he finds he has no money, and for some reason no one will give him credit, even when he explains that his uncle will soon pay them back. For a while he loiters, hoping someone will take pity on him. No one does. Little by little his empty stomach starts to rumble, an unfamiliar, frightening sensation. He wanders around, his bruised body aching, a reek of dried excrement rising up from his crusted clothes. Standing on the corner under the high mansion wall, he has to flatten himself against it to let a funeral procession go past. A smattering of lamp-carrying mourners follows a bier, carried by half a dozen white-masked men. The corpse, wrapped tightly in cotton strips, is strewn with marigold petals. A couple of subdued and portly priests bustle ahead, obviously eager to finish the job.

'Ah, it's the nasty little half-baked bread. Come to beg on my corner?'

The voice is raucous, mocking. Pran looks down to see the old beggar with the withered legs. This man has sat in the same spot for as long as he can remember. His drawn face is grained with dirt, his skin the colour of coal, pocked by some childhood disease. He sits in front of a bowl hollowed out from a piece of orange peel, which contains a couple of small coins. Pran cannot meet his eye. Once, on impulse, he stole the beggar's coins and ran away. It seemed funny at the time. Now he shuffles about and looks at the floor, and at the pair of grotesquely tapering stumps stuck out accusingly at the world.

'I recall the time you stole my bowl and dared me to run after you and fetch it.'

Pran makes a non-committal noise in his throat.

'How I laughed,' says the beggar.

Pran nods. The beggar seems to want to chat, so he decides to ask the question which has been preying on his mind.

'You don't by any chance have some food, do you?'

The beggar stares at him with a look of wonder, and mutters a couple of lines of prayer. Pran takes this to mean he probably does not have food.

'Well then, what am I supposed to do about eating?'

The beggar laughs so loudly that people in the street turn round to look. He thumps his hand against his thigh and drums his stumps on the floor.

'He's hungry!' he shouts. 'He's hungry!'

Passers-by laugh and smile.

'When my uncle comes –' Pran starts, but the beggar only laughs harder.

'What shall I do?' he asks crossly.

When the beggar finally regains control of himself, he curls his lip into a nasty sneer. 'Go and eat with your own people. They'll feed you.'

'Who are my own people?'

The beggar seems to find this even more funny.

'You'll find them at the Telegraph Club. Don't worry, little half-baked. I'll tell you what to say.'

The Agra Post and Telegraph Club is not the grandest club in the city. It is a plain Victorian building, a functional box of red brick with a stone portico attached to the front like a snub nose. Inside lingers a smell of fried food which cannot be eradicated, no matter how hard the cleaners scrub and polish. The cleaners scrub and polish hard, even violently, scouring the surfaces, waxing the floors, dusting until their arms ache. It is never good enough. There is still the smell of food fried in ghee, the rich unmistakable smell of India.

The members of the club have many things in common. The women share a liking for cotton floral-print dresses which, though perhaps not of the best quality, are always clean and pressed, even in the hot weather. These are not the kind of dresses some women order out of the Army & Navy catalogue that arrives from Home once a season. Not the kind of dresses that are eagerly awaited, that take two, even three months to come, and when they arrive will be wrapped in tissue paper that falls open with the musty smell of a storeroom somewhere in Victoria. These dresses are made up at home, from cloth bought in the bazaar. They are worn, sometimes, with a single glass bangle. A discreet bangle, but a bangle none the less. Indian jewellery, not jewellery from Home.

The women wear hats. So do the men. Even when it is cloudy. Even (some people joke) indoors. The Artillery Colonel's wife has seen it done. The wife of the Political Resident in Bharatpur swears she once saw a party of them (them, meaning members of the Agra Post and Telegraph Club) playing a hand of bridge in their hats. Indoors. *After dark.* The sun had gone quite down, and still they sat there, solar topis balanced on their heads, as if they were out riding on a summer's morning. The Resident's wife likes to tell this story. Her friends enjoy hearing it. What a chee-chee thing to do, to wear one's hat at night! It never fails to get a laugh. But despite the jokes, the men and women of the Telegraph Club wear their hats at every opportunity: extravagant, expansive, wide-brimmed hats which ensure their faces are always always shaded from the sun. The sun is definitely a Bad Thing.

For the members of the Agra Post and Telegraph Club, rather a lot of life comes into the category of Bad Things. This, at least, is the opinion of the Resident's wife and her friends. They find them chippy. It is almost impossible to talk to them without causing offence in one way or another. Not that one wishes to talk to them, unless like Ronnie and Clive and Peter and some of the other husbands, one has them on one's staff. If one is something on the railways, or of course the post and telegraph, they are rather unavoidable. What with (the ladies remind each other, sipping tea in the better-smelling and more exclusive Civil Service Club) their awful accents, and their awful chippiness, and the absurd way they talk of Home all the time, they really are rather a pain.

Home home home! Everyone knows none of them has been anywhere near England. One supposes it is sweet, in a way. But ultimately they are rather disgusting, those people. Chewing betel on the sly, their girls chasing after the Other Ranks, squatting rather than sitting when they think no one can see. You can always tell if someone is an eight-anna. Blood always shows in the end.

Ugh, those horrid, horrid blackie-whites.

In the Agra Post and Telegraph Club, the horrid blackie-whites gather together to swap their own stories of disgustingness, the disgustingness of natives, the foul Indian-ness of native ways and the firm manner in which they, the husbands, put down their employees, and they, the wives, chastise their servants, if they have them. The natives are devious, untrustworthy and prone to crime. Their lasciviousness is proverbial. What a contrast to Home, to the Northern rectitude of English ways and manners. They, the Anglo-Indian community, know where their loyalties lie. They know which side of themselves they favour. They wear their hats and read all they can of Home and avoid the sun like the plague, feeling pain with every production of melanin in their skin. Of course they do not call it that. They have other names. Dirt, grubbiness. She has such grubby skin, dear. No one will ever go near her. And her nose. So flat and broad. Not like yours.

Inside the club they can be themselves. They can dance and play housie-housie without having to endure the hostile eyes of the natives and the whispered gibes of the junior officers as they make their way to the Civil Service Club, which will never admit an Anglo-Indian through its doors. For a while they can stop their ears to the jokes and the rhymes.

> There once was a young lady called Starkie
> Who had an affair with a darkie
> The result of her sins
> Was an eightsome of twins
> Two black and two white and four khaki

How often has Harry Begg heard that?

It is so unfair. His shade, his precise shade, is etched in Harry Begg's mind like a serial number. Harry has skin the colour of a manila envelope. Or a little darker. Not a bad hand really, compared to some. He does all right with the girls, though of course most of the ones he walks out with would drop him like a shot if some junior boxwallah or English private showed an interest. One or two have done. It is so bloody unfair. It isn't as though things weren't different once. Skinner, the Skinner who founded the Bengal Lancers, was one of Harry's type. So was Lord Roberts, who commanded during the Boer War. Even Lord Liverpool, yes the Liverpool who was PM – he was one. His grandmother on his mother's side was a Calcutta woman. It is down in the history books, there to be looked up. Once upon a time you could say intermarriage was almost the done thing; back in the Company days, before all those biologists and evangelists made everyone scared of black blood.

When the urchin accosts him, Harry, who stoops slightly as if weighed down by his manila skin, is just leaving the club. The lights are twinkling and he is off to meet Jennifer Cash, who has fine features and a complexion the colour of parchment. This evening he might just feel like a decent human being. As long as they go nowhere there might be other men – other, *whiter* men. Jennifer could so easily be taken away from him. A single stripe. A salary in pounds, not rupees. It is all so fragile. Yet tonight he feels full of hope.

And then the little bastard ruins it all.

The urchin reaches out and grabs his sleeve as if it is the most natural thing in the world.

'Hello,' it says, in treacle-thick bazaar English. 'I am blackie-white like you. I am hungry. Do you have some food?'

The urchin is probably paler than Harry, though it is hard to tell through the dirt. He has an English face, a face one might even say was fine, in another place, in other circumstances. Its very good-looks and whiteness make Harry furious. All his twenty-three years of chippiness and hat-wearing, twenty-three years of trying to raise himself up out of the clinging swamp of blackness, comes rushing up in his throat. It makes him gag, the insolence of that face and the smugly pleading look it wears.

'Get your filthy paws off me, you little sod!'

The urchin recoils. Harry looks at him, goggling. The worst of it is, they are probably of the same blood. If anything Harry is somewhat luckier than him, knowing proper English and having some semblance of good manners. But the same blood, nevertheless. Harry and the street urchin, topped up to more or less the same degree, like two glasses of chai. This is the last thing he wanted to experience on his way to meet Jenny Cash, on a fine evening when he feels so noble and white, white as snow, white as a tennis shoe, white as a little golden angel in fluffy bloody heaven. Damn the little bastard to hell.

In his left hand Harry carries a badminton racket, clamped in a wooden press. He swings it once in his hand, feeling the weight. Without thinking again he brings the racket crunching down on the boy's head, crumpling him to the ground. He whacks the prone body a few more times, kicking it, lashing at it with all the hate he possesses. Dimly he becomes aware that he is shouting, *damn you damn you damn you*, and looks around to see a few of his people gathered at a safe distance, watching him with a tell-tale mixture of horror and pity in their eyes. Some natives make as if to approach him and he brandishes the racket like a sabre, telling them to keep the hell away and mind their business.

As Harry deals with the natives, the dazed urchin takes the opportunity to flee, stumbling away down the street as fast as he can manage. He looks back once, a ghost-face of shock and hurt disappearing in the crowd. Harry lowers the racket, and mops the sweat from his brow with a dirty handkerchief. His evening is ruined already, before it has begun.

Desolately Pran batters on the mansion's scuffed blue door. The chowkidar opens it, and behind him Pran catches a brief glimpse of the moonlit courtyard. Then he slams it shut again.

The beggar howls with laughter as he watches Pran staggering towards him. It is an animal sound and his mouth opens wide as he makes it, displaying an improbably red throat, more of a wound than a mouth. *Pretty little prince,* he sings, in a nautch girl falsetto. *See how beautiful are his clothes! See how his dagger shines as he rides by!*

Pran's face is tear-stained and bloody. His clothes are torn and stinking. His body aches all over. Hearing the beggar's mocking song, his anger boils over and he rushes up and kicks his bowl, scattering its few tiny coins into the dirt.

'Did they not feed you?' the beggar asks, ducking Pran's blows.

'You bastard!' he snarls, sobbing.

'Such is my fate,' admits the beggar. 'Yours too, if I remember correctly.'

'I'm hungry!' Pran half shouts.

'Maybe you should try somewhere else?' the beggar suggests, adopting a theatrical sort of look meant to suggest avuncular concern. Pran glares. The beggar recites, very slowly, an address in the jewellers' bazaar.

'Go there, do what they ask of you, and they will feed you,' he advises.

'Why should I trust you?'

'Take it or leave it,' says the beggar, shrugging. 'Frankly, you should be grateful I'm talking to you at all.'

There is no arguing with that. Pran sinks to the ground dejectedly.

'But you're lying. Something bad will happen to me.'

The beggar considers that for a minute. 'Yes,' he says eventually. 'You're right. I was lying.'

'See!' Pran is triumphant.

'On the other hand,' he ruminates, 'I might be lying now.'

'What?'

'Oh nothing. A little philosophy.' The beggar grins, displaying a charnel-house of decayed teeth. Though he shouts and wheedles, Pran can get nothing more out of him. The beggar scratches his scabs. He picks lice out of his matted hair. He shouts random obscenities at the food-vendors who are clearing away their wares. One of them thumbs his teeth back.

'God the all-powerful!' shouts the beggar suddenly, apropos of nothing. 'You are indeed just!'

Pran shoots him a withering look.

'You should thank God,' he suggests. 'He's giving you a great opportunity.'

He rolls his eyes and hawks expansively into the dust. Then, in one sinuous movement, he slides his withered legs back to the foul-smelling drain which runs along the edge of the street, squats over it and releases an elongated turd. The operation completed, he lies down on the floor and falls asleep, the muscles of his hideous mouth relaxing themselves into a startling smoothness, a calm which might even be described as noble.

The ache in his belly keeps Pran awake. He presses and prods it, hoping to persuade the space to fill up. After a while he gets up and looks around for the coins which fell out of the beggar's bowl, but he cannot find them. As a last resort he scavenges by the shut-up stalls, but finds nothing that has not already been eaten by other hungry children, or by the crafty pariah dogs who slink around looking for a snack. Dejected, he lies down next to the beggar, who is snoring thickly.

He tries not to think about what has happened to him. His father is dead. And he was not his father, anyway. His father was the Englishman in the photograph, and he is dead too. Does this make him an Englishman? He does not feel like an Englishman. He is an Indian, a Kashmiri Pandit. He knows what he is. He feels it.

Hungry and worn out, he tries to parse the problem. You are what you feel. Or if not, you should feel like what you are. But if you are something you don't know yourself to be, what are the signs? What is the feeling of not being who you think you are? If his mother was his mother and his father was the strange Englishman in the picture, then logically he is a half-and-half, a blackie-white. But he feels nothing in common with those people. They hate Indians. They hate him, that is for certain. He remembers the rise and fall of the badminton racket, the man's face as he kicked and swore. He is not the same as those people. He does not think of England as his home. Home is here, on the other side of the blue door.

He begins to cry, and eventually falls into a troubled, shivery sleep.

The city carries on around him. The pariah dogs carry on snuffling about in rubbish heaps and gutters. Policemen, thieves, revellers, carriers of nightsoil, tongawallahs, station porters and other darkside people go about their business through streets which in places are almost as busy as by day.

Pran wakes up, frozen and disoriented, into a grey morning. Over him looms a series of irregular brown shapes, which resolve themselves into a line of scrawny buttocks. By his head a row of rickshaw-wallahs and stall-owners are squatting over the gutter, spitting, gossiping, cleaning teeth and moving their bowels. He jerks his head away to a safe distance and remembers with a wave of horror where he is.

The beggar is still asleep, a speculative fly crawling over one eyelid. Pran shuffles over, his arms clasped over his quivering chest, and prods him with a toe.

'Wake up. It's morning.'

The beggar does not move. Pran digs him again. Nothing. He reaches down and shakes his arm. It is cold and stiff. He steps back, realizing with a dull shock what has happened. The influenza can come very quickly.

Like the rest of the world, he has no time to mourn, because at that moment a tonga pulls up to the blue door of the Razdan mansion. A man steps out, dressed formally in an achkan and an embroidered cap. His beard is neatly trimmed. A pair of wire-framed spectacles perch on his distinguished nose. Pran Nath rushes over to him, his whole being suffused with joy.

'Uncle! Uncle!'

Pandit Bhaskar Nath Razdan, younger brother of the dead lawyer, looks round with an expression of disgust.

'Get away from me, you vile creature!'

Pran Nath stops dead in his tracks. His uncle looks extremely agitated, clutching a silk handkerchief over his face. 'Chowkidar?' he calls. 'Chowkidar, where are you?'

The chowkidar appears in the doorway, brandishing his lathi. His grey moustaches quiver with indignation.

'Chowkidar,' orders the pandit, 'get this vermin out of my sight. I don't want him hanging round the doorstep, giving the family a bad name. Make sure he doesn't come back.'

'Yes, sir!' says the chowkidar, standing to old-soldierly attention. Pran Nath does not wait to be beaten again. He flees, his eyes full of tears. Now he knows it is true. He is alone in the world.

Mumbling and sobbing like a deranged person, he makes his way into the narrow alleys of the sabzi mandi. Assuming he is ill, people avoid him, clearing out of his path as he stumbles towards them. He stops to watch a foodwallah making jalebi, piping coils of sugary dough into a huge skillet of bubbling oil. The fried squiggles are lifted with a ladle, dipped into caramelized coating and fried again. Dip and fry, dip and fry. They look good. Desperate, Pran makes a sudden run for the sweets, snatching up a handful and running off down the street. Behind him he can hear the man swearing, but he tears on, sprinting as fast as he can. Soon the shouts of rage die away. Success. Pran crams down the jalebi in a secluded back street, sucking the juice off his fingers, not caring about the grime and filth that come with it. The sugar gives him a tiny rush of intoxication.

Fortified by this, he feels confident enough to present himself at the address the dead beggar recommended. The house is located at the end of a particularly narrow and foul-smelling alley, pocked by piles of rubbish and puddles of nameless liquids. The door itself is strong, banded with iron and studded with thick square nails; the kind of door it would be very difficult to break down. Pran knocks. There is the sound of shuffling footsteps, and an eye appears on the other side of a peephole.

'We're closed,' says a phlegmy voice.

'I'm hungry,' says Pran.

'So?' says the voice. 'Why should that get you in out of hours?'

'I was told if I came here and did what you said, you would feed me.'

A pause.

'By who?'

It occurs to Pran, uncomfortably, that he never asked the beggar's name.

'I don't know.'

The voice seems to consider this for a moment. There is the sound of coughing, then a jangle of keys and the rasp of a bolt being drawn. The door swings open to reveal a man the size of a bull, dressed only in a chequered loincloth. He has obviously just finished his morning ablutions, and his body shines with oil. His thick hair glistens with it, as does the luxurious black moustache which extends in fantastical war-like curls on either side of his face. The man's oiled stomach juts ponderously towards Pran. He leans on the door lintel and twirls a moustache tip between thumb and forefinger.

'Let's have a look at you, then,' he says, and breaks off in a fit of coughing.

Pran looks back at him. The man's gaze darkens.

'Turn around, you little idiot! Show me what you've got!'

Self-consciously, Pran turns to face the other way.

'Pull them down!' shouts the man, violently enough to dislodge another chunk of lung-lining. It is only after great effort that this is finally expectorated at Pran's feet.

Pran fiddles with the string of his trousers, then lets them fall to display an inch or two of bruised buttock.

'More!' growls the man. Pran reluctantly complies. The man stands and wheezes and coughs for a while, then makes a grunting noise which sounds more or less positive.

'Not bad. You'd better come in.'

Pran follows him into a courtyard full of women. There are women washing clothes, women cleaning rice, women chopping vegetables and throwing the waste into a pile. A balcony runs around the upper storey, and it sags with the weight of yet more women, running in and out of rooms and chatting to each other in doorways. A couple of young girls lean over the balustrade and a third hangs huge silk sari squares on a line which stretches from one side of the house to the other. The enormous man picks his way through this termite mound of females with the bored but lordly air of a bullock in a field of heifers.

Pran has never seen so many women in one place. They all seem young and uncommonly beautiful, and several are in states of undress. Perhaps he is light-headed from lack of food, but this place already seems far better than the street. He decides that if nothing better comes up, he will stay here for a while.

He realizes the girls are talking about him. A group on the balcony shouts something uncomplimentary about the size of his procreative organ, and all round the ground floor of the house a general riot of Pran-appraisal is taking place. He blushes furiously and hurries to keep up with the large man, who is heading into a passageway off to one side of the courtyard. Oblivious to the abuse raining down from all angles, the man strides out of view. With a quick glance back at the courtyard, Pran scuttles after him.

To his joy, Pran is placed in a room in front of a thali of rice and dal. While he pushes food rapidly into his mouth, the room's other occupants discuss him. The conversation takes place in a whispered undertone which, were he less hungry, he would make an effort to overhear. The large man, now dressed in a freshly laundered kurta-pyjama, has been joined by a woman who might be his opposite. Where he is imposing and solid, she is more skeleton than flesh. Her face is all jaw and eyesockets, her arms brittle and twig-like, darting to and fro burdened by a dangerously heavy weight of gold-ringed fingers. A thick red tikka line marks her hair-parting, and her mouth is stained crimson with betel-juice. The overall effect would not be out of place on a dissecting table. Once or twice she reaches forward to pinch and rub the flesh of Pran's arm, judging its texture as one might a bolt of cloth at a tailor's. Pran is too busy eating to care.

Neither the man nor the woman has a demeanour calculated to inspire trust. An objective observer (here, as is so often the case, sadly lacking) might note the sparkle in their eyes as they watch Pran eat. Under his layer of street-filth Pran's extraordinary good-looks are still apparent. The man and woman seem immensely pleased by him, and when he finishes his meal with a resounding burp, they beam as if he has just told a joke.

'Call me Ma-ji,' says the woman.

'And I am Balraj the wrestler,' says the man.

Pran tells them his name and, at Ma-ji's request, narrates the story of how he came to be out on the street, and how the kind beggar told him where to find them.

'And so you're quite alone?' asks Ma-ji. Pran nods sadly and admits that unless his family has a change of heart, he is indeed quite alone.

'The beggar said nothing of what work we do here?' asks Balraj.

'No, nothing at all. What is it you do?' Pran is eager to know why so many attractive young women live under their roof.

'It's a sort of charitable organization,' explains Ma-ji. 'We give a home to these poor girls and in return they do some basic chores and, you know, light work of other kinds.' She waggles her head to emphasize the token nature of this employment.

'Normally we don't take in boys,' notes Balraj. 'But in your case we can make an exception. Obviously you will have to do as you are told, and ride the rough with the smooth.'

Pran promises he will do his best. Already he is picturing a life of kiss-chase and other stimulating games, interspersed with a little fetching and carrying, or some guard duty on the days when Balraj does not feel up to the mark. It certainly sounds much better than being tutored, or wandering around town on his own. It looks as if he has fallen on his feet.

'Have some of my special lassi,' says Ma-ji, chucking Pran's cheek and handing him a metal beaker. 'It's very good.'

Pran drains the yoghurty drink in one go, and is met by two enormous grins. Ma-ji and Balraj have things to do, but suggest he might like to rest for a while before starting work later in the day. They get up, shut the door and leave him alone. Soon Pran begins to feel extremely, irresistibly tired, and, curling himself up on a charpai, falls fast asleep.

Pran dreams of a land made of stacked chapatis and curds, populated by vegetable girls with okra fingers and aubergine breasts and saucy looks in their green-pea eyes. Their relations with Pran are confused but delicious, and course after course goes by in prandial harmony until the beggar who is dead starts running around, grabbing at bits of Pran's partners and stuffing them into his red mouth, which is annoying although Pran supposes there is enough to go round and is honestly prepared to share until the beggar starts plucking at Pran's own arms and legs which is really too much – and then finally turns into Ma-ji, who with the help of a little servant girl seems to be fitting Pran into some sort of silky costume.

His head aches and he has no idea of the time. He supposes it is evening since he can barely see the room around him. The only illumination comes from a couple of candles and a red lamp which throbs alarmingly in one corner. Pran feels peculiar, as if he is seeing the world through several layers of padding. His limbs are now made of a watery substance, which will not respond to the frantic commands sent by his brain. His disorientation is not lessened when he spots himself in a mirror and sees he is being slipped into a gauzy pink silk robe with some kind of flower design on it.

'Hold your head still,' snaps Ma-ji, and Pran finds his jaw clamped between vice-like fingers while something, no, it couldn't be, yes – *rouge*, is applied to his cheeks and lines of black kohl are drawn round his eyes. Pran tries to wriggle away but finds he is held fast. When he winces and shrinks back from the make-up stick he is immediately slapped. Ma-ji calls out for Balraj, who arrives coughing like a sick elephant and grasps Pran in a rigid armlock. When Pran protests, Balraj does something excruciating to his neck and Ma-ji hisses, in a tone shockingly unlike the gentle voice she used earlier, *Keep quiet you little fool.*

Pran begins to suspect the beggar was having another of his little jokes.

Soon he is released, temporarily, to stare at himself in the mirror. With his flimsy clothes and his wide eyes, their pupils dilated by drops of belladonna, he looks completely unlike the filthy boy who arrived at the alleyway door. Another beaker of special lassi is thrust under his nose. He shakes his head no, but Balraj forces his mouth open and Ma-ji pours the whole lot down his throat. They leave, locking the door behind them, and Pran finds himself alone in the room.

He tries to think. During his cogitations, which keep collapsing or getting sidetracked or turning back on themselves, he concludes that Ma-ji and Balraj have designs which are not honourable. What these are, his brain is too fuzzy to calculate. If he tries, he will start getting scared. He must escape.

Feeling as if he is moving through syrup, Pran examines the window and finds that, though it is unlocked, it opens three storeys above the street and there are no obvious handholds to use if he climbs out. Even if there were, the way his watery body feels, he doubts he would be able to cling on. He considers crying for help but the noise of the bazaar blankets everything. No one will hear. Over to the door. Locked and sturdy. He looks around for useful items. Weapons? No. Ropes? No. Perhaps he could tear up a sheet and use that. A sheet. Good idea. Very good.

Pran pulls the cover off the bed and prepares to tear it into strips. It is a worn and greasy square of cloth, with a batik design on it, barely perceptible in the dim light. What is that pattern?

Pran turns it over in his hands, feeling the material. It has an extraordinary texture and somehow he is experiencing it so much more clearly than he remembers ever having experienced a piece of material before. Its *materialness*, its *materiality* leaps into his fingers with such sharpness that it takes his breath away. As if, within this small thing, this insignificant bit of cloth, there could be worlds, whole universes of significance. And what is that pattern? The pattern. It is like a forest. Or a troupe of dancing girls. Or parrots. Yes, it is like a whole flock of parrots, red and green parrots, each one trained to speak in a different way. No, not in a different way. In a sense all the parrots talk the same. Although differently. How exactly do the parrots talk? Have that, and you have everything. The meaning of the pattern. All of it present in that one factor. The speech of the parrots. The answer is simple! The key lies in knowing how the parrots talk.

Pran realizes he has come up with something important, but for the moment he has no idea what it means. Everything seems to have changed. The world is suddenly hectic. It is a lot to take in at once. He was not feeling like this a few minutes ago. He was more sleepy. That is it, he felt sleepy even when they were dressing him up. Now why did they do that? There is a question. They must have had a reason.

Then Pran has a moment which contains an answer and in that answer lies an idea and concealed in that idea is the thought that perhaps the second special lassi has something to do with it. And just as he understands that the second special lassi is special in an extreme and very eccentric way, there is the sound of the door-handle turning and a figure steps into the room. After that he is not sure about anything.

In the days that follow, the special lassi plays a continuing role in Pran's life. He is forced to drink it at least three times a day, with the result that he can never work out which of the things that happen to him are real and which are hallucinations. Most are so unpleasant that he does not care one way or the other.

When he first wakes, bleak and sore, from a night of confusion, he finds he has been moved to a small dirty room which contains only a charpai and an enamelled chamber pot. The floor is dusty, and the tiny window shows a view of a section of cracked wall, perhaps fifteen feet away. In the absence of anything else, the square of wall and the diagonal crack which spiders its way from top right to bottom left of it become his sole interest. Hours of lassi-fuelled staring see it grow into a river bed, a honeycomb, a pit out of which crawl tiny skeletons, an interlocking web of cricket pads and bats, a spinning portrait of the King-Emperor with pale blue face and saffron hair, an ants' nest, a market, and the backdrop to innumerable epic dramas of love, loss, civil war and conquest.

Occasionally his dreaming is interrupted by a visitor. Most of the time it is Balraj. His routine is always the same. Jangling his keys the wrestler will unlock the door, lumber in, look at Pran sourly with his doleful red-rimmed eyes, then turn and lock the door carefully behind him. Sometimes he comes with food or another beaker of lassi. At other times he comes to tie Pran to the bedstead and beat him. He does this with a leather strap, coughing and wheezing as he works. It seems to be both duty and pleasure, and he performs it with the methodical, unhurried air of a rich man demolishing a plate of tasty food. Pran will shout and scream and Balraj will ignore him, hitting hard and rhythmically until his laboured breathing becomes a low gurgling moan, whereupon he will stop, hawk on to the floor and leave.

Other people come, with varying degrees of reality. The beggar drags himself in to laugh. Pandit Razdan visits to shake his head and admonish him for his dirty ways and the low company he is keeping. His mother comes too, the end of her sari pulled over her face, her heavy silver jewellery tinkling musically as she moves. She never speaks, just stands there fading in and out like a candle flame while Pran asks her angry questions. Other figures come, their reeking mouths gaping, curved knives in their hands. They bend down and start to flay him, first scoring lines under his arms, round his wrists and ankles, then tugging the skin off his back like a tight kurta. As he screams in agony, they hold it up to the light, which glimmers through it in an indeterminate bloody glow. Sometimes they arrive with his parents, or are dressed in their clothes, burly men trussed into gold-bordered wedding saris or buttoned up in neat achkans, their pink faces like soft fruit sprouting out of high tailored collars. The girls from the courtyard come in threes and fours to hover above his bed and ask him to play. These are the only visits he enjoys, though they always end in disappointment, the girls fading to nothing as soon as they promise to open the door and let him out.

Sometimes he scratches at the wall with a nail, taking off flakes of plaster with its tip, making tiny drawings of the scenes he sees through the window. The chipped wall fuels new pictures and adventures, and these make the rhythm of daylight and darkness, heat and cold, cycle more quickly. When he is not picking at the wall or talking to his visitors he lies and stares into space, taking sips from the bottle of water that Balraj places on the sill once a day. The bottle is small, and, though Pran is careful to make it last, by evening it is always empty. Night-time means a parched throat and a stricken feeling as the last lassi wears off.

Soon the world outside fades, so that the street noise which filters up to Pran's sweltering box-room seems to come from another country.

One day Balraj does not come. In his place is Ma-ji, accompanied by a thin, nervous-looking man who stands barring the door, his fists clenched as if Pran is about to rush at him. Pran lies curled on the bed with his knees pulled up to his chin. He

looks at these new visitors with some curiosity. He has not seen
Ma-ji since she dressed him for his first night. She looks like a
dead person, a bundle of sticks. As she comes into the room, she
presses a scented handkerchief to her nose and screws up her
face. Pran supposes the smell must be bad. His chamber pot has
not been emptied for some time.

Ma-ji hands Pran a beaker of lassi.

'Drink.'

Pran is obedient. The familiar salty-sour flavour of the drink
hits his throat.

'Balraj is dead,' Ma-ji says bluntly. 'The sickness took him.'

For the first time, for the only time he can remember, perhaps
for the first time ever in his life, Pran smiles. As they tighten, the
muscles in his face feel new and unfamiliar. Ma-ji lifts her hand
as if to slap him, and then lowers it again. In a jerky, darting
movement she turns and leaves.

After she has gone, Pran takes his English father's picture from
its hiding place in his bedding and looks at it, letting the lines of
the face, the shape of the eyes and mouth sink in. He mentally
places it against a thousand memories of his other father – he
can not avoid calling Amar Nath 'father': father looking at his
nails, doing puja at the temple, washing his armpits, calling a
servant to pick something up. The little square of stiff paper
amounts to nothing next to this weight of memory. And yet it
toppled it in a single afternoon. Pran handles the photograph as
if it were a magical item, as if its power is in some way inherent
in its substance, chemicals and paper laced with an energy of
good and evil. He turns it over and over, examining every aspect,
fascinated by a rip on one corner, by the way that at a particular
angle the silvering catches the light and turns the image from a
brown and yellow face to a featureless dazzle. An excess of light,
a god, impossible to look on directly. For that one moment the
silver is whiteness, all the blinding alien whiteness that this new

father has poured into his once-comfortable life. He spends hours tilting the little picture to catch the light, repeating it again again again, feeling each time the thrill, the awe of the transformation achieved by a tiny movement of his hands.

Pran moving outwards from the centre, gathering momentum. Whoever might be in charge, it is certainly not him. 'Him', in fact, is fast becoming an issue. How long has he been in the room? Long enough for things to unravel. Long enough for that important faculty to atrophy (call it the pearl faculty, the faculty which secretes selfhood around some initial grain), leaving its residue dispersed in a sea of sensation, just a spark, an impulse waiting to be reassembled from a primal soup of emotions and memories. Nothing so coherent as a personality. Some kind of Being still happening in there, but nothing you could take hold of.

You could think of it in cyclical terms. The endlessly repeated day of Brahman – before any act of creation the old world must be destroyed. Pran is now in pieces. A pile of Pran-rubble, ready for the next chance event to put it back together in a new order.

Here comes the sound of the bolt being drawn, familiar as the call of the muezzin from the nearby mosque, familiar as the crack or the chamber pot or the column of ants which for so very long now have been using the left-hand wall as a thoroughfare between one ant metropolis and the next. He does not look up.

Two tall women look at Pran from the doorway. Ma-ji hovers behind them, wringing her hands, fingers turning through fingers like wriggling maggots. The women take in the scene. Then, not flinching from the awful smell or knife-thick atmosphere of despair that fugs up the tiny room, they lift Pran upright and half walk, half carry him down the stairs.

Candle-flame visitors? Apsaras? How many times has Pran

dreamt this? Yet their smell of rosewater, their grunts of effort, their tight fingergrip on his upper arms, all seem real.

The rustle of silk. Ma-ji like a caged mongoose, screeching about money. One of the women turns to her and says scornfully, 'You have been paid very handsomely.'

And that is that. Splash of water. Rustle of silk. Pran's quivery limbs are rubbed down. His quivery senses are assailed by the sheer variety, the sheer novelty of another room, a new place. He is dressed in clean clothes, given something substantial to eat, spoken to like a human being. It's all over now. Things will be better.

One small snag.

The clothes. A rustle of silk. A heavy veil hung over his face. The world seen, new and extraordinary, through a cotton grille sewn into the veil. These are purdah clothes. Women's clothes.

'Come on, my darling,' says one of his new owners. 'We're going on a journey.'

Rukhsana

The crowd on the platform at Fort Station throbs like a single body. Dirty-collared clerks, hawkers of tea and sweets, beggars, newspaper-sellers, pickpockets, raucous British Tommies all prickly heat and dirty songs, neatly dressed babus, clipped subalterns soon to be kicking the babus out of their reserved seats, displeased memsahibs leading lines of porters with trunks balanced on their rag-padded heads, peasant families sleeping three generations in a row using baggage for pillows, pompous blackie-white guards striding through to check a manifest or assign a compartment, all the denizens of the various waiting and dining rooms – first second third and purdah, veg. and non-veg., Hindu Muslim and English, all spin together, as, motionless at the centre, snug in his office, the grand master of this invisible college, his lofty eminence the Station Master, moustachioed, dripping gravitas, checks the time of an Up mail or a Down express and intones that sacred information to underlings who take it down in triplicate, quadruplicate or dizzying higher order multiples more grand than beings of lower rank can really comprehend. And all this only a list of people. *The animals* – pariah dogs trotting between legs, terrified songbirds stacked to be cage-carried in third class, a single regal garbage-chewing cow; *the smells* – of food fried in ghee, of coal smoke, sweat, axle-grease and urine; *the noises* – hawkers' cries, shouting, the calling-out of names and the scream of steam-whistles cutting through this enormous brawl of close-packed humanity. A noise so loud that at times you pray for this excess of life to let up, to open a space and make way for you in the world's crush, just a little space, just enough so you can breathe and think.

In the midst of it all, shuffling through the crowd like a trio of voids, come Pran and his new owners. Swathed in floor-length black burkas, they view the world through tightly woven cotton grilles and, tit for tat, absent themselves from the general gaze. Unused to walking, Pran stumbles, feet refusing to follow orders. They hold him up, gripping him tightly by the elbows.

The two tall women walk delicately but with a wicked twist of the hips, never touching the thicket of people around them. They make their way up the train, past third and second, past the guards' van and the dining car to first class. Finding their compartment, which is marked with a typewritten notice, they ascend the metal steps, slide the catch on a dark wooden door and walk into a stale fug of sweat and hot upholstery. The porter puts two small trunks on the rack, is paid, salaams, departs. At once hands are thrust through the window, offering nuts, demanding alms, hands which are still there as the train comes to life, rolling slowly along the platform, only withdrawing as it speeds up beyond running pace. Then come yellow-brown fields flashing past, raw and unprocessed, the sensation of change.

'You can lift the veil now,' says one of the women kindly.

Pran does not move.

'Do you know why you are here?'

He looks out of the window, directly into the sun. He opens and closes his mouth, but cannot find any words.

Afternoon turns to evening. Windows are clicked shut against the cold. A man comes to take orders for food, shouting through the closed door, then returning with metal tiffin-boxes of dal and chapatis which he leaves outside in the corridor. Purdah, complete and airtight, even on the move.

Pran tastes the food in his mouth, but cannot tell what he is eating. None of the objects around him have names. They are just things, vibrations on the eye and ear. Something crucial in his mind has been disconnected and is refusing to recognize the present. All that misplaced consciousness is backed up somewhere, imagining itself lying on the roof of a big house, hearing the swish swish of a maid's broom. Yet his body carries on recording. The rhythm of the tracks, the texture of mashed lentils, the sensation of an old cut on his forehead, the aches and emptiness of weeks lying in a cell: these things filter through, knocking on the door, inviting him to step back out into the now.

Evening to night. Hot sweet tea, handed in through the window from a darkened station platform. The tea is scalding, all sorts of tricks needed to make it drinkable before the empty glasses are collected in a last-minute rush. The two women hoist their veils off their faces, doze, eat fried snacks, speak to each other in lowered voices. Once they join together and sing a song in a language Pran does not understand. They have odd voices, raucous warbling falsettos which grate on the ear. Dimly, he examines them for the first time. Their faces are big and plain, with strong jaws and heavily made-up eyes. He looks away again.

For hours he sits and stares into the darkness beyond the grimy window. Gradually the sensation of movement becomes comforting. The metronomic clatter of the pistons, the rush of displaced air; all of it hints at change, progress. Slowly something begins to congeal in the Pran-flux. The pearl faculty is recovering. So he is travelling. Something new is happening. There is still hope. The women argue.

'What shall we call her?'
'What do you think?'
'Zia?'
'Tuhina?'

'Noor?'

'*Rukhsana.*'

'Call who?' asks Pran. The women laugh, hearty rasping guffaws that show off mossy teeth and viperous tongues.

'Little one,' they say, 'we mean *you* of course. Rukhsana, the Nawab of Fatehpur's new hijra.'

Some questions are better left unasked. Others, if asked, are better left unanswered. All the progress Pran has made in self-reassembly, all the comforting hours of tea and train-travel, falls apart in an instant. Pran has seen hijras. They are frightening women-men who dance outside weddings, banging drums and mocking the guests as they go in and out. When a child is born they appear, as if by magic, heralding the infant with lewd mimes and filthy parodic songs. To make them go away again you must give them money, otherwise they will curse your household. They are outcasts, as ancient as the hills, a human dirty joke which has been told and retold since the hero Arjun was cursed to spend a year as a hermaphrodite conjurer. Arjun the great warrior, going from village to village in his skirts: *Now then, ladies and gents, if someone has a bangle they could lend* . . . Some hijras look after the zenanas in rich noble houses, accompanying the women on journeys, acting as gatekeepers, policemen, chaperones. Rich noble houses like that, perhaps, of the Nawab of Fatehpur.

Pran looks down at himself, at his body modestly swathed in black. He looks across the carriage at the pair of too-tall women, with their raucous voices and strong jaws and exaggerated way of walking. The women smile back. Then he remembers something else, a really bad thing, the other thing everyone knows about hijras. They are eunuchs.

Involuntarily he cups a hand to his lap. The two hijras watch him intently. Their smiles broaden a little, as if they know what he is thinking.

Snip-snip.

The train moves northwards, through Delhi, through Panipat, through Ambala and into the Punjab, land of five rivers and innumerable canals. He listens to the singing of the rails and soon begins to dream of the cell he has just left, the ants, the crack on the wall glittering with strange and beautiful visions. Eventually night turns to morning, and a hazy orange sun swells into life over yellow farmland. He sits up to watch small boys squatting on fieldside banks of earth, women washing their hair at wells or hip-swaying along with brass water jars on their heads, men following ploughs, thrashing grumbling buffalo through shin-deep paddies, all of them stopping for a brief moment to watch the train as it cuts supernaturally through their slow-paced world.

Rajpura ... Ludhiana ... Jalandhar ... and then comes another platform and a sign sliding into view that reads LAHORE. There is a bustle of trunks and lowered veils. Pran's arm is gripped and he steps down from the carriage.

Outside the station, surrounded by gawping urchins, with a uniformed chauffeur standing ramrod straight by its side, sits a car. And not just any car. The gleaming beast squatting like a metallic alien in the Lahore market dust is none other than the star of the coming Paris motor show, imported from France at astronomical expense, powered (mesdames et messieurs) by a v-12 aero engine, incorporating a patent four-wheel braking mechanism, capable of an unearthly top speed of eighty miles an hour, presented in fetching cream with red upholstery – the Hispano-Suiza H6.

'This is for us?' Pran asks the hijras. And it is.

The chauffeur stows the trunks in the boot, toots the horn imperiously and guns the enormous engine. Then in a roar of dust and tumbling urchins they take off through the busy streets.

Pran's heart leaps beneath his sweltering burka, the feeling of propulsion reinforcing his hope that he might yet outrun the forces of confusion scissoring at his crotch.

As Lahore fades into open countryside Pran notices that the car's upholstery is worked with the sign of a dove and a crescent moon, a device repeated on the chauffeur's epaulettes and, in delicate inlay, on the wooden dashboard. The flat farmland rises and breaks into undulating hills. They rattle over potholed dirt tracks unconducive to the achievement of record-breaking top speeds, and by the roadside peasants stand to watch them, then salaam, going down on their knees or bending from the waist as the roaring dust plume passes their fields.

They speed through a small town and the effect is the same, shopkeepers pressing their hands together, people backing out of the way to let them pass. Then, some distance further on, one of the hijras touches Pran on the shoulder.

'There is the palace,' she says.

In front of them, at the end of a long straight road that is lined, at intervals, with peculiar white statues, is a vast mass, a disturbing mirage of spikes and pinkness. As the Hispano-Suiza growls its way closer, the pinkness is broken up by contrasting shades, whites and blues, the occasional flash of other colours, here a lozenge of emerald green, there a bright red stripe. Two or three bulbous central domes (it is hard to tell exactly how many) rise over a complicated arrangement of walls, liberally sprinkled with battlements, crenellations, flying buttresses, decorative rails, urns and other architectural features whose purpose is not immediately clear. On each side of the main cluster of domes perhaps half a dozen spires and minarets poke up, some ending in Rajput domes, some tipped by shining gold crescents, and one tapering into a gothic steeple. At the front, a sweeping gravel drive leads up to a magnificent set of steps, alternately black and white. The Hispano-Suiza rolls past these to a side

entrance, hidden beneath a looming candy-striped wall topped
with a large figure of a bare-breasted woman holding a trident.
Here the chauffeur leaps out and opens the door.

In *The Eighth Lamp*, his 'Critical Introduction to the Architecture of India', G. H. Dalrymple writes that 'the unwholesome confection of European and Oriental motifs which characterizes the New Palace at Fatehpur leads the unlucky visitor to wonder whether some law or treaty could not have been invoked to prevent this devilish work from being undertaken'. Dalrymple, a disciple of Ruskin, had 'the grave misfortune' to spend three weeks as the guest of the fourteenth Nawab in 1895. He had, he wrote, 'no inclination to pry' into the history of the building which upset him so much. Had he been interested, he would have discovered that the palace had not one but three official architects.

The first, a Highlander, produced a set of drawings and models in the Scottish Baronial style then popular in his home country. However, a subcontinental Balmoral was not at all what the thirteenth Nawab had envisaged, so he sacked him in favour of a Palladian who was instructed to incorporate the best aspects of both European and Asian traditions. The Nawab considered the Royal Pavilion at Brighton a suitable model, a structure that embodied an acceptably English species of Indianness. It did not look like anything in the real India, but this in itself was a benefit, distinguishing it from the lavish palaces in Florentine, Indo-Saracenic or Rajput styles then being erected by his fellow rulers. So the new architect was ordered to make something like the Pavilion, only different. The Nawab was, after all, concerned not to appear derivative. One way around the problem was, he suggested, to make everything bigger. He had seen Buckingham

Palace and was shocked to find it far smaller than the homes of many middle-ranking Indian rulers. The English were obviously far too restrained, in architectural matters as in so much else. So the New Palace was to be like a *much* larger version of the Pavilion, bigger, generically Oriental rather than Indian in design, and above all the kind of thing that English people would appreciate if invited to the kingdom to ride or shoot. This brief was set down in writing, for the sake of clarity.

The task proved too much for the second architect, a man of delicate health and fine artistic sensibility. He produced hundreds of drawings, took to opium and nautch girls, and one night sat down at his desk and shot himself through the temple with a silver-inlaid pistol the Nawab had presented to him when he accepted the commission. His papers were cleaned up and presented to the third architect, a syphilitic Italian adventurer called Tacchini, who made up for his lack of formal qualifications with a boundless, if erratic, enthusiasm.

Using the second set of plans as his basis, Tacchini incorporated several elements from the first, including the use of flying buttresses and a spire which was a scaled-down copy of the one on Chartres Cathedral. Then, assisted by a manual called *Elements of Architectural Style*, he decorated his structure with more or less anything that took his fancy. Gargoyles, urns, Islamic arches, Mughal glazed tiles and numerous copies of Greek and Roman statuary all found their way into the completed building. The Nawab was delighted, happily ordering coloured marble from Ferrara, stained glass from Oxford, and employing a team of Venetian mosaic-workers, headed by the architect's cousin.

During the period of construction, Tacchini's behaviour became increasingly eccentric. Apart from changing elements of the design, most radically to incorporate a rococo grotto modelled on one at Siena, 'Il Maestro' (as he insisted on being addressed) began to direct operations in states of semi-nudity.

Eventually clothing was abandoned altogether, in accordance with Il Maestro's theory that creative energy was emitted through the skin, which had to be exposed to avoid dangerous aesthetic blockages. At first this was put down to artistic temperament, and even elicited some praise from the Nawab, who admired committed men. But when Tacchini announced that the women's quarters had to be built by women, also working in an aesthetically unblocked state of nature, a doctor was called. He diagnosed tertiary syphilis, and Tacchini was committed to an institution, where he died some years later, shouting out detailed dessert recipes. In his delusion it appears that he had returned to an earlier phase of his life, in which he had worked as a pastry chef in Trieste. The palace, his lasting monument, is curiously enough thought by many to resemble a large pink iced cake.

So Pran is ushered inside a gateau, a meringue, a three-dimensional projection of a crumbling mind, a game of Chinese whispers frozen and richly rendered in expensive imported stone. Inside it is (of course) a maze, spacious corridors divided and subdivided into paranoia-inducing rat-runs which snake and curl through dark interior cavities and end in alcoves or brass-banded doors or blank walls that would surely reveal secret catches if only your fingers could find the right place. The hijras walk Pran past liveried guards dozing against old-fashioned pikes, up some stairs and along a long curving walkway lined on either side with intricate marble screens. Beyond the beautiful carved birds and flowers he catches glimpses of larger spaces, formal halls, durbar rooms and audience chambers, echoing stone voids that roll footfall sounds like snowballs into a meaningless elephantine booming. More guards and a giant theatrical door, much action with keys and clanking chains, and then Pran enters the zenana, the women's quarters of the palace.

No immediate acreage of unclothed female flesh meets his eyes. There is a promising scent of attar of roses, and an antechamber glazed in variegated pink tiles with an odd slick look about them. At the far end is a gated entrance, more of a slit than a doorway. A pink glass chandelier hangs from the ceiling.

From the other side of the gate comes the sound of a fountain and tinkling feminine laughter, but Pran is not allowed to proceed any further in that direction. Instead he is taken up more stairs, climbing a tower into the open air, where he is met by a cool wind and a breathtaking view of hills.

The Khwaja-sara, chief hijra of Fatehpur, sits under a canopy and stares out across the pink battlements of the palace to the dry winter fields below. A wizened figure, wrapped in a rich gold-bordered sari, he is constructing an intricate paan. Before him is an inlaid brass tray of ingredients, each one in its own round bowl. He chooses a tender leaf, brushes it with a little of this, a touch of that; some sweet coconut paste, a dash of lime. Then, sprinkling a few succulent red pieces of betel on top, he carefully folds it into a parcel and, with a flick of his fingers, tucks it into the pouch of his cheek. Pran hovers by the stairs, watching.

'Stand closer, child. Let me look at you.'

He walks forward. The Khwaja-sara scrutinizes him intently.

'What are you, Rukhsana?' he asks in a lisping voice. 'Boy or girl?'

'A boy.'

'Really? Are you sure? Look at what you're wearing.'

Confused, Pran glances down at his burka-clad body. As he does so, his eye is caught by an unpleasant sight. On the tray among the little bowls of paan ingredients is a long, cruelly curved knife. Following his horrified stare, the Khwaja-sara picks it up and runs a gnarled finger along the blade.

'You can't make me stay,' whispers Pran hoarsely. 'I want to leave. I was brought here against my will.'

This seems to be a mistake. In a rustle of silk the Khwaja-sara sweeps to his feet, brandishing the curved knife. 'Will?' he spits, spraying red betel-juice into Pran's face. '*Will?* Your will is of no consequence.'

'Please –'

'You don't have the right to beg! You are *nothing*, do you understand me? Nothing!'

The hijra makes a couple of waist-level passes with the knife. For such an ancient creature, he is surprisingly deft. Pran starts to feel faint.

'Now,' lisps the Khwaja-sara threateningly, 'who are you?'

'I am Pran Nath –' begins Pran, but is brought short by a slap to the face.

'No!' spits the Khwaja-sara. 'Try again. Who are you?'

'I –' Another slap.

'No! Again!'

This goes on until Pran (who has tried answering *please, stop hitting me* and even *Rukhsana*) mutters, 'Nothing.'

'Good. Now who am I?'

'You are the Khwaja-sara.'

'The impertinence!' Another slap.

'I don't know! I don't know!'

'Good. Well done.'

Pran is confused. It is like being tutored, only in reverse. For the Khwaja-sara, less seems to be more, knowledge-wise.

'Remember you know nothing. You *are* nothing. Now Rukhsana, how many sexes are there?'

'Two?'

'Fool! There are thousands! Millions!' The Khwaja-sara is becoming quite animated, twirling around the roof like a superannuated dancing-girl. Pran, terrified, keeps his eyes on the blade, which is glinting unpleasantly in the lamplight.

'Some people,' says the Khwaja-sara, 'can be so self-pitying.' He sings, in a reedy falsetto:

'Oh, this mortal body will not release me
It will never let me go
Threads of silk
Bind it securely to my soul'

'Such idiocy! All it takes is a cut, one simple cut.' He flourishes the knife. 'This blade is a key, Rukhsana. It opens the door to an infinity of bodies, a wonderful infinity of sexes. As soon as you're free of the thread which ties you down, then you can dance, and fly!'

Like a ragged silken bat, the Khwaja-sara flaps across the roof, performing his own multitudinous freedom for the twilight hills and fields.

'You may think you are singular. You may think you are incapable of change. But we are all as mutable as the air! Release yourself, release your body and you can be a myriad! An army! There are no names for it, Rukhsana. Names are just the foolishness of language, which is a bigger kind of foolishness than most. Why try to stop a river? Why try to freeze a cloud?'

He halts his pirouetting and, ancient again, shuffles towards Pran, holding out the knife.

'It really is a very good idea, you know. You should not be frightened.'

Hands involuntarily clasped over his crotch, Pran backs away until his hips hit the low battlement wall. The Khwaja-sara hobbles towards him, kohl-rimmed eyes drilling into him from the rouged, wizened face. Quivering with excitement, it makes an effort to calm itself, with a toss of long hair and a flutter of a hand becoming a herself, then coughing and straightening up into a himself, then relaxing into something else, something complicated and fleeting, a self with no prefix.

'Sadly, we have other things to attend to before we free you of the tyranny of your sex. You are Rukhsana, which is to say that you are nothing. You have been brought here to perform a service for the state of Fatehpur, and you will do your duty without complaining. If you do, you will be rewarded.' He flourishes the knife. 'If not, you will die. Now, follow me, and I will show you the face of your new master.'

Pran follows the Khwaja-sara through a maze of corridors to a large hall. This is not one of the ballrooms which bubble through the body of the palace like air in a strawberry mousse, but an audience chamber so plain and muted that it might be a part of another building entirely. This diwan-i-am is built in traditional Mughlai style, the style of the founders of this little kingdom. Walls of cool white marble are pierced on one side by a row of arched windows through which a light wind is blowing. The wind tugs at the flames in the ornate brass lamps suspended from the ceiling, sending flickering shadows over the faces of the fifty or so courtiers assembled here. They wrap their shawls closer round their shoulders and pull meditatively at hookahs. Discreet servants wait in the shadows with new coals, plugs of apple-scented tobacco, slim-necked flagons of wine and silver trays of sweets.

The men are richly dressed, expensively set turban jewels and heavy necklaces glowing significantly in the yellow light. Yet none, not even the brother who sits yawning with his foreign cronies near the back of the pillared hall, can outshine the Nawab, who wears seven strands of pearls and carries on his finger a ruby the size of a quail's egg, given to an ancestor by the Emperor Aurungzeb. Though Nawab Murad, Slave of God, Father and Mother of the People, Defender of the True Faith and Shield of the Kingdom, is still a young man, his eyes are recessed in his skull and his forehead is heavily lined. An atmosphere of melancholy hangs around his neck more heavily than the pearls, an atmosphere he has, consciously or unconsciously, spread about him in this hall like a dusty carpet. He appears insubstantial, almost ghost-like, and his sorrow lends a quality of mourning to this gathering, which seems to look back into the past with such a constant collective gaze that the participants take on the appearance of a Persian miniature painting, their faces freezing into serene immobility, their poses as formal as the floral border of carnelian and black marble which runs around the walls.

Reciting his latest ghazal, the poet Mirza Hussein senses this mood and (such are the ways of God) finds it instantly reflected in the lines he wrote for the occasion:

> 'Every corner of the court is decked in shadows
> Only my heart remains, burning through the night'

A murmur of approval goes through the mushaira.

> 'How long, O Mirza, do you think you can you survive
> abandoning all hope, forswearing all delight?'

Mirza concludes the final stanza, naming himself as the convention demands, and his audience anticipates the last word, joining in as he speaks it. The chorus of voices mouthing 'delight' breaks into calls of approval, and the poet receives his applause with a slight inclination of the head. It is a moment of near-perfection, and brings a fleeting smile to the Nawab's face. He has called this mushaira, his love of poetry being one of the few good things he feels is left to him, a powerless ruler in a debased age. His courtiers seem to feel as he does. Only the line of uniformed Englishmen at the back appears unmoved. The Englishmen, on whose pink faces and starched tunics his illusion of a Mughal past shatters like a thrown mirror. The Englishmen, and Firoz, his younger brother, clicking his fingers at a servant and fiddling disaffectedly with the celluloid collar of his London-tailored shirt.

The voices calling 'delight' are the first thing Pran hears as the Khwaja-sara guides him through the last courtyard to the mushaira.

'In a moment you will see the Nawab,' the hijra whispers. 'Whatever happens, you are to be still and silent. Do you understand?'

Pran nods. They emerge through an arch into the audience hall and stand in the shadows, beside a servant who stands very straight, balancing a tray of savouries on one hand. A drawn-looking man begins to read a poem in precise, elevated Urdu.

> 'Why should you quit the chamber of my heart
> Why should you flee this, your safest haven?'

'That is the Nawab, to whom you now belong,' whispers the Khwaja-sara.

Pran studies the melancholy eyes, the bird-like gestures of the man's hands as he speaks. As one sad couplet follows another, the Khwaja-sara mutters approval. 'He is a very fine poet,' he breathes.

Pran looks at the assembly of nobles. In their finery, with their hawkish features and proud bearing, they are an impressive sight. Involuntarily, he raises a hand to his own face, to stroke an imaginary heroic moustache.

> 'How is it that I strayed from my garden
> and in this trap seem to have fallen?'

'And over there,' says the Khwaja-sara, 'is the man for whom you have been brought to Fatehpur.'

Pran follows the hijra's gaze. Intently watching them is an elderly man with a hennaed beard and clothes that are even more jewel-encrusted than those of his neighbours. The Khwaja-sara makes a gesture towards Pran and the man nods.

'Him?'

'No, that is the Diwan, of whom you should be most respectful. I mean the man at the back there, the fat Englishman.'

A line of foreigners is half asleep on cane chairs, the only chairs in the room. Accompanying them is an elegant Indian, dressed in European clothes, his glossy black hair slicked back with pomade. Most of the men are young and wear Civil Service uniforms. One, little more than a blond boy, looks over at the Khwaja-sara and winces as if in pain. By his side, his head lolling on his chest, is a florid middle-aged man. He appears completely, unashamedly asleep.

'Him?'

'Yes, him. That, child, is the accursed Major Privett-Clampe, who is the British Resident here. He is a very powerful man, and a very stupid one. Though he is pickled in gin, he holds the fate of our beloved kingdom in his hands. Luckily, little Rukhsana, he has a weakness.'

'A weakness?'

'Yes. He likes beautiful boy-girls. Like you.'

After the mushaira has ended, Pran is given a meal and dressed in a blue silk sari. 'Now,' says the Khwaja-sara, 'there are some people who wish to have sight of you. Come.'

Lighting a lamp, he leads Pran up a wrought-iron staircase to a region of the palace decorated in a warped version of French Baroque. Gilt mouldings flare from corners and ceilings. Spiralling foliage and faintly obscene curlicues worm around the huge mirrored panels that encrust every flat surface. In places even the floors are mirrored, disorientating and treacherous underfoot.

Pran is ushered through a set of tall double doors into a room where a group of men sit in almost total darkness. Their faces are illuminated only by a pair of oil lamps, their wicks trimmed so that they give off the feeblest orange glow. Pran recognizes the jutting beard and hooked nose of the Diwan. The second face belongs to a thin courtier, a pair of wire-rimmed spectacles hovering beneath a tall turban. The third is that of the young blond Englishman who looked so uncomfortable at the mushaira. Now he looks worse. His hair is plastered to his scalp with sweat, its perfect wax dressing sliding down over his cheeks, giving him the appearance of a varnished wooden puppet. His uniform tunic is unbuttoned to the waist. He is voraciously smoking a cigarette.

'Jesus Christ,' he swears, catching sight of Pran. 'You meant it. This is insanity. You can't expect me to do this.'

The speech is addressed to the Diwan, who shrugs. The young courtier laughs. 'Humbly begging your pardon, Mr Flowers,' he says, 'but we can.'

'You're a swine, Picturewallah,' spits the Englishman. 'I ought to –'

'You ought to?' asks the courtier politely. The Englishman groans, and lowers his head to the table.

'Click-click,' says the Picturewallah, with a giggle.

'Go to hell,' he replies, his voice muffled by his forearms.

The Khwaja-sara turns to Pran. 'Meet Mr Jonathan Flowers, who is a member of the very fine Indian Political Service. He is one of Major Privett-Clampe's very fine junior officers. If Major Privett-Clampe asks you, you are to say that he brought you here, and hid you in the zenana. Do you understand?'

Pran nods:

'Jesus Christ,' repeats the Englishman, who appears to be on the verge of tears.

The Diwan scowls at Pran. 'This is him? I hope he was worth the money. Where did you say you got him?'

'Agra,' lisps the Khwaja-sara.

'Oh well,' says the Picturewallah with satisfaction. 'There you are, then.'

'The brothel keeper assured us that he had been well taught.'

'He's certainly a pretty one.'

'I told them to get the best they could.'

His mouth suddenly feeling rather dry, Pran looks from one face to another. The twin discs of the Picturewallah's glasses; Flowers's slicked cheeks; the Diwan's turban jewel – unpleasantness is reflected back at him by them all. Beyond the dull orange sphere of lamplight the darkness hides further mirrors. More light would not necessarily improve things.

Flowers says again, plaintively, 'But you can't make me do this.'

The Picturewallah shakes his head. 'Once again, Mr Flowers. You have been part of the Political Mission for how long? Eight months? Nine months? You have a comfortable life here.

Certainly you never hesitate to take the hospitality of Prince Firoz – polo, shikar, tennis, his unusual film parties. You are an unmarried man. You have desires. Most understandable. But your choice of entertainment was certainly – individual. You obviously need another reminder.'

He produces a large manila envelope and draws out of it a sheaf of photographs. Pran cannot tell what they depict, but they produce an impressive effect on Flowers, who groans piteously and starts to bang his forehead on the table. The Diwan looks disgusted at this performance and mutters something in Urdu about those who are men and those who are not men and those who are little girls.

'Click-click,' says Picturewallah, looking with pride at what is evidently his handiwork. 'It looks most insanitary,' he comments. 'Surely is there not some government of India ordinance against it? But then you people eat and wipe with either hand. I suppose one thing leads to another.'

'All right, all right' groans Flowers. 'Just put the bloody things away. I'll do it.'

'Naturally. You will tell Major Privett-Clampe that you have procured the boy. He will be waiting in the Chinese room. Be careful that you say exactly what you have been told. We will be listening.'

Flowers rises from the table. The Picturewallah follows him.

'I will accompany you, Mr Flowers. I must get my equipment.'

The Diwan spits, peremptorily, on the floor.

Pran does not have a good feeling about the conversation in the mirrored room. These people do not appear to have his well-being uppermost in their minds. Maybe they have mistaken him for someone else. Maybe he should leave. He suggests this to the Khwaja-sara, who slaps him on the face and tells him that if he tries, he will be hunted down. He decides that he might not leave.

As they are making their way back through the palace to the zenana, there is a commotion in one of the corridors. The Khwaja-sara pulls Pran out of sight behind a life-sized marble discobolus as a completely naked European girl speeds past on a bicycle, a mirror balanced precariously on the handlebars. She is chased by a number of men and women in varying states of undress. For some reason, several of the women seem to be wearing military hats: kepis, shakos, bearskins and forage caps which go oddly with their slips and stockings. They are all shouting at the girl to come back with their cokey. One dark-haired man, dressed in the remains of black tie, is carrying a shotgun. 'I'm going to bring her down!' he growls. 'Get out of my way! Let me get a clear shot at her!' In the midst of the rout is Prince Firoz, supporting himself on a bewildered servant.

'Don't be a ninny, De Souza!' he drawls. 'If you shoot her, she'll spill it!'

They run off down the corridor, screaming and giggling, leaving an empty Dom Pérignon bottle spinning in their wake. The Khwaja-sara looks disgusted.

'You see what we have to contend with?' he mutters, as much

to himself as to Pran. 'How does that puppy think he is fit to rule Fatehpur?'

Back in the zenana he squats down at a low table crammed with a variety of pots and stoppered jars. Monkey-like, long fingers manipulate a pestle and mortar, sprinkling in a little from one container, then the next, and crushing the mixture into a fine red powder. Pran rustles about in his sari, nervously shifting from foot to foot. Perhaps if he hid? Or if he climbed down the outside wall?

'What kind of child have they brought me?' groans the Khwaja-sara. 'Why must I do everything myself?' He digs a small pouch from the folds of his clothing. Sinking further into a voluminous black shawl, her gender seems to fade, recessing into the background to leave behind a neutral, indistinct being. Pran wonders if the Khwaja-sara can become invisible, if the power to remove oneself from sight is merely a deeper form of androgyny. Already, but for the hands, the thing before him is just a shadowy bundle of rags.

Card-trick deft, the fingers hold up a seed pearl, then drop it into the mortar and grind it up. 'This,' they say, less by speech than gesture, 'is asha, the drink of princes. I have crushed thirty-seven ingredients into this cup and it has taken me more time than should ever be spent on anyone not of royal blood, let alone a motherless fatherless little blankness such as you. Now drink.'

Pran hesitates, remembering the consequences of Ma-ji's special lassi. Then, seeing the curved knife appear in the hijra's hands, he changes his mind, and drinks. The asha tastes pungent and bittersweet. Not at all unpleasant.

The Chinese room is not, as Pran expected, decorated with porcelain, silks and images of dragons or parasol-carrying ladies. It is windowless and entirely black. Walls, floor, ceiling and the few sticks of furniture it contains are all either lacquered or stained the same pitchy colour. A simple wooden chair stands in front of a desk. On the desk are writing materials, a few old dictionaries and a pile of little tiles with Chinese characters on one side and English letters on the other; relics, presumably, of some word game. In the middle, dominating the scene, is an ominously expansive bed.

At first Pran does not feel downcast. The asha is warming him from the inside, supplying an intense, almost animal sensation of well-being. He strides around the room, his manly swagger somewhat impeded by the sari. His confidence breaks only at the last moment, when he hears a key fumbling at the double-locked door.

Flowers walks into the room, accompanied by Major Privett-Clampe. The Major wears an expression of beatific joy.

'Oh my boy,' he says throatily. 'Oh my dear dear boy. How can I thank you?' he says to Flowers, thickly. Both are evidently extremely drunk.

'Think nothing of it.'

The Major looks momentarily worried. 'You won't say anything, will you? I mean, if anyone found out – you know – my wife –'

'Of course not. Look, old man, I'll leave you to it. Someone will come and pick him up afterwards.'

'Jolly good,' says the Major. Flowers hastily steps out and closes the door. The two of them are left alone.

Major Privett-Clampe is a man of middle years. He has the kind of sandy reddish hair that afflicts so many northern Europeans, blending in with their sandy reddish skin so that the distinction between one and the other is oddly blurred. This disturbing colouring is accentuated by a finger-thick military moustache. He is wearing the same mess uniform he wore at the mushaira, campaign medals and patent-leather shoes glinting raffishly in the low light. The tight-fitting red jacket and trousers would look good on a younger man, and probably did on the Major himself at some time in the distant past. However, the years have not been kind, made up as they have been of days bracketed by kedgeree at breakfast and port and cigars after dinner, so that his body appears to be at risk of exiting its clothing altogether. Alcohol has not helped his appearance. Over his period of service the Major has, like so many imperial warriors, inched forward the moment of his first 'sundowner' gin of the day. Since the time he was seconded from the army into the Political Service it has been stuck fast at around nine in the morning.

'My dear boy,' he repeats, releasing his beefy jowls from a restraining collar stud. 'They have brought you to me.' Then his joy at the happy occasion overflows altogether. Waving his arms in a windmilling mad-conductor motion, he bounds forward across the room.

Delicacy suggests that this juncture might be suitable for a short survey of the history and geography of the principality of Fatehpur, a fascinating subject which has largely escaped the attentions of scholars of the Punjab. Physically, it is a narrow strip two hundred miles long and about sixty wide, consisting mostly of farmland, though to the east this shades into broken, rocky plain. To the south-east, on the side nearer the course of the Grand Trunk Road, lies a marshy area dotted with small lakes, home to a teeming population of wild birds. Once considered the least productive part of the kingdom, the Fatehpur lakes now play a vital role in the state's social and political life. The presence of such good shikar, with bags sometimes measured in the thousands, means that trigger-happy British officials and other useful personages are always keen to wangle invitations to shoot. Naturally such invitations are more easy to come by for those who do Fatehpur's business, a fact which is well (if only tacitly) understood at the offices of the Lieutenant-Governor, the Punjab States Agency and other such places.

Fatehpur's only major centre of population is Fatehpur town itself. Although some distance from the trade artery of the Grand Trunk Road, which passes to the south of the principality on its way to Peshawar from distant Calcutta, Fatehpur still feels some benefit. Its weavers once made a particular type of chequered cotton cloth, popular across north India. Competition from machine-woven Manchester fabrics has damaged this, but the town is still bustling. Otherwise the Nawab's subjects, a mixture of Muslims, Sikhs and Hindu Jats, are scattered among numerous small villages. Their wealth is considerable, at least in comparison to the peasants in less fortunate places, such as famine-ridden Bihar or flood-struck East Bengal. Thus the Nawabs have always been able to exact stiff taxes and still retain the grudging affection of their people.

Although the ruling family can draw their family tree back to the foundation, this event took place a mere two hundred years ago. In a land where numerous Rajput monarchs can trace their lineage back to the sun and have held exactly the same territory for a thousand or more years, this makes them laughable upstarts.

The kingdom's early years are murky, though it is known that 1,122 years after the migration of the Prophet Muhammad from Mecca to Medina, and some two years after the death of the World Conqueror, Emperor Alamgir, a minor Mughal general by the name of Ala-u-din Khan found himself adrift in the Punjab hills with a company of horse. Having fallen foul of Delhi court intrigue, he had been sent to the Punjab on a mission to pacify the Sikhs, who, despite a catalogue of inducements including the torture and beheading of their ninth guru, had unaccountably refused to convert to Islam and recognize Mughal power.

Riding through the hills, General Ala-u-din found he had lost his taste for warfare. A diplomat by nature, he had never really relished fighting, and had always tried to do as little of it as possible. This was rendered relatively easy by the breakdown of Mughal government after the Old Man's death. Orders failed to arrive. Reinforcements were a thing of the past. Delhi was rumoured to be in the grip of a vicious power struggle and the Punjab Army had long since ceased to be a single entity. Separated from the other commanders Ala-u-din restricted himself to the occasional skirmish, a caravan raid or two. For some months he and his men had been content to roam the fertile countryside relieving peasants of their grain supplies and livestock.

It was a healthy outdoor life, and one can imagine the General, like so many generations of British soldiers after him, enjoying the crisp Punjabi mornings and the plentiful supplies of game. On this particular day, just as he realized that war was no longer for him, he came upon the hut of a pir. The saint blessed him, invited him in and suggested that if he did not want to make war, and did not want to return to take part in the orgy of betrayals and poisonings at Delhi, then he should found his own kingdom. This plan made sense, and so (with fingers crossed) Ala-u-din Khan had the pir's hut razed, proclaimed the site Fateh-pur ('city of victory') and made himself its Nawab.

Fatehpur's first century was a troubled one. The land was unpromisingly located on the traditional invasion route from Afghanistan, and only by paying hefty tribute to the Persian Nadir Shah, and later generations of marauding Afghans, Sikhs, Mughal rump forces and Marathas, were the nawabs able to scrape through it with their territory, if not their pride, intact. When Queen Victoria was proclaimed Empress of India, the eleventh Nawab attended the celebrations and eventually secured the recognition of his kingdom as an eleven-gun-salute state, ensuring that henceforward his descendants would occupy a position near the top of the great table of precedence which governs all official activities in British India, from the lowliest

Sanitary Department tea party to the loftiest imperial durbar.

These days, on arrival in directly ruled British territory (a few miles up the road) or other princely states, the Nawab of Fatehpur sends a servant on ahead to ensure that eleven cannon are to be fired. If not, there will be no arrival. However great this honour, it is, as Nawab Murad does not forget, far less than the twenty-one guns accorded to the fabulously wealthy and important Nizam of Hyderabad, although gratifyingly more than the nine owed to the nearby Nawab of Loharu, another Punjabi Muslim principality with which the Nawab maintains a polite rivalry.

The construction of the New Palace, some distance away from what is now Fatehpur town, was the most ambitious project undertaken by the Khan dynasty. It was also responsible for an increased British presence in the state. The 'vast and reckless' expense involved (the words are those of Sir Percival Montcrieff, first Resident) led to the India Office gleefully concluding that there was every chance the Nawabs would soon prove themselves unfit to rule, so giving the British the opportunity to annex Fatehpur 'for the good of the people'. Duly, the thirteenth Nawab was forced to accept constant administrative interference, which has continued unabated ever since. Although Nawab Murad is still ruler, he cannot tie his shoelaces without the agreement of the Crown's representative, Major Privett-Clampe. The Major can veto visits to Europe, and halt the purchase of new cars, furniture, jewels, polo ponies or aircraft in favour of tedious administrative projects like the provision of a hospital or maintenance of fresh-water supply to the Fatehpur villages. If his opinion is not heeded, a word, a dispatch, would be enough to cause serious, even succession-changing trouble. The Major is a very powerful man indeed.

Luckily the asha dulls Pran's senses. The experience is still painful, like having a fallen log hammered up one's backside with a mallet, but at least it seems to be happening at one remove, the pain-messages arriving at his brain like holiday postcards; brief, belated and mercifully unenlightening about the sender's real feelings. His head has been pushed down into the dusty black bedclothes, so he cannot see the purple face of the man toiling behind him. He is aware, however, that the pounding is punctuated by a rhythm of buttock-slaps and regular full-throated hunting cries. As the Major's excitement mounts, 'Tally-ho!' gives way to 'On! On! On!', and the bed groans with the effort of maintaining its structural integrity.

Some may be tempted to view this as primarily a political situation. It is, after all, Pran's first direct contact with the machinery of imperial government. Sadists, mothers of vulnerable servant girls or those with a straightforward taste for retribution may prefer to call it cosmic justice. Traditionally the consequences of our actions in this life are only felt in the next one, a quick inter-incarnational karmic tally moving us down the evolutionary scoreboard in the direction of sweeper, dog and fish, or up towards Brahminhood and eventual escape from the cycle of action and suffering. Pran's accounting is happening with unusual speed.

Pissed, past it, weak of heart and chronically short of breath, the Major is no sexual athlete. Every so often he has to take a little breather, and it is during one of these breaks that Pran turns round and notices a hatch swing open in the featureless blackness of the Chinese room's far wall. After a moment, the lens of a folding camera pokes through the opening, along with a hand holding a little metal trough of magnesium powder. On cue the Major decides to recommence operations, but, having worked up a muck-sweat, he takes a snap tactical decision and struggles out of his tunic, flinging it away with a stirring 'View Hallooo!' Just as the startled Picturewallah is poised to take his shot, his line of sight is obscured by the tunic and his foot slips off his stool, sending flash-powder all down the front of his achkan.

The sensation of cool air about his armpits is the stimulus the Major needs to finish the job, and he climaxes with a blood-curdling yell. As his brain floods with sobering hormones, he starts to regard his situation with a critical eye. What on earth is he doing? Uncertainty swells to remorse, remorse to guilt and guilt to panic. He buttons himself up as quickly as possible and retires from the field. Being well brought up, when he is halfway out of the door he decides he ought to acknowledge the other fellow with some sort of gesture. Shaking hands hardly seems appropriate.

'Well done, my boy!' he calls gruffly. 'Keep it up!'

As the door closes, a blinding flash of light illuminates the open hatch, like a trench under night-time shellfire. A momentary image of the Picturewallah desperately trying to put out his burning clothes is obscured by billowing smoke, which descends over Pran, enveloping him in a blanket of acrid-tasting grey.

As the asha wears off, Pran is overtaken by a creeping feeling of disgust. Dazed and sore, he lies on the bed, trying to grow a shell over what has just happened. After a while a pair of hijras appear through the haze and march him back to the zenana, where the Picturewallah, whose brocade achkan has a charred hole across the chest, is arguing with the Diwan.

'You incompetent,' the Diwan rages. 'What are we supposed to do now?'

'He saw nothing,' snaps the Picturewallah, gingerly fingering his singed beard. 'I'm sure of it. And he was pleased by the boy. We will simply tell Flowers to bring him back.'

The Khwaja-sara flaps around, hustling the courtiers out, begging them to keep their voices down. Pran is shown into a little alcove, where he lies down on a pallet and drifts into a troubled sleep. As he slides in and out of consciousness, he tries feebly to make out some pattern in what has happened to him, to work out how the proud son on the roof of his father's mansion came to this. Like a little boy, he slips a comforting hand between his thighs. At least that is safe, for the moment. As for the rest, nothing is certain at all.

The next morning the hijras put him to work. He sweeps floors, the hem of the unfamiliar sari dragging on the floor, the choli riding up high over the ridge of his spine. He polishes brass and scours skillets and picks stones out of rice. The floor is the first he has ever swept. The pans are the first he has scrubbed. The feet he presses (hijra feet, with silver anklets and long curled nails) wiggle their toes to remind him that everything about his life is now inverted. He is filled with shame, but so shocked that he cannot find the words to complain. With every swish of the broom, Pran Nath Razdan is falling away. In his place, silent and compliant, emerges Rukhsana.

Day by day, Pran expects to be called back to the Chinese room. The summons does not come, and for several weeks his existence is bounded by the tiny, cramped spaces of the eunuchs' quarters. Nor has he access to the mardana, the men's wing, or to the zenana proper. Rukhsana, floating between worlds.

Through the pink portico lies a paradise of women and running water. There are perhaps a hundred living there, from old crones to babes in arms. Some are the Nawab's wives or concubines. Others are maids or servants, descendants of women who came to Fatehpur as part of a dowry, and were born as the Nawab's property. A few are married to palace men but choose to make their home here rather than outside the walls. Still others have arrived through some eddy in the universal flow of family obligation: widows, distant cousins, obscure aunts come to live out their last days in the rooms around the cool zenana courtyard. The maids scurry after their mistresses, and the hijras scurry after everybody. They are servants, bodyguards, spies, chastisers, cajolers and arbitrators of disputes, living in a warren of quarters just outside the zenana, ready at their mistresses' beck and call. Their raucous voices cut through the space like scissor-blades through cloth.

Time passes. At night Pran lies awake in his little doorless alcove, close to the Khwaja-sara's bedroom. He wants to make a plan of escape, but does not know where to begin. His situation appears hopeless. In the small hours he listens to the elderly eunuch's reedy snores, a steady iamb of suck and rattle which thrums on his nerves as he tries to think. Where would he go if he did escape? He would have to travel miles across country, without money or friends. What guarantee does he have that somewhere else would be any better than here? Night after night, he turns this circle like a prayer-wheel, surrounded by the ponderous stillness of Fatehpur.

Something melancholy pulses through the palace. It is carried in the basic rhythm of zenana life, the heartbeat which underlies all other minor fibrillations: the visits of the Nawab. They are irregular and sudden, but the routine is always the same. The first sign is a racing messenger who skids into the hijras' courtyard. At once someone rushes to the gong room, an upstairs chamber with a grilled window looking down over the entrance courtyard of the zenana proper. The huge gong is sounded and the little room which acts as its resonator disgorges a low syrupy burp of sound which spreads through the wing, vibrating its inhabitants into alertness and hasty toilettes. By the time the Nawab himself appears, accompanied by a few chobdars and bodyguards, an expectant hush has taken hold.

To Pran, secretly peeping through the gong-room grille, the thin man in the rich clothes does not look like a ruler. The silks, the jewelled Jodhpuri slippers, the strings of pearls and the egg-sized finger rings seem less true signs of power than elements of a particularly expensive fancy-dress costume. The bodyguards add to the sense of discrepancy. A gang of giant henna-bearded Pathans, they tower over the Nawab, making him look even slighter than he is. While their master is inside, the Pathans stand to attention by the gate, scratching themselves and making eyes at the hijras, who make eyes back.

The Nawab tends to look even less like a ruler on his way out. He is never in the zenana long, and usually exits at a half-run, as if he has been expelled at high pressure. On his face he customarily wears a limp and stricken look: the look of a man who has failed to live up to expectations. As the Pathans nudge each other and the hijras stare at the floor, despondency settles a little heavier over the palace.

*

Pran starts to despair. He is trapped in Fatehpur; not at its heart but in its gut, like a gallstone or something swallowed by mistake. He is alone, without context, without anyone who cares about him. When he hears one evening that Flowers is going to bring the Major back to the Chinese room, he smashes a mirror and digs one of the shards into his wrist, opening up a deep cut.

Someone hears the crash. Soon he is surrounded by hijras, who bind him up and give him hot tea to drink. For a moment he thinks he will be taken off to bed or to see a hakim, but instead he is dumped in the Chinese room, where, just as before, Flowers shows in Major Privett-Clampe and closes the door. As Pran woozily stares up from the bed, the Major lurches drunkenly towards him, slurs 'My beautiful boy', frowns and passes out on the floor. There is a heavy silence. Gratefully, Pran loses his own grip on consciousness. He is woken by the Picturewallah, who is poking his head through the hatch and shouting at him to take the Major's trousers off. Hearing the noise, the Major wakes up and spots the Picturewallah before he has a chance to close the hatch. Startled and temporarily unable to remember where he is, Privett-Clampe gropes for the door-handle and staggers out into the passageway, which he mistakes for the thunderbox. Some minutes later, considerably relieved, he sets off in search of his driver.

The next day Flowers reports that the Major has no recollection of the specifics of his evening. He has, however, been sitting in his office with all the blinds down, emerging only to invite Flowers in for a long chat about the importance of secrecy in all dealings with his wife. Flowers thinks the Major's state of mind is delicate, probably too delicate to permit suggesting another rendezvous.

Pran is temporarily reprieved. The hijras, perhaps because of his suicide attempt, start to treat him better, speaking kindly to him and letting him assist in some of the life of the zenana. He is permitted to walk on the roof. He helps prepare the begum's bath, laying out her silver bowls of oil, the lotas of herbal waters, the brazier of scented coals over which she will dry her hair. One afternoon he is even allowed out of the palace. The occasion is that most dreaded of all the hijras' tasks: escorting a zenana outing.

In front of the main entrance is a line of Rolls-Royces, their chauffeurs standing to attention in their livery of grey serge trimmed with Fatehpur pink. Maids and mistresses take the first six cars, closed and curtained so they can maintain purdah en route. Trunks, wicker hampers, badminton equipment and eunuchs follow in the next four. Once everyone and everything has found a place, and hijras have been sent back for forgotten combs, jewellery, medicines and shawls, the cortège pulls sedately away.

Their destination is a quiet stretch of tree-lined river bank. As soon as they arrive, the zenana party spill out of the cars like infantry off a troop train. Within minutes the entire area is in their hands, the badminton net up in use, tables and chairs deployed, and elaborate formations of tiffin-boxes and tea urns in motion around the redoubt of the hampers. When one adventurous splinter-group embarks on a walk, hijras have to trot on ahead with whistles and big red flags, signals for any passing farmers to press themselves face down on the earth while the palace women go past. They are unveiled. It is more than a peasant life is worth to take a peep. Throughout the afternoon the hijras are kept on their toes by reconnaissance missions of this kind, but for the most part they maintain a static purdah cordon, firmly gridding zenana-space over one sector of the river.

It feels good to be outside. The labyrinthine confusion of the palace seems to breed uncertainties, always generating new and subtle ways of getting lost. Over the weeks his memories of life in Agra have taken on a hazy quality. It is hard to picture himself anywhere else but Fatehpur. At the river he thinks, inevitably, about escape, but something about the landscape makes the idea ridiculous. Easier to think about immediate things. Easier to lie on the river bank and watch the zenana at play.

Over the course of the afternoon, Pran notices that there are two quite distinct factions. One, the badminton players, consists mainly of younger women, centred around one of the Nawab's junior concubines. An older group gathers by the buffet, picking at choice morsels of food and gossiping under their breath. There is an atmosphere of mutual hostility. Once a maid is returning from the urn with a brimming cup of hot tea when she goes sprawling on the grass. Her badminton-playing friends rush up and accuse the old ladies of tripping her. For a while it looks as if things are going to get ugly, and it takes several hijras to part the two sides. Pran is bewildered, until Yasmin, the youngest of the palace hijras, explains. With the explanation, a lot of other things about Fatehpur become clear.

'Babies,' whispers Yasmin. 'Sons. What else could be the matter? The Nawab comes to the zenana but he cannot perform. The older ladies say it is the fault of the younger ones. The younger ones say it is his. Sometimes he becomes very angry, but still he cannot do the deed. It is almost ten years since his father died, and Fatehpur has no heir.'

'What happens if he dies without a son?'

'The throne goes to his brother. Then Firoz will make hotels and railways, and an airstrip and a cinema, and he will pass a law saying everyone must wear trousers and believe in modern industrial methods.' Yasmin sounds rather excited at the prospect, but he checks himself. 'It will be very bad,' he says solemnly, 'because Firoz loves only things which come from

Europe in crates, and if he becomes Nawab he will spend his fortune on these things, and the great tradition of Fatehpur will be lost.'

'Can the Nawab not make someone else his heir?'

'There is a boy he wants to adopt, but to do that he needs the approval of the British. They do not like him, because they say he is anti-Raj and wants to build the Muslim Khilafat, and kill all the unbelievers.'

'Does he?'

'Of course. The British prefer Firoz because he wears a tie and has promised to let them build factories.'

So Major Privett-Clampe has the power to decide the succession. Everything falls into place.

Click-click.

For a few weeks, Pran is left to his own devices. Gradually the politics of the palace become clearer. Prince Firoz surrounds himself with an ever changing cast of Europeans, a dozen or so at any one time. Sometimes the guests include British officials, but for the most part they are flappers and playboys who conduct a more or less non-stop party in the Prince's rooms. The Nawab's faction could not be a greater contrast. They attend prayers, and talk in hushed tones of the Mahdi, who one day will sweep down on the enemies of Islam and disperse them to the winds like so much dust. They discuss the Holy Places in the Middle East, and the accession of Amir Amanullah in Afghanistan. In the evenings, as gramophone jazz competes with the call of the muezzin, the tension is palpable, and the hijras go about their work with bowed heads, fearful about the future.

Then Flowers sends a message that Privett-Clampe wants to see Pran again. To the plotters' dismay, the Major is refusing to come to the Chinese room. Instead he wants the boy delivered to him at the British Residency. The Residency compound is guarded. There is no time to make a plan. Reluctantly the Khwaja-sara bundles Pran into one of the Nawab's fleet of cars, hissing at him to do whatever the Major tells him, and then report back. This time there will be no pictures.

The Residency lies some distance outside the walls of Fatehpur town. As befits the senior representative of the Crown, Major Privett-Clampe lives in considerable style. Set in several acres of grounds, lovingly watered by teams of gardeners and planted with English flowers, is a sprawling two-storey house in Tudor style. Built at the turn of the century, it is the type of suburban cottage-castle, simultaneously cosy and imposing, which a stockbroker or the owner of a middlingly successful mill might build for his newly wealthy family. Somewhere in its recesses lurks Mrs Privett-Clampe. Elsewhere are a number of offices, used intermittently by secretaries and junior political officers. In one of these, at a comfortable distance from those regions of the house roamed by his wife, Major Privett-Clampe has arranged to receive his young visitor.

Pran is deposited at a discreet distance from the back gate, and taken by a hijra to a side door. At the sound of their knocking, the Major's throaty voice responds. He is discovered sitting at a desk, wearing his mess uniform, the buttons undone to reveal a globular stomach. On his head is a crumpled green crêpe-paper crown, a relic of the religious festival the British have been celebrating that day. The Major has been sweating, and the hat's cheap dye has begun to stain his forehead. A tumbler and a half-empty bottle of domestic whisky ('Highland Paddock', manufactured in Calcutta by the illustrious firm of Banerji Brothers) sit in front of him.

'Run out of soda,' he comments, as the door closes behind Pran. 'Angrezi pani.'

Pran wonders if he is meant to go and get it. He points at the door. The Major shakes his head. 'No, no. I've drunk too bloody much already.'

Pran stands, braced.

'I'm not a bad man, you know,' says the Major, rubbing his bulbous nose with the back of his hand. 'It's not as if I'm some kind of degenerate.' Then he explodes, banging the table with his fist. 'Ye gods! How am I supposed to have a conversation with you like that? Look at that fancy dress they've put you in. You're supposed to be a chap, not a bleeding *girl*!'

He appears to gather his thoughts. 'You've got some English in you. I can tell. Where – no, no, on second thoughts I don't want to know.' He pours himself another burra peg of whisky. 'Happy Christmas,' he says. And again, as if testing the words 'Happy Christmas'. He falls silent for a while, then, to Pran's surprise, says 'I have a present for you.'

By the window, on a battered cane chair, sits a large brown-paper parcel. The Major gestures impatiently for Pran to open it. Inside he finds a set of English clothes: short trousers, a white cotton shirt, knee-length woollen stockings with garters to hold them up. There is also a tie and a cap, both rather old and decorated with the same pattern of blue and burgundy stripes.

'Now at least you shan't look like something from a circus. Well, what are you waiting for? Put them on.'

A few minutes later Pran is attired as an English schoolboy, minus shoes. The bare boards of the floor are rough under his feet. The clothes fit quite well, though the collar is too tight.

'Good,' mutters the Major, his eyes bright. 'Very good. We'll have no more of those heathen dresses. Those were my colours, you know. School colours. You had to play at least one first-team sport to win a tie like that.' He waits for this to sink in. 'I played four.'

Pran nods, to indicate he is impressed.

'Those were good days,' the Major continues. 'Exciting days. Our world was inspiring. Stand up straight!'

Pran stands up, wondering where this is all heading. Privett-Clampe pours himself another peg, even more burra than the last. His hand is unsteady. Whisky splashes on to the scarred morocco of the desk.

'You've got some white blood in you,' he continues, gesturing at Pran with his tumbler. 'More than a little, by the looks of you. With training you might understand. The thing is, boy, you have to learn to listen to it. It's calling to you through all the black, telling you to stiffen your resolve. If you listen to what the white is telling you, you can't go wrong.'

The Major is struck by an idea. Cursing and muttering, he begins rummaging around the desk, then levers himself upright and makes for a shelf of books. Steadying himself against the wall, he finds what he is looking for: a slim blue volume. He tosses it over to Pran.

'Read it out. Page one hundred and twenty-six.'

With an exhalation of breath he settles back into his chair. The book is a collection of poetry, battered and ink stained. It looks like a school text, from the same stratum of the Major's life as the cap and the tie. Pran opens it at the page indicated, and begins to read aloud:

'The boy stood on the burning deck
Whence all but he had fled'

Privett-Clampe snorts in disgust. 'It's *whence*, not *vence*, you nincompoop! Try it again!'

'The boy stood on the burning deck
Whence all but he had fled'

'No! Stand up straight, boy. And say the damn thing as if you mean it. This is exactly what I'm talking about. You have to listen, boy! Listen to what the blood is telling you!'

'The boy stood on the burning deck
Whence all but he had fled
The flame that lit the battle's wreck
Shone round him o'er the dead'

'Lord save us! It's *o'er*, not *oh-ear*! Again!'

And so the recitation continues, Pran starting and being shouted at and stopping and starting and being shouted at and gradually learning to 'puff up' and 'ring it out' and in general to put all manner of ingredients into his performance from back-bone and gumption to spirit and feeling, each of them seeming to consist of puffing up and ringing out still more than before, until the puffing and ringing become so moving that the Major is inspired to shout 'Tally-ho!' He jams himself up underneath his desk, moaning and bouncing up and down on the swivel chair. By the time Pran reaches the final stanza he is slumped back, a disconnected expression on his green-streaked face.

'You can go now,' he croaks. 'Well done, my boy. Keep it up.'

'Poetry?' snaps the Diwan. 'What does the filthy child mean, poetry?'

Pran begins, 'The boy stood . . .' The Diwan's fist slams down on the tabletop. Behind him in the darkness, the mirrors of the Baroque room glint maliciously.

'This is your fault,' he snaps at the Picturewallah. 'It was a simple task.'

'How is it my fault? It is the child's fault. He's not trying hard enough. What about all his Agra tricks? There is a thing the brothel-keepers there teach them to do with their tongues – at least, I am *told* there is a thing they teach them. Perhaps if he was to try something like that?'

'Could we not use some other boy? This one obviously does not meet his requirements.'

Flowers holds his head in his hands. 'He says he likes this one.'

'Well, then, why did he not touch him?'

'How on earth am I supposed to know? He doesn't tell me things like that. All I know is that he wants him to come once a week. The old hypocrite actually had the nerve to tell me he was interested in improving the boy's mind.'

'His mind?'

'That's what he said. He's very suspicious of me. He called

me a degenerate yesterday, in front of all the others. My career is in tatters, you know.'

No one seems to have much time for Flowers or his career.

The Khwaja-sara is practical. 'At least we can work out a way to position a camera in the office.'

'Could we not write a letter?' asks the Picturewallah nervously. 'Would that not work as well?'

'We need a photograph,' says the Diwan. 'That is the only thing these Angrezis believe in.'

So Pran starts visiting Major Privett-Clampe on a weekly basis, to wear school uniform, recite poetry and watch him jiggle around under his desk. He puffs and rings and is told to keep it up, and gradually his English accent improves, and he learns stirring passages from Victorian poets about martial prowess and the sacred duty of keeping one's word. The poetry baffles him, with its stiffness and violence and thumping horseback rhythms, but he discerns that it is in some way responsible for Privett-Clampe's importance, and the importance of Englishmen in general, so he pays attention to it, hoping to divine its secret.

Meanwhile the plotters try to work out a way of insinuating the Picturewallah into the Residency, but after one of Mrs Privett-Clampe's dogs savages him as he is creeping through her flowerbeds, he refuses to go back. Anyway, he argues, since the Major (who, Flowers claims, is consumed with guilt about his drunken lapses) never touches Pran, just bounces and tugs and shouts hunting cries, there is nothing much to photograph. Their plan is falling apart.

Meanwhile the life of the palace continues. The Nawab still strides into the zenana, and slinks out again crushed and unhappy. The only time he looks pleased is when he mounts his favourite white mare en route to one of the frequent parades on the Fatehpur maidan. On parade days he has a spring in his step, bossing around his attendants and waving his whip in imperious gestures. The Nawab adores his little army, stinting nothing on their training and occasionally redesigning their uniforms himself. A touch of braid here, a stripe there, and the whole lot ordered from a firm of regimental tailors in Calcutta as often as twice a year. His pride in his soldiers is so great that when the European war broke out, he forgot his dislike of the British and insisted on sending the Fatehpur Army to France. His enthusiasm was short-lived. On hearing that the cavalry would be forced to dismount and fight in the trenches, and worse still that they would all have to wear plain khaki, he withdrew the offer. Consequently the Fatehpur forces have never seen action. This is of course something of a tradition, diplomacy having been preferred to force by generations of the kingdom's rulers. So the newly suspended Great War for Civilization has more or less passed Fatehpur by, much to the despair of Major Privett-Clampe. In the event, the Nawab's contribution to the war effort consisted of a single donation, a trio of old Rolls-Royces he thought might be useful as troop carriers.

Not to be outdone by his older brother's military parades, Prince Firoz also initiates his fair share of spectacle. In normal circumstances he would spend most of the year in Europe, but the war and Major Privett-Clampe's policy of financial restriction have conspired to keep him in India. He is extremely angry about this, but has put a brave face on the situation, announcing drily that if Muhammad cannot go to the Riviera, then the Riviera must come to Muhammad. His house guests seem to like the change of scene. Some years ago he had his rooms remodelled in the then fashionable *Jugendstil*. Now they echo to the sound of feminine bicycling and indoor lacrosse, pursuits which take a toll on the interiors, and lead to an ugly meeting with Major Privett-Clampe, who turns down a request for more redecoration funds.

Though Firoz is, if anything, more profligate than his brother, he remains the obvious favourite of the Raj officials. For all the Nawab's cars, songs and uniforms, he remains a Mughlai prince, the type of traditional monarch who takes little interest in irrigation, land surveys or the rational distribution of agricultural resources. It is obvious to the British report-writers that the Nawab is happier eating from a metal thali set on the floor than the fine Meissen table-setting which is brought out when they dine at the palace. They sense the passion in his eyes as he recites a Persian couplet or turns over a piece of enamelwork, and know that in his heart he considers them an interruption, their eighty years of ascendancy over his land an incident in a longer history, unfolding under the crescent moon of Islam.

Firoz, on the other hand, has a mania for novelty. Though it alarms British sensibilities attuned more to past than future, it is (they feel) in keeping with the progressive spirit of the times. Nothing embodies the Prince's modernity more completely than the private cinema he has installed in the smaller of his two ballrooms. Several times a week he shepherds the Brazilian gamblers and American actresses, the racing drivers and lady flyers and feckless younger sons, into a darkened room where, amidst groping and spillage of Martinis, they watch Mack Sennett comedies. As Fatty Arbuckle takes another pie in the face and Carol or Clara pretends she has not noticed the hand exploring her underwear, Firoz peers through the darkness and reassures himself that he is no cringing native, ignorant of the ways of the world.

By day the house guests are entertained with polo and tennis and shikar, the one activity where all the factions of the palace, from the stiffest Britisher to the limpest dandy, the fiercest Mughlai courtier to the most timid heiress, can take part and be as one. The massacre of gamebirds at the Fatehpur lakes is a release, a complex ritual that soothes the passions which dominate life within the palace walls. A Fatehpur shooting party is always a jolly affair. Even one or two of the zenana women are allowed to join in, which is how Pran comes to attend, and to have his first sight of the celebrated Mrs Privett-Clampe.

As usual, protocol is at the root of things. The wives of the various players in Fatehpur politics are expected to support their husbands in the Raj's most delicate cottage-industry – the production of entente. Thus, although Mrs Privett-Clampe was twice winner of the Annandale Ladies Cup and has shot everywhere from Gilgit to Bharatpur, she is obliged once in a while to suffer the indignities of the purdah-butt. Located at a discreet distance from other butts, this structure looks over the Sultan Jheel, the largest of the Fatehpur lakes, and is camouflaged from prying eyes (both duck and human) by a cunning set of screens. From the outside it looks like another of the tangles of high reeds which dot the marshes, but inside is just as well appointed as the other royal shooting butts. Canvas chairs, pegs for coats and hats, a chest of refreshments and a table whose numbered compartments are crammed with shot and cartridges all serve to make a morning's shooting pleasant and comfortable. Religious complexities arise with loaders and retrievers, since obviously palace men cannot do the job. Instead specially trained maids and a few grumbling hijras are drafted in.

To Charlotte ('Charlie') Privett-Clampe, being surrounded by a bunch of chaps in saris is only slightly more bearable than the sight of women in trousers would have been to her father. Still, the burdens of the Englishwoman in India are heavy, and it has never been her way to shirk responsibility, especially when Our Mission to Civilize is at stake. When the party reaches the lakes and positions are assigned, she makes no complaint as the men and the other European Ladies head excitedly off to their places, her husband taking comradely nips of whisky with a visiting colonel from Hodson's Horse. Instead she grits her teeth and attempts to make conversation with Zia Begum and Amina Begum, the Nawab's junior wives. Neither of them has an opinion on the weather. Neither of them actually speaks any English worthy of the name. It will, she fears, be a long day.

Pran, for his part, is rather awestruck by the stern middle-aged memsahib striding along between the two court ladies. Even Zia Begum, known for her foul temper, looks cowed and diminutive next to this athletic figure, whose battered topi towers at least a foot and a half over the bobbing heads of her companions. As Mrs Privett-Clampe's commanding voice rings out over the quiet lake, Pran wonders whether the Major prefers boys because he is afraid of her. Asking such a woman to perform sexual acts might be unwise.

Sexual congress does not rank high on Charlie Privett-Clampe's list of pleasurable pastimes. Certainly not as high as shooting duck or riding to hounds. She and Gus have not had children, and it has never occurred to her to view this as a disappointment or a failure. Her maternal instincts are largely directed towards the pair of Purdey twelve-gauges she is holding, one crooked under each arm. Arriving at the butt, she loiters outside for a while, breathing in the damp morning air and adjusting the padding on her shooting shoulder. Her loader, a palace maid who winces at her kitchen Urdu and looks as if she is more used to cosmetics than cartridges, is obviously going to be a dead loss. Still, if she is lucky, she might bag a brace or two of the Gadwall flying insouciantly overhead.

Pran is disconcerted to find that it will be his job to retrieve the dropped birds. He is even more worried when Yasmin pushes him into a narrow flat-bottomed boat and begins to punt him out into the water in front of the butt.

'But won't they kill us?' he asks the young hijra, who is having trouble keeping his pole free of weeds.

'Very likely,' says Yasmin gloomily. 'Amina Begum is a terrible shot. And Zia Begum might shoot low just for the fun of it.'

This does Pran's mood no good at all, but he has no time to reflect, for a whistle rings out over the lakes, and the beaters begin their distant racket of drumbeats and catcalls. A wave of snipe take flight over the water, and all hell breaks loose as twenty-five guns start trying to bring them down. Involuntarily Pran flings himself full length on to the bottom of the boat, almost pitching Yasmin into the lake.

For the next two hours Pran cowers in the boat, reaching over the side to pull in bird carcasses and sometimes, under Yasmin's direction, slitting their throats to make them halal. He lives in constant fear that the next target will be him, although, as Yasmin points out, being steersman he has to stand up straight and so is in far more danger than Pran. As the sun climbs higher, their hands and clothing begin to reek of bird-blood, which makes death seem still more present and tangible.

Meanwhile in their separate butts the Privett-Clampes are having an excellent morning's sport. The Sultan Jheel is a resting place for all manner of migrating waterfowl, and today precious few of them are destined to escape alive. Pintail Snipe and

Bar-Headed Geese fall in numbers, but it is the duck who come off worst. Death comes to Mallard, Teal, Pochard and Shoveller alike, and soon Pran's boat is piled high with feathered corpses. In the purdah-butt Charlie completely outclasses the two palace women, who find it hard to concentrate as the Amazon beside them shouts at her cringing loader and provides a running commentary on their performance, a string of Hurrahs, Dash its, Bad shows and That's the ways which leads Zia Begum to wonder why the English send their sons rather than their wives to fight their wars. Elsewhere the Major, always more introverted than his wife, is shooting steadily, phlegmatically, acknowledging his loader's cries of 'Good ehshot, sahib!' with a grunt and a sideways look to Carter of the Hodson's, to check he has noticed his latest feat of arms. Carter invariably has, but stoically pretends otherwise.

For the Major, the day's slaughter is a respite, a moment out of a life he finds increasingly baffling. Augustus Privett-Clampe is a man whose existence was once knowable and controllable, a thing to be turned over in the hands and examined from every side. It was a life, he remembers, like the flask at his hip or the gun whose barrel is heating his hand so comfortingly through its protective leather glove. If you were to open his file at the India Office you would see nothing but success written there. Alcohol and sodomy do not feature in the memoranda. So why does the Major have his first whisky at nine? Why does he forsake his loyal wife for the corruptions of a half-caste boy? Why does he brood for hours in his office, thinking (as is the tradition among failed men) of the service revolver in the locked drawer by his side?

Under the scorching sun of the North-West Frontier, such a thing would have seemed impossible. There a young Privett-Clampe, newly arrived in India, newly shouldering the burden of a Queen's Commission, looked up at the snow-capped peaks of the Pir Panjal mountains and believed that he had arrived in heaven, never more to leave. The garrison town of Abbottabad was a marvellous place for a young officer, especially for a man commissioned in the station's senior regiment, Prince Albert Victor's Own 1st Punjab Cavalry. Peshawar, 'Pindi and Simla were in easy reach, and though the town itself was undistinguished, the Officers' Mess was like a blue and scarlet brotherhood, where strenuous games of High Cockalorum (games which left civilians debagged, eyes blacked, chairs and tables smashed and a fellow's monthly bill painfully inflated) were not only tolerated but encouraged by the CO.

A Daly's man (as they were still called, from the Nabob days when they were simply Daly's Horse) had the run of the place, and once morning parade was over there was nothing to do but take advantage of it. The country around afforded excellent sport, and it was only natural, only right and proper, that Privett-Clampe should become a devotee of pig.

There was, as a 23-year-old Privett-Clampe would remark to anyone who came within range, nothing on earth so fine as the camaraderie of the Abbottabad Tent Club. The CO was known to agree, and decreed that weekends could begin on Thursday, to give the regiment's numerous pigstickers more time to develop their art. It was his keenest wish that a Daly's man win the Kadir Cup, and for a while it looked as if young PC might be the chap to do it. Everything about pigsticking agreed with the young officer's temperament, from the heft of the nine-foot bamboo long-spear to the look of a 'big un' 's curved tushes mounted above one's bed in the Cantonment. Nothing, he declared, gave him a greater thrill than the head shikari's cry of 'Woh jata hai!', as a large boar broke cover.

If he could find no one in the mess to listen to him, Privett-Clampe would play out pig exploits in a kind of shadow theatre

as he lay under his mosquito net after parade. Fingers became
heats of riders, lined up between the flags at the start of a beat.
The beaters, swishing through the long grass prodding likely
thickets with their poles, dissolved to a whooshing noise made
with the mouth. After that it became more physical, fist smacking
into open palm as a pig made his first spurt for freedom, then a
terrific creaking of the bed-frame as the adrenalized gallop
gathered speed, the pig accelerating away for a first uncatchable
half-mile with the leading man straining forward in the saddle to
see if it was rideable. Too small? A female? Then the disappointment of a horizontally held spear, an exhalation of breath, a
sharp pull-up and a return for another beat. But oh! if it was a
goer! (And here in the re-enactment nothing but the shout itself
would do.) The call of 'On-on-on!', and it was time to ride like
billy-oh and the bed-frame would take a real bloody pounding
and brother officers would sometimes put their heads round the
door thinking something else was going on entirely and end up
in stitches as PC in the role of the pig began to tire, jinking from
left to right, the cunning old devil leading his pursuer into the
very worst kind of country, almost-but-not-quite dropping him
into ditches and nullahs, on to hidden logs or copses of thorns
or tamarisk and oh! at last came the moment but only after the
heroic young nimrod had driven his horse to the verge of
exhaustion and the other riders were far far behind, only then
did the pig turn and charge and it was time to lower the spear
and drive it home into the sweet spot just over his shoulder,
feeling the sudden shock of his weight jar all up your arm as he
ran himself on to your sharp spade-shaped blade and in that
passionate instant it was all over, time for a quick glass of the
chaiwallah's cold tea and back behind the line to begin it all
again. Nothing like it. Nothing in the world.

Young PC got his tent-club button (for ten 'first-spears') in his
maiden season at Abbottabad. He never did win the Kadir,

narrowly losing out to a fellow from Skinner's, but his second place was enough to make him the toast of the regiment and win him a permanent place in the CO's heart. Life was wonderful. A hard schooling had taught him that the only way to be certain of a situation is to keep it clamped tightly between your legs, and, having been on the wrong end of the House Captain's spear on too many occasions, Privett-Clampe's joy in pigsticking went deep. The thunderous beating of a horse's great heart as he rode it hard over the rough, the thrill of knowing that one mistake could lead to a fall or a terrible goring, the delicious conjunction of judder and squeal as 'Old Crusty' impaled himself on to nine feet of hardened male bamboo – all of it reminded him that he was a man, that he had the upper hand, and the world and the creatures in it were his to dispose of as he saw fit.

This same sense of mastery was reflected back to Privett-Clampe in the admiring faces of his proud Pathan Sowars as he inspected them at morning parade. They were a marvellous body of men, tall, well made and protective of their honour to a near-pathological degree. Like all Indian Army officers, their young Captain had been trained to distinguish the differing martial characteristics of the races of the Subcontinent. Since the disaster of the Mutiny it was known that the Hindu Brahmin was both wily and untrustworthy, a far inferior soldier to the average Indo-Gangetic Mussulman, who himself was inferior to the war-like Sikh and the Pathan. These were the races with whom the Englishman felt an instinctive sympathy. By recruiting almost exclusively among them, he ensured generations of loyal soldiery who understood their privileged place in the hierarchy of things, and would strive to protect it. These racial differences were clear-cut, and obvious to even the greenest India-hand. When compared to the hair-splitting Calcutta babu or the timid Kashmiri, it was undeniable that the Pathan was a truer breed of man altogether. Of course they treated their women abominably and had an unfortunate predilection for sodomy, but neither of these tendencies ever interfered with army discipline. Privett-Clampe led his Pathans into the mountains on several occasions, burning villages to punish border raids and tracking down bands of horse-thieves. Those were the days long before the mechanized slaughter of trench war, when fighting was conducted with honour and decency. Privett-Clampe (and all those who ever shared a billet or a dinner table or a railway carriage with him) would never forget the day when some of the infantry chaps were exchanging shots across a valley with a party of Waziri tribesmen, and one of the enemy called out that the English were firing too low, and stood up to give them range. There was your Pathan. Not a finer man in the Empire, even when he was the enemy.

Between Pig and Pathan, Privett-Clampe was a man with both his hands and heart full. To the polite inquiries of the CO's wife about his marriage plans, he would reply bashfully that he had none, suffering her questions with the stoic but mournful air of a wounded man undergoing field surgery. This was his typical response to matters feminine, for he found interaction with women a feat of endurance.

To the invisible college of elderly matchmakers who ran the station's social life, such a prize as the young nimrod could not be allowed to escape. Tea parties were arranged with the sole purpose of marrying Augustus off, and he was forced to endure frequent and excruciating picnics where young ladies of the 'fishing fleet', fresh out from Southampton, would attempt to hook him with parasols and big eyes and well-timed fainting fits. PC would stand them up, dust them off and take them briskly back to their chaperones, disappointingly safe and unmolested.

Just at the point when the matchmaking cabal were about to turn nasty and brand him unsound, Augustus met Charlotte Lane. If not love at first sight, it was at least admiration. He first noticed her taking a tricky ditch as a guest of the Peshawar Vale Hounds. The PVH hunted jackal over some of the best country in India. Privett-Clampe was a valued member and universally reckoned to look very fine indeed in his scarlet coat with its pale blue collar. The thing that struck him about the girl was how well she took the jump. As the horse stretched out for the far bank, she leant forward over its neck, easing smoothly back into her seat as it landed. He could not help but think it finely done, and told her as much in the club that evening.

Born under the sign of the horse, their courtship was charmed from the start. To the hunt they added polo, paper-chasing and tent-pegging as reasons to meet each other, always doing so as if by accident and then standing around with their hands in their pockets, rocking backwards and forwards on the soles of their booted feet. Neither of them was much on dancing, though Privett-Clampe was delighted to find that the young lady shot as splendidly as she rode. When he saw her bring down a black buck with a .275 at a hundred and fifty yards he decided he must be in love. She was tall and rangy, with big hands and a shock of blonde hair which was usually shoved up under a 'Bombay Bowler' topi. PC appreciated all of this in much the same way as he did a good gait or a well-turned fetlock in a polo pony. What Charlotte looked like under her clothes never really occurred to him, and it took a lot of coaching from 'Stage-Door' Johnny Balcombe before he understood how and where and when to try to kiss her.

It was a bad business, the first kiss. Gus prepared more or less as he did for any close-quarters engagement, and beforehand was just as tense. He had chosen for his ground the swing-chair on the rear veranda of the Abbottabad Club, which gave a commanding view over a suitably romantic mountain vista, and afforded at least two lines of retreat in the shape of the garden and the billiard room. He made the assault by night, during the latter stages of a leaving 'do' for a civilian polo chum who was changing station. Despite the advantage of surprise, and a weakened enemy in the shape of a Charlotte who had been plied with several glasses of slightly stiffened fruit cup, he was entirely routed. After softening up her position with some Stage-Door-taught phrases about the beauties of the wild and the fragrance of the evening, he imagined he had made his intentions sufficiently clear and embarked on a frontal assault of such vigour and poor direction that his forehead slammed hard into the bridge of her nose. Fruit cup splashed on to new dress, followed by several drops of blood. Both of them were mortified. Gus immediately withdrew his forces, but Charlotte, who had been sent to India by her mother to do exactly this sort of thing, was not going to give up so easily. She clung to Gus's neck and pulled him back downwards, and although there was a deal of smoke and many alarums and excursions, by the end of the action the two sides had come to an understanding. A week later they announced their engagement and were duly married in the English church at Peshawar three months after that.

The wedding night was as disastrous as the first kiss had portended. After several bruising falls before the walls of the citadel, Gus attempted to force a breach and was finally and definitively unseated by a furious Charlotte, who thought the whole thing an outrage and a frank imposition. The newly-weds forgave each other, neither being the grudge-holding type, and fell to playing Old Maid on the bed. Things progressed slightly over the following weeks, but they never thought it a priority, and by the time they took a long leave in Kashmir the following year they were living as chastely as brother and sister.

Time and again, the last form imprinted on fading duck eyes is the glittering lung of the Sultan Jheel, the black dots of the shooting butts ranged across it in a bowed line. The birds spiral downwards in a flutter of blood and feathers, splashing into the water for Pran to scoop up. The killing seems endless. When his arms are slick with blood and there is no more space in the shikara, he sinks down exhausted, his head resting against a warm cushion of duck corpses. Yasmin does the same, the pole trailing in the water beside him. Overhead the slaughter continues, an irregular crackle of gunshots echoing off the surface of the lake.

The boat drifts and gradually they find themselves close to the butt where the British officers are shooting. Sharper eyes than theirs, the eyes, perhaps, of the spirits the peasants sometimes see flittering through the reeds of the lake, might be able to make out the avid expression on Major Privett-Clampe's face. It is mirrored on other faces, Charlotte Privett-Clampe's most closely, a tightness about the mouth and a brightness in the eyes that seems to intensify at the moment of pulling the trigger. Discharging one gun and taking the next from his loader, the Nawab displays it as a cruel curl of the lip. Even Firoz's girls, more used to the kind of kicks to be found on dancefloors, in nightclub bathrooms or the darker reaches of house-party gardens, find themselves oddly moved by the pounding recoil against their shoulders, the heft of the hot barrels in their hands. No one feels it more than the Major, for whom this discharge has to substitute for all others, his sole relief from the urges he finds welling up so powerfully and problematically inside.

The early days of his marriage were the happiest of Privett-Clampe's life. He felt he was at the zenith of human existence, and could look forward to an unbroken eternity of pigsticking and Pathans with his wife at his side. It was then, naturally enough, that disaster struck. Like the heroes of the Shakespearean tragedies that had bored him so powerfully at school, young PC had a tragic flaw. Unlike them, his was not a particularly dramatic fissure. It lay concealed under the surface, manifesting itself in a certain nonspecific air of gravitas he would adopt when confronted by conversations he found puzzling or irrelevant. His face would cloud for a moment, and then an expression of noble rumination would pierce through it like a shaft of sunlight. This expression had a peculiar quality, in that whatever he said next, even if it were just to shout for another nimbu-pani, would always sound like the very last word on the matter in hand.

So striking was his facial tic that Privett-Clampe gradually earned a reputation as a man of piercing intelligence. Though it was perhaps not entirely deserved, he made little effort to repudiate it. Who would? This is the kind of petty failing that anyone but the most pox-ridden Renaissance dramatist would feel bound to forgive. Yet it was enough to exile him from the Eden of Abbottabad, and mire him in a bog of uncertainty from which he has never freed himself.

The occasion of his fall was a conversation with a certain Mr Wiggs; its cause, a sneeze. Wiggs was an unwelcome guest in the Daly's mess, because he insisted on talking politics. Like women, politics was the subject of an absolute prohibition. But Wiggs, who had trained as a lawyer, considered that the term comprehended merely party politics, whereas his topic was the evils of nationalist agitation, a staple of clubs and common rooms across India. Technically he was correct. However, by 'politics' an officer of the first Punjab Cavalry means 'anything I find boring', which described Mr Wiggs's monologue perfectly. When he demanded that every last rioter, distributor of seditious pamphlets and jumped-up babu be transported to the Andaman Islands for the term of his natural life, though his opinion was considered sound, it was received with stony indifference. All down the long table, fingernails were examined and toothbrush moustaches wrinkled against the bottoms of noses in a uniform expression of froideur. Privett-Clampe, his deep-and-grave look set fair on his face, did not even notice the exposition drawing to an end. He was too absorbed in a daydream about Victoria sponge cake, a hard thing to come by in India.

It was at this moment that he sneezed.

The sneeze brought him to the attention of Mr Wiggs, who was looking around nervously for allies in the sudden chill of the mess. He noticed the young man's contemplative expression, and formed the opinion that here at least was one fellow who appreciated the subtleties of an argument. Foolish puppet of fate, Privett-Clampe looked up and made eye contact with Wiggs. Thinking he had better make some remark, he said, 'Yes, rather', and nodded, feelingly.

This clinched it. To Privett-Clampe's dismay, Mr Wiggs (who did something deadly at Delhi) collared him when they retired to smoke. He said, in a tone unpleasantly full of darkness and mystery, that Lieutenant Privett-Clampe was a young man whose talents were being wasted. Privett-Clampe, who felt that barely a drop of them was being spilt, still thought better of disagreeing. He simply told the old chap thanks awfully and, as soon as was decent, fled. How was he to know that in the loneliness of his guest room, Mr Wiggs (who despite his social failures was a man of influence) would decide to 'give him a hand up'? How could he foresee that this intention would be immediately made flesh in a letter that contained a passage describing 'a young man of acute political judgement, with genuine feeling for the problems of the region'? Who could predict that its recipient, a certain Colonel Brightman, would put the acute youth's name into a memo which, in time, would pass over the desk of none other than Sir David Handley-Scott? Who would have thought that Sir David would pause briefly over that name, and deciding it was indeed the fellow from the PVH, would mark it with a red pencil?

But it happened. Three months later Privett-Clampe was promoted to Captain and seconded into the Indian Political Service, one of the most sought-after postings in the Empire. To any other man it would have been a time for celebration. PC was aghast.

It was a desk job.

There must have been some mistake. But however hard he complained, however many times he went to the CO or wrote to London or got drunk and cursed Wiggs for an interfering poodlefaking swine, no one would take him seriously. They either thought he was pulling their leg, or put it down to a sudden crisis of confidence.

There was nothing for it. At the age of twenty-nine, Captain Privett-Clampe entered a world of paperwork and plots in Simla, helping with the fiendishly complex business of negotiating relationships between the Crown and the hundreds of native states. In the IPS, only two things counted – protocol and cunning. Failure to stab the correct person in the back at the correct time, and to do so whilst meticulously observing all the canons of precedence and tradition, could have dire consequences. One slip, a single word out of place, and one could have an 'incident' on one's hands. It was bewildering, and even though there was still polo, pig and the PVH, Privett-Clampe found that his work followed him around like a pariah dog, stubbornly howling even in the midst of the most delightful chase or hard-fought chukka. Within a year the first lines were etched on his face, and a regular pattern of whiskies had started to emerge.

To make things worse, the combination of tedium and secrecy in his new work distanced Privett-Clampe from his wife. Charlotte was a straightforward woman, and found it very hard to understand what Gus *did* with all the papers he glumly hawked back to their bungalow every night. Her questions filled him with despair. How was he to tell her he spent his days in fear, checking first one and then another of the hastily scribbled lists he stuffed into the pockets of his uniform?

Charlotte chose to make the best of things, and threw herself into the ordained business of the Burra Memsahib, terrorizing the servants and double-checking the cook's account book. The mali had to try harder to make the delicate English flowers grow in the hot weather. The dirzi had to copy the master's suit exactly to the stitch, and use less material than he would have needed to cover the back of a child.

The years progressed on a gentle downward slope. Despite Privett-Clampe's lack of aptitude for his job, and despite the reputation of the IPS as a service where only the most talented could shine, in truth it was still a bureaucracy, where his undoubted punctuality and the impressive piles of paper he kept on either side of his desk were enough to keep his career on track. Had he realized, he would probably have taken care to turn up late and put his feet up whenever his superior passed in the corridor. Sadly he did not, and his record remained exemplary.

Eventually he was posted as a junior to one of the larger Rajput states. To the dismay of the Paramount Power, the Maharaja had a taste for the sexually bizarre, and a series of rape claims had been brought against him. Privett-Clampe immediately found himself embroiled in the details of the Maharaja's private life, in which Argentinian tango dancers, Borzoi dogs and a certain regimental harness-maker in Jaipur all featured. Gus was shocked. The further he delved, the worse it got. English women. English breeds of dog. He had to keep a French dictionary at his elbow just to decipher the reports. When he found out it was his job not to give the fellow a sound thrashing but actually to smooth things over, he had a fit of despair and embarked on a mammoth drinking binge.

Perhaps it was inevitable. Charlotte and he had ceased exchanging all but the most basic pleasantries. The case of whisky was fine, brought over directly from Glen-somewhere-or-other by a chum. The sheer volume of work had left him little time for pig that year. And so, his head full of *cuissade* and *frottage* and *soixante-neuf*, he found his way into a native brothel. There the perceptive madam, seeing he had no genuine interest in her girls, left him in a room with a boy.

The next day, filled with disgust, he applied for a transfer back to the cavalry. The transfer was denied. A strenuous programme of tennis and early-morning rides did nothing to alleviate a creeping sense of doom. Try as he might to bury them, lewd thoughts, oddly mixed with pig and schooldays, kept surfacing in his head. The only thing that kept it at bay was drink, but one night he drank too much and found himself back at the brothel. A cycle was set in motion. The final blow came when a bad polo fall left him with a broken leg. The leg set badly, and felt permanently stiff. Returning to the cavalry was now entirely out of the question. Privett-Clampe realized, with a kind of blank horror, that he was now thirty-nine years old and would spend the rest of his life behind a desk.

Charlotte noticed her husband's boozing, and was genuinely upset that the old boy did not find riding as easy as he had. However, she certainly did not feel she could actually *talk* to him about it. She had her own life, running the household and organizing a charitable venture dedicated to retired cavalry horses, saving them from the glue-factory and putting them to pasture on some land near Rawalpindi. PC thought this pointlessly sentimental. Their roles became as fixed as the cook's Thursday night meal of 'lamb cutlash' and 'pudding with cushter'.

The outbreak of the war raised a glimmer of hope in both their hearts. Surely with the Home Country in such dire need, the Captain could escape his desk? Yet in response to Privett-Clampe's letter offering his services in the European theatre of operations, London promoted him and posted him to Fatehpur. He tore the memo up and wrote again asking for Palestine, which he thought (being halfway) might be a compromise. But the confirmation came, with orders to present himself at his new station forthwith.

So for Major Privett-Clampe, Fatehpur is the end of the world. In this backwater his staff consists of a floating group of ICS-trained juniors like Flowers. With their 'heaven-born' arrogance and their habit of speaking to each other in sentences which consist entirely of Latin tags, they make him feel even more desolate than he did already. He can barely think of them as human – in their pressed shirt-fronts and neat frock coats they look more like a flock of wading birds. When nursing his morning hangover, just the sight of one of them perching in his doorway with a file makes his trigger finger itch. For their part the juniors make no secret of the fact that they consider themselves (*si parva liceret componere magnis*) far more competent than the Old Walrus, and note (*pro pudor!*) the unmistakable signs of *delirium tremens* as he struggles to light his pipe in the morning conference.

Pickled in domestic whisky, the Walrus has also given up struggling against his sexual tendencies. He plumbed new depths by allowing Flowers, a man whom he detests as the worst kind of desk-bound pansy, to introduce him to the beautiful boy he thinks of as Clive. Clive has aroused so many conflicting emotions in his breast that he barely knows where to begin. There is no doubt about it. The Major feels *romantically* towards him. There is, he tells himself, nothing exploitative about his desire. One of the few things which stuck in his head about the Greeks was their admirable tradition of man–boy love. His sodden toilings appear to him in an improving light. Now he knows for certain that a degree of white blood courses through the young man's veins, this sense of being a mentor, a guide through the perils and pitfalls of life, is getting stronger.

Clive's unwillingness to talk poses a problem. The Major would feel better about things if the boy did not give such an impression of being there under sufferance. He imagines trips to the mountains. He could even teach the lad to shoot! Yet despite his suspicions that most of his IPS juniors and just about all the palace nobles are at it too, there is a need for secrecy. As the weeks progress, the Major's guilt takes hold more strongly. The whisky-dampened suspicion that he might be doing something wrong looms ever larger in his mind.

Gradually, as the weather grows hotter, Privett-Clampe makes Clive do less turning round and more reading out loud. To his surprise, after a nearly text-free lifetime, the Major finds himself turning willingly to the written word. Naturally he has no truck with the kind of tedious high-flown nonsense (Tolstoy indeed! Sheer Bolshevism!) favoured by the IPS chaps. *Jorrocks's Jaunts and Jollities* is more to the Major's taste. A good rhyme will also do the trick, anything with a clear metre and stirring sentiment. He often has Clive recite *Gunga Din* or *The Charge of the Light Brigade*, while he does something pedagogical in his trousers.

Eventually, in the way of things, Privett-Clampe's noble fiction starts to coincide with reality, and even the trouser-fiddling stops. Clive's accent improves and the Major contents himself with mistily watching his protégé as he stands up straight and declaims.

'Oh yes,' murmurs the Major. 'Ring it out. That's the way.'

The whirr of a projector. White light spills on to a screen, silhouetting a dozen fashionably empty heads. Slicked, marcelled, shingled and pomaded, Prince Firoz and his special friends are slumped on red plush chairs in a darkened ballroom, limp flesh pendants to their rigidly set hair. The remains of some activity lie underfoot: sporting or sexual, or conceivably some fashionable Riviera combination of both. Whatever it was, it is over now, and servants are picking up camisoles and fencing foils and arranging the room for one of Firoz's notorious cinema shows. Liveried retainers have coaxed the opiated chorus girls and satiated shipping heirs from a tangle on the floor, wiped them down and propped them up in front of the screen. In position, despite a few skewed double-windsors and misaligned bandeaux, they appear startingly, intimidatingly attractive. This ability to look perfect even when under the influence of the strongest intoxicants Firoz's money can buy is their shared skill, the talent which has marked them out from the merely modish herd and brought them here to Fatchpur. Tonight they are excelling themselves, because tonight Firoz has promised a very special show.

Yes, sir, Cornwell Birch is back in town. Birch, fresh from the City of Angels with a consignment of the latest in motion-picture entertainment. Birch, dressed in an Angeleno tailor's idea of tropical evening dress (yellow silk suit, green spats) and smoking a totemic double corona. Birch, changed from Burcz at Ellis Island, Cornwell for that toney back-East ring. Whoever introduced him to Firoz should be ashamed of themselves, but they certainly started something. Birch comes to Fatehpur both to show his latest work and to make some more, maybe a little newsreel stuff, scenes of life at the Maharaja's palace, that kind of thing, but more often movies of a highly specialized nature, which he would prefer not to discuss unless someone round the table can vouch for you.

For now he is smoking and half listening to Firoz, who is cursing and fuming about the latest political developments. Political in the loosest sense. To Firoz, politics is mainly a matter of allowances, or rather *his* allowance (pitifully inadequate size thereof), and whether he is ever going to be able to get his hands on any of the capital tied up in the royal lands. Then he could convert it into something useful, like cufflinks. Or an aquarium. Whatever it is he needs (he is not quite sure, but he knows he needs *something*), it would be far easier to get it if he were Nawab. And now his brother is making trouble. O Mighty Sword and Shield of Fatehpur! O Ruler Incapable of Sustaining an Erection Worthy of the Name! Like trying to push an oyster into a slot machine, apparently; he has it on good authority. Perhaps not an aquarium. Perhaps a spa, with hot springs and attendants in white uniforms. Anyway, if he is ever to stand a chance of some real money, his impotent brother must not be allowed to adopt an heir.

Which is where the politics comes in.

The latest news is that in three days' time Sir Wyndham Braddock, Combined Punjab States Resident, will be arriving with Lady Aurelia to shoot some tiger, eat too much and have himself inventively pampered at the expense of the state of Fatehpur. A protocol visit. No doubt Murad will ask his permission to adopt, and he in turn will consult his man on the ground. Thus the power to decide Firoz's entire financial future will fall into the lap of that appalling dunderhead Privett-Clampe. Ordinarily, he would not worry. Everyone knows the British would love to get rid of Murad. The thing is, Firoz is not sure that Privett-Clampe approves of him. The recent redecoration spat was mistimed. So was the hoo-ha over trying to buy that zeppelin. For pity's sake, the vendor said he was Swiss!

However, there are ways of ensuring the right outcome. 'Apparently he likes boys,' Firoz snarls to Birch. 'Ned Flowers told me. And then I had another one of my fabulous ideas! Jean-Loup? Are you there?'

Jean-Loup is indeed there, sitting in the back row, coiled up like a lithe Gallic spring. Jean-Loup, dragged out of a gutter in Marseilles, cheekbones like razors, solace of sailors, willing to do absolutely anything with absolutely anybody, as long as – well, as long as nothing, really. He just will. Someone woke up with him in Cannes, someone else on a yacht off the Cap d'Antibes. Eventually he ended up here, and might well have made the voyage in someone's luggage for all Firoz knows. He says he is twenty-one, but most put him at seventeen. No one would care either way, were it not for the notorious bulge in his unnervingly tight trousers.

'So Jean-Loup – my idea was that you should do something unbelievably twisted with Major Privett Clampe, and *you*, my dear Cornwell, should film it. Then I will threaten to show Sir Wyndham the reel, unless the old pig supports me as my brother's successor! What do you think of that?'

'What do I think of what?' asks Privett-Clampe, who has just wandered in at the heels of a wildly gesticulating Flowers.

'He just came along,' mouths Flowers. 'I couldn't stop him.'

'Hello, chaps,' says the Major, who is quite tipsy. 'Flowers said you were putting on some sort of a picture show. Haven't had the chance myself, so I thought I'd come and see what it's all about. You don't mind, do you?'

'Major, of course not,' purrs Firoz. 'How delightful to see you. Jean-Loup? Come and keep the Major company.'

*

'Rukhsana? Wake up.' Yasmin shakes Pran by the shoulders. 'They want you.'

Rubbing his eyes, Pran walks into the Khwaja-sara's cramped quarters, to find the Picturewallah and the Diwan there, deep in conversation. Sir Wyndham Braddock's imminent visit is causing as much consternation here as in Prince Firoz's wing of the palace. The Nawab wants to know if they can assure him there will be no problems with the adoption. It is vital that he can name his little cousin as his heir, so the kingdom does not become Firoz's piggybank. So far, he does not feel reassured at all.

'Boy,' says the Khwaja-sara, 'it is time for you to show your art. Great things are at stake. The honour of the kingdom. Your safety. I have just had word that Major Privett-Clampe is with Prince Firoz. Now is our chance to act. You must lure him back to the Chinese room. Then at last we will be able to make an end to this.'

Before Pran is fully awake, he has been dressed in his school uniform and taken to the end of a long corridor. At the far end of the scarred parquet is a set of double doors, through which comes light and the sound of laughing. His escort vanishes, and Pran is left wondering what on earth he is supposed to do.

As he gets closer, he can clearly hear the Major's gruff tone.

'Absolutely not. Don't you worry. O'Dwyer will keep a firm grip on things.'

'But,' comes Firoz's drawl, 'these troublemakers have a lot of support. There are many ignorant people for them to mislead. In Fatehpur we should really be doing much more against them.'

'Couldn't agree more. That's why we needed the Rowlatt powers in the first place. Come down hard on the bastards. It's the only way.'

Pran peeps his head round the door. The room is darkened. A few straggly rows of chairs are lined up in front of a large white screen. From the back of the room, a humming projector throws out light as a servant fits a reel of film on to the spindles and threads it in. There is evidence of a party. Champagne bottles roll lopsidedly on the floor and a few bodies are slumped in decorative attitudes on the chairs. Among them Pran spots several people he recognizes: the South American, the naked cyclist and the strangely dressed man who arrived this morning with all the steamer trunks. Major Privett-Clampe sits in the middle, a portly shadow among stick figures. No one notices as he slips through the door.

'There you are,' says Prince Firoz, pouring Privett-Clampe a Scotch.

'Thanks, old man,' responds the Major nervously. Though he is grateful for the chance to have a crack at Firoz's imported whisky, the young fellow beside him is sitting uncomfortably close. Privett-Clampe has never had much time for French people, and this one has his hand on his thigh.

Against the screen their silhouettes contrast comically. Jean-Loup's head wilting on the Major's shoulder, Firoz's angular profile threatening to burst Privett-Clampe's heavy jowls and swollen nose like a blown-up balloon. Pran edges further into the room, almost slipping on some kind of ladies underthing which gets tangled round his foot. He has to grab on to a chair to right himself. The chair crashes loudly into its neighbour, and Pran squirms underneath, his heart pounding.

'Are you awake, De Souza?' calls out the Prince. 'You're just in time for Mr Birch's latest discovery.'

Pran lies very still. Firoz swears loudly. Then there is a yelp and a smashing of glass against the back wall. Evidently, the Prince has launched a champagne bottle at his projectionist.

'What are you doing, you silly black bastard? How long does it take you to make the damn thing work?'

The projectionist stammers apologies in Urdu.

'And speak English to me! I hate it when people speak that bloody monkey-language!'

'Sorry, sahib!'

Prince Firoz apologizes effusively to his guests. Pran takes a peek over the row of chair backs. As the projectionist tries to make his machine work, Privett-Clampe carries on talking politics, saying things which Pran does not completely catch, about the defence of India and marching and protests and detention without trial. The other guests seem less than interested. Only Firoz appears to be paying attention, but every so often he shifts about in his chair, as if he would rather be doing something else.

As Pran's eyes become accustomed to the darkness, he spots other figures – the sullen French boy who hangs around the Pathans, Flowers, a scandalous Swedish dancer whom the zenana women have read about in the illustrated papers.

'Aha!' shouts Firoz. There is the crackling sound of a needle being placed on a gramophone, and dramatic piano music begins to billow out into the room. Pran peeps above the chair back and sees a title flash on to the screen:

SYLVIA
OR
TERRORS OF THE WHITE SLAVE TRAFFIC

Firoz begins to applaud loudly, and one of the dead bodies in the back row lurches upright and rubs its eyes.

'This is very special!' Birch announces to the darkened room. 'It wasn't made for public exhibition.'

Pran has never seen a moving picture before. The flickering images take him up like a fist and sit him on one of the Prince's high-backed wooden chairs. He forgets where he is. He forgets that he is in danger. The people on the screen are like ghosts, memories that have been drained of all colour. He wonders how they have been persuaded to show such intimate details of their lives.

Sylvia, the eponymous heroine, is a young immigrant girl arriving in the USA. Almost immediately on landing, she is plucked out from the crowd of arrivals by a young man in a straw boater. Saying he will make her famous by putting her in moving pictures, he takes her off to a tall brick house. Pran is confused by this, since Sylvia is already in a moving picture. Still, the action is taking place in America, where the meanings of things may be different. It soon becomes clear that the young man is not a maker of moving pictures at all but a ruffian with designs on Sylvia's virtue. Once she is inside the house she is locked in a room with an old woman who grimaces and wears a lot of kohl around her eyes. Pran can sympathize with this. Then the straw-boater man (who has been making plans with some moustachioed associates) returns. Little time is wasted in stripping Sylvia of all her outer garments.

'Good Lord,' expostulates the Major. Birch laughs.

'Hold on to your hat, please. This is only the beginning.'

Birch is right. Item by item, Sylvia is divested of all the rest of her clothing bar a pair of black stockings. When the young man begins to undress as well, Major Privett-Clampe can contain himself no longer and leaps to his feet in shock. For a moment he stands swaying, his silhouette obscuring most of the screen. The semi-conscious man in the back, De Souza or whoever, slurs an incomprehensible complaint and makes flapping sit-down gestures.

'How on earth do they – that's disgusting.' The Major clearly cannot believe his eyes.

'I'm told it gets much better. Birch promises us a very piquant scene where she falls into the hands of three evil Arabs. The contrast of the light skin and the dark is –'

Prince Firoz has overstepped the mark. Even though the Major is full of his host's whisky, even though the host is of royal blood, even though he is the *host*, God damn it, still Privett-Clampe cannot let this kind of thing pass.

'You scoundrel!' he shouts. He is squaring up to punch the Prince when he is distracted by the screen. The straw-boater man is now wearing nothing at all but his trademark headgear, and standing side-on to the camera is approaching Sylvia with a villainous erection. Like a deflated balloon Privett-Clampe sits down in his seat to watch coitus take place. Behind him Pran too is open-mouthed in amazement.

The scene comes to a conclusion, and is rapidly replaced by one in which Sylvia is joined by another female captive. The sight of not one but two white women in peril floods the Major with memories of his darkest days of maharajas and *le vice Anglais*, and soon he is back on his feet, accusing Firoz of all manner of wickedness, in an apparent confusion of on-screen events with those at Fatehpur. Ignoring the Prince's suggestions that he sit down and have another drink, he starts clearing chairs out of his path, attempting to get to the door. Too late Pran remembers that he was supposed to be discreet, but, before he has a chance to hide, finds the Major directly in front of him.

'Clive? What are you doing here?'

Prince Firoz looks round, peering into the darkness. 'Who the hell is that?'

'I –' says Pran, and flees.

An atmosphere of crisis descends on Fatehpur. At the British Residency, Charlotte is organizing an enormous garden party. At the palace, where the Braddocks will be staying, the Nawab's retinue are making preparations for a parade and a ceremonial durbar, while Firoz's servants are putting the finishing touches to a programme of entertainments designed to demonstrate their master's taste, thoughtfulness and self-evident fitness to rule.

It is merely their visitor's due. Sir Wyndham Braddock, IPS, KCIE, His Majesty's Resident in the Combined Punjab States, is an imperial demi-god. His tours of the twenty-five principalities under his tutelage always take place in this cloud of gifts and entertainments and durbars, and are conducted according to protocols so fine and rare as to be almost ethereal, the Platonic form of politicking. This year, Sir Wyndham has left Fatehpur until very late in the season. The hot weather is coming, when Englishmen become irritable and indecisive. It looks as if he will have to be pleasured even more vigorously than usual. Cars travel back and forth to pick up supplies from Lahore. Silver is polished, glassware is shined. Much rests on tiny details.

Among the Nawab's faction, there is despair. It is surely too late now. They have no way of making Privett-Clampe do their bidding. Firoz will inherit, and the future will be a European horror of production lines and grinning faces. The Diwan cannot control himself and strikes Pran across the mouth, splitting his lip. Pran sprawls on the floor of the Baroque room, watching drops of blood multiply on the mirrored surface by his head.

Elsewhere in the palace it is all his friends can do to calm Firoz down. Dom Miguel De Souza, whose hangover is already tightening a ratchet around his temples, is sure everything will work out for the best. Firoz cannot believe the attitude of these freeloading fools. For the best? Easy for him to be blasé with property on three continents and a million head of beef cattle chomping grass in the far-off Mato Grosso. For the best? Does he know how insecure Firoz's finances really are?

De Souza thinks that if Firoz is going to behave like this he will have to order a prairie oyster. That might help. Would it really be too much to ask? In reply, Firoz launches a well-aimed highball glass. Brief curtain of Tom Collins. De Souza ducks. One of the women, the famous 'Eastern' dancer (Swedish star of the 'Rite of Shiva', as performed for all the crowned heads of Europe), screams and runs out. Firoz reflects that she is really very highly strung. Someone is dispatched to go and find her, before she gets herself into trouble.

In the darkness of the hour before dawn the Nawab, eyes gummed with sleep, gives orders for the chauffeur to ready a car. He carries his troubles into a curtained rear compartment and is driven down a bumpy road, sliding from side to side on the leather-upholstered banquette seat.

There are layers to the confusion at Fatehpur, a millefeuille of guilt going back years into the past. The Old Nawab spent more than usual one summer, and found himself embarrassed for funds to buy the uncut ruby shown to him by a Rajput jeweller, the one which caught the light *just so*. For political reasons the loan had to be made in secret, so the Nawab approached an outsider, a Hindu banker of the Charan caste. The terms were easy, the ruby changed hands; it was duly set into a turban jewel which the present Nawab still wears on official occasions. It is a badge of secret shame. Shame because there were other creditors, many others, and the Charan lived in far-off Mewar. Shame because the Old Nawab weighed up his obligations and defaulted on the debt, thinking there would be no real consequences. Shame because the Charan still followed the old, hard traditions of his caste, and when he realized he would not be paid he mixed a poison and committed ritual suicide. On his deathbed he grabbed his son by the collar, and, pulling him down close enough to whisper, cursed the family which had brought such shame on his own.

Deathbed curses are the strongest kind. But what was the curse's substance? That is the question. Only the Charan's relatives know for certain, but the rumour persists that the Nawab's house is doomed to die out within a generation. All the signs are there. Harvests have been bad in recent years. Astronomers have noted unhealthy conjunctions of the moon and Venus. And of course there are less publicly visible phenomena, eased out of loosened pyjamas only in the lamplit secrecy of the zenana. Cold fingers of destiny are cupped tight around the Nawab's testicles, stunting the sperm and softening the erection which ought to be securing Fatehpur's future. Fate has him firmly by his silk-wrapped balls.

The Nawab is en route to an obscure hill village, his difficulty curled between his legs like a small sick animal. As the sky lightens, the big British car grumbles over a rutted cattle-path that leads to the hut of the only bona fide saint currently resident within the Fatehpur borders. There the Sublime Ruler, Confounder of Darkness and True Sword of Islam, prostrates himself before a blind pauper, touches his calloused feet and begs him to lift the curse.

Charlie Privett-Clampe is also up as early, keen to fit in a morning ride before the day's labours begin. She takes Brandywine for a quick canter and is already back, washed and ready for her chota hazri, before the head cook has even made an appearance in the kitchen. This is only a temporary delay. Soon enough tea and toast has been delivered, and the Burra Mem' is supervising the unpacking of cups and saucers, cutlery and plates, the first stage in the preparation of tomorrow's official garden party. Two hundred to be fed and watered on the lawn. A big job, no doubt about it. But she is an Old Hand at garden parties, and more than up to the task.

Charlie would be in the thick of it, were she not interrupted by that insufferable Firoz, arriving out of the blue with an escort of over-dressed dagos and some kind of fancily wrapped present which he insists on giving to Gus right away. Gus, the bloody fool, is barricaded in his room with a bucket, looking like the victim of a railway accident and refusing even to let the boy in to dress him. So the unctuous Prince is under Charlie's feet, and she has to drop everything to dispense lime soda and small talk while all around her the extra help is visibly slacking on the job. What a bore!

The sun climbs higher and the Diwan discovers there is not enough gunpowder for the salutes, and the red carpet is a little threadbare and should have been replaced. Then he recalls Lady Braddock's embarrassing kleptomaniac tendencies and orders that all small objects in the audience rooms be removed for safekeeping.

In the zenana the question of What to Wear is uppermost in everyone's minds, and errands are urgently run for new and hard-to-find cosmetic supplies. The legion of dirzis encamped in the outer courtyard sew as if their lives depend on it, which in some cases is exactly what they have been told. All this chaos takes place despite the fact that no one will actually see these outfits. The essence of dressing up for the zenana women lies more in preparation than in actual display. In a snatched moment the Khwaja-sara pincers Pran's chin between ring-encrusted fingers, examines the broken lip and informs him in a vivid tone that the time has come for concentration. The choice is a simple one and Pran will not be told again. There will be one last attempt. It will succeed. If he seduces Privett-Clampe, and they get a suitable picture, then he will be given money and allowed to leave. If not, there will be no further use for him. The silence between the words falls away, grey and heavy. Pran realizes, with a chill, that his options are running out.

He would be even less happy were he to bump into a certain casual stroller in the palace. Jean-Loup stalks the corridors, a purposefully aimless flâneur. He suspects he has a rival. Jean-Loup hates rivals. Jean-Loup's rivals get cut. So he looks around the palace for a good-looking boy dressed in English school uniform. He will not be so pretty soon, hein?

Later that morning the Nawab emerges from the hut somewhat lighter of heart. The pir has assured him that, despite his family's past misdeeds, it is not Allah's will that he lose his throne. They have sat together and the old man has laid his hand on the affected part, an experience which was not altogether unpleasant. He has assured Murad that his potency will return soon. The ruler is taking away a little newspaper cone containing a concoction of herbal ingredients. He has been instructed to think of himself as a tiger. If he follows this advice, he will soon feel the power of his ancestors coursing through his veins. The pir waves him off, and stoops to gather up the gold mohurs the grateful ruler has sprinkled in front of him on the floor.

The sun reaches its zenith, and Major Privett-Clampe says how kind and how nice as he unwraps the framed print of a pink-tinted King-Emperor. A good safe present. One which lets you know on which side the giver's loyalties lie. Prince Firoz wishes his fervent apologies to be conveyed, his sincere apologies. Surely the Major will be able to find it in his heart to forgive and forget. Last night? An aberration. A lamentable failure of taste.

The Major grunts gruffly and hands the present to a servant. Firoz departs with all his doubts still intact. If only he had not been so drunk last night.

Firoz spends a mildly diverting afternoon looking through Cornwell Birch's new titles. *The Yellow Man and the Girl*, *Three Little Negro Maids*, *Country Stud Horse*, *Jazz Godiva* and the latest of the *Big Bellhops* series he distributes to his more discerning clientele. But Prince Firoz is more interested in Birch's next project. A hunting picture. A *tiger*-hunting picture.

The light fails. Darkness inks in corners, passageways. An orange dot waxes momentarily bright in the shadows of the zenana's outer courtyard. The tailors finished long ago. Everyone should be asleep. But Jean-Loup is still wandering. He throws the cigarette butt on the floor, grinds it flat under the sole of a handmade two-tone co-respondent shoe. Things have become clearer during the day. The zenana seems to be where the little fool is hiding. And here he comes, shuffling sleepily down the stairs, on his way to the latrine, picking up his skirts as he walks. La mignonne! Jean-Loup is grateful. He was starting to get bored.

This is his cue. Unsheathed from a snug hip pocket is a razor, glinting as it is opened out, twirled in practised fingers. This is what they call the Marseilles grip. Pran scratches his arse, thinking of nothing but his bladder, as he shuffles along. Jean-Loup walks faster, gaining, coming up behind but is suddenly met by light and voices. A group of people hurrying towards them. He shrinks back behind a pillar.

The unknowing seventh cavalry consists of the Nawab and a pair of sleepy torchbearers. He wants them to pick their feet up, because there is an unaccustomed stirring in his loins. He barely notices the little hijra salaaming to the floor as he passes. He has better things to think about. Those women are going to see something. They are going to see Magnificence! Make way! It is satisfying to yell in the darkened courtyard and to watch the scurry and tumble as the doors are opened. Nothing like a surprise visit for keeping them on their toes.

Lila Bai, junior wife, has the rudest of awakenings. The Nawab framed in the doorway. Behold him! Indeed, the pir's herbal decoction has had a noticeable effect. See that? Damascus steel. And she knows where that is going. Lila Bai barely has time to beg for mercy before he is on top of her. Tonight he knows he is fantastic. He is first class. The drug does, however, seem to be making him very vocal. Not words. *Roaring*. He finds he has to growl, deep full-throated growls that stretch his jaws and rattle his chest. This is not normal. Still, it is working. Really. Really. Really. Working. And then, with a mighty roar, the royal climax occurs, every drop of it worth its political weight in gold. At once he pins her down, panting into the hollow between neck and shoulder. She rubs his back. He pulls himself together, makes a speech about how she will never doubt him again, slaps her face a couple of times and departs well pleased with himself. Wah!

Sir Wyndham Braddock smiles and waves. Lady Aurelia smiles and waves. The little brown people smile and wave. They wave paper Union Jacks and stare up at the decorated elephant parading through the streets of their town. The band marching behind the elephant plays 'The British Grenadiers', with a distinct nasal wail. Sir Wyndham winces. However long he is in India, Sir Wyndham will never get used to native orchestras.

The streets are packed. People sit in rows along the roofs. They have climbed on to awnings and dangle their legs from windowsills. Sir Wyndham looks about nervously. Swaying inside the howdah he feels exposed. He peers into windows and scans the swelling, shoving mass of people, kept out of his path by lathi-wielding policemen. The Nawab has organized a good turn-out. A three-line whip, most probably. Like all native chiefs, this one is doubtless no stranger to coercion.

Had it been at all possible, Sir Wyndham would have cancelled. The situation in the Punjab is worsening. Even so, it is impossible. The thing has been arranged for months. He has to go through with it, even if riding about on an elephant makes him feel like an empty bottle on top of a wall. He is the representative of the Crown and the Crown must be seen to be unafraid. There it is. End of discussion. He wonders what is known about yesterday's events. He has had Intelligence check with the Post and Telegraph people, and they told them it is indeed possible that some traffic to Fatehpur last night related to Dyer's action at Amritsar. Possible? The incompetents. That means more than bloody likely. So whoever the local Congresswallahs are in this flea-bitten little kingdom, they know. Which means there may well be trouble. What a day to make a state visit.

Sir Wyndham does not know exactly what happened at Amritsar. Only that some kind of meeting was held in defiance of a prohibition on public gatherings. Only that Dyer went in hard. Two hundred dead, said the first reports. Must have been a bloody business. Still, everyone knew it was coming. Even the natives.

Smile and wave.

Opposite him Lady Aurelia has a set expression. Little droplets of sweat stand out on her high white forehead. Lady Aurelia is obviously Bearing Up. He leans forward and touches her on the knee.

'Minty?' he asks, his voice tender.

She says nothing. Minty is obviously having one of her Days. Smile and wave.

Over the years, Sir Wyndham has learnt to interpret his wife. With Minty one is never told. One is expected to guess. She is hot and, he supposes, frightened. When she is like this, she would rather be Left Alone. This is how Sir Wyndham organizes his understanding of his wife. Two-word headings. A column for every one of her various states, all the way from Fast Asleep to Hysterical Fit.

At least they have managed to keep Gandhi out of the Punjab. And most of the other bigwigs are in preventative detention outside the state borders. Firm action has been taken. In times like these the response is simple enough. It is simply a matter of nerve.

Smile –

There is a sudden rattle and crack. A rending. A tearing of the air. Instinctively Sir Wyndham ducks. Lady Aurelia does the same, dislodging her hat. For an instant their heads are close together, almost in each other's laps. Sir Wyndham is sure he knows what has happened. Someone in the crowd has thrown a Mills Bomb. An assassination attempt. But neither he nor Minty appear to have been hit, and their mahout is looking round at them quizzically, heels braced behind the ears of his mount.

The howdah smells of fresh paint and elephant dung. Sir Wyndham cautiously straightens up. The noise is continuing. Firecrackers. Someone has lit firecrackers. A group of men are dancing about in the crowd, their hands in the air. They have opened up a space between them, a clearing in which a string of fireworks fizzes and bucks. His heart still pounding, Sir Wyndham silently curses himself for his skittishness. Minty is fiddling with her hat, trying to adjust the mother-of-pearl pin which fastens it to her hair. She will not look at him. Maintaining Order. Another one of her usuals. Sir Wyndham straightens the brim of his own topi, and risks a glance back behind him. A glance to see if any of his staff have noticed his cowardice. From the elephant behind, Vesey gives him a mocking salute. Damn. That means it will be all over every mess and common room in Lahore within a week. Fortescue taking cover from firecrackers. Damn damn damn.

Smile and wave.

He reminds himself he has a job to do. This will not happen again. He will not show he is afraid. As the howdah lurches from side to side, he finds himself suffused by a physical shame, a sickness in the pit of his stomach which is only made worse by the trembling pitch and yaw of the elephant's massive hips as it plods towards the palace. He sits up straighter, unpleasantly aware of the weight of the row of medals on his chest.

He has a job to do. He has to smile and wave. At the moment the procedure may seem ridiculous, but it is vital to the British project in India. Sir Wyndham has explained it around any number of dinner tables, the importance of his popinjay life. His lavish tours, the presents, the sightseeing, the hunting. None of it, he tells them, is for him as an individual. If one were to mistake the respect one is accorded as an official for something stemming from one's own personality or talents, one would find oneself in hot water. Go off the rails. Get delusions of grandeur. No, one is simply there as a sort of projection, a magic lantern image of the Viceroy, who is himself no more than a magic lantern image of the King-Emperor.

One just puts up with it. The lavishness.

The procession passes through the town, and approaches the maidan beside the hideous wedding-cake palace. This is Sir Wyndham's first visit to Fatehpur, and the sight of the giant edifice makes him feel worse than he did already. The building looks feverish, decadent. As he approaches, he could almost swear it was throbbing. A gland. A great pink growth. Minty is watching it too, one hand clapped over the brim of her hat as if caught in a high wind. For the only time on their journey, husband and wife catch each other's eye. A shared instant of horror, immediately smothered. Face to face with the embodiment of all the runaway madness it is their job in India to curb.

Waiting for them on the maidan is, of all the godforsaken things, another band. A military pipe band. Dressed in grey jackets and – is it? – yes, pink kilts, they are wheezing something raucous and threatening which alludes distantly to the 'Skye Boat Song'. The band walking in the procession increases its volume, and for a while the two sounds clash, the howdah a mountain peak in a roiling flood of noise. Sir Wyndham is sure some of the musicians are taking the opportunity to add their own inventions, little trills and whooping drum rhythms that seem to have arrived out of nowhere. For a while it seems as if everyone is playing something different until, with a few last petulant stabs of brass, the procession band is silenced and the pipers, like a malevolent swarm of wasps, float their victorious humming unchallenged over the hot parade ground.

The salute. Twenty-one guns welcoming him. Welcoming him, Wyndham, not as Wyndham for Wyndham's sake but as the King-Emperor's shadow. The shadow flinches involuntarily at the noise, tries to hold the flinch inside, a crawling of the skin against the lining of his uniform. Then the flinch is countered by a little twitch of pride. He, Wyndham, the equal in guns of any maharaja.

From an upstairs window Pran watches as the Braddocks are helped out of the howdah at the palace's Elephant Gate. A deputation awaits them on the high platform. Flanked by assorted guards and servants is the Nawab, dressed in an extraordinary get-up of blue and white paisley. He is draped in strings of pearls, as well as the sashes and stars of the various Orders he is entitled to wear. His white silk turban is set with a huge blood-red ruby. The Diwan is equally opulently attired, and Firoz elegant in his sleekly tailored morning suit. Beside them are Major and Mrs Privett-Clampe, he beetroot-faced in his white undress uniform, she standing as militarily as her husband, stiff in a summer dress. All smile winningly at their guests.

As he stoops to descend from the howdah, Sir Wyndham notices their shoes. Beneath their finery, both the Nawab and the Diwan are wearing plain black slippers.

Those entitled to wear uniform will wear undress uniform, white. Those not so entitled will wear morning dress. Patent-leather shoes should be worn by all Indian gentlemen who do not attend in morning dress.

Plain black shoes. As the dignitaries execute a little dance, trying to walk in the correct order down the narrow steps of the elephant platform, Sir Wyndham tries to read it in their faces. Is it deliberate? Are they mocking him with their shoes? What reason could they have? He realizes someone has just asked him a question. Prince Firoz, making small-talk. He begs his pardon.

They sit in a gaily decorated grandstand and the Fatehpur armed forces march past in their Ruritanian uniforms. Pink. Why so much pink? Privett-Clampe leans over and says something disparaging about their drill technique. The Nawab leans over and says something proud about their turn-out. Sir Wyndham is still thinking about shoes. Finally he can stand it no more, and twists round to the row behind to whisper in Vesey's ear.

'Their shoes. Do you think they mean anything by it?'

Instantly he wishes he had not. Vesey's face is first blank, then lights up with scarcely concealed amusement. That blasted undergraduate wit of his.

'Their shoes, sir?'

'Oh never mind!'

The march-past ends. Refreshments are served. Sir Wyndham sips a lime soda and says yes very to the people crowding round him. Especially eager, this lot. No one letting anyone else get a word in edgeways. There is an atmosphere, a sort of vivid quality to the conversation which makes him uneasy. At least the public part of the thing is over. There should be no danger now.

They move in to the diwan-i-am for the durbar. Embroidered awnings have been hung between the pillars of the huge hall. A slight breeze blows over the marble floor, cooling hot English cheeks, bringing slight smiles to sweaty faces. As they take their places, fragments of conversation come to Sir Wyndham's distracted ears.

'I will give you the name of my London tailor,' says Prince Firoz to Vesey.

'It was at the Borders,' says Minty to Mrs Privett-Clampe. 'Or was it that tennis party at the Retreat?'

'The Nawab-Sahib has undertaken many large programme of

reformations,' says the Diwan. Silence. Oh, are you talking to me? I beg your pardon. His accent is really very bad.

'Lochinverarie,' says Mrs Privett-Clampe. 'I'm sure it was a dinner at Lochinverarie.'

'That would be too kind,' says Vesey.

'Yes, very,' says Sir Wyndham, settling himself on his mock-Louis Seize chair, careful to copy the Nawab's easy posture, one foot up on the footstool, arms resting on the gilt arms of the chair. From the upper gallery he can feel the eyes of the palace women on him. Invisible women behind carved marble screens. Occasionally he sees a shadow up there, catches a susurrus of barely audible whispering.

One by one the local dignitaries are introduced. The Treasurer, the military and legal members of the Council of State, the Household Treasurer, the Commissioner of Public Works. Sir Wyndham shakes hands or returns an adaab, cupping his hand and raising it to his forehead. Beside him the Nawab embraces, nods, clasps. Behind him unseen juniors shuffle their feet. May we present the Senior Medical Officer, the Chief Inspector of Police, the Superintendent of the Gaol, the Head of the Department of Forests and Lakes. Indian gentlemen in patent-leather shoes.

When the last Junior Commercial Minister Temporarily Attached to the Excise Department has passed, Vesey hands Sir Wyndham a telegram.

'Just in from Simla' he whispers.

The telegram says that Dyer fired without warning on a crowd at a political meeting, and that the death toll is currently estimated at five hundred. Sir Wyndham folds it neatly and slips it into a pocket.

The necessary balance of hospitality must be maintained. Home and away. So after the durbar comes a ritual exchange of farewells and a short separation before the performance of the Return Visit. Sir Wyndham (not as himself, as England) is to receive the Nawab at the Residency. Then luncheon for two hundred on the back lawn. A big job.

The Nawab's arrival is slow and stately. Preceded by a dozen attendants. Followed by fifty Fatehpur Household Cavalry, this season wearing pink trousers, blue tunics and (in an innovative touch) dyed pink bearskins. A few English flowers, clinging on to life in the beds by the driveway, are dusted Empire-map red as the car swings past. Stray flagwavers cluster by the gate, kept at bay by khaki-uniformed chowkidars. Then the chauffeur's clockwork salute, the car door opening, a (plain-black-shoed) foot touching gravel – and the Nawab is out of the car. Next come the steps.

At the foot of the steps are two uniformed ADCs, twin heel-clicks synchronized (how do they do that?) to the millisecond. They escort the Nawab halfway up – a total of eleven steps – to where Vesey (not as himself but as Punjab States Senior Political Officer) salutes and escorts him the remaining ten. The uneven number of steps has been the subject of a long exchange of memoranda. Simla's arbitration on the meaning of the term 'halfway' was needed to settle anxieties about the political implications of one division over the other. At the top of the steps is Sir Wyndham, who escorts the Nawab the short distance between the front porch and the drawing room, where he offers refreshment – another lime soda? – and has his offer declined. This short moment has its potential for intimacy (the conversation, the look into the eyes, the murmured *so how are you really?*) dampened by the presence of the Nawab's six chobdars. Three attendants carrying maces in the shape of peacock feathers, another three with rather natty silver-mounted yak tails, all of them frowning, as befits the solemnity of the occasion. Sir Wyndham stoically ignores them, pretending to clear his throat.

'If, Your Highness, you'd care to follow me.'

To the garden. As they stand on the back veranda, a ripple of applause washes over the crowd. Both the Nawab and Sir Wyndham permit themselves a smile. And a wave.

Then into the thick of it. Indians and Englishmen. English men and ladies. Indian ladies? No. All chatting in little clusters like an enormous social spore-culture, an experiment grown on the petri dish of the Privett-Clampes' well-watered lawn. White-gloved khidmutgars circulate with silver trays. A string orchestra plays light classical music by the new gazebo, an architectural innovation of Mrs Privett-Clampe. To one side is a long table of Ango-Indian foodstuffs, curries, plain chicken pieces and rice salads, veg. and non-veg., all compromise-spiced to suit the various palates present. Charlie has been working overtime to ensure there are no hiccups, no hardboiled eggs with black fingerprints, no cold drinks salted instead of sugared. It looks as if she has held her end up well. There will be no incidents today, at least none sparked off by the food.

As Sir Wyndham and the Nawab descend the steps to the garden, they are instantly drenched in conversation, like a movie double-act taking a bucketful in the face. Sir Wyndham fidgets. He is finding the proximity of other people difficult. Why will everyone insist on talking at once? And all of them watching each other! He decides there is definitely something unhealthy about Fatehpur. He can tell from the kind of people who are at the party. So many cameras! A loud American keeps interrupting to take moving pictures, shouting at him to turn around or strike poses as if he were a mannequin. A Fatehpuri nobleman with an absurd yellow outfit and smoked eyeglasses keeps waving another apparatus in his face. All manner of European flotsam and jetsam seem to be present too, drinking too much, sneaking off in pairs into the house. A white boy walks past, dressed incongruously in school uniform. How the dickens did he get here?

'I know,' says the Nawab, a sudden raffish grin appearing on his face, 'that you are perhaps reflecting on the silent patter of tiny feet.'

Sir Wyndham begs the Nawab's pardon.

'Silence. The absence of patter. The absence of my son, so very eagerly awaited.'

'Oh yes,' says Sir Wyndham, still bewildered. Son? Then he recalls the bit of swotting he did last night. No son. The Nawab has yet to get off the mark, sonwise. Intelligence seem to think he might be firing blanks.

'Well, Sir Wyndham,' the Nawab continues, 'perhaps you will soon not be disappointed!'

Behind them there is a commotion centred around Prince Firoz, who has dropped his glass, spilling champagne all over his morning suit. The Nawab smiles. He is seized by a sudden desire to slip away from the party and try himself out on one or two of the other concubines. Really, he hasn't felt like this in years.

'Yes,' says Sir Wyndham, distracted by Vesey, who is making signals at him, 'very.'

'GGRRRHHAWW!' roars the Nawab. Heads turn. Sir Wyndham is temporarily at a loss for the correct response.

Pran peers across the lawn to see where the noise came from. He walks gingerly around the party, trying to look as if he is having a good time. He is startled by the Picturewallah, who grabs him tightly by the arm.

'Now, Rukhsana, we must go to work.'

Before he can answer, they are elbowed aside by Dom Miguel De Souza, accompanied by two delightful friends whose names escape him, barging through the party singing show tunes with all the hysterical vigour of a trio who have not been to bed since the night before last. Travelling in their wake, the Picturewallah steers Pran in the direction of Major Privett-Clampe. Dug into a position giving a commanding view of the bar, the Major is in conversation with Vesey, who wears the drawn, elevated face of a man looking around hopelessly for an escape route.

'Old Crusty's favourite trick,' reveals the Major, 'is to gallop full pelt up to a well or what have you, then jink sharply off to the side –' His jollity is forced. Actually he is not feeling his best. He has not had a drink all day, and the shakes are setting in. Steadying himself on Vesey, he shuts his eyes for a moment. When he opens them again, the party, every surface of it, is covered in pink and grey insects.

'Jolly interesting, old man,' says Vesey, patting the Major on the back, 'but ours is to serve. Guardians of the Republic and all that. I must circulate.'

Privett-Clampe nods. They are on him too. All over him. He lurches towards the bar. By the fourth glass of champagne, the insects are beginning to crawl more slowly.

'A woman,' the Major says to a silver-suited fellow, 'can catch a pig on the maidan, but it takes a man to kill one in the jhow.'

'Fascinating!' purrs Jean-Loup.

Inside the house De Souza and the girls are trying to cheer up Prince Firoz. Firoz is convinced everything has gone to hell. Buck up, old man! Have a little joy powder! He manages a couple of petulant sniffs, which only serve to make him more determined than ever, yes determined, that even if his accursed brother has done the unthinkable and managed to sow a viable seed, still the child will never, and yes as God is his witness he means never, sit on the throne of Fatehpur.

'Perhaps you should calm down?' suggests De Souza, alarmed.

The Diwan storms by. He is looking around for the Nawab, who seems to have disappeared. As he sweeps past De Souza's huddle, his robe brushes the vial out of his hand.

'Hey! You spilt all our cokey!'

Imelda (it is Imelda, isn't it?) is in no mood for low tricks like that. She takes off a shoe and aims it, badly, at the departing Diwan's head. Cream high heel sails past turban, then arcs elegantly over the veranda into the garden, striking Jean-Loup hard on the back of the head. Instantly his street-fighting reflexes kick in (unless you are quick, you are dead, hein?), and he wheels around, looking for his assailant.

The Diwan is reduced to asking Charlie Privett-Clampe, 'You have seen His Highness?'

'No, I bloody well have not!' With that, she charges off, a livid expression on her face. For although privilege of rank has to be respected, and we would be nowhere without hierarchies, and though you might say in some circumstances turning a blind eye is a virtue, there are still limits and some things are just not to be tolerated, no matter who perpetrates them.

Seeing Mrs Privett-Clampe bearing down on him, Sir Wyndham pales visibly. He can spot these situations at fifty paces. Minty has been at her tricks again. He scrunches the latest telegram into a little ball, the telegram which says that the estimated death toll at Amritsar has risen to eight hundred and the native press are claiming double that, and tries to head disaster off at the pass.

'Can I help?' he asks, his voice freighted with diplomacy, tact, finesse.

Charlie does not know what to say. This is precisely what Sir Wyndham intended.

'No,' she says eventually, trying to make it sound firm. 'Have you seen Gus?'

'I think he's talking to that American fellow. The moving-picture chap.'

Charlie nods distractedly, and heads off.

'Gus? Gus!'

'Charlie?'

'What on earth are you doing?'

'They're everywhere, Charlie. Absolutely everywhere.'

Charlie ignores him. He often spouts this sort of nonsense. 'Gus,' she hisses, 'shut up and listen. It's that – that Braddock woman. I found her in our bedroom, bold as brass, helping herself to one of my favourite little Kashmiri boxes. You know, the papier mâché ones we got that time in Gulmarg. The cheek of it! When I walked in she didn't look worried at all. Not in the slightest. She just said how darling and popped it into her hand-bag. I didn't know what to say. So there you are, Gus. What are you going to do? Gus?'

Gus makes a flapping gesture with his arms.

'Ointment,' he says weakly. 'Maybe that would do the trick.'

Inside the house something marvellous has happened. A rare thing. One of those conjunctions which many people dream of and few are lucky enough to experience. Minty has met the Nawab. Official meetings are one thing. A person encountered formally so often appears to be no more than the role they fulfil. Here, now, things are different. She, sauntering towards the garden with a newly bulky handbag. He, striding through the hall on his way to his car. Though she is no longer a young woman, Minty Braddock's poise is arresting. The Nawab notes her long arms, her high white forehead, the small neat bow of her mouth. Minty finds herself slightly shocked at his gaze. This fierce young ruler with his hook nose and dark eyes – and so very many jewels! That brooch in particular. Absolutely irresistible. When he approaches her, takes her hands in his and makes an extraordinary wordless sound in his throat, she knows she will do anything he asks.

'GRROAAH!' says the Nawab, to the base of Minty's neck.

'Oh Your Majesty!' whispers Minty, completely forgetting her protocol. 'Oh!'

'Minty?'

It can't be. Damn. Her husband's plaintive tones. The old boy is standing behind the Nawab's shoulder, moustache wriggling in embarrassment, pretending to cough into his clenched fist. The Nawab whirls round and, in an inspired impulse, vigorously shakes Sir Wyndham's hand.

'Well done, sir. Jolly well done.'

Sir Wyndham, used to being praised for reasons not immediately obvious to him, says a reflexive thank you.

'I shall see you at the hunt later on,' he adds, but finds he is talking to the Nawab's departing back. There is the sound of a car engine, and the ruler of Fatehpur leaves the party in a spray of gravel.

That afternoon, throughout Fatehpur, lunchtime hang-overs barely impede preparations for the hunt. Khaki clothes and solar topis are laid out on beds. The barrels of .375 magnum hunting rifles are cleaned, oiled and squinted down. There is checking of electric torches, application of patent anti-mosquito preparations, careful filling of hip flasks and tiffin carriers. The light will not fail for a few hours yet, but every mind is fixed on the thought of a night in the forest.

Well, not every mind. There are distractions. Charlie finds Gus even more helpless than usual, unable to get a single thing for himself. In the guest bedroom Sir Wyndham can get no sense out of Minty, even after he has emptied her bag of its clinking booty of boxes, lighters, cigarette cases and ivory ornaments. At the palace the Nawab has disappeared into the zenana, although the sound of screaming, growling and nervous feminine laughter gives his sniggering servants some idea of his location. In his dressing room Prince Firoz cannot decide between the belted English jacket and the German stalking coat the Margrave of Stumpfburg gave him last year. Sartorial indecision is always a sign of stress with Firoz, and eventually the problem is solved by flinging both items out of the window.

Some hunters seem to have more complex packing to perform than others. Mr Birch's servants gingerly lift a box stencilled with red US Army WARNING markings into one of the cars. The Khwaja-sara is filtering something green and sludgy through a muslin bag. Pran is left to wait, sitting in his alcove, dressed in brand new white-hunter garb, his socks pulled up to his knees and his oversized hat shading his eyes so completely that he has to crick his neck backwards to see the world outside. He has tried to mention certain things to the Picturewallah, such as his suspicion that the silver-suit boy is trying to kill him, and the way the other side seems just as keen as the Nawab's party on taking compromising pictures of the Major. No one has time to listen. He swings his legs, banging his heels nervously against the stone seat. He is not looking forward to the hunt at all.

Jean-Loup is upstairs in the palace, helping Imelda, De Souza and the Swedish exotic dancer to polish off the last of the joy powder. Most of them have made some attempt to change into hunting gear. A few hats. An artistic khaki wrap. Everyone has a gun, at least. That is the important thing. They like guns, this crowd. Guns and cokey.

At the appointed hour of five o'clock a line of cars is assembled. There is a certain strangeness round the edges of the scene. Men lope around, peering into car windows. A fashionably attired hunter experiences a sudden and violent nosebleed, while his screaming companion is forcibly parted from her weapon. Here is the Khwaja-sara, discreetly directing a servant with a tray of refreshments to offer drinks to some people, but not to others. Here are the chauffeurs, standing by passenger doors, then running round to gun the engines and spin the wheels in the dust. Pran finds himself sandwiched next to the Picturewallah in the last car of the convoy. During the long boneshaking drive to the Fatehpur forests, he dozes as the noble lectures him about the honour of the kingdom and the fabulous rewards which will accrue to him for helping persuade the sisterfucking English to maintain the Nawab's line of succession.

When the Picturewallah shakes him awake, the rest of the convoy has disappeared. Their car has stopped in a clearing and the chauffeur is standing beside it, smoking a bidi. Around them tall forest trees rise up towards a grey sky. It must be shortly after sunset. Pran climbs out of the car, stretching his cramped legs, trying to shake the long drive out of his body. Ahead of the car the road, already a narrow rutted track, peters out into nothing. He peers into the green darkness. A dense, breathing world, smudged here and there with pink and red rhododendron bushes. All around the dusty car the trees quiver with birds, their blanket communication enveloping everything, a flow broken only by the sudden thrash and rustle of a langur monkey leaping from one branch to the next. The Picturewallah looks at the scene disdainfully, poking his wire glasses back on to the bridge of his nose.

'Come,' he says, and Pran notices a villager, skinny and dark, salaaming at them from the trees. The man picks up various cases of camera equipment and balances them on his head, beckoning them to follow him into the darkness. The Picture-wallah immediately unslings his rifle, carrying it in front of him like a stave. He is wearing a hunting outfit of thick Shetland tweed and a matching tweed turban. Twin cartridge belts are slung bandit-fashion across his chest. Pran sees the set expression on his face and wonders for a chilling moment if the whole seduction plan is a ruse, and he has been taken out here to be killed.

By the light of an oil lantern they pick their way along a dried-up watercourse, made into a closed tunnel by a lacy canopy of creepers. Above them the forest communicates in whoops and trills and buzzes, passing news of the three walkers far ahead into green space. Once something large breaks cover up ahead, a blur crashing heavily into the trees. After half an hour or so, just as the Picturewallah is beginning to wheeze and wipe his sleeve across his forehead, a smell of cooking starts to overlay the forest's clean pungency and they arrive at another clearing.

Loinclothed men lounge around a fire, scooping rice and sloppy dal into their mouths out of big steel dishes. Their skins are leathery and dark. Tribal men. A pair of their women squat further off, ears, ankles, arms and noses heavy with silver, scouring pans and whispering together. Yellow eyeballs dart round, then settle with impersonal curiosity on the newcomers. The women tug the pallas of their saris over their heads and look away again, focusing meekly on the ground. The Picturewallah starts giving orders, and the men stand up, unhurriedly, to obey.

Behind them are two large mounds, covered in branches. Pran makes his way round the fire, walks towards them, and is greeted by a rich, deep, rasping sound. A roar. With a start he realizes he is face to face with a pair of caged tigers. They look lazily at him, tongues lolling, their liquid eyes seeming barely to register his presence. He turns to the Picturewallah for explanation. All the men are grinning at him, as if he has just been let in on a joke.

'When the Angrezi come to hunt,' the Picturewallah laughs, 'there are some things it is better not to leave to chance.'

One of the tribals dances forward to a cage, sticks his arm through the bars, and actually strokes a broad velvety snout. The tiger brushes against his hand like a cat.

'You haven't given them too high a dose?' asks the Picturewallah. 'You'll have to drag them over to the machans.'

'No, sir. No. They're awake just enough for the shoot. Anyway, these foreign people will not know the difference.'

'True enough,' grunts the Picturewallah, and settles down to wait.

Some distance further into the forest, the main party takes a light supper. Hampers. Wine coolers. Collapsible tables unpacked and spread with white cloths. Prince Firoz strides among the foreign people, more opulently foreign than his guests. He cannot settle. Occasionally he casts a glance at the drunken Major, who is wandering around among the parked cars with a leg of chicken and a hip flask, his upper body making involuntary jerking movements. Is he? – yes, he seems to be talking to himself. Jean-Loup should not find him too much trouble. If the man will not make the right recommendation after that silly business with the pornographic film, then he will have to be persuaded. Birch has brought a mountain of equipment, and right now he should be setting himself up in a suitable vantage point. Everything should be fine. Unless, that is, his accursed brother is telling the truth. Unless, God forbid, he has managed to propel one of his stunted sperm far enough into one of his women to impregnate her. Firoz thinks this impossible. And yet – and yet his sources in the zenana have supplied some alarming reports. Damn. He really wishes he had chosen a different hat. This one has such an *Indian* feel to it. Damn.

The Diwan also has photography on his mind. He does not trust the Picturewallah, who had to be reminded that he would be working in darkness. How will your machine see? Oh, he had not thought of that. Of course if the imbecile had taken a good picture the first time around none of this would be necessary. And the Major seems not to be himself. Ill, perhaps? The Nawab-Sahib has also been behaving strangely. As soon as they alighted from the cars, he sidled up to Lady Braddock and did a very lewd thing. A sort of rubbing. Naturally everyone had manners enough to pretend they had not noticed, but Sir Wyndham appears angry. His good English lady wife should have been able to stop the Nawab fondling her breasts, even if he is her superior in rank.

A signal is given and the party heaves itself on to elephants to travel the last few miles to the hunting ground. The mounting goes more or less smoothly, apart from some antics involving the Swedish dancer, who wishes to be lifted by her animal's trunk. Eventually they move off, a single file of beasts swaying hip-deep in the high meadow grass. The atmosphere of plotting, of fierce concealments and scratch calculation, spills over the elephants' grey hide like a static field, a nervous aura of itchy trigger fingers, weird brain chemistry and paranoid virtualities which makes the animals edgy and skittish. The mahouts dig their heels behind large and sensitive ears, murmuring to their little pearls to step boldly, not to worry, not to fear.

The grass turns to forest and the party dismounts, walking a short way to the site the Nawab's Royal Huntsman has decreed most likely to attract a tiger. The Huntsman himself, an ancient retainer with a moustache that extends in extravagant curls on either side of his face, leads the way. A dry nullah runs beneath a slight ridge, a single cut-off bend still filled with reasonably fresh water. Around this area, in a ragged semicircle, wooden machans have been mounted in the trees. The platforms are large and sturdy, spreading amply over lower branches, furnished with stools and bedding. 'No one,' cries the Nawab, in his first intelligible speech for some hours, 'need suffer as a guest of the Lord of Fatehpur!' He receives a smattering of applause.

'Quite the place for a tiger, this,' Vesey remarks to the Diwan, with the knowledgeable smirk of a man who has shot a big cat or two in his time. The Diwan agrees politely. He cannot, alas, summon up much enthusiasm for the hunting aspect of the evening, mainly because he already knows what is due to happen. At around two hours after midnight Sir Wyndham will bag a large male, which will miraculously turn out to measure two inches more from nose to tail than the tiger his predecessor shot three years ago. If things go exactly to plan, one of the other English visitors will take the second. This degree of predestination might disappoint some of the guests. However, their hosts take the view that politics demands certain sacrifices from sportsmanship. Sir Wyndham must, above all, associate Fatehpur with success. Even if this were not the overriding consideration, some lack of spontaneity would be inevitable: the last genuine wild tiger was shot here in 1898 and in recent years the royal family has imported its animals from Assam, where they have a surplus.

Three spindly legged calves are tethered at strategic positions around the waterhole. The huntsmen make long knife-cuts across their backs, deep enough to draw blood. The calves scrabble at the earth and low in fear, as if aware their scent is now wafting enticingly through the forest. A complex ballet takes place as the Royal Huntsman assigns the party its places. The confusion is partly caused by his moustache, which muffles his already eccentric pronunciation of names, and partly by a reluctance on the part of some of the hunters to go where they have been told. Mrs Privett-Clampe and Lady Braddock, for example, seem unaccountably reluctant to spend a night up a tree with one another. Sir Wyndham is swiftly ushered into the best spot, accompanied by both the Nawab and Prince Firoz. Privett-Clampe, who has great difficulty even seeing his tree, let alone ascending the rope ladder to his machan, is eventually helped up by Vesey and De Souza, the latter casting longing looks at his lady-friends, who have been placed out of harm's way at one end of the row. By the time the hunters are in position and the ropes have been pulled up, darkness has fallen. They settle down to wait.

Pran sleeps. He is woken by the Picturewallah, who looks as if he has just woken up himself. His voice is thick and phlegmy, and he appears agitated.

'Hurry up!' he whispers. 'We're late.'

The campfire is a pile of embers. The men have gone, the tigers with them. The Picturewallah gathers up his things and the two of them trot through the trees, thorns and creepers catching their clothing, tugging at their ankles like beggar children. Pran does not understand the urgency, does not understand anything about this blind stumble except that it seems to knit together everything about his life into one act, a pelting through clammy resistant darkness. The thought makes him laugh, and he runs along panting and giggling, light-headed, hysterically careless.

Tiger hunting requires two main qualities: silence and patience. If a change of wind direction carries the hunter's scent to his prey, any but the hungriest man-eater will stay away. Likewise, the slightest noise can ruin things. Loud giggling, for example, or the popping of champagne corks. Charlie Privett-Clampe, quite pleased with the hint of moonlight illuminating the nullah, and the clear line of sight she has to the tethered bait, does not want her chances ruined by the commotion coming from the end tree. What are they doing up there, holding a cocktail party? She hisses a sshhh!, much as one might at the theatre, but when it has no effect on the festivities, she goes back to glowering over her rifle barrel, propping herself in a comfortable position and trying as far as possible to ignore Minty, who is coquettishly brushing her hair.

It is not only the goodtimers in the far tree who are having trouble keeping still. Several people in the party are sharing a rather unpleasant experience, an experience which began when they accepted one of those queer-tasting lemonade drinks that were being handed round at departure. That queer taste has been hanging around at the backs of throats, developing into something distinct and metallic, accompanied by a gradual increase in what can only be termed 'gastric awareness'. Stomachs (organs which are usually only intermittently present to their owners) have been changing state, becoming mobile, active, uneasy. Vesey is suffering badly, his innards acquiring a treacherous and marshy feel which, once up in the machan, immediately develops into a sensation of full-scale bubbling swamp. No amount of clenching or mind-over-matter exercises will alter the inevitable. It is only a matter of time.

'I'm terribly sorry,' he says to Privett-Clampe, 'but I'll have to get down for a moment.'

Prince Firoz is feeling something similar, but is determined not to leave his brother alone with Sir Wyndham. Conversation has been slight, but the risk that in his absence Murad might bring up the matter of the succession is too great to take. Still, a crisis is imminent, and Firoz is unused to physical discomfort. He digs deep, searching for some nub of perseverance not worn away by years of pleasure-seeking. Alas, his resources are meagre, and neither surreptitious wind-breaking nor sips of water seem to help. He pulls his knees up to his chest and tries to think of polo, light aircraft and other strong, manly things.

Activity in the undergrowth grows by the minute. Hunters, mostly those associated with Prince Firoz's faction, are answering urgent calls of nature. Other hunters are twitchily training their rifles on these sudden movements, surprised to find the jungle so full of life. Squatting in a spiky bush directly in Sir Wyndham's line of fire, Imelda works out how many hours she is away from the nearest flush toilet, and begins to cry. Sir Wyndham, who in thirty-five years of foreign service has never seen a woman in the act of excretion, watches her through his sights with mingled horror and fascination. Minty must do that. God. There is movement behind him. The Nawab has thrown down the rope ladder, and is descending.

'Not you too?' asks Sir Wyndham. The Nawab does not respond. Almost as soon as he has gone, Prince Firoz, who has been rolled up into a kind of foetal ball, unwinds with a strangled exhalation, and scrambles after him, leaving behind a nasty whiff. Sir Wyndham is left quite alone.

Also alone is Major Privett-Clampe. Vesey and De Souza have vanished, leaving him wrapped in velvety, crawling blackness. The Major finds his world has been hollowed out as if by maggots, leaving him suspended in space, a plump and florid web-bound fly. That is how the criss-cross branches look to him. A spider's web. The horrors multiply in the corners of his eyes, and he cannot stare them all down at once. Only staring, hard concentrated staring, works to resolve the jerks and writhings of this awful place into a conventional arrangement of objects in space. The darkness makes it worse. There are dangers all around. Rustlings. Particularly from a tree some way behind him. Something is up there, watching. The Major takes a firm grip on his rifle and thinks of the Four Hundred and the Valley of Death. If it comes to that, he will not shirk. He will ride forward.

'Do you absolutely *have* to hum?' Charlie hisses at Minty. She has had enough.

'Yes, I think I do, rather.'

'Well, even if you don't want to bag a tiger, I think you might show some consideration for those of us who do.'

Minty sighs, an extended and dramatic chest-deflation intended to indicate equal measures of pity and boredom.

'Oh, you are being tiresome. No wonder Augustus drinks so much. You know, I rather think I shall go for a walk.'

Charlie cannot believe her ears. 'A walk? We're in the middle of the jungle.'

'Yes, precisely. Such a romantic spot. I think it will be delightful.'

And with that she throws down the rope ladder, and descends. Charlie tracks her through the sights of her rifle, wrestling with a set of very un-English impulses. Around and below her, the hunt unravels, all sense of purpose lost. She feels herself the last repository of order in this place, a tiny island in a sea of chaos, a lone rock battered by black waves and topped by a ragged Union Jack.

Finally the Picturewallah slows down, and ahead Pran hears the lowing of frightened calves. They have reached the place.

Together they peer through the foliage into a clearing where three unfortunate animals are tethered, shuffling from side to side in agitation. Grabbing Pran's collar, the Picturewallah points out the Major's machan.

'That one. Go. I will follow you in a few minutes.'

Pran has a thought. 'What about the tigers? Have they released them yet?'

'No. Of course not.' He sounds unconvinced. 'There have been no shots yet, have there?'

Cuffing Pran round the head, he propels him forward.

In subsequent months, various accounts will be given of what happens next. Some will be dictated to officials, others written or submitted as verbal depositions to Civil Service superiors. Most of these statements will differ wildly from one another about even the most basic facts, although by the bureaucratic alchemy of the India Office these differences will eventually be resolved and a unified narrative presented in the form of a two-page memorandum. This document, bearing eight signatures (including those of two cabinet ministers), will be marked Top Secret and henceforth viewed only by those sections of posterity in possession of the relevant British government security clearance. It will be seen as forming the final and definitive word on the Fatehpur Incident, and will, needless to say, be incorrect in almost every particular. The presence of armed insurgents in the forest, the politically motivated assassination attempt, the reckless and tragic gallantry of certain British serving officers – none of it is strictly true. The exception is the growl. All sources agree that the growling came first.

Pran hears it as he creeps towards the machan, and stops dead. The tigers, he thinks. They have let the tigers loose. This is destined to be his last coherent thought for some minutes, because the growling is swiftly followed by a volley of shots, screams, thumps, furious rustlings and a sudden whooshing sound. A trail of vapour shoots upwards from one of the trees, and the sky explodes in a ball of blinding light.

Many things are revealed.

First is the bombardier himself. Cornwell Birch knows there are no second takes in the blackmail business. Deciding to leave nothing to chance on such a complex night shoot, he has employed the radical but effective lighting technique of launching a military flare, as used by Uncle Sam's Doughboys on the murky Western Front. From a neighbouring tree, he has a grandstand view of Major Privett-Clampe's machan. Unfortunately the star of the show is not present. The platform is empty but for Jean-Loup, in full Major-seducing kit – a touch of rouge, tight shorts bulging artfully, khaki shirt unbuttoned to the waist. Jean-Loup stumbles, shading his eyes. His camera propped on an overhanging branch, Birch wobbles and swears – then (true professional) recovers his composure and turns his lens on the action at ground level.

This action is, to use a Hollywood term, sensational. The camera tracks the Nawab emerging from a bush, naked but for his topi. He is both tumescent and covered in blood, although most of this seems to belong to Minty, who, also naked, is running around him in circles clutching her wounded shoulder. Whether the Nawab is the source of the growl will never be entirely clear, because the larger of the two tigers is also trotting about the clearing. A swift pan to Prince Firoz, whimpering in fear, as he tugs at his soiled underwear and scrambles away from the huge, panting beast. A few shots thump into the ground around the Prince, answered by more gunfire that seems, bizarrely, to be aimed up at the machans. Then Major Privett-Clampe, the absent film-star, materializes wild-eyed from the trees, blasting to left and right like Tom Mix cornered by Injuns. From his wife's machan comes an answering hail of fire. Minty and the Nawab take cover from another blast which appears, perhaps understandably, to come from the direction of Sir Wynd-ham. Someone yells out in pain. Imelda screams, runs for cover, and instantly knocks herself out cold on a tree trunk. All is terror. All is panic.

Pran watches, open-mouthed. Behind him the Picturewallah catches his breath, then inexplicably starts forward, perhaps thinking to take a photograph. Instantly he is felled by a stray shot, collapsing into the undergrowth in a quivering tweedy pile. Birch sends another flare into the night sky, in the process losing his balance and (an occurrence he will regret for the rest of his life) falling out of the tree and smashing his camera. Somebody calls out for a doctor. Other figures, Indian and European, flit among the trees in varying states of undress. Pran watches with a strange sense of disconnection. This is nothing to do with him. Fatehpur has breathed him in, and now it is exhaling. He takes a single, dream-like pace backwards. No reaction. No one will notice. No one will care. He turns, takes another, then another. Slowly, steadily he begins to walk away through the forest.

A crashing sound behind him. He whirls round. It is the Major, haggard and spectral in the phosphorescent light. He is bleeding from a wound to the head, and clutching his rifle in both hands, his knuckles white on the barrel.

'My boy –' he says, his voice small and strained.

'I'm not your boy,' Pran answers. The Major's eyes widen, as if in surprise, and he sinks to his knees, the rifle sliding out of his grip. Then, in a movement of infinite slowness, he collapses backwards to the floor.

Pran stands, looking at the lifeless bulk of his body, white knees and stomach pointed up at the night sky. Then he carries on walking. After a while he realizes he is not alone. Four reflective eyes. A rumble of hot breath. The tigers have also had enough. They are leaving too. Together they walk on, heading towards the border with British India.

White Boy

The Amritsar road seems quiet to Jiwan Singh. He makes a sucking noise against his teeth and points this out to his brother. Abhay, a head shorter and a year younger, nods warily. The road is quiet. The day is hot. The two boys dangle their legs and squint into the sun and suck their teeth, the splayed yellow mouthfuls that are their most obvious inheritance from their father. The cart grumbles its way through the dust, its freight of clay pots clinking with each bump and rut in the road. The Singh family's nameless buffalo pulls in the shafts and uses its tail to switch flies off its scrawny haunches.

The village women say that the potter Bishen Singh is not a clever man. All he is good for is getting sons. Six of them, and only two dead. This is no mean feat, but all the sons have Bishen Singh's slow wits and bad teeth, which spoils it. Truly Bishen Singh's wits are very slow. Only he would send his sons to market in Amritsar with the countryside in such a state. Only Bishen Singh's sons would be incurious enough to give a lift to the stranger dozing beside them in the cart, and not ask a single question.

The cart rolls towards Amritsar. The sahib who does not speak like a sahib wakes up and scratches himself.

'How far?' he asks.

'One more hour, sahib,' says Jiwan Singh. The strange young man nods and tweaks at his sweat-soaked khaki shirt, wafting air to his glistening chest. Then he goes back to sleep. He has been asleep all morning. Had he been awake, he might have noticed the nervous faces of the guards by the railway bridge, or the rubble in the last village they passed, where the sahib aeroplanes had thrown down bombs as a punishment. Or the ominous quality of the silence. All morning the little cart has been travelling into it, curd-thick and fearful.

A silence like this takes time to form. It has been churned little by little out of the terrible things that have happened here during the past months. The Punjab is the breadbasket of the British Raj, and also its army recruitment ground. This landscape of flat fields crossed by irrigation channels and low mud banks means everything to the sahibs, and lately they have felt it slipping from their grasp. First there were rumours. Indians talking secretly to Russians and Germans, of Bolshevism, sedition – the inevitable fruits, said the hardliners, of educating natives. Handbills were pasted in public places. *Prepare yourself to kill and die.* Then, soon afterwards, small omens. A Hindu procession joined by Muslims. Shouts of *Mahatma-Gandhi ki-jai.* Street dancing and drum rhythms. Religious enemies seen drinking from the same cup. The sahibs began to count their guns, and say to each other that the time for talking was over. There were not enough of them. So many troops sick with the influenza. So few white faces in such a sea of brown. Throughout the Punjab, club smoking rooms filled with talk of firm government, of hitting first, and hard.

The mixture began to thicken. At public meetings, Congress babus called strikes. A crowd at a cricket match poured on to the pitch, ripping up the matting wicket and waving stolen stumps in the air. Then night-time arrests, nationalist leaders transported outside state borders. Another crowd, milling about in Aitchison Park, angry, aimless, uncomfortably close to sensitive places like the railway station and the telegraph exchange. A stone's throw across the tracks were the Civil Lines, neat rows of bungalows sheltering neat angelic wives and neatly dressed cherubic children. Of course the soldiers opened fire. Soon bodies were strewn over the parched brown grass. That was how it started.

Gradually the city walls materialize through the heat haze. The sahib wakes up as the cart passes through the Ghi Mandi Gate, watched open-mouthed by the English Tommy guards. One of them walks forward, rifle levelled, but does not flag them down. Jiwan and Abhay and the sahib drive into the charred, silent city.

'I will walk now,' says Pran. 'Thank you.'

The boys nod and suck their farewells. Pran is left standing by a charred heap of rubble, the ruined shell of the Alliance Bank.

Terrible things happened here. Horrors. The place bears its memories near the surface, memories of heavy wooden bank furniture dragged out on to the street and doused in kerosene. The image of Mr Thompson, the manager, his screaming face blackening in the flames as he is cremated by the chanting mob.

As Pran walks down the street, people stop and glare at him. For almost two weeks now the sahibs have only entered the city in military patrols. Their women and children are in the Gobind Garh Fort. Why is this boy strolling about, looking at the damage like a tourist? The gleaming dome of the Golden Temple peeps over the soot-blackened roofs. Oblivious to the reaction he is causing, Pran heads towards it.

All around the city, memories. Burning and looting. After the banks, the post office. The police station. The English shops in the Hall bazaar. White men beaten to death. Mrs Easdon, the zenana hospital doctor, splashing her face with a bottle of black ink, struggling into a sari while downstairs bottles were smashed in the dispensary and the Anglo-Indian nurses raped. Elsewhere, in the quiet town of Jalandhar, the General's dinner party is interrupted by a telegram. Yes, he says to the nervous messenger. I have been expecting this. There is a big show coming. His guests carry their drinks on to the porch of Flagstaff House to wave him off.

Pran does not walk down the side-alley into the Jallianwala

Bagh. He feels the weight of absence hanging over the place and hurries past. The only motion is in the air, a pair of kites, still hovering hopefully, even though it all happened a week ago. The entrance is tiny, and beyond it is the thing Pran does not know about but still does not want to see. A large open space with high walls all around, perfect for public meetings.

A week ago. The afternoon shadows lengthened while as many as fifty thousand people listened to a speech, a speech made in defiance of the General's newly proclaimed martial law. The entrance was so narrow that the General could not get the armoured cars in, which irritated him since he had hoped to use their large-calibre machine guns. It was fiendishly hot and he, as usual, was in secret pain. The General's pain was constant and severe, as it had been for years. Though his sclerotic twice-shattered legs were sending streams of tiny daggers up his back to his head, he was the Officer Commanding, and considered it a matter of honour not to display frailty in front of subordinates. So he did not complain, but went in with fifty rifles, Sikhs and Gurkha hillmen, and deployed them in a line.

The editor Durgas Das was standing on the platform, looking up at the spotter plane circling overhead. He had stopped speaking. The noise of its rotors was too loud for him to be heard. As the soldiers doubled in to the Jallianwala Bagh, he looked over the crowd and raised a newsprint-blackened hand to his forehead. People turned to face the disturbance. The soldiers knelt and for the briefest moment, like a premonition, there was silence.

Then, without warning, they started to fire.

Das saw the first wave of bodies fall, a breath of wind rustling a cornfield. Then he was caught up and pulled away. The only exit to the Jallianwala Bagh was behind the line of soldiers. Panicking people trod on top of each other, trying to scale the walls. The General directed his troops to aim where the crowd was thickest. The men fired and reloaded, fired and reloaded, and every so often, between volleys, there was another gulp of silence as they changed magazines.

The Deputy Superintendent of Police stood beside the General and watched. You are teaching these people a lesson, he said. They will not forget it in a hurry. The General nodded. His troops fired 1,650 rounds.

Like the Deputy Superintendent of Police, the General thought of his bullets in pedagogical terms. Ethically, the dark-skinned races are like children, and the General was fulfilling the primary duty of the white man in Asia, which is to say that he was laying down a clear line. His bullets were reminders of the meaning of law. Repeat after me.

After ten minutes or so the General gave the order to withdraw. As he returned for dinner, the kites and vultures were already circling overhead. Corpses were piled in drifts around the walls of the Jallianwala Bagh. The well in the corner was choked with them. As darkness fell, relatives looking for their dead were attacked by jackals and feral dogs. Under martial law there was an eight o'clock curfew. Most of the townspeople were now too scared to break it, so the wounded remained where they lay until morning. The Jubilee Hospital was run by Europeans. Not one person applied there for treatment.

The next day bodies were burnt five to a pyre. People made haste to hide the evidence that their relatives were at the gathering. No one knew how many were dead. The Europeans held a meeting, where the Civil Surgeon tried to canvass support for bombing the city. He would finish the job, if only it were his decision. In the afternoon the General summoned Indian leaders to the Kotwal. I am a soldier, he told them in clipped parade-ground Urdu. For me the battlefields of France and Amritsar are the same. Speak up if you want war. If you want peace, open your shops at once. You will inform me of the badmashes. I will shoot them. Obey my orders.

Pran hurries on past. A week of martial law has left a stink in Amritsar. Charred wood. Uncollected refuse. The sweetness of cremated flesh and the sharpness of burnt sari silk, powdered and used to staunch bleeding. He catches a glimpse of gold and water at the end of a street, the Temple in the middle of its huge tank. A tailor sits outside his shop, blank and impassive. A few people pass by on the narrow street. They are on foot, as the General has requisitioned all the tongas and bicycles for military use.

Turning a corner, Pran is confronted by an unusual sight. Three English soldiers, big brick-coloured Somerset men, stand over a Sikh labourer. They are following him as he crawls on his belly down the lane.

'Jaldi! Jaldi, you brown bastard!' barks the Sergeant. The crawling man complains that he lives here, and why will they not let him walk? The white men give no impression of understanding.

'Get on down there and shut up. Chalo!'

But he has no other way to go. How can he do this each time? His wife does not dare to leave the house. God the merciful knows this cannot be right. Above the lane faces peer from high windows, then disappear again. The young ones, the two privates, follow on either side, occasionally poking the man with their rifles. His white kurta is already smeared with filth. He tries to avoid another pile of dung, but the Sergeant's boot comes down on the small of his back, pressing him hard into it. He crawls on, in silence.

Pran has stumbled on another lesson, this one occasioned by the General's belief in the sacredness of women. It is a point of faith with him, as in his opinion it ought to be with any man. Unfortunately it is not universally held. During the rioting a woman was violated on this street. The missionary, Miss Sherwood, was riding her bicycle (typical bloody missionary, trying to 'live among her flock', look where it got her) when she was attacked by the mob. The General has been to see her in the Jubilee Hospital, and his visit made him very angry. An English-woman, weak, soiled, mummified in bandages, hovering between life and death. He paced up and down in the antiseptic-smelling corridor, racking his brain for a suitable punishment. Something exemplary. Something to fit the crime. So, in prep-aration for a round of public floggings, he has had a whipping triangle set up halfway down the street and decreed that any native wishing to pass along it must do so on all fours. If they will behave like animals, they shall be treated as such. The order has been in force for two days. The watercarriers and the clearers of nightsoil are avoiding the area. No one but the trapped residents will brave the soldiers. The gutters are clogged with rubbish and excrement, steaming in the summer heat.

'Bloody hell,' says one of the privates. 'What are you doing out here?'

Pran realizes with a rush of fear that the man is speaking to him. The Sergeant and the other private look round, identical expressions of surprise on their faces. Any moment now they will attack him, arrest him, make him crawl and grovel like the man at their feet. He cannot force his mouth to form words. He should run.

'Are you mad?' asks the Sergeant. 'You should be back at the station, or wherever you've been billeted. Where did you come from?'

Pran understands. They think he is one of them. Despite the sweat, the dirt of five days' travelling in the same clothes, the way he holds his head and hands, the terrified expression on his face, they think he is one of them.

'Are you all right, boy? Where are your parents?'

Pran cannot speak. As soon as he speaks they will know. They will flog him on the whipping post. How can they be so blind? How can they not tell?

'Look at me, boy,' says the Sergeant, the note of gentleness in his voice chiming weirdly with the filthy man prone at his feet. 'Are you all right? Can you tell me your name?'

Pran shakes his head mutely. He has to say something. He can feel colour streaming off him like sweat. He wills his pores to close. Skin to statue. White marble. Impenetrable. He stands as still as he can.. One move will betray him. But he must move. Otherwise they will take him away.

He points down the street, towards the Civil Lines. He tries to hold Privett-Clampe's voice inside his mouth.

'I am going,' he says. 'I am very well.'

The soldiers stand, looking at him. The man on the floor scrabbles in the dust with his calloused heels.

'I am very well. I am going. Forthwith.'

Pran starts to walk. The Sergeant calls after him, 'Look after yourself.'

Pran turns and nods, trying not to run until he is round the corner. As soon as the men are out of sight, he cannot hold it back. His feet barely touch the ground. His heart hammers in his chest. The people of Amritsar watch as he tears past, an insane grin on his face. He is filled with exhilaration. He hardly thinks of the man on the floor, and each running stride seems to take him further away from him, another yard of clean starched space.

Now all he has to do is get out. He left Fatehpur without a plan, without really believing that he would make it. For five days he has been out in the wide world, and it has sucked him towards this dead city like a hair towards a plughole in an Englishman's porcelain bathroom. But he cannot stay here. He will be killed. He stops and asks a startled woman the way to the railway station. Wordlessly she points it out. He carries on in the direction she indicates, jogging slower and slower until the mazy streets end abruptly in the dead brown lawns of Aitchison Park.

On the other side is the station and the regimented rows of bungalows in the Civil Lines.

Walking into whiteness. In spite of his luck with the soldiers it takes all his courage. As he approaches he sees that the station windows have been blocked with sandbags, and English soldiers are manning a gun emplacement at the entrance. He falters for a moment. How can he go in there? But there is no choice. No one questions him as he passes by.

The place is packed with people waiting to be evacuated. A stench of sweat hits him like a fist. Frightened people jammed together on the platform, in the waiting rooms, the canteen, the ticket office. Jammed black-hole tight. The stink of their bodies, suddenly isolated from all the other stinks of India, is shocking. One attar note smelt raw on a perfumer's glass rod, nasty and unblended. Pran has been taught the rhyme. Fee-fi-fo-fum. Be he alive or be he dead. This is the smell of Englishmen, an incitement to the mob, the ogre, to attack. They are mostly women and young children, and they must have been camping here for days. Each family group has demarcated its little patch of floor, sometimes using improvised screens of rugs and bedlinen to separate them from their neighbours. As if propelled by instinct, by the European's animal drive to segment the world, to grid and order space. Every family's own little pink territory, drawn on the map of Amritsar Railway Station.

They look haggard and wretched. The children hang limply about their tight-lipped mothers, whose grimy faces seem at first sight to be masks of defeat and worry, the grinding effect of hours and days of dehydration and poor sanitation and constant fear of death. But seen closer the women's eyes are bright. Underneath the dirt something in these memsahibs has been elevated by their plight. It connects them to history, to their grandmothers of the Mutiny, to the symbolic destiny of the Englishwoman in tropical climes, which is to make do, to endure.

They are becoming the angels their husbands imagine them. Sacred. Worth spilling blood for.

These women frighten Pran almost as much as the soldiers guarding them. He is a trespasser, a black cuckoo in the nest. He tries to make himself as inconspicuous as possible, acutely aware that there are no other boys of his age present. The real English boys are all away in boarding schools at Home. Some of the women start to watch him, visibly sifting through their memories, trying to place his face. Each time he spots someone fixing on him, he moves, takes up position elsewhere. For a long time he stands beneath a peeling poster. *Visit Bombay. The Gateway of India.*

Just when he thinks he is about to be approached, the sound of a steam whistle pierces the fug. Pran steps out on to the platform to see a train puffing into the station. At once there is bustle and action. Soldiers stretch and climb down from a goods wagon, which has been converted to house machine guns. Food and supplies are unloaded by Sikh soldiers, closely monitored by their English officers whenever their work takes them close to women or children. In the midst of the confusion Pran slips on board. Soon he is watching fields slide by, heading south.

Pretty Bobby

A little courtyard opens out behind high Bombay tenement walls like a thumb pot opened out of a lump of clay. On the far side lies all the afternoon noise and chaos of Falkland Road. On this side, a youth is sweeping the floor. He does it in a desultory way, flicking the broom away from his long legs in a petulant motion designed to keep the dust off his new European-cut trousers. This is not his job. It is the sweeper-woman's job.

After a few minutes the youth considers his task done. He throws the broom aside and straightens up, lighting a cigarette. He holds it elegantly, instantly transformed from servant to cocktail-party guest. To complete the picture he leans on the wall beside him, crossing one leg over the other. A fashion plate. A man of leisure.

The wall is unsightly and poorly built. It rises more or less to the eye-level of an adult man, and divides the courtyard, already cramped, into two unequal sections. On the smaller side, against which the youth is leaning, the wall bows alarmingly in the middle. Crumbling mortar seeps between the bricks, which have been laid haphazardly on top of each other, with little care or craftsmanship. The poor quality of the wall appears incongruous, given that the buildings on either side of it are sturdy, although in need of plaster and lime.

As the youth takes another languorous drag on his cigarette, he is startled by the appearance of a bearded white face on the other side of the wall.

'Robert?' says the beard. 'Have I not told you? Have I not said it often enough? Tobacco is a lever which the devil uses to wrench open your heart!'

'Yes,' replies Robert, sulkily stubbing out the cigarette with a sandalled foot.

'Yes, what?'

'Yes, sir, Reverend Macfarlane.' Though the two look nothing alike, the youth's accent is strikingly like the beard's, with all the prim inflections of an educated Lowland Scot. Reverend Macfarlane raises one bushy eyebrow, a movement like a small hairy animal breaking free of its herd. Grimacing, Robert stoops to slip the crushed butt into his trouser pocket.

'I'm very disappointed in you, Robert,' continues Reverend Macfarlane. He is bobbing up and down on the other side of the wall, standing on tiptoe to deliver his homily. 'I know that you cannot be expected to rise beyond a certain level. You mustn't think I don't make allowances. However, you're a bright boy. You stand a good chance of transcending the affliction God has, in his wisdom, seen fit to bestow upon you. But it will only happen if you struggle. You must fight it, Robert! Fight!'

Reverend Macfarlane's tone and volume rise, until by the time of his exhortation to fight, his voice is ringing out through the courtyard with a force honed by many years of street preaching. The sound attracts a woman, who appears in the doorway on Robert's side of the wall. Though European, she is dressed in a sari. Younger than the Reverend, whose explosion of wiry grey attests to perhaps sixty years of combat, her own straw-coloured hair is drawn back from her face in a severe bun.

'Chandra?' she calls out.

'Yes, Ambaji?' replies Robert.

'Have you finished your chores?'

'Yes, Ambaji.'

'Does he want you for anything?'

Reverend Macfarlane grunts. 'Tell her yes I do. Some new equipment has arrived. I want to try it out.'

'Yes, he does, Ambaji.'

'More skulls? Very well. Tell him not to keep you too long.'

Chandra-Robert turns back to the beard and the wall. 'She says –'

'I heard,' mutters the Reverend. 'Now climb over and help me unpack the things. They have come all the way from *Edinburgh*.' He emphasizes the name of the town, as if to underscore its importance and specialness.

The youth pulls a packing case close to the wall and uses it to climb over, dislodging a loose brick with his foot. The Reverend rolls up his sleeves in anticipation of hard work and leads the way indoors to a low-ceilinged hall fitted out as a church. The furnishings are plain and unornamented, a heavy table and lectern facing rows of backless benches. Stacks of hymn books are crammed on to bookshelves at either side. At the far end a pair of double doors open out on to the street, barred by a heavy wooden beam. City sounds, tonga wheels and bicycle bells and hawkers' cries, seep in through a two-inch gap beneath them. The place is scrupulously clean but pointedly spartan, its single concession to comfort being a ceiling-mounted fan.

'You must call my wife by her proper name,' Macfarlane snaps. 'I don't want to hear you using this gobble-gobble she's adopted.'

'Yes, sir, Reverend Macfarlane.'

'She is Mrs Macfarlane. Anything else encourages her. And don't allow her to call you Chin-whatever it is either. Robert. Elspeth and Robert. Perfectly adequate names.' Dust motes dance in the light, swirling about them as they pass through the church and climb the narrow flight of stairs to a room which serves the Reverend as both sleeping quarters and laboratory. Robert hovers in the doorway as Macfarlane strides over the creaky floor and throws open the shutters. The street noise jumps closer and the dim room is unveiled in all its meagre glory.

The Reverend Andrew Macfarlane is a man who believes that tidying up is a minor species of prayer, handmaiden to more major forms like spring cleaning and the practice of callisthenics. As a result he lives in a space whose contents are arranged with a kind of right-angled vigour, the hundreds of books placed in exact alphabetical order on well-dusted shelves, the hard cot bed made up with soldierly precision, the battered writing desk free of stray papers and the cupboards containing his more unusual study tools shut tight and bolted. No graven image sullies the white-painted purity of the walls, no frivolous rug or matting besmirches the honest boards of the floor. Personal vanity is imprisoned in a metal travelling trunk of clothes, liberated twice monthly to occupy the small exercise yard of a shaving mirror, a mirror turned face down on the washstand when not in use. Were beard-trimming to take place more frequently than this, sinfulness might be the result. Religious prophylaxis, rather than self-indulgences like convenience or (heaven forfend) actual aesthetic preference, dictates the condition of the Reverend's wild patriarchal growth. Like the room, nothing about the man is the product of chance or carelessness.

Yet, through a chink, sentiment has seeped into this airless world. The absence of images is not complete. A hinged bazaar-bought brass frame stands on the writing desk, containing two photographs. Robert, who has often been in this room, nevertheless sidles over to look at them, the two young infantry soldiers staring unreadably into the camera. Two different studios. Two different tones of sepia. The dead sons. He finds their faces endlessly fascinating, though nothing particular about their undistinguished shuffling of their parents' features catches the eye. They are frozen and powerful, the repository of all the backed-up emotion which rules the life of this household. They are, he realizes, the reason Ambaji took him in, and the reason the Reverend allows him to stay.

'You're supposed to be assisting me, not standing about day-dreaming.'

Macfarlane's voice brings him back to earth, and he helps to lever open a small packing case and lay the lid carefully to one side. They lift out various pieces of grooved and slatted wood, along with several little leather cases containing sets of callipers, adjustable clamps and heavy brass rules. There is also a folding screen on a metal stand, rather like those Robert has seen used to project cinema pictures, but black.

Macfarlane reaches into his pocket for keys and opens one of a pair of large wooden cupboards. Inside, arranged neatly on shelves, are several rows of human skulls. The Reverend looks at them affectionately.

'Ah, my little Golgotha. Hello.'

He stoops and drags out a heavy tool chest from the bottom of the cupboard.

'We'll put the Lamprey Grid together first. You hold and I'll tighten the screws.'

As he presses down on the slats of wood, Robert looks up at the dead people. The dead people look down at him. However hard he tries he cannot get used to the Reverend's collection. The idea of them all packed in there fills him with horror. Men and women who once walked around and ate supper and played music and had arguments, all reduced to scientific specimens. The first time he saw them, he almost screamed. 'Base superstition', Macfarlane called it, musingly rapping Robert's head with his knuckles. 'Quite natural in a mind such as yours.' Robert pulled away. The gesture chilled him. He felt as if, in the Reverend's eyes, his own walking eating arguing existence was provisional, that the boundary which separated him and the cupboard of specimens was easily crossed. Now, under the hollow gaze of the skulls, he helps Macfarlane string silk threads through the wooden frame, creating a chequered grid which they mount on a stand before the black screen.

'There it is,' says Macfarlane, full of satisfaction. 'Now at last I can make proper photographic studies. You, young man, shall have the honour of being my first subject.'

Robert squirms uncomfortably. He has assisted the Reverend before, and though the work is neither arduous nor painful, it always makes him uneasy. Several times they have performed an experiment which Macfarlane refers to as 'following in the footsteps of the great Morton', upending the skulls and filling them full of fine lead shot. The shot is packed tight and then carefully poured back out into calibrated glass beakers. In this way they have found that the Naga tribal woman's skull holds less than the Bihari farmer's. The Gujarati Kayastha holds more than the Bihari. The Tibetan herder holds more than the Kayastha or the Bihari or the Naga or the Orissan fisherman. All these discoveries are held by the Reverend to confirm the great Morton's greatness, though the large size of the Tibetan's skull appears to irritate him. Through all of it Robert's help has never seemed strictly necessary. His main role is to listen to the Reverend expound his theories, derived from the vast library of books on anthropological subjects he has acquired during his thirty years as a missionary.

It turns out that through the incontrovertible methodology of science, craniometry has revealed the foundation of British imperial domination of the world. The scale of cranial capacities which Reverend Macfarlane has confirmed for a selection of the subject races of India can, he explains, be extended to show how differences in brain size correspond exactly to degree of civilization and capacity for rational thought throughout the world. At the bottom, atavistic creatures like the South Javan and the Hottentot demonstrate capacities (as well as facial and maxillary structures) little different to those of the higher apes. The Indostanic group, to which most of the Reverend's dead people once belonged, falls somewhere in the upper middle of this global league. At the top is the European, whose capacious 100-cubic-inch capacity gives him room for brain development far in excess of such benighted fellows as the 91-inched Peruvian or the savage 86-inched Tasman. Hence, Empire. Of course the Reverend acknowledges that simple capacity measurement is crude and old-fashioned, but he has had to wait until now to get his hands on the tools which will take his inquiries to the next level.

He stands Robert side-on in front of the grid, fixing his neck and back with rigid steel clamps and extending one arm, similarly immobilized, out in front of him. Then, mounting a camera on a tripod some distance away, he takes a series of photographs. The boy seems to have a distaste for having his picture taken, and Macfarlane has to shout at him to stop him wrinkling up his face. Finally he settles down. Through the viewfinder his marble-white skin almost glows against the black calico background. To the Reverend his fine nose and thin, sharp lips appear strangely pure. For a mongrel, incredibly pure. Really almost too pure. Almost European.

'Quite, quite remarkable,' he mutters. 'Really, Robert, your taint of blood hardly shows at all.'

Robert is unscrewed and placed on a chair, as the Reverend employs his new measuring devices on the various parameters of his head. Facial angle is fixed at ninety-three degrees, the nose found to be leptorrhine and eyes mesosemic, with a certain upturning at the corners which is announced to be a tell-tale indication of Asiatic origin. The jaw is pleasingly orthognathic, a contrast to the jutting prognathous jaw of the Negro skull illustrated in Nott and Gliddon's *Indigenous Races of the Earth*. This interesting volume is given to Robert to flick through while the Reverend jots down his results. He looks at the pictures of noble

Greek statuary and twisted soot-black nigger faces, and feels, as he often does, a peculiar relief at his resemblance to one and not the other.

Like most of the Reverend's books, *The Indigenous Races of the Earth* is very old, its once-fine pigskin binding cracked and mildewed by many years of exposure to the monsoon. With his fingers Robert traces the bumps and bubbles on its cover, not displeased at the turn the afternoon has taken. At least the arrival of the Lamprey Grid and the gauges means that the Reverend's obsession with measuring the body might be channelled away from the dead to the living. In the past it has meant some unpleasant errands to St George's Hospital, walks back through the busy streets with square brown-paper parcels that made him feel like a ghoul or a murderer.

As Robert is thinking about death, Macfarlane is making a note of the 'unusual luminous leucochroicity of the subject's skin', and wondering whether perhaps the very fineness of the features, their uncanny quality, places them under the heading of one of the great Lombroso's criminal types. The tendency to crime of the mulatto has, after all, been well documented in the Americas, and Robert's peculiar disguised form of hybridity might conceal all manner of antisocial tendencies. His excessive care for his personal appearance and his enjoyment of tobacco certainly point in that direction, while an examination of the nose and ears reveals a certain hawk-like aquilinity in the former and a pointed tubercle in the latter (more pronounced on the left than on the right) that the Italian anthropometrist identifies as features of the born criminal. For a moment he wonders if it would be wise to dismiss the boy, who, after all, turned up at the Mission completely out of the blue. On the other hand he has lived there for well over a year without incident. And he is a bright boy. Even brighter perhaps than Duncan at that age. Certainly brighter than Kenneth.

As soon as this disloyal thought rears its head, Macfarlane quashes it. Better not to think at all than to think that. He resolves to do nothing. Let the boy stay, even if he is a hyphenate.

'All right. No time for lessons today. You're free to leave. Tomorrow I shall test you on the *Aeneid*, Book Five, and on your knowledge of Paul's Letter to the Corinthians. If you speak to my wife, you must remind her that I forbid her absolutely to associate with that Pereira woman. I have an idea that she intends to do so this evening. I'm counting on you to stop her. Do you understand?'

'Yes, sir, Reverend Macfarlane.'

Robert bounds down the stairs, two at a time. Quickly he hops over the wall, and into a doorway on the other side of the courtyard. Inside a little parlour, decorated with framed prints and vases of flowers, he finds Elspeth Macfarlane chopping vegetables with Shobha the sweeper-woman. They look up as he barges in.

'Are you going out, Chandra?' asks Elspeth.

'Yes, ma'am.'

'Well, don't be long. I shall want you to escort me to Mrs Pereira's at eight.'

'The Reverend said –'

'Yes, I'm sure he did. How was your skull?'

'Very good, Amba – I mean, Mrs Mac – I mean, very good. I am almost English.'

She looks up sharply.

'I mean Scottish.'

'I think you should be content to be an Indian, which is more or less what you are. It is a fine thing. I am reliably told that in all your past births you have been an Indian, apart from once when you were Egyptian, and once born on the planet Mercury. Now, make sure you are back to take me at eight.'

'Yes, Ambaji.'

Chandra-Robert disappears up to his room, a little garret almost entirely papered with portraits from illustrated magazines. American film actresses, politicians, soldiers, jockeys, famous writers and artists, cabaret artistes, society ladies and cricketers mingle with religious pictures, Ganpati, Vivekananda, Saint Francis Xavier, the Buddha, Shiva Nataraj. There are tinted postcards of British views arranged around the washstand. Hyde Park Corner, Lake Windermere, 'afternoon in the New Forest', Balmoral from the air. Somewhere buried in the middle of the faces is a group photograph cut out of a periodical called *The Harvest* depicting a missionary tea on Hampstead Heath. Mr and Mrs Macfarlane are just visible among the halftone figures, standing at the back with cups and saucers in their hands.

For a few minutes, he lies back on his bed with his arms folded behind his head and stares at his constellation. He has a game in which he half closes his eyes, or opens and shuts them rapidly, smearing or flickering the faces together, making them into new ones, more fantastic, more interesting. He begins to play, but remembers that he should go right now if he is to make a little money and be back in time for eight o'clock. So he jumps up and stands in front of the square of mirror hanging from the back of his door, and carefully runs a comb through his thick hair. Then he scoops a little dab of wax on to his fingers, rakes them through his hair and combs again, turning his head so the light catches the hint of copper in the shiny blackness. He kicks off his sandals, slips on a pair of Argyll socks and takes a pair of black Oxford brogues from under the bed. They are heavy well-made shoes of a type rarely seen on Indian feet, and very rarely indeed on those of the menial classes. He considers a collar and tie, but decides he has no time, and rushes back downstairs and out of the door, followed by the disapproving stares of the women in the parlour.

Once he is outside on the street, he stands for a moment at the double doors of the church, under its flaking painted sign.

Independent Scottish Mission among the Heathen (ISMH)
Falkland Rd. Bombay. India
Minister – The Revd A.J. Macfarlane
'Dare we let them die in darkness when we have the light of God?'

Some of the text is unreadable, obliterated by splotches of red and yellow dye, a remnant of last year's Holi festival when Hindu revellers (all in a spirit of fun, of course) almost stormed the Mission. Robert retrieves something from his pocket – a wrist-watch with a brown leather strap. Furtively looking behind to check neither of the Macfarlanes has followed him out, he straps it to his wrist, breathes on the dial and polishes it on his trousers. Now he is ready, his outdoor identity complete. The young gentleman steps into his domain. Pretty Bobby, crown prince of that most notorious of all red light districts, the sewer of India: Falkland Road.

The Road is undergoing its evening transformation, from day chaos to night chaos. The change in rhythm is subtle, perhaps imperceptible to the outsider. The street vendors are still trudging up and down, selling ice-cold water, fruit, snacks and bidis. The handcarts and tongas and bicycles and impatient horn-honking black cars are still pushing and shoving their way through the sullen crowd, grinding slippery refuse into the dirt. The smell of stale fried onion and lamp-oil still floats over everything and, of course, the street's star attractions, the girls on the steps and wooden balconies, are still screeching come-ons and insults to anyone who catches their eye. But as the light fails and the daytime heat lessens, the composition of people on the street is changing. The huddles of men at the paan-stalls become more intent, their conversations more freighted with secrets. Women, ordinary women, rare during daytime, have completely evaporated. Single walkers are hurrying along, not looking around, retreating to their houses to eat dinner and tell their wives about the events of the day. The Road now belongs to the groups of hand-holding boys who saunter slowly past the open doorways, their eyes bright with cheap toddy, the volume of their dirty jokes rising and falling with their proximity to the girls and the groups of scowling goondas who have gathered to lounge on the corner waiting for a fight or a fast rupee.

Robert walks out into it, weaving nimbly down the street with a city-dweller's quick paces and half-glances to left and right. He does not know exactly where he is headed, does not need to know, because meaning and purpose will, as always, be delivered to him without too much thought or effort.

'Bobby? Bobby!'

He waves up to Maria Francesca, sitting at the first-floor window of the Goa House with a new girl he does not recognize. She leans over the rickety railing, her big doughy breasts spilling out of her tight blouse.

'Hello, Maria!'

'Hello, Pretty! Good thing you come along now, yaar! One of the customers wants a bottle! You can run to the corner for us? Wait, I'll throw the money down to you!'

She wraps some coins in a rag, twists a knot in it and drops it into his hands, like a sweetheart throwing a favour to her lover. Bobby catches it and makes in the direction of the liquor stall. The change, he will pocket.

Ten minutes later, smelling of Maria's rum and rosewater thank you hug, he has another commission, this time from one of the more expensive houses. Mamma Paul's Anglo-Indian girls have shown a young British merchant seaman too good a time, and now they need someone to take him safely back to his ship.

Mamma presses a couple of coins into Bobby's hand. Just so long as the man does not pass out in the street, or decide he was robbed and lead the police to her door.

'And was he robbed?' Bobby asks cheekily, looking at the slumped figure on the parlour floor. Mamma Paul makes as if to slap his face, and grimaces.

'We think he's called Norman, but we can't really understand what he says.'

The sailor is so drunk he can barely stand. Once out on the street he decides he cannot remember where his ship is.

'Its name? What is its name?' Bobby asks him, staggering slightly under the man's weight.

'Who gives a toss, like? I certainly don't.'

'You will in the morning.'

This remark is unwise. The sailor looks belligerent, and makes an effort to stand unassisted.

'You little bugger!'

Bobby lets go of him and he crashes heavily into a passer-by, setting in motion a brief and poorly coordinated fight. The journey continues in this way, and by the time the man has been deposited at the government dock in front of a likely looking vessel, Bobby's wristwatch (a 'present' from another drunken sailor) shows a quarter to eight. Damn. He starts running. Mrs Macfarlane is a little more observant than her husband, and she is beginning to suspect that her servant's acquaintance with the Mission's neighbours is closer than it should be.

Since the evening he arrived on the Mission doorstep, asking whether he could work in return for food, Bobby has changed considerably. He was calling himself by another name then and claimed to be an English boy down on his luck. Elspeth Macfarlane did not believe him. It was plain he was a mongrel, some Tommy's child who had grown up on the streets, but he was fine featured and his manners were good, so she fed him rice and dal in the parlour, and, in half an hour of watching him eat, persuaded herself she needed a servant. Hindu-fashion, she decided to name him after the full moon which was shining in through the window, and when he had cleaned his plate she told him he could stay.

As Chandra settled into the little room upstairs, she surprised herself by how keenly she felt the pleasure of a young man's presence in her house. The clattering of his feet on the stairs, the sight of his thin forearms resting on the table as he read a book, even the musty smell of the dirty sheets he brought down for the dhobi could give her a pang, a sudden pressure-valve sensation of pain and love. Entirely inappropriate emotions, of course. Silly-woman thinking. This was not her son. Her sons were gone.

When he realized what she had done, her husband temporarily forgot the Christian virtue of charity and insisted the freeloading little wastrel be told to leave immediately. However, as years had passed since he had spoken directly to his wife, making his views known was not straightforward. Chandra stayed, and after a couple of months Andrew switched from furtively watching the boy over his ridiculous wall, to sending him on errands, lecturing him on points of morality, and finally teaching him Latin and history and English grammar.

So in spite of herself Elspeth is unable to be too angry when Chandra arrives, out of breath and at least ten minutes late.

'Where have you been?' she says, gathering her things to take to Mrs Pereira's.

'I – I went for a walk. To the Apollo Bunder. To see the ships.'

'You spend too much time there. Have you nothing more constructive to do? No studies? Your room is tidy?'

'Yes, Ambaji. No. Yes. Nothing.'

'We'll be late for the meeting.'

'I'm sorry.'

She shakes her head, and they leave for Mrs Pereira's house.

As they walk Elspeth watches Chandra's eyes take in the sights and sounds of Falkland Road. Several shopkeepers nod hello to him. The boy is such a chameleon. Everything he touches, he seems to absorb. When he arrived he was so gawky, so *foreign*. Now he has become part of the place. They are turning into Grant Road when she notices a wristwatch peeping out from beneath one of his neat white cuffs, and, not for the first time, is worried about him.

Mrs Pereira lives tucked away in a cramped compound off the Grant Road, a battered neem tree in the courtyard screening her dealings with the netherworld from prying eyes. The neighbours keep their children away from her door, in case they make too much noise and the old witch puts the evil eye on them. Sometimes the more intrepid ones come to her for advice, while others go elsewhere for rival charms to ward off those they believe she has put on them. Useless to explain that she is not a magician but a *scientist*. Useless to say it is not hocus-pocus but a message of hope. These days, rather than explain, she prefers to rise above the rumours. Her reputation has its conveniences, privacy among them, and this is a woman with higher things on her mind: in the secrecy of her green-draped parlour Mrs Pereira has conquered death.

Bobby follows Mrs Macfarlane up the stairs to the third storey and stands a pace behind her as she knocks on the door. The sound of singing filters underneath. Elspeth looks accusingly at him. The meeting has begun. They are late. There is the sound of a bolt being drawn and Mabel, Mrs Pereira's daughter, ushers them in. Her mother, enormous, sallow, swathed in a washed-out yellow silk robe, is leading the participants in a harmonizing song. Waving her swollen fingers in the air like an orchestra conductor, she makes a sour face at the newcomers and beckons Elspeth into the circle. Bobby turns to go and wait outside, but to his surprise Elspeth looks at the hostess for permission, then motions for him to stay. She has never done this before. He shifts his weight from foot to foot, unconvinced that he wants to be part of the experiment.

The people singing around Mrs Pereira's unvarnished table make a motley group. The tall middle-aged Englishman stands ramrod straight, his hands clasped formally behind his back, projecting the words like a prefect singing a school song. The dapper young Hindu next to him keeps fingering his starched collar. Quiet gaunt Mabel stands next to the Hindu boy, flicking longing glances at him out of the sunken troughs of her eyes. At her mother's request she cranks the handle of a gramophone and they sing:

'See the chain of angels brightly dancing
Bringing blessed peace to those on earth
Life and death are hand in hand advancing
Fear is banished, all is joy and mirth'

The other European woman does not appear to know the words. Her eyebrows, startled black arcs pencilled halfway up her fore-head, are crinkled with concentration. She mouths what she can through her rouged lips, and, as if to indicate her willingness to participate fully, sways a little to the music. Bobby thinks he has seen her before, somewhere on the street. When the gramo-phone needle skips to the centre, Mrs Pereira lifts it off and places another heavy shellac disc on the turntable. Out of the brass horn a distant organ crackles into life, leading the group in a second song.

'Bright spirits, wise spirits, show us the way
We seekers of knowledge who make darkness our day
Will lift up the veil and cast sadness away
For that mighty spirits we humbly do pray'

When they have sung four or five doggerel verses, Bobby following even less of it than the young white woman, Mrs Pereira puts the record back in its sleeve and, wheezing a little, settles her bulk into a wooden chair at the head of the table.

'We are now in harmony. The atmosphere is positive. I bid welcome to the newcomers. Mademoiselle Garnier and –'

'Chandra,' says Mrs Macfarlane.

'Chandra. Welcome. Please everybody, seat yourselves. Chandra, if you could come to my left. Mr Arbuthnot, to my right. Mabel next to Chandra. Then Mr Shivpuri, yes, that's right. Mademoiselle Garnier between Mr Shivpuri and Mr Arbuthnot. Now Mabel, my dear, could you extinguish the light?' The girl gets up and turns down the lamp on the sideboard, the flame dying inside its glass bell to leave the room in darkness. Someone coughs. Mademoiselle Garnier giggles nervously.

'I must ask you first to join hands. Please spread flat on the table and press down. Do not hold hands, put your hands on top of one another. What we are about to do is very powerful, so I will remind you of the rules. If you do not follow them the consequences could be grave, especially for me, since I shall be receiving in my body the spirits of the dead. Please do not break the circle for any reason at all. Especially do not make any sudden movements, or light. I must emphasize this. Make no lights in this room.'

Mrs Pereira lingers over her vowels, stretching words out into long lilting flows which seem to lap around the table, at once soothing and perilous, like water running over a weir.

'Keep your hands joined, and your feet please very firmly on the floor. The feet on the floor are most important, as together we are to be a battery, charging up with psychical energy. The feet on the floor will ground us to the earth. So keep them please. No crossed legs or lifting up. Very important. You may talk if you like but if any spirit addresses you through me I advise politeness. I don't think we have any scoffers in this room, so I am sure we will make true contact, but politeness, politeness, politeness. Very important. And again, please to remember that there is great risk in this, and if you break the flow in any manner I am at risk of possession by a hostile spirit. Now I shall enter the trance, and call upon my spirit guides.'

Despite himself Bobby feels uneasy. On one side Mrs Pereira's fat ham of a hand is pressing down hard and sweaty on his, on the other Mabel's dry claw is doing the same. Beneath his palms he can feel the rough scarred wood of the table. The medium's breathing comes hard and ragged in the darkness.

'Blue Pearl? Blue Pearl? Can you hear me? It is I, Rosita, calling you. Blue Pearl, come to the portal. Rosita wishes communion.'

Bobby peers through the darkness. He can see nothing. Mrs Pereira's hand is pressing down ever harder, half crushing his. He wants to pull away. The air feels close and foetid, though this is probably just the medium's overpowering perfume, which is robbing him of breath, lacing his throat and nostrils with cheap musk.

'Blue Pearl? Blue Pearl? Is that you I hear?'

A series of sharp raps pierces the darkness. Around the table, the sitters shift in their chairs excitedly. Mrs Pereira's voice takes on a thick gluey quality.

'Blue Pearl?'

More knocking sounds. Then another, deeper voice.

'Is it thou, sweet Rosita? Callest thee? Is it thou who callest me out of the light?'

Mrs Pereira makes a low gurgling sound.

'I have been watching thy circle from up above. My brethren in the realm of light are mightily pleased with thy researches.'

Once again Mrs Pereira's voice is clear.

'Thank you, Blue Pearl. Thank you. You do us all a great honour.'

'I have a message for one among you. The one who harnesses the great machines.'

Mr Arbuthnot calls out excitedly. 'That's me! I mean, it is I, Blue Pearl. Arbuthnot, the railway engineer. What do you want to tell me?'

'I have a message from the one you lost.'

'Oh God, David? You've spoken to David? What does he say?'

'David is here beside me. He has not yet the power to speak of his own accord. He says to tell you that he is treated with great honour here in the realm of light. He wishes you to know that he is watching over you.'

'Oh heaven. Thank you. Thank you. And has he seen his mother up there? Is Thomasina with him?'

'The twain are united, and they give you their blessings. David is free of all pain now. He was borne aloft out of the icy waters. He hath fought on the waves and is become a hero, now and for ever. He has escaped the cycle of birth and death.'

'Oh thank you. Thank you.'

Mr Arbuthnot's voice catches, and Bobby hears muffled sobbing across the other side of the table. This moment of grief is interrupted by a sudden crack. The tabletop starts rolling and bucking like a wild animal. Beside him, Bobby can hear Mrs Pereira inhaling and exhaling hard, as if performing some kind of heavy physical exertion. Weirdly her breathing seems to be coming from somewhere near his knees. Her hand has squirmed into a different position, its heel pressing down painfully on his fingers.

'Watch out!' It is Mabel, her voice suddenly loud and excited. 'Don't break the circle. My mother is in the grip of some other spirit.' Around the table the sitters cry out in alarm.

'Watch over her!' calls out Mabel. 'Watch for her!'

The table starts to rise up, until Bobby's hands are almost in front of his nose. Then with a clatter it falls back to the floor. Mrs Pereira makes more gurgling noises.

'Be careful!' shouts Mabel. 'It is a young spirit who doesn't know its own power!'

The table stops moving, and for a minute or two the only sound in the parlour is the medium's laboured breathing. Then, so quiet as to be almost inaudible, there is a tinkle of bells. A tiny girlish voice, broken by phlegmy coughing, comes out of Mrs Pereira's throat.

'Tra-la-la! It is I!'

The sitters are silent.

'Hey-la. What fun, what fun! So glum, so glum, why so glum?'

Mr Shivpuri speaks up, in a tremulous voice. 'O spirit? Who are you please?'

'Who am I? Am I? Why I am myself, of course! You silly, silly.'

'I say again, who are you?'

'They call me Little Orchid, you silly, and I have been young since the beginning of the world. I like fun! So much fun! Fun for you and fun for me!'

'Please?' It is Mademoiselle Garnier's voice. 'Is it very pretty there?'

'Pretty pretty! All is light and happiness. All is joy, tra-la!'

'Please?' asks Mademoiselle Garnier. 'Do you have perhaps anyone there from Charleroi?'

Mrs Pereira is suddenly taken by a fit of coughing. Bobby feels her moving around in her chair. Once again there is the sound of distant bell-ringing and the table begins to judder.

'Please?' Mademoiselle Garnier sounds desperate. 'Charleroi? You have seen? Please? You have seen?'

Mademoiselle Garnier is to be disappointed. Little Orchid does not speak again. After more bells and rocking, Blue Pearl's voice comes back into the parlour.

'Verily, the spiritual frequencies are busy this night. The golden chain between the two worlds is most strongly manifested. I have two more spirits here, taken in their prime. Young warriors who seek a mother.'

'Oh Lord,' whispers Elspeth. 'Can it be true?'

'They have not yet the power of speech, for it is hard to keep the ethereal charge flowing.'

There is a banging and clattering at the table.

'Quick!' cries Mabel. 'My mother is at the end of her strength. I don't know how long she can hold the portal open. Perhaps we can communicate using the spirit code. O spirits, spirits! Answer our questions, we beseech you. Knock once for yes, twice if you don't know and three times for no. Do you understand?'

A single knock.

'Is there one in this room with whom you wish to speak?'

A knock.

'Is your mother here among us?'

A knock.

Elspeth Macfarlane's voice is choked with emotion. 'Kenneth? Duncan? Is that you?'

Again, a single knock. Elspeth breaks into uncontrollable floods of tears.

Long before he tore them apart, God brought Andrew Macfarlane and Elspeth Ross together. Elspeth and her sister had been invited by the Johnstone boys on an outing to Melrose Abbey, to take a look at the ruins and, as Petie Johnstone put it, 'Just to imagine how all the old monks and nuns used to spend their days.' The girls thought never in a million years, but, in a rare fit of good nature (and because the Johnstones were the chemist's boys, and had prospects), father had given his permission. However, when the two excited girls opened the curtains on the appointed Saturday morning, the world outside was wet and grey. Low clouds hung heavily over the trees on the hillside, and rainwater was already coursing in rivulets down the cobbled street below their bedroom window. There was nothing for it. The trip was cancelled.

Afterwards Malcolm Johnstone could have kicked himself. He would always put it like that when he told the story. I could have kicked myself right the way from here to the Border. Nevertheless it was his idea to look in on the public lecture at the kirk hall. Better than nothing, he thought. At least it was a chance to sit next to Elspeth for an hour, an hour in which there would surely be sixty minutes' worth of opportunities to touch her hand, or brush her leg with his, or to scrape his foot inch by inch over the parquet until the side of his shoe was touching the side of hers. He did all of that. On the other side of him, Petie and Susan were doing the same, but with one big difference. When Petie's searching fingers made accidental-on-purpose contact with Susan's, they found themselves accidentally touched back. There was hand-holding. There was pressing of calf against calf. What Malcolm could not see directly, he could tell by the colour of Petie's face. Red as a beetroot, the lucky beggar.

Malcolm, on the other hand, got nowhere. Elspeth ignored him with a resoluteness that was both shocking and hurtful. She sat listening to the bushy-bearded missionary as if he had cast a spell on her. Here was a local man, from Kelso just along the Tweed, who had swapped the pale watery light of Scotland for the scorching sun of India, who though still young had already spent ten years braving the most appalling hardships, walking for months through the Eastern jungles and living among savage tribesmen who worshipped devils and hung the painted skulls of children outside their huts for decoration.

Oblivious to Malcolm's mute and yearning presence at her side, Elspeth listened to tales of poor benighted people bowing down to idols and trusting themselves to the wiles of native priests, and fell in love. As he told his story, Reverend Macfarlane's eyes burned with such passion that in a few moments the vague images of Malcolm which had begun to forge themselves into a band in her mind, images which were all mixed up with the tinkle of the Johnstones' shop doorbell and the smells of cold medications and scented soap, were completely incinerated. To her he was Andrew immediately, even as she sat there in the hall, ignoring Malcolm's questioning toe and listening to the lecture, even before she had spoken a word to him.

Andrew.

Andrew had lain for three weeks in a savage's hut, praying to God to deliver him from the fevered hallucinations of malaria. Andrew had seen the Assamese tribeswomen shamelessly parading their nakedness, and called upon them to cover themselves. Andrew had healed their sick and made a mortal enemy of their witchdoctor, who collected snake venom and shook his bone rattle, trying to cast a curse on the powerful white devil who was so destroying his prestige. With his own hands Andrew had cut down jungle trees and raised high the beams of the Mission Church, bringing the Word of God for the first time in history to this forsaken corner of the Empire. Andrew told of all this with wonderful humility, saying that it was his duty, the measure of his Christian faith, the least that could be expected of someone who had the good fortune to have been born in the knowledge of God's grace. When he finished speaking and asked everyone to join him in a short hymn, Elspeth sang so loudly and enthusiastically that people in the row in front turned round to look. Afterwards Malcolm hung around gloomily at the back of the hall as she stood beside the lectern, shifting from foot to foot, asking the speaker a hundred questions and, finally, inquiring whether he might not perhaps care to take tea at her father's house. By the time Petie and Susan were married the following spring, Andrew and Elspeth Macfarlane had already taken ship for India.

At first the joys outweighed the disappointments. The stern clarity of Andrew's faith made the world seem certain and secure. Elspeth felt armoured by his firm rules, protected by his pronouncements that such a thing was sinful and such another thing the only possible course for a Christian. She loved his coarse sunburnt skin, his fierce patriarchal features, even the way his sleeping body was drenched in sweat when the old fever made one of its occasional reappearances. In the privacy of the marriage bed her eighteen-year-old body knew revelations, as her husband took his rights with an abandon that, had she not been reassured it was lawful, would have seemed to her the very definition of carnal sin.

Elspeth's trust in Andrew was complete, so she swallowed her disappointment at hearing, in their little room at Mrs Butler's Travellers' Boarding House at St Pancras, that they would not be going to Assam. Some dispute with the Mission Society meant that Andrew was no longer the minister of the church in the jungle. Also, as he gently explained, his work there was done. The job of keeping savage minds fixed on the Lord belonged to another man. His calling was taking him in a different direction. Looking out over the soot-blackened roofs of King's Cross, the London skyline hazed with green-tinged fog, Andrew painted a picture of another city, darker still. Amidst the teeming slums of Bombay were souls crying out for the word of God, souls who had nothing but three million Hindu idols, every single one diabolic in origin, to satisfy their spiritual cravings. On his lecture tour Andrew had raised enough money to start a mission in the very heart of the slums, where the degradation and depravity was at its worst. He asked her to think of it, the honour of bringing true Christianity to a city where fire-worshipping sects exposed their dead for the birds to pick clean, and Jesuit priests, almost as idolatrous as the Hindus themselves, went among the poor and needy spreading distorted versions of His Word. He knew the road they were about to travel was hard, but he would never have dreamt of asking Elspeth to join him on the journey had he not believed implicitly in her fortitude. She bowed her head and told him she would follow wherever he led.

Her first taste of disillusionment came a few weeks later, as she was walking on the deck of the Peninsular & Oriental steamer, squinting out at the bright glare of the Red Sea. The rubber soles of her deck shoes squeaked with each pace she took past the first-class passengers, who reclined on folding chairs, attended by solicitous young stewards in starched white uniforms. When she had first climbed up the gangplank and was handed the passenger list, she thrilled at the thought that she would be mingling with such exalted, interesting people: Civil Servants, Indian Army officers, all the aristocracy of the Raj. However, it was rapidly made clear to her, through silences, seating plans and acid politeness, that a missionary's wife was not the honoured rank she had been led to believe. Her second-class cabin on the starboard side of the ship, the inferior side which caught the full force of the sun, marked her as unfit to eat with, or even talk to, the Heaven-born or the business nabobs, who appeared in their tails each night at dinner to take possession of the ballroom, spinning their shimmering wives and daughters around in their richly tailored arms. Now, as she passed a gaggle of elderly memsahibs surveying some of the young folk playing deck quoits, she heard one cut-glass English voice remark to another, insolently loud, not caring if she heard, 'There. That one.'

'Her? That's the Scotch God-botherer's wife? Poor little thing. He seems so completely insufferable.'

'I imagine so. Arthur says he simply never shuts up.'

It should not have touched her, but it did. Somehow she had thought everyone saw Andrew as she did. The idea that he might be boring had never crossed her mind. Naturally she did not mention it to him, and, as she lay awake that night, wrapping the memory tightly inside her, she told herself it was a test of faith, a little trial sent by God. All the same, she remembered the words, and something inside her began to stand apart and watch.

Bombay shook her even more. Her image of the Orient was vague in the extreme, a misty vision of palm trees and coconuts and brightly dressed native women. She knew the city would be a terrible place, but in the abstract its awfulness had presented itself as an exciting challenge, to be faced with gritted teeth and a prayer, a trial which would soon evaporate in the face of good Scottish resolve such as her own, to be transmuted into a harmonious Christian East of hard work and smiling brown faces shining with the light of the Lord. The crush of porters at the Apollo Bunder, the hundreds of beggars tugging at her white cotton dress, the furnace heat and the alien smells all hit her like a dirty black hand slapping her face. Following Andrew into the worst of it, where the streets narrowed into stinking alleys, she first thought she would faint – and then did, collapsing in the middle of a crowd. She came round again in the dilapidated courtyard which was to be her home for the next thirty years.

For a long time she existed in a state of suspended animation, trusting herself entirely to Andrew. She followed his lead in every thought and action, mechanically running the household according to his instructions. As far as possible she blocked out the nightmarish place in which she lived, holding it at arm's length like a soiled rag she was taking out for the laundry. When she felt alive at all, it was inside her imagination, fuelled by battered English books that she saved up to buy second-hand from junk dealers in the Crawford market. She read romances, fairy stories and tales of gothic horror, the more extravagant the better, hiding them from her husband and selling them back to the bookwallahs when she had finished.

When she fell pregnant, Andrew relented and allowed her a servant. The old woman helped with some of the cooking and swept the floor of the makeshift church at whose doors he stood waiting every Sunday, ready to welcome a congregation which had yet to materialize. At night she comforted herself with memories of grey hills and white faces. Thoughts of Malcolm Johnstone and tall glass jars of miniature scented soaps presented themselves often to her mind, bringing with them painful silent tears.

Duncan's birth was difficult. She almost died in the stifling ward at the women's hospital, and though Andrew was keen for her to get back to her work at the Mission, she spent two months recuperating, lying in a cot by an upstairs window, weakly nursing her baby and watching the street life unfold below her. Perhaps it was this angelic distance, this sense of floating above the world she watched, that first allowed her to love India. She watched the people go about their business, buying and selling, cooking their food, begging for alms, washing their clothes, squatting to brush their teeth over the gutter, and finally found something more complex in Falkland Road than a mass of unsaved humanity. Day by day she watched more carefully, saw the figures carrying racks of tea glasses, hods of bricks, bales of cotton, papier mâché idols and flower-strewn corpses, and started to marvel at how full this world was, how full of things she understood nothing about.

Andrew was overjoyed at her return to health. She threw herself into Mission work with new vigour and attempted, for the first time, to make friends with the people among whom she lived. She now felt she truly loved Andrew for bringing her here, and he responded by taking her with him as he roamed the slums, seeking converts.

'What is it that I, a man from faraway Scotland, intend to do? Only to raise you up! Only to take your hand and show you the way! Only to ennoble your hearts by inspiring that moral fibre which is the mainstay of the Scottish character! I pledge this to you! I shall live among you as an example of righteousness, and if you come to my church, when you go back out into the world, they will say of you – he is a good man, she is a good woman . . .'

Sometimes passers-by would stop and listen. More often they would walk past. Because Andrew spoke in English, his message went unheeded by most of the people he was trying to reach. Though Elspeth pointed this out to him, he seemed reluctant to learn the language, let alone preach in it. He explained this by saying that the English language had an innately moral character, that it was in itself a route to God. She asked what he had done among the tribesmen in Assam, and he told her he had learnt some of their tongue, of course, but had concentrated on teaching them his own. English and Christ, Christ and English. Inseparable.

To Elspeth, it did not seem a very satisfactory method. Something else about it nagged her as well. She had thought Andrew was the open one in the marriage, the one really living in the

India she tried to push away. Now she began to see a different figure, arrogant and closed. Because of the strength of its religious traditions, missionaries had always had a hard task in India. It was not like Africa, where, she had heard, they would prostrate themselves in the hundreds after a single sermon. Yet Andrew seemed to have so very little success. When Elspeth fell pregnant again, after almost three years in the country, the Independent Scottish Mission among the Heathen had only two converts, both untouchable men who did odd jobs around the compound in return for food, and on Sunday often had to be dragged out of the paan shop on the corner to attend service.

Andrew decided it was too great a risk for her to give birth in Bombay again, but they did not have enough money to travel back home together. It was arranged for her and little Duncan to stay with the Gavins, an ex-missionary couple in Edinburgh. Kenneth would enter the world there. As she waved goodbye to Andrew from the deck of a Liverpool-bound B & I steamer she felt a surge of excitement. She was going home! She tried hard to keep the image of her husband before her, but too often on board ship it drifted away, obliterated by a sighting of a school of dolphins or the tangled plot of the Marie Corelli novel on her lap.

Scotland was wonderful and alien. On the ship she had worried that she would love the place too much to leave again, but when she arrived she realized to her amazement that part of her had taken root in the Bombay slums. Coming home felt like revisiting herself as a child, both emotional and slightly embarrassing. The first meal of roast beef and potatoes made her cry, and when Susan and Petie came to meet her, she hugged them so hard that Petie asked if she really wanted to crush the life out of them so soon in her visit. Father was too ill to travel. A week later she sat by his side in the old front parlour and cried again, holding his hand while he stared confusedly out of the window, asking her for the third time if she was not Mrs Ferguson come to bring his supper.

The Gavins had known Andrew in Assam, and they spoke of him in a way that sometimes troubled her. How is his resolve, asked Mrs Gavin. There must be terrible temptations in such a place. Elspeth replied that she had never known so firm a resolve, and Mr Gavin spluttered into his tea. Several times Mr Gavin mentioned Andrew's decision to work among fallen women, as if it were somehow a questionable thing. But he has Elspeth, Mrs Gavin admonished him. She is his strength.

Kenneth's birth was nearly as hard as Duncan's, and the Infirmary doctor told the new mother that she would be putting her life at risk by going through such an ordeal again. Abstinence, he said. It may be hard on your husband, but he is a man of the cloth, and he loves you. I'm sure he will understand. They gave her a letter explaining the precariousness of her health. The doctor looked over the rim of his spectacles as he pushed it across the desk. Perhaps this will help to persuade him, he said.

Arriving back in India with her two sons, she realized that all the alignments had changed. Before she left she had revolved tightly around Andrew, caught in him like a moon in the pull of a large gaseous planet. As soon as she smelt Bombay from the deck of the liner, the faint note of woodsmoke travelling across the surface of the sea, she knew this was no longer true. India was part of her personal orbit.

Elspeth's new gravity changed the Mission beyond recognition. Ignoring Andrew's complaints, she engaged a munshi to teach her the language and began to tour the slums and brothels, discovering for herself the place where she lived. She spread the word that anyone needing medical attention should come to her husband, and that after the Sunday church service English lessons would be held. Within a few months the ISMH was a hive of activity, and several new young converts had been made.

Her success both elated and shocked her. Why had it been so easy to accomplish? It showed her a new Andrew, a lost Andrew, purposeless beneath his veneer of conviction. The watchful part of her grew, a distance reinforced by the physical gap announced in the doctor's letter. Her husband's face as he read it, purple with suppressed rage. There was nothing to say. At night she could feel him beside her, tense with resentment. She would try to comfort him and he would push her stroking hands away. Worse than nothing, he muttered. Worse than before you came.

He made her feel as if it were her fault, as if she had done it on purpose. He did not understand that it was a loss for her too. This was how they had always connected with each other. They had used their bodies to guarantee the rest of it; when he was angry, when she had doubts. So she too was in mourning, though the watching part of her also held its breath, secretly relieved not to have to give itself now her faith in her husband was ebbing away. Sometimes she could not stand it and called him to her, but it always ended badly, with fumbling, tightness, apologies. Being together became worse than being alone.

For some years all this was buried beneath the bustling new life of the Mission. There was always a queue of people waiting for Andrew's rough doctoring, which consisted mostly of dispensing lectures about personal hygiene. The Falkland Road women began to use the school as a sort of occasional crèche for their children, and the Mission gradually found a niche in the ecology of the road. Elspeth would smile at the gaudy mothers, and they would smile at her, each trying to hide their mutual fascination. Elspeth also noticed how Andrew looked at them. Agonized glances. Forced disapproval. She began to wonder what game he was playing, what kind of test he had set himself.

He seemed to draw violence towards him. Once he almost caused a riot, haranguing a Muslim procession as it passed by the Mission gate. Another time a young English policeman put his head round the door of Elspeth's parlour. Sorry to intrude, but they had her husband in custody. A, ahem, *fracas* with a Catholic clergyman. As he escorted Elspeth to the kotwal, he could barely hide his amusement. It was always the same. Andrew against the world. Him right and everyone else wrong.

The boys grew up. It came time first for Duncan and then Kenneth to be sent back to Scotland to school. After her little boys faded to handkerchief-waving dots on the horizon, Elspeth had nothing left to distract her from her husband. The truth was, she had fallen in love. Not with another man, but with another way of thinking, which was worse. Gradually the visits to the munshi had been supplemented by a deeper research. Trips to the museum and to historical ruins soon led to lectures, bouts of night-time reading. She made Indian friends, and went to dinner at their houses, feeling wild pleasure at sitting close to the floor and eating with her hands. She went to the beach to watch the Ganpati Festival, jostled by worshippers as the huge idols of Ganesha were dipped into the sea. She peered into the sanctuaries of temples, trying to make out the greasy ghee-smeared forms of the gods in the darkness. One year during Holi, Andrew came out into the courtyard and confronted his grinning wife, her drenched, clinging clothes splotched with dye. You're becoming one of them, he shouted. They are dragging you down into the mire.

For her it was all to do with magic. The new world she had found was infused with secrets. Her instincts had always drawn her towards the fantastic, and now she realized this was opposed completely to everything Andrew thought – and was. His certainty, once so attractive, now appeared childishly presumptuous. How did he dare? How could he set up his foolscap and balsawood purity against the infinite mysteries of the universe?

As their little constellation flew apart, Andrew, impelled by opposing forces, started talking of science and rational religion and the superiority of the European mind to that of the Asiatic. When there was enough money for them to come out for the holidays, the boys found their parents civil to each other, more or less. Once the family had parted again, its members marginally less strange to each other than before, life in the ISMH returned to a state of guarded hostility. The Mission began to suffer. Elspeth's centre had moved outside it, and she saw no reason to encourage others into a faith she herself was leaving. When she first put it as bluntly as that, forming the words in her head as she bicycled down a busy street, she had a sense of furiously peddling guilt, an exhilarating fresh sweat of betrayal that broke out under her arms, between her breasts, the residue of the missionary wife soaking out in rivers through her pores.

Imagine a secret doctrine. Imagine ancient wisdom. The ideas were not her own. Nor were they pure Hinduism. Elspeth had been introduced to other seekers, people who believed as she did, in wonder, in the mystic synthesis of things. She attended lectures where she sat as rapt as she had in the kirk hall years before, except that now she listened to stories of the Great White Brotherhood of Himalayan masters, the Lord of the World, the Buddha, Mahachohan, Manu, Maitreya. The speaker, an enthusiastic Englishman dressed in a plain white kurta-pyjama, told of the key held by adepts, attained only after long esoteric training and fierce spiritual discipline, the key that confers immortality and a chance to join the illustrious ranks of Cagliostro, Abraham, Lao Tzu, Mesmer and Plato. The names themselves were dizzying. Hilarion the Greek. Beautiful Serapis and blue-eyed Koot Hoomi. Boehme and Solomon. Confucius and the Syrian Jesus. It seemed that throughout history men and women had strived for a richer understanding of the world, for a fleeting grasp of the dizzying recess of meanings and hierarchies that lay beneath the surface of life. In the modern age, East and

West were coming together in Theosophy, a scientific spirituality which sought the only true wisdom, the knowledge of the occult laws which govern the universe.

Elspeth did not join, not yet. It was all too far away, too great a translation from what she knew. Plain whitewashed walls to intricate carvings. Moderation in all things to joyous excess. She concealed herself from Andrew exactly as he concealed himself from her, and while they were held in this stasis, unable to escape each other completely, the Mission withered. Converts drifted back to their old ways or were sucked up by more dynamic slum churches, the Baptists or the American Lutheran pastor who had set up on Grant Road. Then came the war, and the news that both Kenneth and Duncan had volunteered. Andrew was proud. Elspeth only felt angry. Her sons had already been away for most of their lives, and now they were being taken still further from her, little boys with white handkerchiefs lost among the smudged type of the news reports. It was everything she detested. Lives reduced to black and white brevity, bodies she had washed and cradled straitjacketed by infuriatingly abstract accounts of 'actions', 'fronts' and 'offensives'.

For a while she and Andrew prayed together; they had long since ceased sharing a bed. It was a gesture. Elspeth spent her evenings with circles of Theosophists and other seekers, meditating on the troops, trying to throw a psychic shield over the ones they loved. She heard terrible things about the war, how the Germans were servants of the Lords of the Dark Face, implacable opponents of truth, how the dead warmonger Bismarck had planted magnetic talismans at his borders to prevent occult resistance to Teutonic domination. As news of casualties filtered through, some of her Theosophist friends became Invisible Helpers, patrolling the far-off front in their astral bodies, shepherding the souls of the dead towards the afterlife. With terrible foreboding, she tried to make contact with Kenneth and

Duncan. Just once. Just (she could not form the thought) one last time. But she could not leave her body, could not unground herself from Bombay. Perhaps, she reasoned, she lacked spiritual technique.

The two telegrams came in quick succession. Kenneth at Ypres. Duncan at Loos. Only the thought of reincarnation sustained her. Someone pointed her to Mr Leadbeater's 'Lives of Alcyone', with its list of incarnations, famous lives intertwined across the cosmos from 40,000 years before Christ until the present day. Julius Caesar. Mrs Besant. Lives lived on Mars, in Peru, on the moon. The immensity of it was comforting. This horror was simply the termination of a single visit by her sons. They had met before and would meet again, hundreds of meetings, hundreds of receding figures, waving across time. With the two telegrams in front of her on the parlour table, she found she was not afraid any more and told Andrew what she believed, calmly laying it all out like a carpet unrolled down a flight of steps for a visiting dignitary.

He was appalled. He told her she had been seduced by Satan. They were no longer man and wife. That afternoon he carried hodloads of bricks into the courtyard, stripped to his shirtsleeves and began to build a wall.

When Bobby first arrived, he marvelled at the construction which had such power over his new employers. It was an uneven wall, crumbling and bowed at the centre, yet with the husband's life on one side and the wife's on the other, it seemed both absurd and mystically potent. He has come to suspect that even the Reverend could not explain how he had brought it into being. It was a thing which sprang fully formed out of pain.

It was as much to keep himself in as to keep her out. No one understood that. Slamming the bricks down one on top of the other he felt like the very last man. The tide of filth had swallowed even his wife. Even Elspeth.

Oh Lord.

All his failings. All the previous walls. None of them would have been necessary had he not failed so badly and so often. What the rest of the world saw in him he did not know and did not really care. What God saw was all that mattered, and he knew how he must appear to that giant blue eye. A dripping bucket. A leaky bag of skin.

For a while he thought of laying the bricks in a square. Make a tomb. Shut himself in. It did not come to that. Despair is among the things God does not permit. So he built the bricks up to eye-level, moved the last of his things to the attic over the church, and began to watch Elspeth as she lowered herself gradually towards the level of the monkeys.

He could have made it final. Either of them could have done it, by moving away or returning home. He could have forced his will on her by withholding the money that came from her sister. Susan and Petie, made rich by their chain of chemist's shops. Yet something in both of them resisted it. By living on either side of the wall they made their lives provisional, unfinished. They put off the final moment of failure.

On Elspeth's side people came and went. Andrew watched them furtively, peering from upstairs windows or standing on tiptoe behind the wall. They were always in groups, these Theosophists. They seemed to need to band together. Though the same faces appeared again and again, they did so under different banners. The Daughters of India, the Order of the Rising Sun, the Preparation League of Healers, the Prayer League, the Brotherhood of Arts. So much hocus-pocus. So much confusion. Men and women, Indians and Europeans, promiscuously mingled together. He did not see how Elspeth could stand it.

He never had the capacity for vagueness. He was not proud

of this. It was a sign he was weak and faltering in his faith. All his life he had known that were he to give way only once, he would be lost. The baroque mysteries unfolding on the other side of the courtyard were the devil's work, of that he was sure, but he had always eschewed even more innocent forms of imprecision. Lack of limit. Blending. Multiplicity. To him these were just other names for Doubt.

When he fell, he fell hard.

A light flickers in a hut on an Assamese hillside, slivers of oily yellow escaping between loosely lashed staves of bamboo. A young Andrew paces up and down inside, the print of his naked body left behind in dirty sweat on the sheets of his cot. He drinks water from the covered jug on the table. He kneels to pray. His hands brush himself, bitten nails scraping his mosquito-bitten chest. Each touch sears his skin. The tropical climate is doing its evil work, dissolving Europe in heat and moisture, turning this man of God into a sensuous thing, a streaming naked body fronted by a bobbing, straining cock. He rolls on the floor, groans. He is twenty-four years old. On other nights like this he has given in, hands working guiltily until it is over. Tonight there is a noise outside his door, and he realizes he is being watched. He clutches an old shirt around his waist and opens it, comes face to face with Sarah, one of the Mission girls. Tiny cat-faced child-woman, both hands pressed over her mouth to stifle her giggles. She has removed her cotton print dress, the Mission clothes he and the Gavins have such trouble getting them to wear. She is squatting there, a twist of rushes round her waist, heavy brass rings piercing her distended earlobes. Otherwise naked. His eyes stray down to the little studs of her breasts, her rush-fringed vulva. It is too much. He circles her upper arm with his hand and brings her inside.

It happened once, twice, a third time. No more. By then he was revolted at himself. It was over. He vowed it. But a few months later little Sarah was to be seen waddling round the compound, hands smoothing the faded rose-print stretched over her belly. He avoided her. The Gavins knew she was not married, but they put it down to some failing on her part, yet another event in the tribe which had taken place outside or beneath the limits of European understanding. Perhaps she has a husband, guessed Mr Gavin one day. Some fellow who is not a convert. He had not noticed how the other Mission girls looked at young Macfarlane. He had no idea what his assistant heard as he lay awake at night, whispering prayers into the humid darkness. The scratching at his door like the clawing of small animals. Sarah, and not just Sarah. All wanting favours. Wanting to be the woman of the young white priest.

A little girl was born, and Sarah held her up to her father as he strode past; he did not dare to meet her eye. It was a pale creature. He thought the Gavins could hardly fail to notice. They said nothing. The child was always there, playing in the dirt, clapping its chubby hands. Accusing him.

He had seen villages near to the big tea plantations where whole families of half-breed children lined up to watch the missionaries ride past. Boys and girls of various sizes holding hands in front of their huts, each one bearing the tell-tale crook nose or jug ears of the Plantation Manager, or the Engineer, or the District Medical Officer. A shocking conversation with a man in the mildewed smoking room of an upcountry club. Helps while away the long evenings, what? Bugger all else to do.

But not for him. He was supposed to be better than that.

He resolved to try harder. He threw himself into work, conceived a project for building a proper hospital at the Mission. Four solid brick walls with full facilities, large enough to serve the whole district. He was winning. His thoughts had found a channel. Then Mr Gavin came to visit him one night and found the girls at the door, three of them curled like puppies on the veranda while inside Macfarlane innocently wrote funding requests to the authorities in Darjeeling. Why were they there? What kind of degenerate harem was he running? Eventually his protégé's face persuaded him that things were not as bad as he had thought, but the damage was done.

One day, the inevitable conversation as they rode for supplies, monsoon water sluicing off their broad-brimmed hats, deep green jungle smell high in their nostrils. This is a hard country for a single man. Perhaps it is not the place God has ordained for you. Go back, Andrew. Find yourself a wife. We will of course support you completely, but I have to tell you the Mission Society may not be able to find you another place here in the hills.

He had fallen. Yet he would not give in. He went back Home and tried to gain support for his own mission. Duly his perseverance was rewarded. In his mercy God brought him a wife, and out of gratitude he decided to test himself, to strive as hard as possible to prove worthy of God's gift. A plan unfolded. He would walk among the harlots, make his home in the most depraved place he knew. Thus, by resisting temptation, he would prove his strength and redeem himself in the eyes of the Lord. It was the same impulse that leads other men to lift heavy weights or volunteer for dangerous duties in wartime. He consulted no one, so no one was there to ask him if this was indeed fortitude, or merely a desire to pick, like scabs, over his weaknesses.

Elspeth arrived, fumbling questions to him at the front of the draughty kirk hall. Donations were made for a Bombay mission. The two seemed part of one thing: an end to his worthlessness. He concentrated on this spiritual goal and the world shaped itself around it. The marriage was celebrated, and two second-class tickets purchased on the P & O. Only back in India, with his hysterical young wife stowed inside a dilapidated tenement on Falkland Road, did he stop to think, to draw breath and look properly at the challenge he had taken on.

In truth he was lost. He did not know what to do. It had been like that many times in Assam. He wanted a force to push against, hard work to help him learn about himself. Instead he was frictionless, a flailing skater nudged by the city across its own impenetrable surface. The problem was people. He needed them to do a job, which was to form a mass, a single object for his spiritual striving. Instead they remained stubbornly unassimilated. The unsaved men and women of Bombay watched him preach or did not watch, chewed betel, wandered off, passed comments, and with every sign of amusement or indifference they seemed to flaunt their individuality. How could they? This was teeming Asia, where the individual counted for nothing. He screamed at startled rickshaw drivers in the street, and felt it a shadow of God's own anger. The whole thing was an affront, made more galling because these people were so servile to other forces: to money, to false religion and the lead weight of their traditions, to the other white men who ruled them. He wondered if he lacked some vital quality these other men possessed, some organ of whiteness and command.

Maybe he was the kind of debased white man who diluted his precious blood.

Everything became knotted together. Duty. The Mission's failure to get a foothold. Semen. Giggling native women. He wanted to know the exact shape of his sin, and found it in scientific books. Andrew Macfarlane of the Leucodermi, cymotrichous of hair and mesocephalic of head, had coupled with Sarah of the Xanthodermi, exotically leiotrichous but woefully brachycephalic. Their daughter was a collapse. A blur.

Compared to the parent of the higher race, the children are a deteriorated product. The mixture, if general and continued through generations, will infallibly entail a lower grade of power in the descent. The net balance of the two accounts will show a loss when compared with the result of unions among the higher race alone.

What had he brought into the world? He could not remember

what the child looked like. Gradually her face was obliterated by those of his two young sons, born whole and unsullied by their father's previous failure. They were his pride, yet sometimes the price seemed too high. The denial of his wife's body was a torture. Though he had the doctor's letter, something in Elspeth's manner told him that she would have held herself back even without it. Falkland Road became a place with many pitfalls.

These are the signs of racial inferiority: simplicity and early union of the cranial sutures. Wide nasal aperture, with synostosis of the nasal bones. Prominence of the jaws. Recession of the chin. Early appearance, size and permanence of 'wisdom' teeth

These are the parts of women. High foreheads. Eyes rimmed with kohl. Breasts fastened into tight coloured blouses. Bare stomachs. Red sucking mouths, open, waiting.

A flat and retreating forehead is also a 'low' feature, but a somewhat bulbous forehead, such as is characteristic of Negroes, does not necessarily imply high intellectual ability

His young wife flourished. Her energy seemed boundless. She was a pulsing living thing, and she was denied him. By rights she was his. It was impossible. Impossible. His jealousy became like a living creature.

The European has crossed with every known race of humanity in the course of his conquest of the world. This miscegenation has resulted in an inextricable mass of mixed peoples, perfectly comparable with our street-dogs and roof cats

Fucking. Make the shape of the word with your red mouth. Lower lip flicking off the teeth, breathy vowel guttering in a strangled click of the throat. Fuck. Fucking.

Examining the angle and direction of the Negress's vagina and the corresponding angle and structure of the male genital organs, one can clearly see

Fucking. The whore who, as he walked past one morning, lifted up her pink skirt to show her *periodic erethism of the sexual centres*

The missionary walking among the harlots. The valley of mouths. Fearing no evil.

the labia are much flattened and thinned, approaching in type that offered by the female anthropoid ape

Fucking.

The missionary toils over a splayed girl. Nails dig hard into brown skin. English words. Gibber gibber glub-glub. Screaming. He makes a fist. All the years. Hit hard. Harder. Somewhere else his forbidden white wife. Oh Lord God.

Men came and pulled him off. Brown men who smelled of sweat and garlic and punched his stomach and cut his face and dragged him outside and threw him on to a rubbish heap. Half naked, his bare feet pressing into shit and rotting orange peel, he stumbled around looking for his trousers. The missionary, watched by a little knot of street children.

He told Elspeth it was an argument with Hindu thugs. He could tell she did not believe him. It was around that time he began to take seriously the ideas of the polygenists.

Maybe, he decided, there had been other families apart from that of Adam and Eve. The sacred author of Genesis had no reason to be concerned with those creatures, and so they had existed down the years, undescribed and unmemorialized. Today's lower races showed such distinct and separate characteristics that one could hardly help concluding they were actually a separate species, descendants of these less human men. All this made crossing doubly unnatural, no better than bestiality. How he had fallen! At least most authorities agreed that the products tended towards sterility. He imagined his huge-headed yellow daughter, breeding a litter in the muck of the jungles, his own features distorting step by step until the line petered out into a last hideous stillbirth.

Meanwhile Elspeth was drifting away from him. She ceased

asking his permission for things, and spoke to the monkey people in rapid syllables which he could not follow. She would not touch him, but would dandle monkey-children on her knee. It was like watching one's wife debasing herself with a dog or a horse. Afterwards he realized that the outbreak of war had saved him from doing something terrible. All sorts of ideas were stewing in his head, Old Testament images of blood and revenge. The Kaiser wiped them out, or rather redirected them, the *Illustrated News* caricature of the bloodthirsty monster in a spiked helmet doing the work the people of Bombay had never managed, rendering the forces of darkness single and visible. He began to hate the Germans with an overwhelming passion. For a while they became the sole topic of his streetcorner sermons. People gathered to watch him rage over the evils of the Hun, goggling at this whirl of spittle and balled fists perched on a tea chest in the market. He was even prepared to overlook his wife's occult activities, especially since for the first time in years the two of them knelt together to pray.

Despite his eagerness for war he assumed sacrifices would be asked of him. Sacrifice was, after all, what he craved. Perhaps it was a lack of imagination, but even though Kenneth and Duncan were in France he never thought God would demand them. Abraham placed Isaac on the altar but the Lord stayed his hand. Andrew was never granted the favour of such a personal test, and nothing stayed the German machine gunners. The telegrams left him too stricken to be angry. When Elspeth told him she no longer believed in his God at all, and laid out her fairytale of reincarnation and silvery spirits, part of him wanted to reach out and clasp her to him. If only the boys could come back. If only something could bridge the chasm that had opened between him and the world.

Instead he built the wall. One brick slapped down on top of the other, sealing in the last shreds of his virtue, a sparrow in an experimenter's glass bell, fluttering as the sustaining air is pumped out. He felt he had no other choice. The wall gave the Macfarlanes a kind of equilibrium, allowing Elspeth room to try to reconnect with her sons in the astral plane, and Andrew to brood on God and guilt and Reason. He gradually conceived a project large enough to occupy him for the rest of his time on earth, the search for a physiological basis for spirituality. Surely, he reasoned, the white man's unique capacity for faith must stem from some quality of mind or body. Comparative anatomy would hold the key. He began research in earnest.

When the boy arrived, Andrew was existing somewhere near madness, floundering in statistics and calibrations. He heard a noise in the courtyard and came down from his laboratory to peer over the wall as Elspeth showed the dirty khaki-clad urchin her half of the Mission. Later he noticed she had put him to work around the house. He was instantly suspicious, and when he discovered that despite his fair skin and noble looks the child had a taint of blood, he felt that all his worst suspicions had been confirmed. Elspeth was moving further down the ladder. She would be robbed and cheated. He wrote a letter detailing his objections and wedged it under her door. She showed no sign of having received or read it. The boy stayed.

Andrew spied on him over the wall, watching him go about his household tasks. It was as if a ghost had come to haunt him. To have to live so close to the thing he feared most: white yet not white, a diffraction both of his dead sons and his monstrous daughter. One day the lad was out in the yard, mending a broken chair. Elspeth came out and stood behind him, watching him work, a peculiar half-smile on her face. Almost unconsciously she put out a hand and ran it through his hair. The boy looked up and smiled at her. Andrew's chest constricted. That afternoon he called out to the boy and gruffly ordered him to sweep his side of the courtyard.

Soon he was teaching Robert to write and speak proper English, and giving him the rudiments of culture. It was done in an experimental spirit. What effect had the child's mongrel heritage (about which he was understandably reluctant to speak) on his intellectual and moral capacities? As he taught, he studied his pupil. The boy was amazingly quick and eager, almost *desperate*, to learn. To his surprise, Andrew found himself dispensing praise as well as admonishment. And of course the boy did the job of a messenger, a celestial intermediary between his world and that of his wife.

An angel.

The cold weather follows the rains. Hot follows cold. During the year after the visit to Mrs Pereira and the arrival of Reverend Macfarlane's scientific equipment, Bobby's body hardens and his face acquires a lean cast. The Falkland Road women still call out as he walks past, but the tone of their voices has changed. There is something hungry in the dirty jokes, something wishful and appraising. He has grown out of his old clothes and bought more. Clothes please him. He enjoys the feel of a clean shirt, the glint of a collar stud. The act of choosing a tie from the selection hanging inside his wardrobe door has a ritual quality to it. Spots or stripes. Who to be today.

Though he still lives at the Mission, everyone knows that Bobby's position as the Macfarlanes' servant is only nominal. Those two are more than half in love with him, say the gossips. Well, they're not alone there. I wouldn't mind. Nor I. What I could teach him if I had the chance.

Bobby has been busy. His Bombay business interests have been considerably extended. He is not rich. Who is in this place? But he is perhaps even better than rich: he is connected. He still runs errands for the houses, but smaller boys are sent out for paan and bottles now. Bobby works on commission, brokering deals and procuring hard-to-find services for those with a discreet manner and an open wallet. Whether your tastes run to the florid curves of Madame Noor's Baghdad Jewesses (*Habibi! Habibi!*), the threadbare geisha at the Japan House, or those specialized and painful activities that only the Blue Butterfly is properly equipped to provide, Bobby will be able to point you in the right direction.

Rumour has it that he is not above a little freelance work himself. Heaven knows the offers are there. However, he lets on that he is not interested, and people accept that, more or less.

No one can find anything out about Bobby's background. Nothing so unusual in that. You would not dream of asking Shyam Sen why he can't go back to Calcutta, or quizzing China Tony about his mangled fingers. Some things are private. But Bobby has a quality which is different from secretiveness. When he is talking to you, he seems to fall in with the rhythm of your voice. He will stand how you stand, making remarks that seem somehow tailored to your sense of humour. For all his swagger and beauty and flamboyance, there is something in Bobby which craves invisibility.

Bobby's capacity for mimicry helps in his work. He can reduce British Other Ranks to fits by imitating regional accents. Oroight there, mate? Och ye dinnae wanna worrit yersel'. Now then, sirs, if you please to follow me I know a very good place . . . Bobby deals in stereotypes, sharply drawn. Sometimes he hangs around near the doorways of expensive places, paying the doormen to let him stay. He has short one-sided conversations. 'How are you today, sir?' 'Good evening, can I be of service?' There often does seem to be something he could arrange. Especially late at night outside Green's or Watson's, or at the Byculla Club on race day.

Bobby is a ghost, haunting thresholds, pools of electric light. He hovers at the limit of perception, materializing in his collar and tie like someone only semi-real, ethereal enough to trust with your secrets, safe in the knowledge that he would melt in direct sunlight. Bobby has never been inside the places he watches. He just catches the people who fall out of them. However, he knows one of the waiters at the Royal Bombay Yacht Club, and once stands for a whole evening watching a ball. Flaming torches are set on the lawn, and strings of bulbs illuminate a floor of wooden boards around which the members dance each other's wives and girlfriends, a whirl of white backs and arms watched intently by twenty pairs of Indian eyes.

Sometimes by day Bobby is a student. Under Reverend Macfarlane's beady eye he recites Key Dates. The Battle of Hastings. Magna Carta. Glorious Revolution and War of Jenkins's Ear. His Latin grammar is excellent. In return for his tuition he brings the Reverend photographic subjects. The routine is always the same. Tell them I won't pay, he says, but he will, though only if the subject is from a caste or class he has not covered, and they will pose undraped.

Bobby wonders what Macfarlane thinks. What does he choose to believe about his pupil's street friends? Or his clothes, or his manners, or his eagerness to learn the Reverend's lessons? When Macfarlane looks at him, it is not with love, exactly. There is a challenge. An appraisal.

Actually Macfarlane is most surprised by the way Bobby studies his scientific books. One day he sneaks a look at a notebook to find, alongside lists of second declension nouns and the battles of the English Civil War, the sequence *Eskimo, Palaearcticus or Ugrian, Sinicus, Northern Amerind, Turki, Paroean or Southern Mongoloid, Polynesian, Neo-Amerind, Tehuelche, North-West Amerind* . . . And so on. All the racial subgroups, as listed by Haddon. There are other things. Charts. Tables of distributions and frequencies. His fascination with classification seems almost as intense as Macfarlane's own.

No extraneous word is spoken in the classroom. The two of them communicate in raw data, streams of facts, typologies. Though he feels he ought to be flattered, Macfarlane finds it peculiar. He has a disciple, but there is something almost too avid about his concentration. Something aggressive. He has an instinct to cover himself. It is like having the marrow surreptitiously drained from his bones.

As they turn over information in Macfarlane's attic room, both find it sinister. Perhaps, thinks Bobby, it is a kind of staring game. Who will blink first? He does not understand why he persists, what is the source of the weird fascination he finds in his lessons with Macfarlane. He feels closest to an answer when watching the Reverend at work on a photographic study. How his clawed hands arrange the model, clamping a body rigid in front of his grid. How they take measurements. The width of a pelvis. The angle of a breast. Dimensions calibrated, then noted down in a ledger. As Macfarlane peers into the camera, his hunched old-man's body is merely a massive grizzled vehicle for an eye. A single line of force, drawn through the aperture like a wire. There is always strain in his face as he surfaces. Once a girl starts teasing him. Touching herself and striking poses. He stands away from the camera and stares. He seems appalled, unable to think. Finally Bobby bustles her out of the room, afraid Macfarlane is about to do something appalling.

On Tuesdays and Thursdays Mrs Macfarlane introduces Bobby to scientific spirituality. The Theosophical Society meet in a large hall, hung with banners proclaiming the wisdom of the Himalayan Masters and the nobility of the hermetic quest. Bobby attends these with his mistress and is much admired. How his soul shines through, murmur the middle-aged ladies and gentlemen. He is surely destined to be an Adept. Bobby discovers that good-looking boys have always played an important role in the work of the Society. The World Teacher himself, currently on a lecture tour in Europe, is by all accounts an extremely handsome young man.

They sing songs and take collections and listen to lectures about the significance of the pyramids, the authority of the Vedas in the modern world, and the need for a synthesis of Eastern and Western thought to heal the psychic wounds of the war. Sometimes Bobby pays attention. Sometimes he just looks around and marvels at the peculiarity of this congregation, where Indians and Europeans mingle without seeming to notice. The atmosphere is fevered, millenarian. Throughout history, the people of the world have cried out for knowledge of a Key, a Path. Now is the time for that wish to be granted. Now, with the world rent apart, with the war-driven increase in traffic between dead and living, between the astral and the gross materiality of the physical, it is finally time for the Society to lead mankind forward into Bliss. Membership is blossoming. The meetings are packed, and from the lectern the officers read out dispatches from Australia, from the Netherlands, California, Brazil. Cast your thoughts westward, urges a speaker from Adyar. Out of the waters of the Pacific will rise a future race, one that will supersede the Indo-Aryan leaders of today.

There is controversy when a meeting is addressed by a German woman. Swiss, insists the Chairman over the uproar. Frau Doerner is a distinguished teacher of Eurythmics. And she is Swiss. Some members walk out in protest, but Frau Doerner is allowed to speak, tugging nervously at the border of her sari as she outlines her philosophy of sensuous ritual movement and the liberation of the Instinct.

Politics and spirituality have become oddly mixed, since on the material plane Congress has promised swaraj within one year, and every few weeks Bombay is paralysed by another strike. Mill workers, dockers and sailors walk out, and a general hartal shuts down the city for several days. Union leaders stride on to Theosophical platforms, following speakers on occult chemistry and Christ's training as an Egyptian Mason. Theosophists are urged to work for Indian Home Rule, for such is the message the Lord of the World gave to Mrs Besant when the immortal Rishi Agastya (Himalayan Master with special responsibility for India) arranged for her to have an interview at Shamballa, the Brotherhood's secret mountain HQ. Political freedom for India means spiritual freedom for the world. Please put your change in the tin.

Bobby discovers that for people so focused on mind and spirit, the Theosophists still find an unusual amount of time for the body. At an afternoon party, while the others are standing around in their robes drinking tea, the formidable Mrs Croft (wife of the Assistant Inspector of Works) manoeuvres him into a storeroom. There she informs him she is a Sensitive, and thus she knows of his sacred mission. However, he is not to worry since his secret is safe with her. Then she tears open her blouse to expose her breasts. Anoint me, Chandra, she breathes. Place your lips upon these rosy aureoles. Bobby, whose mind is filled with images of court rooms and all-white juries, tells her he has taken a vow. Of what, she asks. I think I hear someone coming, he lies. You had better button yourself up. On another occasion young Mr Avasthi happens upon Bobby in the WC and wonders aloud whether he might, just once, beg leave to perform a particular service. Bobby lets him get down on his knees, then tells him that unless he hands over a certain sum of rupees, he will tell the other members of the terms of their arrangement. Mr Avasthi pays up, and flees. Afterwards Bobby feels a twinge of guilt. Mr Avasthi is shy and works as a clerk in a shipping office. Unfortunately business, first and foremost, is business.

Mrs Macfarlane is pleased by Chandra's inquiring mind, and his touching willingness to attend to higher matters. She would probably be disappointed were she to learn that his main reason for attending Theosophical meetings is to spy for Mrs Pereira. Mrs P. has many Theosophical clients, and finds information about their personal lives, likes, dislikes, hopes and dreams immensely useful in producing satisfactory contacts with the spirit world. She maintains a network of drivers, hotel porters, ayahs, bearers and punkahwallahs who supply her with tidbits of information. Bobby has been a committed team member since the week after his first seance.

Bobby made it a condition of service that Mrs P. showed him how she did it. It took a lot of argument, but eventually, with much wheezing and grumbling, she sat down at her seance table and demonstrated certain technical aspects of mediumship not known to the general seance-going public. Displaying unusual agility for such a large woman, she showed him how to tip a table by flicking it up with the nape of the neck, how to free a hand from the control of a neighbouring sitter and how to use various parts of the body to produce spirit clapping; she also briefly outlined the advantages of a light construction when attempting table levitation. With a certain pride she pulled up the rug to show the system of bells and electrical control switches she had installed to help with more complex manifestations. Warming to her topic, she even sketched (thankfully without demonstrating) some of the methods of storing and producing ectoplasm, techniques which explain why female mediums have such an advantage in this fast-growing area. Mrs P. explained that she no longer made a habit of ectoplasmic manifestations, after a scrape where a sceptic forced her to drink a cup of coffee before the sitting, and the muslin came up brown. Bobby went away thoroughly enlightened, though a little depressed for Mrs Macfarlane.

Because of the unusually fluid moral outlook imposed on him by his work, Bobby often finds himself lost. Though the Macfarlanes have given him a home, there are certain barriers to emotional honesty. No one else takes an interest in him. He belongs to no group or gang. There is nothing much he feels connected with at all. Bombay is large, and the violent flows which surge through it are enough to scare highly trained British administrators, with uniforms and codes of honour and portraits of the King to give them backbone. So it is hardly surprising that

Bobby sometimes jumps at shadows, and has recurrent dreams about spider-webs and being chased through forests. When he feels like this he goes to visit Shuchi, who is a year older than him and works at the Red House. If she has no clients she will curl up with him on her bed and watch him sleep. Bobby also sometimes turns up at Madame Noor's on a quiet night, to visit the girl the others call Gul. Madame Noor used to deduct it out of his commission, but she stopped. Something has to come for free in this life, she says, sucking philosophically on her waterpipe.

One morning Bobby strolls out of the Mission on his way to pick up a new suit. He is full of anticipation, though disturbed to see that someone has daubed red paint over the church door. A hammer and sickle. Reverend Macfarlane will not be pleased. He already suspects that his wife has Bolshevist sympathies, and believes that the new unions springing up across the city are satanically inspired. Bobby shrugs. Not his problem. Today is a good day, too good to be spoilt by one of the old man's moods. Later he will call at the Red House to show Shuchi how he looks. Perhaps he will even take her out for a promenade. He imagines her dressed like an Englishwoman in a long embroidered dress with a big straw hat on her head. And a parasol. Amused by the idea, he bounds up the step into Shahid Khan's shop, stepping past the apprentices hunched over their sewing machines and calling out to the tailor, who is drinking tea in the back.

The suit is a delight. Shahid Khan has lined the cream-coloured linen with yellow silk, and done so at half the price he initially said was the minimum necessary to subsist for a single day in this debased age. The jacket is tight and double-breasted, its flap pockets fashionably angled down. The trousers end in generous turn-ups that break on Bobby's leather shoes just so. Full of praise, Bobby pays up, and Shahid Khan tells him he is taking food from his children's mouths but looks pleased all the same, in the way that a tailor always looks pleased when his work is being worn by someone who shows it off well.

Bobby decides to take a stroll down the Hornby Road, to look in the glass windows of the European shops. He slides down the street, feeling (with some justification) that he looks a thousand times better than all the sweating English and scruffy Indians he shoulders past on the busy thoroughfare. He is looking at a display of portable typewriters ('light and sturdy enough for travel and camp use') when the shop door opens and an elderly white man in the uniform of an infantry officer steps out, carrying a wrapped parcel.

'Good morning,' he says.

'Good morning,' replies Bobby, surprised to be addressed.

'Hell of a day,' says the officer. 'You sure you should be out without a hat? Terribly fierce sun, you know. Pays to be careful.'

Bobby is about to speak, but the man has already started off down the road, whistling tunelessly. He is puzzled. That oddly complicit tone. One man to another. No distance. No reserve. A hat? Then he realizes. The man thought he was English. Two Englishmen, talking about the weather. An hour later, Bobby goes into Laidlaws and buys an enormous Curzon topi, which sits on his head like a minor classical monument. Instead of going to see Shuchi he spends the afternoon walking around, tipping it to English people. Sometimes they tip their hats back.

After the hat incident Bobby starts to play a new game. He loiters in places where English people are to be found, and tries to engage them in conversation. Not for money. For fun. The Apollo Bunder is a good spot. When the huge packet steamers make port, the dock is alive with people, and among them are always plenty of newcomers in need of assistance. Weaving between piles of mail sacks and chalk-marked luggage, he scouts for candidates, avoiding those being met by friends, searching for the ones who look hot and confused, who will be grateful for a helpful young man to shoo away the touts and recommend a good hotel.

The point is to tell them a story. Any story will do, so long as it is English. Or rather about *being* English. Hello, my name is Walker, Peter Walker. John Johnson. Clive Smith. David Best but call me Bestie. Everybody does. I work for a petroleum company. A rubber company. The school board. A department store. I'm here visiting my cousin. An old school friend. And you?

The thing is, they believe him. They hear an accent and see a face and a set of clothes, and put them together into a person. After a while, a few begin to sense there is something wrong, something they cannot put their finger on. Were you brought up in the colonies, Mr Best? Rarely does this sense congeal into anything definite, and by then Bobby has moved on. Unless, that is, he makes a mistake.

There is the time with the old woman and her niece. He is at the docks, watching a car being lifted out of a cargo hold by crane. Disinterred from its crate, it sits on a wooden pallet, gleaming expensively. Chains have been passed underneath, which jerk tight as the stevedores shout to each other, winching it round. The car clears the deck and swings precariously overhead, a large black shadow shivering across the quayside. Bobby hears a gasp and sees the two Englishwomen scurrying out of the way.

'Oh – my case!'

Bobby nips back and rescues a little valise, hands it (with a tip of the hat) to the elderly lady. He is rewarded with a gracious smile.

'Oh, you are kind.'

'Not at all. Just arrived?'

'Yes. On the *Viceroy*. You too? We didn't see you on board.'

'Oh no. I was waiting for my sister. I thought she was due on today's boat, but I think I must have got the date wrong. I'm such a duffer with dates.'

'Oh I do know what you mean. You poor thing. I'm sure she'll turn up.'

Soon he is rounding up porters and arranging for their luggage to be transferred to the Taj Mahal Hotel. They believe him implicitly. Nigel Watkins, Junior Land Surveyor. The old lady fusses around, loses things, finds them again, worries that someone will 'make off' with the smaller items, and all the time thanks her white knight profusely. The young one, who is pretty, dispenses seductive smiles from beneath her hat. Everything is going well. Perhaps too well. Before he knows it Bobby is inside the hotel, following his new friends through one of the small courtyards. You must stay and take tea with us. We absolutely won't take no for an answer. I'm sure Virginia has a hundred questions about Bombay.

While they go to settle themselves in their rooms, he waits at a table under a big canvas umbrella, looking up at the rows of wrought-iron galleries which loom over the garden on all sides. The place feels like a prison yard. Bearers sleep on mats outside their masters' rooms, or squat in groups to gossip. He starts to wonder if any of the men idly leaning over the railings will recognize him. Not impossible. A lot of people know Pretty Bobby. He begins to feel nervous, exposed. Perhaps this is not such a good idea. Just as he has made up his mind to leave, the Englishwomen come back and sit down with him. Virginia starts talking about tigers and snake charmers and other things she has heard are to be found in India. He answers distractedly. Yes, it is true that scorpions can be dangerous, but as long as one remembers to shake out one's shoes in the morning, one is unlikely to be stung. A waiter brings tea. And winks at him, he is sure of it. The man walks away, his elaborate puggaree bobbing up and down as he disappears into a passageway. He is probably en route to the manager, to tell him about the conman in the garden.

'Where did you say your family were from?'

It is the aunt, teacup poised between saucer and chin. He has not thought about this part of the story, and answers without thinking.

'London.'

'Oh really, which part?'

'The – the east of the city.'

'The East End? You surprise me. Whereabouts?'

'Where?'

'Yes, where?'

Bobby has heard of the East End. It is the opposite of the West End. But East End place names are beyond him.

'Brighton' he says uneasily. It is obviously the wrong answer. The two women look at him quizzically.

'I thought you said London,' says the niece, with that flirtatious relish for tripping up young men that nice English girls are taught at boarding school.

'I did?'

'You did.'

'Well – my ancestors came from there. I was brought up in India, for the most part.'

'But – you said you only came out to take up your present position with the Survey.'

Bobby could easily have said that. He doesn't remember.

'Oh, you must have misunderstood. I have been here a long time. Look, it has been lovely meeting you but I – I forgot that I have an appointment at three. I really must be going.'

He knows he is behaving oddly, but he cannot help it. His unease communicates itself to the aunt. Warning bells ring visibly in her head. Scanning the garden, she appears to be looking around for someone official. Bobby stands up. Her face clouds with a sudden intense suspicion.

'Virginia? Did I leave my handbag here? I'm sure I had my blue bag with me.'

'I think you took it upstairs, Aunt Dorothy.'

Aunt Dorothy looks sharply at Bobby. He looks wanly back at her. She notes the strain in his face, and takes it as an indication of guilt.

'Mr Watkins. Have *you* seen my bag?'

'Absolutely not. And now, if you'll permit –'

'Waiter? Waiter?'

Aunt Dorothy is convinced she has sniffed out a plot. She glares fiercely at Bobby. Already two or three hotel staff are converging on the table. Though he has done nothing wrong, Bobby does not think he could brazen out an explanation. He scrapes his chair back over the flagstones, and flees.

'Stop, thief!' calls out Aunt Dorothy in a bell-like tone.

Bobby heads rapidly for the main entrance. Luckily, no one in the lobby is of a vigilant cast of mind, and he reaches the street without being stopped. The only casualty is his Curzon topi, which falls off as he makes his escape. He runs through the afternoon heat and is soon comfortably lost in the maze of tenements. Later, holed up with Gul at Madame Noor's, he decides the hat is no great loss. Real English people don't seem to wear them, unless they are attending some sort of official function. A few days later he goes out and buys a plain pigsticking topi to replace it. A far less imposing item of headgear. Discretion, he is beginning to realize, is the key.

Luckily for Bobby, incidents like that of Virginia and Aunt Dorothy are few and far between. Once a middle-aged tax inspector, country-born, leans towards him and says, 'You're an Indian, aren't you?' but most of the time Bobby is free to reinvent himself, slipping into a new gora identity like one of Shahid Khan's jackets. His pretences are flimsy at first, and he soon learns that looks and accent are not enough. There is, for example, the question of smell. Like everyone, Bobby has always wondered about the grim English war against cookery, their inexplicable liking for tasteless slabs of meat, unspiced vegetables and sweetened concoctions of flour and fat. A conversation with a naval rating reveals a side-effect of a diet devoid of garlic and onions. Bobby is pretending to be a man of influence, heir to an Edinburgh import–export business. The sailor snorts with laughter and tells him frankly that, money or no money, he stinks like a wog. Unless you sort yourself out, lad, you'll die a bleeding bachelor. Bobby is too intrigued to be offended. What do wogs smell like? Is there a typical English smell? The question fascinates him. He starts to avoid garlic (at least before going out), and tries, surreptitiously, to inhale the scents of the people he accosts at the docks. It is not enough. One day, in desperation, he pays a servant at Watson's Hotel a couple of annas to let him sniff the piles of dhobi. The man thinks he is a pervert, but is prepared to take his money anyway. Face buried in burra mem's smalls and burra sahib's dirty shirts, he finally puts a name to it.

Rancid butter. With perhaps a hint of raw beef. The underlying whiff of Empire.

One can choose to avoid introspection. If Bobby makes himself invisible to others, shape-shifting, changing names and keeping his motives hidden, he does so no less to himself. Secrecy hints at depth, and this is what people fantasize about when they see him. The prostitutes and Theosophical ladies, the Cook's tourists and the layabouts at the paan shop, are all prisoners of the conviction that, if they stared hard enough, they could unearth what lies beneath the beautiful mask of Bobby's face. It is a kind of addiction. It makes him tantalizing, precious. Yet this aura would not be there if Bobby knew why he does what he does. It is cowardice, of course, but he tells himself he does not want to understand. Better, he thinks, to live an unexamined life. Otherwise you run the risk of not living at all.

So Bobby is a creature of surface. Tissue paper held up to the sun. He hints at transparency, as if on the other side, on the inside, there is something to be discovered. Maybe there is, maybe not. Maybe instead of imagining depth, all the people who do not quite know him should accept that Bobby's skin is not a boundary between things but the thing itself, a screen on which certain effects take place. Ephemeral curiosities. Tricks of the light.

Stitch a personality together. Calico arms. Wooden head. A hat and a set of overheard opinions. How perfectly impossible it is to grow a good lawn in India. The positive moral effect of team sports. The unspeakable vileness of Mr Gandhi, and the lack of hygiene of just about everything. Lay them out one by one, like playing patience. It does not matter if you believe them. Belief is nothing but a trivial sensation in the stomach. Nevertheless, as Bobby builds and inhabits his puppets he grasps that there is something marvellous about English people. Their lives are structured like pieces of engineering, railway engines or steamers unpacked and bolted together at the heads of new rivers. Each one is rigid and assured, built according to blueprints of class and membership that are almost noble in their invariance, their stern inflexibility. Noble, at least, in the manner that a suspension bridge or a viaduct is noble. English lives, conquering and functional. Industrial lives.

Bobby is drifting towards something. It happens in imperceptible stages, a continuum rather than a leap, but if there is such a thing as the crossing of a line, it takes place on the night he meets Philips, the Singapore planter. Destiny electroplates the meeting, for Philips accosts Bobby, rather than the other way around, asking him for a light as he walks along Marine Drive. Bobby pulls out his new petrol lighter, and the man cups his hands over the flame. A little conversation accretes to the surface of the encounter, conversation of the nice-night-tonight variety, and for a while they stand and smoke, watching the running lights of the dhows on Back Bay. Philips introduces himself, and Bobby does the same. Bobby Flanagan, of Johnson & Leverhulme, Calcutta trading house. Philips is on his way home, first time in ten years, and to be honest, no offence intended, he doesn't think much of Bombay. Not a patch on Singapore. Far more life over there, and by Jove a fellow needs a little life. However, by a stroke of luck he did meet some chaps who invited him to play in the billiards tournament tonight. Bobby must know it. The one at the Majestic. Only trouble is he needs to find a partner. Awfully irregular, but would Bobby consider . . . ?

Philips has a disturbingly smooth face, round as a football, and his hair is slicked to one side by some kind of dressing that makes it shine in the moonlight like a gramophone record. He smokes in a stiff clubman's attitude, one hand behind his back as if he is about to perform a recitation. Shellac man. Bobby is not convinced, but something about the conjunction of glittering surfaces, the water, the pale road, Philips's absurd shiny hair, forces him to nod. They take a gharri, and head in the direction of the Majestic.

Bobby has often hung around the door of the Majestic Hotel. It is, by convention, a place where Indians are usually not welcome except as servants. When it comes to billiards, this informal rule is strictly applied. Heading through the lobby into the games room, Bobby is greeted by a sea of pink faces, half-drunk men in their shirtsleeves, chalking cues and downing chota-pegs at a great rate. Englishmen relaxing, venting all the frustrations and anxieties of India in alcoholic competition. He realizes with a shock that there will be no getting away from this until it is through.

Philips finds the men who invited him, and, amidst much shaking of hands and standing of drinks, 'Philips and Flanagan' is chalked on a board with the rest of the entrants. It is lucky for Bobby that the principles of the game of billiards are relatively easy to grasp, and that the standard of play at the weekly Majestic tournaments is notoriously low. Soon he is moving around the green baize table, listening to the Englishmen laughing and swapping stories of deals made, natives outwitted, game brought down and time still to serve. Bobby makes a difficult shot and Philips claps him on the back, his big hand casually sliding down to brush against his buttocks. Bobby turns round to find a sly grin on his partner's face.

'Glad I met you, young fellow.'

Bobby nods silently and hands him the cue.

They win the first-round match, and Bobby slips out on to the balcony to smoke a cigarette. He is elated, tense with the suppressed energy of the successful spy. The confidence of the billiard players has rubbed off on him, and he accosts a passing waiter, tersely ordering a gin and tonic and taking a white man's pleasure in the brown man's deep salaam. Taking the drink when it comes, he clenches a hand behind his back in unconscious imitation of Philips. The waiter disappears and Bobby is left to swirl the ice-cubes around his glass, their tiny bright clink like the sound of money. Suddenly he hears a woman's laughter piercing the basso of male conversation from the billiard room. A couple have walked out on to one of the neighbouring balconies. The man is making some remark and the woman's head is thrown back in amusement, one long white arm caressing the back of her partner's neck. They appear intimate without being close. Bobby has the impression that they do not really know each other. The woman is beautiful. Her dark hair is cut daringly short and her clinging gown makes her body a theatre of pale yellow silk and bare skin, glowing lasciviously in the spill of electric light. She screws a cigarette into a holder and Bobby finds he is forgetting to breathe, so intense is her presence. The man is many years older, dull and solid next to his companion. How can he cope? How can he be immune to the operatic near-nakedness of this woman? For a moment Bobby catches his eye, and the man inclines his head, as if acknowledging his stunned homage.

'I say.'

It is Philips, a shiny messenger to take Bobby back in for their second-round match. At the sound of his voice, the woman turns round and for a moment Bobby looks her in the eye. She returns his glance blankly, her face insolently gorgeous, not a flicker of reaction, even of appraisal. Pretty Bobby is not used to such indifference. In a deliberate gesture, she turns back to her escort and leads him inside.

In round two Flanagan and Philips are soundly beaten. It is mostly Flanagan's fault, his play embarrassingly erratic compared to his assured first-round performance. Philips is drunk and indulgent, calling out bad luck and never mind, steadying himself on one of the bearers as if the man were a pillar or a wall. Soon

Flanagan makes an attempt to leave, but his partner hurries after him, drunkenly crushing him against a wall on the Majestic's main stairs, oblivious to the appalled glances of the men and women passing by on their way to bed. The encounter soon turns ugly, and when Flanagan hurriedly leaves the building, brushing away the doorman's offer of a cab, the lapel of his jacket is torn. Yet during the course of the evening something else has knitted together. Pretty Bobby knows what he wants to be.

The woman at the hotel preys on Bobby's mind. Her self-possession and her indifference. Her long white back and oval face. He wonders about her age, and decides she is probably very little older than him. What would it mean to stand on a balcony with her? What would it mean to look out over the smoking chimneys of the Mill districts and feel the presence of so many tens of thousands of people who would never climb up so far?

He does not want to be Pretty Bobby any more. He stops visiting Gul and Shuchi, and whenever possible leaves the cages of Falkland Road altogether, hurrying off into better areas of town to wander in the arcades and tip his hat to white people. He is always looking out for the girl. He imagines her wealthy, some rich Englishman's daughter, and prays she is still in Bombay. He peers through the window of Evans & Fraser, hoping to see her shopping for dresses. He eats an ice at Cornaglia's, willing her to come in and sit down at one of the marble tables. His various jobs are neglected, Elspeth Macfarlane's chores entirely forgotten. To make up for the money he loses, he touts at the docks as a guide, riding with tourists out across the bay to Elephanta Island.

On the launch, he sits quietly until it slides between the island's tangled fringe of mangroves. At the landing place, he shoos away other would-be guides and helps his party up the winding stone steps, only speaking when he begins to show them the caves. After the climb, the sight of the monumental carved faces can also reduce the guidebook-clutching tourists to silence, at least for a moment or two. Bobby takes them past the triple-headed Shiva at the entrance and shows them the hermaphrodite figure of the God, man on one side, woman on the other. He stands back as the women titter and the men make ribald jokes. Then discreetly, when they are not looking, he reaches forward and touches the stone for luck.

He is too preoccupied to think about politics, barely registering that around him agitation against the British is growing to fever pitch. Mrs Macfarlane's parlour is full of other young men, students who have obeyed the call to leave their English-run schools and work full time for liberation. They are neat and serious, Parsis, Muslims and upper-caste Hindu boys who sit down together to read aloud from pamphlets and argue about the latest pronouncements of Gandhi, Patel and the other leaders. Elspeth brings them tea, glowing with the energy of the thing that is taking place around her. As Bobby slopes in and out, he can feel her eyes boring into his back. The unspoken question: won't you join us?

Bobby senses the young nationalists' distaste for his well-cut suits and newly minted accent, such a contrast to their own proud-Indian attire of Congress caps, white kurta-pyjamas and high-necked achkans. One evening as he is leaving (to go and stand outside the Byculla and wait for the hotel girl), a few of them bar his way. Brother, where are you going? Comrade, will you not stay and work for your country? He shakes his head and pushes through them. As he walks off they spit on the floor and mutter insults. Mongrel, English lackey. When the day comes, one shouts after him, you and all your kind will be swept away.

'I'm worried about you, Chandra,' says Elspeth as he comes down one morning to eat. 'You're losing your direction.' Bobby stares at her in disbelief. She struggles on. 'You should be proud of your nation. Think of its future. You should be proud of what you are.'

'So what am I?' he asks, then slams the door and walks out without waiting for an answer. He wanders over to the maidan, where a hockey tournament is taking place. A Muslim youth team is playing against a side from the Railway. A group of British Other Ranks are standing at the touchline, passing a bottle and cheering on the Anglo-Indians.

'Go on, the Railway! Go on! Smash the black bastards! That's the way!'

The Railway team play hard, puffing up their chests with pride. Bobby looks at their eager faces with disgust. Their supporters would desert them in an instant if they were playing a fairer-skinned team. They are the true mongrels, wagging their tails for scraps.

One night Bobby's prayers are answered. She is going through the door of Green's on the arm of a well-known jockey. Quickly he follows her in, glaring at the sceptical doorman who briefly considers barring his way. The bar is packed. Every walk of Bombay society is represented, from the table of young ICS men making a daring visit to this haunt of the demi-monde, to the pair of Russian whores slow-dancing with each other near the bar, their eyes raking the crowd to see which of the men is watching them. The girl and the jockey join a large party of racing people who have secured the best table in the house, and are laying on a fine show for the rest of the admiring clientele. Two white-gloved waiters are putting the finishing touches to a pyramid of glasses, while a third is removing the foil from a jereboam of Krug, ready to pour a champagne fountain. The host, a wealthy Parsi breeder, is obviously celebrating something special. As the girl and her escort arrive, he effusively kisses her hand and clears a space for them to his side. Right on cue the champagne cork pops, and to general applause the wine waiter climbs on to a chair and begins to pour.

At nearby tables, minor moons orbiting this particular sun,

are lesser lights of the Bombay turf world, bookmakers, trainers, hungry gamblers on the look-out for tips. Bobby spots a fat Englishman eyeing the action with particular intensity. He sits down next to him and asks what is going on.

'Readymoney's horse won again.'

'Which one?'

'Which one? Pot of Gold of course. Now would you mind vacating that seat? I'm waiting for someone.'

'Certainly. But tell me, was Torrance the winning jockey? He's obviously a lucky man. His wife is stunning.'

The fat man laughs.

'That woman? She's no more his wife than I am. Not that you should get your hopes up. From the looks of you, you couldn't afford her. Now will you go away?'

Bobby gets up and slips over to the bar, where he orders a soft drink and stares at Torrance's not-wife. She is, if anything, more beautiful than when he saw her before. Her hair is cut high at the back, falling forward over her face to expose a neck so sensuous that it appears somehow indecent in its whiteness. As she laughs and drinks with her companions, her eyes sparkle mischievously.

'Bobby? Bobby! What are you doing here?'

The pancake-encrusted face of Mrs Pereira's Belgian client. The young one who always wants news of her sister – what is her name? – Ga – Gal – Gan – Gannay? She is eager and inquisitive and high, her darting hands trailing cigarette ash and slops of gin-and-it behind them as they fan the air. He makes a guess.

'Miss Garnier?'

'Bobby! I did not think to see you in such places. Not – such *expensive* places!'

'Perhaps I could say the same about you.'

Her expression hardens. 'I am often in Green's. I am a European.'

'So you know many people here?'

'Of course,' she says defensively. Bobby notices dark circles under her eyes.

'Such as the people over there with Sir Readymoney?'

'That is Readymoney's jockey and Elvin who is one of the stewards at the Gymkhana, and –'

'And the woman with Torrance?'

'Why do you want to know about her?'

'Mind your own business.'

Miss Garnier's mouth forms a small outraged 'o' and she turns on her heel. Cursing himself, Bobby grabs hold of her arm. She squirms and looks at him furiously. He summons his best melting look into his eyes.

'I'm sorry.'

'Let go of me.'

'I am sorry. I didn't mean to be so rude.'

'I should think so.'

Her resolve is wavering. She relaxes slightly in his grip. 'Please let go of my arm.'

Bobby does. Instead of moving away, Miss Garnier steps towards him. She is wearing some stifling kind of orangewater perfume, and his back is soon arched against the bar as he searches for air.

'You are very bad,' she tells him. 'I think you are already very bad.'

'Already?'

She tuts at him. 'You are only very young.'

A cigarette-holding hand caresses his cheek, narrowly missing one eye. She smiles at him acquisitively, and is about to say more when a man appears and brusquely taps her on the shoulder. His face is ruddy and pockmarked.

'Come on, Diane, or whatever your name is. I haven't got all night.'

He glares at Bobby. Miss Garnier winces, but forms her mouth into a smile.

'Of course, darling. I am just coming.'

'What is her name, Diane?' Bobby pleads. 'Tell me her name?'

She looks at her escort, who is tapping the dial of his watch. Then she turns back to Bobby. Suddenly she looks infinitely tired, the architecture of her face on the point of collapse.

'Her name is Lily Parry. And mine is not Diane. It is Delphine.'

Bobby nods. She says it again, separating the syllables. *Delphi-ne.* Then she leaves, half pushed out of the bar by the impatient man. A moment after she disappears Bobby has forgotten her, transfixed by Lily Parry.

She is perfect. And Bobby is certainly not the only one who thinks so. It is as if the bar has subtly rearranged itself around her, pillars tilting forward, rails warping and chairs shuffling their occupants into alignment. The men of her own table are leaning up towards her like the dinner-jacketed slopes of a mountain. Around the packed main room and out on to the terrace, each vantage point where an observer might casually stand and smoke is occupied, and there appears to be such a fashion for this activity that several would-be leaners and loungers have been reduced to sauntering and strolling, which in the confined space of Green's on a Saturday night is definitely the second-class option.

Miss Parry herself is not bothered by the attention, it being the atmosphere in which she lives. Indeed she shortly hopes to receive more of it, and in a more formal setting, as long as that old skinflint Readymoney keeps his promise to bankroll her musical show. So when, en route to the powder room, she is surprised by a very young man who bows to her, she is surprised not so much by the bowing per se, as by its insolent theatricality. As if he is mocking her. When she comes out he does it again. Unbelievable! Naturally she ignores him completely.

Obviously her snubbing technique needs polishing, since Miss Parry finds herself surprised in this manner quite often in the next two or three weeks. An epidemic of stealth bowing breaks out all over Bombay. The bower appears without the slightest warning at the Willingdon, the Yacht Club, under the arcades on Rampart Row, even popping out from behind a palm tree as she drives to a party. Lily Parry has an unusually busy social life, and everywhere she goes people are pleased to see her. But there should be limits, even to adulation, and, though he is a pleasingly handsome boy, the bower represents something she will not admit into her life.

In order to conduct his clumsy wooing campaign, Bobby has put his entire network into operation. Domestic servants, porters, doormen, tonga drivers and legions of small boys are pressed into service. His chance-meeting opportunities are contrived by the simple expedient of following Lily from her home, a lovely villa on Malabar Hill, lent to her by some relative of the Governor. Historically speaking, his informants tell him that she came to Bombay two years ago as the fiancée of some upcountry Civilian. The engagement was quickly broken, and she has since rapidly risen to become, in the words of one of the desk clerks at Watson's, 'the most celebrated young lady in Bombay'. It appears to be a lucrative position. Though the jockey Teddy Torrance spends most of his prize money on gilding his Lily, his gifts are more than matched by those of a certain Colonel Marsden and are probably exceeded by those of Mr Barratt, the government contractor. Sadly for Torrance, this is not even the full extent of the field. His horsey baubles are completely eclipsed by the lavish presents of Gebler, an infatuated German ship-owner, and against the absurd largesse of the Raja of Amritpur they do not even seem worth adding to the balance sheet. On occasion even Sir Parvez 'Readymoney' Mistry contributes to

Miss Parry's well-being. If I were Torrance, concludes Bobby, I should be discouraged.

Strangely he does not apply the same logic to himself. Although he has learnt most of what Falkland Road can teach on the subject of romance, he has (lately at any rate) always done so from a position of clarity. Love, real love, has never entered into it. However, when he watches Lily Parry laugh, or contemplates her remarkable neck and the scarlet cupid-bow shape of her lips, he feels that love is undeniably the name for what he is experiencing. This, he reasons, makes him different to other people. All those rajas and contractors and other old beasts have to back up their amorous suits with presents because, logically, they would never otherwise be in with a chance. Love is not for them. They are just too stupid to see it. For him, on the other hand, it will be plain sailing. All he has to do is place himself in Lily's way often enough and the rest will happen naturally. His mind is full of romantic carriage drives, coded fan gestures, bowers (whatever they are) and other things gleaned from reading the novels gathering dust on Mrs Macfarlane's bookshelf.

One day at the track he decides she is ready for conversation. Teddy Torrance is lining up for the third on Wicked Lady, Readymoney's second-best Arab. By a combination of bribery and cheek Bobby has gained access to the members' enclosure, where Lily is conversing with a group of English racing gents, all of whom (naturally) are vying for her attention. One holds her champagne glass, a second her parasol and a third her bag, as she makes minor adjustments to her new hat. A fourth has been dispatched in search of a hand mirror which will not be needed by the time it arrives, and a fifth has, despite the presence of a dense cluster of bearers, insisted on fetching her glass of iced water himself. Suddenly Lily remembers that she should watch the race, and, with a show of petulance that no one saw fit to remind her of dear Teddy's imminent exertions, she leads her swarm of drones up to the stand. As Bobby follows them he feels confident. Shahid Khan has made him another new suit, a copy of a very fashionable one temporarily liberated by the Taj Mahal dhobiwallah for the purpose. His tie (silk, purple) is also new. He just has to choose his moment. How can he fail?

Lily is also attempting to choose – between the five pairs of binoculars which have been offered to her to view the race. As she picks one, its owner wilts with satisfied desire and the defeated rivals try to cover their disappointment, shooting envious glances at the victor and his superior equipment. An expectant buzz rises from the bustling Grand Enclosure, rolling through the cheaper native stands, gathering volume and power. The bookies are doing frenzied last-minute business, and the tea kiosks are deserted as people struggle to the barriers to get a view of the start. Bobby positions himself between Lily and the track, perching a couple of rows down so that she will have to focus on him.

As the horses thunder down the dusty opening straight, he knows he has been successful. Lily lowers her binoculars and glares directly at him. He raises his hat and stares back at her, taking no notice whatsoever of the race. For a while she stoically ignores him, but as Wicked Lady struggles home fourth, she seems to make up her mind to do something about the stealth bower. Jerking her head in the direction of the members' bar, she skilfully divests herself of her beaux, who are waving their programmes and shouting at each other, momentarily distracted by the sport. Bobby follows her, his heart pounding with anticipation. Instead of entering the bar she leads him past the door and behind a large kitchen marquee. As soon as they are discreetly out of sight, she whirls round, her eyes fierce.

'Right, you. What the hell do you think you're doing?'

Bobby has memorized an opening speech concerning the

blessed effulgence of the dawn and Lily's likeness thereunto. Unwilling to be put off his stride by her angry expression, he launches in, addressing her as 'Dear Heart' and clasping his hands together in demonstration of sincerity.

'Shut up!' she barks. 'I suppose you think I'm going to give you money?'

Bobby is nonplussed. 'Money?'

'Look. I know what you are. You may think you're pretty good, but I can see through you. I know people in this town, and whatever you spread around, you won't damage me.'

'Damage you? Why would I damage you? I love you.'

Now it is her turn to look confused. 'What on earth do you mean? Like I say, I know people, and you could wind up very seriously hurt –'

'I do. I love you, Lily. You're the most beautiful woman I've ever –'

'Don't start with any of that rubbish. So we're the same, you and me. So what? All that means is you know what I've had to do to get here. So you must know I won't let you drag me back down. I'm not going back there. Why don't you leave me alone? Turn round and go away.'

Bobby is really confused. Does she mean? She couldn't – she couldn't be. 'But I love you,' he says again. It seems like a safe starting point. At least he is sure of that much. Feeling there is a space to be filled, he tries 'I adore you' for variation. Then 'I really do', which sounds somehow weak. Then he breaks off. Grabbing hold of one of the marquee guy ropes to support herself, Lily Parry is laughing like a drain.

'Go on,' she says in between giggles. 'Say it again.'

'I love you,' repeats Bobby, suddenly diffident.

'You love me? Oh darling, do you love me?'

Perhaps things are moving in his direction. Bobby opens his arms.

'Just you stay over there, soldier. You love me? God, you poor thing. You poor little half-and-half. You don't have a clue, do you?'

'Yes, I do,' protests Bobby unconvincingly. Half-and-half? Hang on. What does she mean by that?

'Oh, don't worry,' she says, seeing his expression. 'You're very good. Very convincing. You can fool them' – waving a hand in the direction of the members' enclosure – 'but I'm different.' She fumbles in her bag for a cigarette, and lights it. 'You really don't know, do you? The very idea. You, coming for me. As if I had something to give you. It's sweet, I suppose, but what are you after, yaar? Go on, you can tell me.' She looks at him with an odd directness. As she talks, her voice, her clipped English accent that is so very like his own, has changed, slipping, thickening, warming. All the Northern ice and suet falling away.

'Nothing,' says Bobby, still trying to cling on to his script. 'I'm not after anything at all.'

Instantly, her face slams closed. When she speaks, her perfect voice is in place again, and once more she is Lily Parry, the most celebrated young lady in Bombay.

'Run away, little boy,' she says. 'Go on. Piss off and don't come back. If I see you again, here or anywhere, I'll tell them about you. They'll put you in prison. No one likes niggers who play at being white men.'

For a moment he hesitates, fishing blindly for some phrase that will improve things. There is nothing. Dejected, shattered, he raises his hat to her, and walks away.

'Hey!'

At the sound of her voice he turns around. 'What is it?'

'Don't do that with your head. It's a dead giveaway. The two cardinal rules are never to waggle your head, and never let them see you squatting on your heels. All right?'

Bobby nods in mute thanks and walks away, leaving beautiful Lily Parry smoking the last of her cigarette, smoking it right down to the butt.

As Bobby walks away from the racetrack, he tries to believe Lily Parry never existed. With each step he buries her a little further. He is determined; a hand pushing her face below the surface. The next day when Gulab Miah the porter asks about the lovely memsahib, Bobby rounds on him and swears he will cut his bastard throat if he mentions her again. Gulab Miah nods nervously, but thumbs his teeth at Bobby's departing back. Later, at the toddy shop where he goes after work, Gulab tells his drinking buddies how Prince Pretty Baby has fallen down at last, and how he had always told the boy such a time would come, because God willed it.

Bobby is not thinking about God. He is thinking about Other Things. He badly needs money, so he goes to see Mrs Pereira. Sallow-faced Mabel lets him in, an undisguised look of pleasure on her face. Bustle, bustle. Hello Bobby how are you Bobby long time no see. Her mother is in the parlour, submerged in a sagging armchair doing violence to the dead skin on her feet. As he comes in, she leaves off picking and waves for him to sit down.

'Well, looking very smart, I see. You've not been here for some time.'

'No.'

'Just that? Just no? Such a well-presented boy and not a shred of conversation? You aren't very happy. Still, I can't say I'm surprised.'

Mabel brings tea, rubbing up against Bobby's leg like an oversized cat as she puts down the clinking tray. He shrinks away from her cotton-print rump, searching in his pocket for cigarettes.

'What do you mean?'

'You're not the only one with eyes and ears in Bombay. It was always going to be this way. What were you thinking? She a rich English lady and you a street boy, even if she is – what is so funny?'

Bobby's face is twisted into a bitter smirk. 'Nothing, Amma, nothing. So, do you have any work for me?'

Mrs Pereira grunts, and, as Mabel pours the tea, starts to excavate something unwholesome out of her right heel. As she works she tells Bobby about Mr Dutta, a Theosophist who hopes desperately for a message from his dead brother. Something about the title deeds to a house. She doesn't expect Bobby to find anything specific, just a little local colour to help her understand how the brother should appear in manifestation. Bobby copies down the address. Perhaps, he thinks, he even knows the man. Didn't he see him talking once to Mrs Macfarlane? Before he leaves, Mrs P. shows off her new trick, a button concealed under the rug which triggers celestial music from a gramophone in the bedroom. It does not work perfectly yet. The needle tends to skip, but she is sure it will prove a big hit. Bobby says very nice, and tells her he will be back in a couple of days.

It is not an arduous job. When he returns, he is able to inform her that the brother died in Calcutta three years previously, and took with him the exact location of some land deeds which had been walled up in the old family mansion. It seems the documents are the key to Mr Dutta's future financial happiness, and it is this, rather than filial love, which fuels his desire to make contact with the Other Side. There are a few other details, which Mabel carefully notes in Mr Dutta's file. Her mother nods in silent satisfaction, scratching her chest with one hand and methodically cramming rice and dal into her mouth with the other. When she has finished eating, she rummages inside her dress, peels a few greasy banknotes off a thick wad and gives them to her visitor.

Unfortunately, as he is leaving the Pereiras' chawl, Bobby runs straight into Mr Dutta himself. They do an awkward side-to-side dance in the narrow stairwell, each trying to get past the other. Dutta nods in confused recognition, obviously trying to place him. With the briefest of acknowledgements Bobby hurries on.

He thinks nothing of it until he is confronted, a day or two later, by Elspeth Macfarlane. She actually stands in his way as he propels himself through the parlour, his usual ruse to avoid a conversation.

'I want to talk to you, Chandra.'

Bobby sighs and shuffles his feet. 'Amma, I'm tired. I want to go and lie down.'

'Look at me.'

He looks at her, and is worried by what he sees.

'A friend of mine tells me you have been loitering around his house, talking to his servants.'

'No –'

'Chandra.'

'So? I have too a friend there. The – the chowkidar.'

'I see. And he says he saw you coming from Mrs Pereira's apartment. I didn't know you visited her without me. Look at me.'

He looks up again.

'I went for a reading. I want to know my future.'

'Why do I think you're lying to me?'

'I, lying? I'm not lying. Why should I lie to you?'

'I don't know, Chandra.'

'I'm not lying.'

'You make me so angry.'

'I'm sorry, Ambaji.'

'For what?'

Bobby says nothing. Mrs Macfarlane sits down heavily on a chair.

'Are you sorry? What in your life actually makes you feel sorry? What are you sorry *about*?'

'I'm tired, Amma.'

'You? At eight o'clock in the evening? You only get up at eleven.'

Bobby stares at his feet, listening to the street noise. After a while he realizes Mrs Macfarlane is crying.

'Why are you like this, Chandra? I took you in. I helped you, and now look. Why are you like this? Mr Dutta thinks you're spying on him. I had to tell him not to be stupid. Because you aren't spying on him, are you? Are you, *Robert*? What do you do? What do you do all night?'

Her questions pour out one after the other, a dam bursting. Bobby is frozen. Only once before has he seen her cry.

'Mr Dutta says you run errands for Mrs Pereira. He thinks you spy on him for her, and that you spy on all of us for the British and someone ought to get you. He says Mrs Pereira is a fraud and he will call the police. I told him not to be stupid because Mrs Pereira is a very great – she is very sensitive. And he says even if they don't put you in prison and just let you go we'll still know and you won't be able to do your damage to the cause. Mrs Pereira has a gift, Chandra. You think she has a gift, don't you. Don't you?'

Now she has him. He should agree, but he cannot. He feels sorry for her, this woman with her dead sons, and for all the other people clutching at their dead across the void, with Mrs Pereira picking her feet in the middle.

'Mrs Macfarlane, you should not go to Mrs Pereira any more. She is not a good –'

Before he can even finish his sentence she slaps him round the face.

'Did you spy on me as well? Is that why you stay here, so you can spy?'

He cannot answer, tries to make 'no' come to his lips. She says, very quietly, 'You can go now. Take your things and leave.'

'Amma –'

'Mrs Macfarlane?'

'I'm not your Amma.'

'Mrs Elspeth Macfarlane? Excuse me, Mrs Macfarlane?'

Behind them is an acutely embarrassed English police captain, flanked by two Indian constables. Elspeth turns round, astonished to find them there.

'Mrs Macfarlane, I'm afraid you're going to have to come with us. We have orders to place you in preventative detention under the terms of the Defence of India Act.'

Mrs Macfarlane is given time to collect some clothes, then led outside to a lorry. Three Indian detainees are already sitting in the back, looking silently at the large crowd which has gathered to watch the arrest. The mood is ugly, and Bobby sees the British Captain unclip the leather strap on his holster, freeing his revolver for quick use.

While his constables push onlookers away, the Captain helps Mrs Macfarlane climb up. He takes her bag and shows her to her place on the grimy wooden bench, his manner oddly obsequious, like a theatre usher who has suddenly found himself in uniform. All the time he keeps up an embarrassed flow of conversation, assuring her that nothing too awful will happen, that it is only for forty-eight hours, that she has his personal assurance about something and his word of honour about something else. She ignores him, sitting ramrod-straight, fitting disordered strands of grey hair back into her bun.

Finally the Captain stops babbling and jumps down. He makes a brief address to the crowd, telling them to disperse quietly, go back to their homes, let the King-Emperor's officers do their duty. Then he slaps the lorry's side and tells the last of his men to get in. As the engine coughs into life, Bobby runs to the tailgate, but no matter how many times he waves or calls her name he cannot make Ambaji look at him. Finally one of the constables gets up and pulls the canvas flap closed. The driver inches forward, leaning on the horn, pushing the front bumper up against the jostling mass of people. The crowd parts reluctantly and the lorry drives away into the darkness.

Bobby finds Reverend Macfarlane standing at the door of the church, staring at a group of youths who are loitering around on the opposite side of the street.

'Go on!' he shouts at them in English. 'Go away! Godless rabble.'

'Reverend,' implores Bobby. 'Mrs Macfarlane has been arrested.'

'Yes, I saw. Go *on*! Get away before I take a tawse to the lot of you!'

'What shall we do?'

'Do? Nothing, boy. She is reaping what she has sowed, cleaving to Bolshevists and Satanists. Where have you been? I expected you this afternoon to assist in an experiment.'

One of the youths throws a stone, which clatters against the church door. 'Imperialist!' he shouts. 'Capitalist lackey!'

Reverend Macfarlane strides across the road and the boys scatter, calling more Communist slogans as they run away. The Reverend comes back, red-faced and out of breath, to extract a promise that Bobby will help him with the work in the morning. As soon as he can, Bobby makes an excuse and goes up to his room.

His collage of pictures looks down at him, all the hundreds of magazine faces, stars in the sky. They make him feel earthbound, insect-like.

He is worried about Mrs Macfarlane. She is old. She loves him. Yet as soon as she returns he will be homeless, so maybe it is good they arrested her. Is it bad to think like this? He has a sense of collapse, of scaffolding falling away. Something like this has happened before, but then it was sudden and unforeseen. Now he feels as if he is leaking, all the particulars that go to make up Pretty Bobby draining away to leave behind nothing but an empty vessel. A husk. When he falls asleep, the watercarriers are already moving through the streets, making their early-morning deliveries.

The next day Bombay is shuttered up. Only the European shops in the Fort remain open, their owners posting men at the doors to ward off trouble. The trade unions have called a one-day strike, aimed mainly at shutting down production in the cotton mills. The streets are filled with a roiling crowd of workers. Mrs Macfarlane and her friends have been arrested to prevent them from marching and making speeches, but despite the wave of detentions the city is at a standstill. Bobby spends the morning measuring shin bones with Reverend Macfarlane, listening distractedly as he outlines a plan to quantify relative degrees of moral rectitude in north Indian racial groups by weighing (postmortem) sections of the frontal lobe of the brain. Through the open window comes the sound of engines, troop carriers roaring past to deploy platoons of English Tommies at strategic locations around Bombay.

By lunch-time Falkland Road is a rumour factory, centred on the paan stall. The red-spittled gossipers say some strikers have tried to hold a meeting on the maidan, but it was broken up by a police charge. They say anarchists tried to torch one of Readymoney's mills, but were shot. Or they were Communists and got away. Motilal Nehru will make a speech. A woman was run over by a military vehicle. The Governor has left the city. The British will use aeroplanes. Hindu fanatics are attacking Muslims in the suburban slums.

People are feverish, tense. When Bobby goes out, he notices an atmosphere of hostility. It is odd, barely tangible, but people who normally greet him are avoiding his glance. His sense of foreboding worsens during the afternoon, as he spots the stone-throwing Communists of the previous night hanging around outside the Mission, looking up at Reverend Macfarlane's shuttered window.

At dusk a column of smoke is clearly visible, rising up from the slums near the Tata Mills. Falkland Road is unusually full, and something about the ebb and flow of people strikes Bobby as odd. There is no impression of fun or pleasure-seeking. These men are ready, waiting for something. An hour or so after sunset, a ragged march goes past, garlanded satyagrahis punching the air to the sound of drums and wailing trumpets. It leaves behind a restless wake of men and boys, looking for action, a focus, something to bring the strike day to a climax.

A fire of rubbish is lit in the street, and people stand around in its orange light. From his window Bobby sees a motor car turn the corner, a white face visible behind the wheel. The car stops dead, hesitates, then turns round to go back the way it came. Gradually more people crowd around the fire. Bobby spots men carrying staves, one a long curved knife. Then a lorry of policemen growls down the street, and the crowd dissipates, leaving the fire behind to burn itself out. The constables hang around for a few minutes, kicking over the embers and peering up at the tall rickety wooden buildings. Then they leave.

Afterwards, things quieten down. Maybe tonight will pass peacefully after all. Bobby is bored sitting at the window. He needs air, space to think, so he pulls on a linen jacket, knots a tie around his neck and goes out for a walk. As soon as he steps outside he feels the difference. People stare at him, and once or twice men try to block his way, until he speaks to them or some other person pulls them back, explaining who he is. It is not good to look English tonight in Bombay.

Bobby's walk leads him into the Fort. Here he has the streets to himself. The office windows are unlit, the tramlines are silent, and apart from a few beggars and the odd hurrying cyclist he could almost imagine that this is the moment just after the end of the world, Pretty Bobby wandering around on a stage set which all the other players have vacated. He amuses himself by occupying the space in suitably lordly fashion, strolling in the middle of the road and stretching out his arms to become

275

as large as possible. Pretty Bobby, Lord of Endtime Bombay.

Progressing with giant steps through the abandoned city, he arrives at Flora Fountain. A stockade of gas lights illuminates this underwhelming piece of scenery, a little outcrop of soiled statuary jutting out of a tarmac plain. As he walks towards it, he discovers that he is not the only bit player to be left behind. Under the lights, still performing for all they are worth, are two others, an English boy and a cow.

'God almighty,' slurs the youth. 'What does one have to do to be treated civilly in this hole of a city? Rude, that's what it is. Bloody rude.'

He seems to be talking to the animal. Bobby advances cautiously, until he reaches the edge of the pool of light. The boy sways on his feet, fumbling in his pockets. He locates a hip flask, drinks from it and appears to come to a decision.

'Right, cow. If you're not going to play fair, the gloves are coming off. I say to you – just a shot across the bows, you understand – *Horseradish sauce and Yorkshire pudding.*'

The cow looks at him impassively. The boy looks annoyed.

'Steak, you idiot! Jerky! Stew! I'm not mucking about. I don't give a fig for your bloody Cow Protection Societies or any of the rest of your Hindustani fan club. I'm bloody going to eat you, you pig of a cow.'

He looks as if he is squaring up to punch the animal on the nose, but spots Bobby. 'Hallelujah!' he shouts. 'Someone with vocal cords. The name's Bridgeman. This beast is a bloody disgrace. Now, you wouldn't happen to know where one could purchase a tart around here, would you?'

Bobby nods cautiously. Bridgeman's face lights up. 'Ha!' he shouts, like someone who has just won a particularly difficult point in a game, and slaps the cow's rump in satisfaction. 'Take me there, right now. What did you say your name was, old fellow?'

Bobby has not said, and is yet to be convinced he is taking

anyone anywhere. This Bridgeman is in a sorry condition. Though he cannot be above twenty, his rough skin is livid with the effects of a day's drinking, and his clothes bear the remains of more than one meal eaten standing up. Even sober, his face would not inspire much confidence. It has a doughy, half-formed quality, small eyes and a blunt porcine nose swimming over it like dumplings in some sort of fatty soup. Drunk, his entire head seems unpleasantly mobile beneath its fringe of lank brown hair. Jelly-like. Unstable.

He does, however, have money. He proves this by taking it out of his pocket and waving it around. 'So, old lad,' he slurs, 'we are going to have ourselves a time. A grand finale. Right, where's the bloody bovine gone?'

He is adamant that they should take the cow with them. Even when he realizes it has trotted off, he seems inclined to go looking for it. Eventually he accepts its loss and allows Bobby to walk him in the direction of the red light district, keeping up a flow of conversation that fills Bobby both with wonder (at its volume, dexterity, total unconcern for listener) and with a creeping, unmistakable sense of fate.

Before they have reached the end of Esplanade Road, Bobby has found out most of what there is to know about Jonathan Bridgeman, from his premature birth on the floor of a dak bungalow in Bihar to the reasons for his intense intoxication in Bombay nearly eighteen years later. He is, it turns out, within a month of being the same age as Bobby, and is a second-generation drunkard. Son of a dipsomaniac tea planter and his similarly inclined wife, he spent his early life up in the hills near Darjeeling, helping his father knock together a series of makeshift stills under the gaze of the mighty Himalaya.

After mother Bridgeman fell off the veranda and broke her neck (an event which took place when Jonathan was still small), her grieving husband vowed never to send his son to school in

England, indeed never to let the Only Thing He Had Left out of his sight. Thus by the age of ten Jonathan knew how to ride, shoot and mix an excellent gin and tonic, but was unable to read or write. This did not bother his father. Literacy was, to his way of thinking, the root cause of his wife's demise, she having slipped on a copy of *Blackwood's* magazine which had been carelessly discarded on the front steps.

In those moments when he was capable of directed behaviour, Bridgeman senior's energies were entirely devoted to a project to distil a new type of spirit from tea leaves. When perfected, this elixir was to replace Scotch whisky in the affections of the British populace, and so make its creator wealthy beyond the dreams of avarice. Unfortunately, either due to faults in the production process or to the innate unsuitability of tea for the purpose, most batches of 'Bridgeman's Old Malt Tisky' tended to induce seizures and temporary blindness, and its creator eventually decided to amend the recipe to include rice.

Much given to bouts of depression, during which he would take melancholic potshots at his estate workers with a small-bore hunting rifle, Mr Bridgeman eventually realized that even rice would not rescue his dream from ruin. The disappointment made him more than usually morose, but following negotiations with the District Officer (backed up by a platoon of Gurkha infantry), he finally freed his hostages and allowed himself to be committed to the care of the Little Sisters of Violent Contrition, who ran a discreet institution in Calcutta. Little Jonathan was put into a nearby boarding school, with the instruction that he should visit his ailing parent once a month.

In the first few years, Bradshaw's Calcutta Boys' Academy beat the rudiments of an education into young Bridgeman, teaching him to eat with his mouth closed, grapple meaningfully with Roman numerals and the alphabet, and keep silent through-out even the longer morning chapel services. Everyone expected him to return to the hills and engage in some rugged pastime, perhaps of a military nature, which would take him to a remote spot where his unpolished manners and already flourishing alcoholism would cause least upset. They reckoned without the miraculous healing powers of the Little Sisters, and their head psychiatrist, Mother Agnes.

Agnes, a burly Slovenian nun with a face like a polished walnut and the temper of a pack-camel, had no truck with mad people. Taking her cue from the traditional customs of her tough mountain village, she employed a regime of cold baths, incarceration and religious invective that produced startling results in her patients. It was said (erroneously) that she literally scared them into sanity. In fact, when sudden temperature changes and a colourful lecture on the torments of hell were insufficient to effect a cure, her technique of last resort was the wrestling pit. Stripping off and oiling herself down, she would take her more recalcitrant charges round to the back of the convent, and there give them a thorough drubbing, moving systematically through the sequences of throws, grapples and locks that had once so effectively protected her chastity against the predations of local shepherds, maddened by lonely months in the high pastures.

It was in this way that Jonathan's father was returned to sanity. After he cried mercy and promised never to drink again, he made a spectacular recovery. No one had ever expected him to be released, but shortly after his son's fifteenth birthday he arrived at the school gates, properly dressed and sober, to announce that he wished Jonathan to continue his education, and eventually to go to England to study at one of the great universities. He was truly a changed man. The masters shook him by the hand, raised eyebrows at the large silver crucifix he wore round his neck (fanatical adherence to the Church of Rome being a side-effect of the Mother Agnes cure) and privately considered his hopes for his son laughable. However, Jonathan did his best, mastering various multisyllabic words and acquiring a veneer of wit and culture that impressed even his harshest critics at Bradshaw's Academy.

Sadly, years of Tisky-tasting had taken their toll on Mr Bridgeman's health, and a year after his release from the care of the Sisters he died. At the reading of the will it was discovered that he had bequeathed half his estate to Mother Agnes and the rest (a surprising amount) to his son, to be administered by the Bridgeman family solicitor in London, one Mr Spavin.

'And so, old boy, that's why I'm here,' says Jonathan, clapping Bobby heartily on the back. 'Tomorrow morning I sail for England. This Spavin chappie is to act as my guardian until I'm twenty-one. Frankly I don't know what to think. Never met the fellow myself. Some kind of friend of my grandfather's. I mean to say, what if he's an old tyrant? Bloody inconvenient to have to go begging to him every time I want a few shillings. And to be honest I don't like the sound of Blighty much. I know you're not supposed to say that, but I hear it's damn cold. You've been, presumably?'

'Yes,' says Bobby. 'That is, no. Not really. I've lived here for the most part.'

'Hmm,' nods Bridgeman sagely. 'Thought you were country-born. One can always tell.'

'So, you've got no relatives at all?'

'None that I know of, old boy. Last of the line. Anyway, strike or not, there was no chance I was going to spend my last night of freedom cooped up in some hotel room. All my stuff's already on the boat, and so long as I'm there for the medical tomorrow morning, it doesn't matter what condition I'm in, does it?'

'I suppose not.'

'No it bloody doesn't! And I don't mind telling you my balls are like two ripe melons. Tried to get my leg over with a little half-caste nurse on the train, but she wasn't having any of it. Told me she would pull the emergency handle, frigid bitch. One would have thought she'd be grateful, but there really is no pleasing some of them. Now, what I'm really after is a big girl. You know, one carrying a little extra ballast in front and behind. It's how I like 'em. Nothing worse than a skinny tart, don't you think?'

As they turn into the maze of back alleys off Falkland Road, Bobby looks around nervously. He is taking a chance bringing this Bridgeman here tonight. For the moment everything seems quiet. A few people watch them go past, Bobby trying to saunter casually, Bridgeman putting one deliberate foot in front of the other. Two cocky English boys out for a stroll.

For big girls the place to go is the Goa House. Maria Francesca is surprised to see them, shooting a nervous glance at Bobby as Bridgeman lumbers up the stairs and through the door. There are no other customers, so the whole household is in the parlour drinking tea and snacking on sticky coconut sweets. A row of smiling chewing faces. Bridgeman claps his hands in glee at the sight of such a buffet of plump disrobed flesh, and immediately drags Tereza, by far the largest in this household of binge-eaters, through the bead curtain into one of the bedrooms. Bobby paces up and down, smoking pensively, half listening to a story of Twinkle's about a client who always arrives with a mango.

'Are you mad?' Maria asks Bobby. 'Why bring this fellow here tonight? People are out for blood, you know.'

'Nothing will happen,' Bobby snaps. 'I'll take him home after this. We all need to eat, you know,' he says, gesturing sarcastically at the ravaged plate of sweets. 'What is life without risk?' He likes the sound of this phrase, which he found in one of Mrs Macfarlane's novels. It has a manly, adventurous ring. Maria snorts derisively.

'Look at you – you coconut. You can't leave the English alone, even when it means you might get your throat cut.'

'Fuck your mother.'

'I've had everybody else. No, I take it back. Not a coconut. You look white on the outside too.'

She says it with a smile, and Bobby lets the insult go. From the bedroom comes a deep melon-squeezing bellow of pleasure, accompanied by Tereza's professional sounding trills and ornaments. A few minutes later Bridgeman reappears, a beatific look on his face.

'Drink, old man?' he asks Bobby, taking a swig from his hip flask. The girls look impressed at this familiar tone. Pretty Bobby, so suave that even the feringhi treat him as one of their own. Bobby sips a little, for form's sake, feeling the liquid searing the inside of his throat as it goes down. An unpleasant thought occurs to him.

'This isn't – is it?'

'Oh no,' laughs Bridgeman. 'Old Malt Tisky? No, there's been none of that around for years. This is *my* recipe.'

Bobby is not reassured. Bridgeman, however, is in the best of moods. Barely noticing that he is the only one drinking, he polishes off the rest of his flask and asks Maria, with a rakishly appraising glance, whether she has some kind of discount rate for special clients. Though his voice is so slurred that she has trouble understanding, she finally discerns that he wants to 'go again', this time with her. Another bedroom interlude ensues, punctuated by Maria's unique yelling. She really plays to the gallery, pulling off some spectacular pitch-shifting moans which go down particularly well in the parlour. Arré, says Tereza, she sounds like a factory siren. After a while there is silence. Not bothering to dress, Maria comes out to tell Bobby his friend has passed out.

'He can't stay here,' she says, rolling her eyes and waggling a scornful little finger at Tereza. Tereza makes the same gesture back, and all the girls fall about laughing. Bobby sends one of them out for some water.

An hour later, he and Bridgeman are on the road again. Bobby is half carrying him, a beefy post-coital arm lying across his shoulders, heavy and damp as a forest log. 'The thing,' Bridgeman is telling him 'about old Blighty is that it's different from here.' The street is deserted, but he feels uneasy. The air has a charred smell, and stumbling out of the Goa House they stepped over a single shoe, forlorn in the middle of the roadway. Now that the majority of this drunken idiot's rupees have been transferred to his own pocket, Bobby wants to get shot of him. As soon as they are somewhere near the big hotels, he will let him go.

Not to be.

Bridgeman is wondering whether the mountains in Blighty are like the mountains here, and guessing that they couldn't hold a candle, when one of the shadows ahead of them splits up and filters into several smaller shadows, each carrying a stick or a bottle or a knife. Bobby goes cold. Seven, eight men? Even from a distance they reek of smoke and toddy. The leader has a rag wrapped round his head and an iron bar in his hand. There is a smear of blood across his cheek, as if he has already been fighting tonight. As he steps into the light, Bobby sees his eyes are bloodshot with bhang.

'Sisterfucking feringhis,' he spits.

Self-interest is deep-rooted in most people, and in Bobby deeper than most. The decision to drop the semi-conscious Bridgeman is made, more or less, in the time it takes for the relevant synaptic messages to travel from brain to legs.

He runs.

And behind him hears yells, thuds, sickening sounds.

So he runs faster.

After a while he realizes they have not come after him, and stops. He hugs his knees, his breath coming in huge ragged gasps. When he has recovered, he starts to feel guilty. He should have stayed with Bridgeman. He should have buckled his swash and flourished a rapier and fought them off. All eight of them? Swearing, he takes off his tie and folds his jacket under one arm. Then he gingerly starts walking back the way he came.

The men have gone. He makes sure of that first. Bridgeman has been dragged into an alley, between the high walls of a tenement and a builder's yard. He is lying on his back, his arms limp and formal at his sides. He looks peaceful, from a distance. Still.

Bobby waits and watches for several minutes. Yes, they have gone. It is safe to approach.

Bridgeman looks no better dead than he did alive. The left-hand plane of his face is a single huge contusion, black and swollen. His jaw has a lopsided look, one side caved in by a blow. The grubby shirt, once decorated with food stains, now glistens a uniform blood-red. Bobby examines him with a kind of detached pity. The alcoholic boy who was to go to England. One last night of fun. An odd touch: through all of it he somehow managed to hold on to his hip flask. Bobby bends down and prises it out of the dead hand. Turning it over, he traces the initials JPB, engraved on the side, and this makes him feel guilty again, for a moment.

Bridgeman's empty wallet is lying near by. Bobby is about to leave, nervous about being found next to a corpse, but something makes him stop. By his foot is a little leather document folder. Inside is his steamer ticket to England, a passport in the name of 'Jonathan Pelchat Bridgeman' and a blank sheet of notepaper with an engraved heading: 'Spavin & Muskett: Solicitors and Commissioners for Oaths', of the Gray's Inn Road, London.

He looks at the photograph on the passport. A dark-haired young man stares out at the camera, his face so washed out it is almost blank. Not much of a likeness.

It could be anybody.

He puts the documents in his pocket and starts to walk back to the Mission. The idea is already fully formed before he has reached the end of the street. He knows what he is going to do.

He can smell kerosene on the air. Bridgeman, the actual physical Jonathan Bridgeman, is already fading. Someone known for a few hours only. Emptied and reinhabited. He grins. How easy it is to slough off one life and take up another! Easy when there is nothing to anchor you. He marvels at the existence of people who can know themselves by kneeling down and picking up a handful of soil. Man was created out of dust, says the Reverend. But if men and women are made of dust, then he is not one of them. If they feel a pulse through their bare feet and call it home, if they look out on a familiar landscape and see themselves reflected back, he is not one of them. Man out of earth, says the Reverend. Earth out of man, say the Vedas, like the sun and the moon and all other creation, born out of the body of the Primal Man. But he feels he has nothing of the earth in him at all. When he moves across it, his feet do not touch the surface. So he must have come from somewhere else, some other element.

As he turns the corner on to Falkland Road, he hears a sound like heavy rain falling through trees.

The street is full of people, jostling and shouting. Over all their earth-coloured faces something casts a livid orange glow. He is so wrapped up in his transformation that he is in the midst of the crowd before he knows what it is.

The Mission is on fire.

Flames lick over its wooden frontage like fingers on the strings of an instrument. They make a crackling sound, a low awful roar that momentarily bursts open into a rush, a crashing. The speech of giants. He tries to force his way forward, suddenly horrified at the loss of this place, of his room with its collage of half-tone faces, the cupboard of clothes, the familiarity of the walk downstairs to the parlour. The Mission sign has almost been consumed, only a few words still legible: *Dare we let them die in darkness when we have the light of.* At the front of the crowd someone is waving a home-made red flag. A kerosene stink catches in his nose and mouth. What will Mrs Macfarlane say? After all her work, her love? And the Reverend?

As if in response to his question, the shutters of the garret above the church are suddenly flung open. The crowd seethes and pushes, those at the front trying to back up to protect themselves from the scorching heat, while those further back press them forward. He elbows forward, feeling his face, *Bobby's* face, baked dry by a searing wind. Fists punching the air. Chanting. Burn! Burn! Bright faces, bared teeth, howling red mouths. On to the balcony stumbles the Reverend himself, like a vision of damnation. His face and clothes are covered in soot, his hair and beard standing away from his head in a haze of smoking grey. His eyes are wild, and he shouts something down at the mob, inaudible over the sound of the flames. Seeing him, the crowd draws back, and some people try to run. The chanting falters, and stops. Cradled in his arms is a pile of skulls. For an instant the scene is suspended in time and ever afterwards Bobby will remember it like that, still and silent as a photograph. Then, with a sickening tearing sound, the balcony collapses inwards, and, like a pile of rags, the Reverend disappears into the flames.

Bobby pushes back through the crowd, fighting to break free. There is nothing here for him any more, nothing to make him stay. He feels the earth moving swift and frictionless beneath his feet.

Jonathan Bridgeman

Jonathan Bridgeman stands at the stern rail of the SS *Loch Lomond* and watches its wake, which looks like a line of whitewash painted on the black water. Though he is crossing the black water, the kala pani, he feels no ill effects, no draining away of caste or merit. Close under the rail the churned-up white actually appears a pale phosphorescent green, the colour of ghosts or radium cure-alls. The night air is warm, and beneath the scrubbed decking turbines are turning giant propellers to make billions of light-emitting algae glitter expensively, just for him, as if to prove that the water can also be the very opposite of black, if it chooses. Bridgeman smiles and hooks the collar of his jacket up over his head, to shield himself as he lights a cigarette.

So the black funnels will carry on pumping out coal-smoke to blot out the stars, and couples will carry on strolling upon the buff-coloured deck, and the ship will carry Jonathan Bridgeman into the mouth of the Red Sea and through the Suez Canal and ease him out into the Mediterranean, so called because it is the centre of the world and around its shores civilization was born in a conjunction of war and law and democratic institutions and the disciplined observation of nature. Leaving the Mediterranean, the black and buff coloured ship will round Cape Finisterre, *finis terra*, the end of the earth, for beyond that, beyond the earth altogether, lies England.

Ah, the mystic Occident! Land of wool and cabbage and lecherous round-eyed girls! The girls must be quite something if Bridgeman's reception aboard the *Loch Lomond* is anything to go by. The presence of a 'spare man', and such a high-grade one (so *very* spare, so *very* manly) has left the losers of last Autumn's Fishing Fleet, the inglorious 'Returned Empties', all in a tizz. Still husbandless after spending the Cold Weather in India, all they can look forward to at Home is a further period of husbandless-ness and then some form of compromise. Less tall. Less rich. Less well bred. Bridgeman, despite the fact that he looks very young and his clothes are singularly ill fitting, appears to represent More. One or two of the Empties are quite determined, and he has been forced to wedge a chair under the handle of his cabin door when he goes to sleep at night. Despite this precaution, both Miss Emily Howard and Miss Barbara Hollis believe they have come to an understanding with him, and Miss Amanda Jellicoe, who has seen rather more of life (and Jonathan) than they have, believes that were she to die tomorrow she would do so contentedly. As the spare man watches the luminous wake stretch away into the darkness, Amanda is sitting back down at the table with Mr and Mrs Devereaux, her chaperones, who think she has been lying down in her cabin, instead of grappling with Jonathan under the canvas cover of a lifeboat on the lower deck. Mrs Devereaux is remarking how *well* she looks, and Amanda is hoping that she will not notice the damp patch on her dress or the rich male smell rising up off her body.

Amanda is an exception. Jonathan has been attempting to avoid such encounters, hoping in fact to do nothing to draw attention to himself. He spends as much time as possible in his cabin, and when he goes out on deck buries himself in the most forbidding-looking books he can find in the ship's library. Rare indeed is the Empty who can find much to say when the answer to her eye-fluttering 'So-what-are-you-reading?' is 'Volume two of Motley's *Rise of the Dutch Republic.*' Amanda, quicker than the others, covered her ignorance of seventeenth-century history by talking about windmills and her home in Suffolk and inventing a picture-postcard view of it which she simply had to show him after dinner.

If she knew what she represents, Amanda would probably press her case further. To Jonathan she is a first, a revelation, as much of a crossing as that of the black water itself. Her smell, her colours, even the texture of her hair, are all tiny victories to him, and, as he stands at the rail with her scent in his nostrils, each time he lifts his cigarette he feels like an explorer.

However hard he tries, Jonathan is finding even a basic level of inconspicuousness hard to achieve on board ship. His luggage was a disappointment to him, consisting of a trunkful of screw-top bottles of a brown spirituous liquid, and a second much smaller trunkful of dirty clothes. Apart from a tennis racket in a press, a rifle, ammunition and the skull of some kind of deer, this constitutes his entire estate, and, once he had hefted the bottles over the side, the remainder made a pitiful heap on his bunk. The worst of it is that the clothes do not fit. The previous Bridgeman's waist was bigger. His feet were larger and his arms shorter. For an incarnation who cares particularly about tailoring, this is a torture. There is only so long that one can walk around in a dinner jacket with a cigarette burn on the lapel, and a pair of trousers with the waistband rolled over and frayed cuffs which flap indecorously about one's ankles.

Desperate times call for desperate measures. Luckily Ganesh the junior cabin steward is another of Jonathan Bridgeman's admirers, and behind closed doors has been encouraged to think that he too is in possession of a certain understanding. Ganesh has been induced to liberate certain items from the wardrobes of some of the better-equipped passengers. A shirt-front here, a pair of braces there. Even more daringly, a system of high-risk temporary loans has been instituted. Thus Merriwether, the young Kerala DO, sometimes misplaces his second-best linen suit, and Dickie Carson notices something dashed familiar about the cut of Bridgeman's dinner jacket. Yet since Dickie has three of his own, he does not make the connection, and Jonathan is able to appear at least adequately (if not actually *well*) dressed.

Ganesh's dress-hire service brings with it its own problems, and when, after Aden, he begins to demand payment and physical relief from the tensions of stewarding, Jonathan has to come up with something special. Money is a particular difficulty. He has almost none of it, and though certain shipboard services are free and a tab can be run for others, bribery is a cash-only operation. He thinks he will find the solution in the regular engine-room poker game, but on his second visit one of the stokers catches him cheating and things turn very ugly indeed. It is all the chief can do to stop the boys throttling the little bastard and dumping the body over the side. As it is, Jonathan's face is so cut up that he does not appear in public until after Gibraltar, and for the rest of the voyage he has to watch his back when he ventures anywhere off the main passenger deck.

A storm in the Bay of Biscay alleviates the awkwardness of the situation, transforming most passengers into vomiting wrecks too caught up in their own misery to notice Bridgeman's bruises, or his sudden return to shabbiness. Spirits aboard the *Loch Lomond* only lift again when the white cliffs of Dover come into view. One or two particularly sea-sick passengers actually cheer (despite the fact that the English coastline has been visible for some time), and there is much discussion of the beauties of Home and the first things people will do on landing. Amanda Jellicoe stands beside Jonathan at the rail and asks him, Aren't you glad to be back. Jonathan says yes, hearing as he says it how unconvincing he sounds.

Squinting over the water at the green-rimmed chalk cliffs, he is struck by something like awe. To the people around him this has meaning. Only now does he realize that though he has studied England obsessively, he has never really believed in it. The place has always retained an abstract quality, like a philosophical hypothesis or a problem in geometry. Imagine a cube, rotating about its axis . . . Imagine the Lake District and the Norfolk Broads and the white cliffs rising up out of the green-grey water, circled over by gulls. He tries to feel what the others feel, and wonders nervously what he has become.

Samuel Spavin employs a quintet of long white fingers to trill the fringe of beard beneath his chin. His chair creaks venerably, a delicate ornament in the fugue of age and tradition that is the special music of the firm of Spavin & Muskett. On the wall behind him hangs a portrait of an early-Victorian gentleman with a fierce look and a high starched collar. Visitors often remark on the resemblance between Mr Spavin and the man in the portrait, most assuming that the sitter, who has been depicted beside a table of books and documents, is a Spavin ancestor, some long-dead lawyer whose wisdom and probity form part of the firm's professional inheritance. In fact, despite a cultivated similarity of manner and aspect, Mr Spavin is unrelated to the painted man. The picture was purchased in a house clearance sale in the early days of his career, to give precisely the impression of long establishment that his clients have subsequently found so comforting.

Today Mr Spavin is looking across his desk and finding himself pleasantly surprised. He would never have thought it possible. True, the boy is a trifle scruffy, but then he is an orphan. Scruffiness, believes Spavin, is a natural attribute of the orphan, one of the accidents that gives orphaned substance its specific pathos. Spavin is an admirer of Dickens, and Jonathan Bridgeman's appearance accords perfectly with the old boy's template for such a person. A little old, perhaps. And male. It would certainly be more piquant if he were a she. Being already that most Dickensian of things, a lawyer, Mr Spavin is now about to become Bridgeman's guardian. A moment like this, when life takes on the formal quality of literary art, is to be savoured. Spavin shakes his head in silent wonder at the depth of his own sensibility. His appreciation of these matters is so keen that he sometimes wonders whether he missed his vocation.

'There, and there.'

He points out the spaces on the document where Jonathan is to sign, and watches indulgently as the boy writes his name. He is hesitant, forming the characters slowly and purposefully, no doubt as aware as his patron of the special poignancy of the moment.

'There, my boy. It is done. Just as your dear departed father would have wished it.'

Bridgeman nods. He is really a rather good-looking fellow, which in itself is a miracle. Spavin casts his mind back to the day when this Bridgeman's grandfather, also called Jonathan, marched his lump of a son into the office, and announced that he wished to make arrangements to set him up in the tea trade. Even the most charitable of observers, a class among whom Spavin has the honour to count himself, would have found little to commend in Bridgeman junior. An ill-favoured fellow, coarse and loutish, with what might be termed an *Irish* look about him. His drunkenness (at eleven in the morning!) only added to the negative impression. Who would have thought that from the loins of such a brute could spring so fine a figure as this? Spavin cannot remember whether he ever met the poor woman who was this boy's mother. Probably not, since the marriage took place after the move to Darjeeling. Yet it is clear that she must have been extraordinarily beautiful. As befits a man of poetic sensibility, Spavin believes that character shows itself in physiognomy. One could tell in an instant that the potato-featured dolt who slurred his way through the interview those twenty years ago would never amount to anything. But this one . . . What a woman the mother must have been!

'Do you have a photograph of your dear mamma, Jonathan?'
'No, I'm afraid not. My father didn't believe in photographs.'
'Didn't believe in them? I see. How peculiar.'
'That's right. I have none at all. Not one.'
'That is indeed a shame.'

A shame indeed. As far as he can remember, the grandfather was not the most handsome of men either. How proud he would have been to know that his line was to be continued by such a one as this! A profile like the Apollo Belvedere! The thought of continuity leads Mr Spavin to cast an eye around the legal clutter of his chambers, the bundles of papers, the shelves of morocco-bound books, the whole tangle of sealing wax and red ribbon that is his working life. Yes, he knows about continuity. Every facet of his existence, from the headed notepaper on which he conducts his correspondence to the regular one o'clock light luncheon he takes with Mr Muskett at the chophouse on the corner, attests to his position as a guardian of tradition, a small but honourable conservative force in the life of a great nation.

It is all a considerable relief. When the telegram arrived saying that there had been some kind of trouble at the docks, and could he send a sum of several guineas to procure the release of his charge from custody and allow disembarkation formalities to be completed, he experienced feelings of apprehension. Could the son be as worthless as the father? Nevertheless, in accordance with his obligations, he sent the money, and the boy turned up with a heartbreaking story which instantly dispelled his fears. He had been robbed in a Bombay alleyway by a gang of cut-throats, and though he defended himself gallantly, knocking two of them down before he was overpowered, they took almost all his travelling money. The misunderstanding about the suit stemmed from a simple and overzealous Indian steward, who made a present of it to the destitute boy, neglecting to tell him that it belonged to another passenger, the Mr Carson who lodged the complaint. Spavin's intervention had cleared the matter up, and Carson accepted an apology.

'What would you have done without me, eh, boy?'

'I honestly don't know, sir.'

In London the streets are paved with gold – electric light reflected on the wet flagstones. Walkers leave fierce trails behind them, flashbulb memories of raincoated arms and spattered striding legs. Piccadilly is criss-crossed by forces as modern and purposeful as factory machinery, and even the pigeons, fat and grey and rat-like though they are, appear to be coursing with something imperial and rare, some pigeon-essence that powers their strut and their pompous inquisitiveness. In London the rain sparkles with stray energies, and the dirty water that runs in the gutters is notable because it is London water, and carries along with it Morse-code oddments, leaflets and sweet-wrappers and cigarette ends that telegraph clues to London life and thinking.

Jonathan dodges pedestrians and taxi cabs, hearing the metallic clattering of the rain on his big black umbrella, a sound so unlike the roaring of the Indian monsoon that he can never forget what he has done, how he has come here and made himself giddily, vertiginously new.

London has blue-uniformed policemen and red omnibuses with advertisements on the side. The parks that open out between its tall buildings yield expanses of rich green lawn, and for the first time he understands what the British have tried unsuccessfully to replicate in India. Velvet green. Pulsing with life. The homesickness that India's brown and patchy open spaces must inspire in these people! Here in their own place, in the fug of their dampness, they finally make sense. In their London you can shake the rainwater from your umbrella and step into a

Lyons tearoom where pale girls in black and white uniforms serve cake as heavy and moist as the lawns, accompanied by brown milky tea that is almost the only thing in the city not subtly different to its Indian namesake. They are called 'nippies', these girls, and Jonathan wonders if this is due to their sharp, pinched look. It is a type of Englishness entirely new to him. This sort of face, washed out and poor, is not exported to rule the Empire.

Everywhere Jonathan finds the originals of copies he has grown up with, all the absurdities of British India restored to sense by their natural environment. Here dark suits and high collars are the right thing to wear. Here thick black doors lead away from the electric streets into cluttered drawing rooms, with narrow windows to frame squares of cold watery London light. Cocooned in a leather armchair, Jonathan understands for the first time the English word 'cosy', the need their climate instils in them to pad their blue-veined bodies with layers of horsehair and mahogany, aspidistras and antimacassars, history, tradition and share certificates. Being British, he decides, is primarily a matter of insulation.

Mr Spavin has rented him an attic room in Bayswater, with his own little window on to a view of roofs and chimneys. It is only a short let, because in September he will go to school to prepare for The University. This is spoken of like firing a pot or varnishing a piece of furniture, a final craftsman-like transformation he must undergo before he is saleable. He will spend a couple of terms in the workshop of Chopham Hall, and be turned out as an Oxford scholar.

After the door of this room closes for the first time, he stands looking at the empty mantelpiece and the neatly blacked grate and the rug and the washstand with the square of speckled mirror hanging above it. Until this moment he has not thought about the contents of his new life. The life itself, *an English life*, was enough. The sight of all these empty things waiting for him to fill them up with himself sends a knife of panic into his chest. He locks the door and slumps down against it. He has grabbed this life; he is an Englishman. But there are more requirements, things that hitherto have escaped his attention. The empty book-case next to the bed. The dark square on the wallpaper where a picture once hung – where a picture is *supposed* to hang. What picture? What should be there? He does not know, and the answer that would come to other people, to real people (*Whatever picture I like*), surely cannot be right for him. He does not feel he could like something without checking to see if it gave him away. Before he *is*, he is an Englishman, and should have the taste of an Englishman.

Which is?

He thinks long and hard about this. An Englishman would hang up a hunting print or a photograph of the King or a painting of his dead relatives, like the mutton-chopped old man over Mr Spavin's desk. Having no painting, Jonathan settles for the King, bought from a stall in Berwick Street and slipped into a gilt frame. So, for his first months among the lawns and the rainlit streets, he goes to sleep under the hand-coloured image of George V, resisting the temptation to pray to it, to ask the jutting tinted beard to point him on the path to selfhood.

Until September he has nothing to do. Jonathan is quite happy about this. The idea of Chopham Hall fills him with trepidation; when British people talk about school, they use words that other people use about prisons. Spavin, however, is concerned, and asks young Mr Muskett, his partner's son, to show him around. In due course, after a polite exchange of notes, a golden-haired youth in tennis whites materializes on the Bayswater doorstep. 'Hullo,' he says, peering with visible distaste into the dim recesses of the hall. 'You must be Bridgeman. I thought we could play a couple of sets.'

Muskett stands in the dim hall, and receives the obeisances of Mrs Lovelock, the landlady. Mrs Lovelock evidently finds him an impressive figure, and fusses round him in a kind of bobbing spiral meant to indicate deference and pleasure. Muskett ignores her, fully occupied in curling his sculpted lower lip at the hall decoration. When he is offered a seat in the front parlour, he declines, saying that if it is all the same to Mrs Lovelock he would rather stand. His lower lip is employed once again when Jonathan reappears, wearing a pair of brown shoes.

'Don't you have plimsolls?'

'Afraid not.'

'Oh well. I suppose we can buy some on the way.'

A detour via Piccadilly, and then the two of them walk out on to a springy grass court tucked away behind a house on the good side of Regent's Park. Jonathan's feet are sheathed in fresh white canvas. The handle of his racket is already drenched in nervous sweat. The game is a disaster. He throws himself after the ball, chasing it left and right, slamming bodily into the net and failing to return a single one of Muskett's shots. After a while the golden youth surveys the panting figure on the other side and, employing his expressive lip once again, asks whether he would perhaps like to have a break. Jonathan nods mutely.

'I thought you said you played.'

Jonathan is non-committal.

'I'm surprised. You colonial fellows are usually so sportif. The healthy Punjab lifestyle and all that.'

Ruefully Jonathan remembers the British-Indian habit of building tennis courts on any available piece of land, even in the hills, where they carve them into the mountainsides like Jains do the images of their saints. It is inconceivable that he would not play. He can think of no satisfactory reason for his failure, so he says that he has hurt his hand, hoping this will be enough to save him. Muskett obviously does not believe him, but politely half

301

masks his disgust and suggests they go and drink lemon barley water on the terrace.

Jonathan feels obliged to rub his wrist occasionally, and Muskett talks about parties and the people who go to the parties and their relationships with the hosts and each other and him. Muskett has money and a motor car, and invitations for the next five weekends to The Country, which is where Everyone goes when not at Parties or on the tennis court. Muskett tells the story of Lady Kynaston's dance, and of Mr and Mrs Huntington's dance and the amusing things he said at the dinner the Waller-Waltons gave beforehand. It appears that all these occasions were deathly and most people were at all three, except the ones who had an invitation to the reception at the Swedish Embassy, which Muskett didn't. He didn't mind because he expected it would be even more deathly (embassy things always are) and of course afterwards Everyone said that is exactly how it was. Muskett has already done two years at The University, and he has debts that the Old Man will sort out and an understanding with Anne Waller-Walton, and expects that when he goes down he will probably go into The City, which is not, Jonathan gathers, the opposite of The Country but something altogether more technical involving the controlled flow of capital, equity and lunch.

Muskett says he will call again the following week, but does not. Jonathan knows he has failed some sort of test, and realizes he has a lot to learn before he is fit for the kind of circles in which young Mr Muskett moves. In a notebook he jots down his deficiencies: *tennis, dancing, motor car*. Most of his allowance has already been spent on clothes, but he starts to reserve a small sum for lessons. Tennis or dancing? Dancing is cheaper, especially if he travels out to Shepherd's Bush, where according to a classified advertisement in the *Post* a woman called Madame Parkinson holds a Monday evening class. Madame Parkinson turns out to have bright red hair and a French accent that even Jonathan can tell is fake, but she is a good teacher all the same. *Left one two, right one two, and viz elehgaanz – yes!* Soon he is spending evenings at the Hammersmith Palais de Danse, where the Brylcreemed band punch out foxtrots through the cigarette smoke, and shingle-haired girls let him tread on their toes, and then take him down by the river where it is dark and quiet.

Gradually he begins to relax into the city, his senses attuning themselves to the different qualities of London space. People have different boundaries from Bombay, different thresholds for invasion and anger. He travels on the underground, and forces himself not to hold his breath, to adopt the same expression of nonchalance as the other passengers hurtling along through the earth in their metal capsule. He sits in the cinema, bathed in white light, thrilling as the organist coaxes gunshots and creaking floorboards out of his futuristic machine. Between the petting couples in the back row, he eats an ice and feels Englishness begin to stick to him, filming his skin like city grime. This is what he wanted. This is enough.

It all ends abruptly when Mrs Lovelock mentions the Palais to Mr Spavin, who calls him into his office and explains that this is not the sort of behaviour he expected from his ward. Jonathan does not know what exactly is the problem, but apologizes profusely, terrified that everything will be taken away. Mr Spavin believes he is becoming unruly, and it would be best if he went up to Chopham Hall forthwith. Discipline is what he needs. Discipline and the rigours of academic life. It would be pointless to delay. He is to take the morning train from Liverpool Street Station.

At the moment of his death, Sir Peregrine Haldane is said to have sat bolt upright in the Great Bed at Chopham Hall, and shouted, 'Let them be chastised, O Lord! Spare them not!' Afterwards these last words were variously interpreted. The parish priest of Chopham Constable (a man Sir Perry had always suspected of dangerous and levelling opinions) considered them prophetic of the fate of all rich men, and preached a sermon which dwelt heavily on the fate of the citizens of Sodom and Gomorrah. An anonymous London pamphleteer claimed that 'Sir Poxridden Halfmast' was actually imagining himself back at the scene of one of his legendary five-wench debauches, an opinion which was shared by most of London society, despite the gallant protestations of friends who maintained that Sir Peregrine had meant to say, 'Let *me* be chastised, O Lord! Spare *me* not!', but had, in his final agonies, become confused.

Whatever the truth, after the reading of the will, no one could deny that the old man had repented. On hearing its contents, Oliver de Tassle-Lacey, Sir Perry's nephew and heir, realized he was ruined. Having heavily engaged himself on the expectation of his inheritance, he felt he had no option but to commit suicide, and jumped from a box at the Theatre Royal, impaling himself on a spear carried by an attendant in a production of *Alexander and Poros*. The combination of Sir Peregrine's appalling reputation and Oliver's flamboyant death kept the matter of the will in the public eye for several weeks. That the old rake should choose to found a school for 'the sons of the deserving poor', instead of passing on his house and land to the next generation, was considered eccentric to the point of folly. Still, some at court thought it touching, and the King even had a description of the foundation read out to him during his morning evacuation.

During the subsequent two and a half centuries Chopham Hall has gone through many changes. The initial bequest was supplemented by various others, and for a period the school was even fashionable enough to attract sons of the lesser aristocracy to its doors. Sadly, by the August afternoon that Jonathan's train pulls into the sleepy station of Chopham Constable, such days are long gone. Chopham Hall has settled into a middling niche in the great hierarchy of English public schools, some way below the Harrows and Etons and Winchesters, though still far enough up the social ladder for the villagers to doff their caps to the young masters, and sometimes spit at their departing backs.

To Jonathan, Norfolk seems a very long way from London. Rattling over the flat countryside he is reminded of the Punjab, and these memories make him uneasy. When he sees Briggs, the school porter, waiting to meet him, a stiff and bushy-bearded figure in a bowler hat, he is tempted to stay on board and take his chances with King's Lynn. However, he steels himself, dismounts, makes himself known, and is duly driven through the village in an ancient pony trap.

Conversation is sparse. Briggs makes a single gnomic pronouncement about the weather, which he reckons about fair, considering. Considering *what* exactly, Jonathan does not ask, and Briggs does not see fit to tell him. They reach the school gate in silence.

First impressions are pleasant. The grounds are ample, a line of rugby and cricket pitches stretching off towards the Brand, the little stream which marks the eastern limit of the park. The Elizabethan manor house has altered little since Sir Perry's day, though generations of headmasters have added amenities like the new boarding houses, and the gymnasium-and-chapel. Housed together in a single Victorian gothic building, this architectural curiosity stems from one educationalist's theory about the close relationship between worship and physical exertion, which he put into practice with the help of a progressive staff and a subscription fund. The chapel tower, a round structure with a slight curve and an oddly bulbous tip, is all that remains of Sir Perry's folly, built at the height of the old man's hellfire days. Disguised by buttresses and topped by a cross, it is nevertheless still known by the villagers as the Big'un, and the legend persists that it is an anatomically correct rendering of Sir Perry's favourite appendage, executed in an attempt to win the favours of the Duchess of Devonshire.

As Briggs hefts his trunk off the back of the pony trap, Jonathan walks into the oak-panelled entrance hall and for the first time smells the combination of carbolic soap, mud and boiled cabbage that is the unique aroma of the English boarding school. Since there are three weeks before term starts, everything is deathly quiet. The gold-leafed names on the scholarship roll and the plaster busts of past headmasters look down on a scene of weird calm, like sentries during a cease-fire. Jonathan peers into a glass case of sports trophies, until Briggs coughs loudly in his ear, suggesting that they might as well think about climbing up, considering. He follows the old servant upstairs, past rows of closed doors and through the cavernous, scarred space of the junior prep room. Finally they reach a wing once occupied by the Haldane family guest rooms, and now by the sixth-form studies of School House.

A door. Another empty room, waiting for him to fill it up.

He is given time to settle himself in, and told that the headmaster expects him for tea in the glasshouses in an hour. Having delivered this information, Briggs hovers in the doorway until Jonathan presses a coin into his hand, whereupon he shuffles off down the hall.

*

Rising up behind the main hall, the glasshouses appear like a miniature crystal palace, glittering in the sunshine. Mesmerized, Jonathan is approaching them across the back lawn, when a voice bellows out, stopping him dead in his tracks.

'Boy! BOY!'

He wheels round to find a red-faced man leaning out of an upstairs window.

'What on earth do you think you're doing?'

'Going –'

'What?'

'Going –'

'WHAT? I hardly think you should be *going* anywhere over the *grass*! Regard! What you have wrought!'

Jonathan looks down, and sees that his shoes have left a trail of little bruises on the sleek green-striped surface.

'Lawn!' shouts the man. 'Parents, masters and senior domestic staff only! Exceptions! Prefects on Sundays! All upper-form boys on Founders Day between two and four in the afternoon! Now get off!'

Gingerly Jonathan steps on to a gravel path. The window is slammed shut. He thinks for a moment, takes out his pocket book and writes: *further demonstration of the significance of lawns*. Englishness seeps a little deeper into his skin.

Finding the glasshouses is one thing. Finding a way in is another. The structure appears to be divided into three sections, each one crammed with foliage. Certain areas are screened from the light by canvas blinds. Others are so misted up that it is impossible to see inside. A complex system of pipes passes over the gravel, pumping out heat. Finally Jonathan spots a yellow-hatted figure moving about inside. Following the perimeter, he discovers a door, and is transported back to rainy-season India, the air as heavy and thick as flannel.

Dr Noble, Headmaster and orchidist, is discovered in the act of hybridization. He has a lush red Dendrobium by the petals, and is stroking a pollen-coated toothpick over its sex organs, coaxing it like a recalcitrant chorus girl. His wide-brimmed yellow panama is pushed back on his head, revealing a bony scalp and a single lock of grey hair. Transmitting frowns down a long sculptural nose, he appears not to notice Jonathan's arrival, concentrating absolutely on his task. Only when the pollen transfer is complete does he straighten up from his workbench. He stretches, then surveys his new pupil with a post-coital smile.

'Bridgeman,' he intones. 'Fresh from the tropics.'

'Yes, sir.'

'Lately arrived from Asia, like my new box of Paphiopedilums.' He indicates a wooden crate at his feet, and together they stare into it. Jonathan sees an unpromising mess of dirt and tubers. Whatever Dr Noble sees must excite him, because he lets out a low moan.

'Gorgeous,' he murmurs.

'Yes, sir.'

'Follow me to the Alpine House, where I trust we shall discover that Mrs Dodd has laid out tea.'

They make their way through the mass of greenery. Orchids are everywhere, lined up in long planters, hanging from baskets, curling over logs and artful contraptions of bark and wire. They take every imaginable form and colour, large waxy flowers with trailing roots, tiny stars, spikes, fans, columns and rosettes, flowers in the shape of pouches and flowers with little pointed tails. They reach frilly lips up from beds of moss, and hover overhead, trailing clusters of aerial roots which catch at Jonathan's face and hair. The Doctor appears more their leader than their gardener, controlling his hordes by force of will.

The plants in the Alpine House are grouped around little tableaux of rocks, and the temperature is a good twenty degrees colder than the tropical zone next door. Dr Noble pours tea and explains the school philosophy, which is essentially that boys should work hard, play hard, and under no circumstances enter the portals of the Blue Badger or Edith's Café, the fleshpots of Chopham Constable. Jonathan's guardian has, he mentions, indicated a certain gravitational tendency towards fleshpots. He has been assured that Chopham Hall will effect a cure. Business dispensed with, he returns to orchids, describing his plan to cross certain difficult species of Cattleya. The result to be presented to Kew. The hybrid to be called *C. haldaniensis*, or perhaps *C. emiline*, after a girl he knew at Oxford. Mention of the university brings him back to the topic of Jonathan's education, and he switches to Greek, uttering a long peroration in that language, then pausing expectantly. He appears to want an answer. When Jonathan confesses that he does not understand, he is told that this is extremely serious, and the process is repeated in Latin. Together they manage a stilted conversation about the war-like character of the Germanii east of the Rhine, before Dr Noble loses interest and starts to talk about the huge number of plants he lost in the recent drought. The toll on the tropical epiphytes was particularly heavy. As he describes the losses, Jonathan thinks for a moment that he is going to break into tears, but he collects himself, pours more tea and announces that he believes Jonathan would do best in the history sixth.

'That is what you shall put in for at the university. Classics is not for you. I realize this may be a disappointment, since in your journey along life's winding path you may encounter fellows who believe an affinity with the Ancients is the mark of a gentleman. However, you must bear their barbs with fortitude and trust me when I tell you that it is for the best. Though the bees in our gardens transfer pollen indiscriminately from flower to flower, still we do not find crosses between dahlia and delphinium, or between geranium and gentian. Why? Because their essential natures are different. Just as it is with flowers, so it is with boys. Each boy has his essential nature, and yours, Mr Bridgeman, is historical. Surely, as observers of creation, we must look upon these boundaries as a good thing? Were there none, the flowers would lose their identities in a hybrid swarm, and nature would be in a desperate mess.'

Jonathan thinks about this for a moment.

'History will be fine, sir.'

'That's the spirit. Now you may go and unpack your things.'

Jonathan spends the three weeks before the start of term reading in the library and assisting Dr Noble in the glasshouses. He sands and paints rotten wood, and learns to mist the tropicals with water at sunrise and sunset. Noble seems to have taken a liking to his new pupil. Or, if not exactly a liking, at least an interest in. Jonathan will laugh or make a gesture and find the Doctor intently watching him. Analysing. Tracing him back through the generations to the pure botanical forms from which he originated.

One afternoon Jonathan helps the Headmaster bed microscopic seeds in layers of watery jelly, packing them into stoppered flasks and talking to them as he does it, his lisping tone totally unlike the clipped voice he uses to human beings. These potential orchids are empresses, queens of the night; they are houris and goddesses and once, startlingly, 'black-breasted Madonnas of the jungle'. Noble seems unaware that the boy can hear him laying bare this interior life, so full of sensuality.

At night Jonathan walks around the grounds, smoking contraband cigarettes and wrapping the holiday silence tightly around himself. Chopham Hall feels clenched, expectant. On the first day of term it explodes into life.

Dawn breaks with Briggs coughing his way on to the front porch. There is an hour of quiet, then an ominous rumble in the distance. Like invading motorized cavalry, a convoy of parental cars sweeps into the drive, disgorging stern fathers, tearful fox-furred mothers, their sons, chauffeurs, maids and dogs into a mêlée of cricket bats and parcels. The fathers bundle the mothers back into the cars and drive away. Then things begin in earnest. Trunks are bumped up and down stairs. Small boys are kicked and whipped from dormitory to bath to chapel to breakfast to form room to assembly, while larger ones, the kickers and whippers, are sent five miles over the fields, or taught to drill with wooden rifles, or lined up against one another and made to ruck and maul. The chaos is regimented by masters, capped and gowned like ragged black crows, and by prefects, waistcoated sadists alive to the slightest sign of insubordination. Jonathan soon learns that the prefects are the true masters of this universe, and that he, as a new sixth-former, is a suspicious anomaly in it.

School House, to which Jonathan has the honour of belonging, is captained by one Fender-Greene, a straw-haired thug with a wispy moustache and a garish green silk tie, symbols of his privileged rank. Calling Jonathan into his study, he administers a crushing handshake and makes a short speech, to the effect that he does not know what sort of a life Jonathan has led hitherto, but he is now part of something larger than himself, and will be expected to act in accordance with the principles of the house. Then he takes a breath and screams 'Boooooy-up!' through the open door, which produces a panting eleven-year-old fag, carrying tea. As the little boy rattles cups and saucers, Fender-Greene leers at him proprietorially.

'He's a lovely little lusher, ain't he? Does boots too, and a super omelette.'

After tea, Fender-Greene escorts Jonathan in front of the assembled house, where he is introduced, applauded and sung to:

'Striving we for glory
Striving all for fame
Giving of our utmost
In the School House name'

Then Fender-Greene and his prefects turn their attentions to hazing the new ticks, leaving him free to slip upstairs.

In his study he finds a dark-haired young man picking out a tune on a sort of misshapen guitar. The unused side of the room has miraculously filled up with books and pictures, along with a number of unusual objects, such as a typewriter and a little bronze bust of a man with a pointed beard. The boy stops playing, stands and holds out his hand.

'Hello. I'm Gertler, and you might as well know straight off, I'm a Jew.'

'Bridgeman. How do you do.'

'You don't have to like it, but there it is,' he says, picking up his guitar again.

'I don't mind.'

'That will make it easier.'

Gertler returns to his practice, constantly repeating the same figure, slapping the body of the instrument in irritation when his fingers refuse to follow instructions.

'So what are you?'

'I'm sorry?'

'C of E, I suppose.'

Jonathan makes no answer. 'Who's that?' he asks, pointing to the bronze head.

Gertler smiles. 'Comrade Vladimir Ilyich Lenin. I'm a Communist too. You can ask to switch studies, if you like. They'll probably let you, and I certainly don't care. Fender-Greene already wants me out. Old Hoggart only keeps me in the House because my father's rich.'

'If you're father's rich, why are you a Communist?'

'Might as well ask, why am I alive? I believe everyone should be equal. Money shouldn't come into it. It does, but it shouldn't. How's that for a surprise?'

'Surprise?'

'Coming from a Jew, I mean.'

He doesn't understand. Gertler sneers at him.

'Don't you believe in something?'

'No,' says Jonathan.

Gertler snorts, and goes back to his guitar.

And so a routine begins. Jonathan's year at Chopham Hall is governed by two things: numbers and lists. The school is a machine for producing belonging, and accordingly everything is done in groups, from showering in the morning to the composition of essays in evening prep. Every gesture of Jonathan's day is honed to its functional minimum by two hundred years of institutional evolution, like some upper-class version of Mr Taylor's factory system. Accustomed to total freedom, he often wonders how long he will be able to stand it. In his notebook he writes: *Englishness is sameness*, and *the comfort of repetition*.

Numbers and lists: lists of school rules, masters' names, prefects' names, names of the first eleven and fifteen, lists of school colours, lists of areas out of bounds, lists of the dates of battles of the English Civil War and lists of its causes. All of these Jonathan is expected to be able to recite when called upon. Sometimes he can. Sometimes he cannot. His punishment for failure is more lenient than that handed out to first-year new boys, who are often flogged for believing that the middle-school rugby colours contain a narrow gold stripe, or placing Mr Russell above Mr Hoggart in order of staff seniority.

Mr Hoggart is the red-faced shouting man, and his first impression of Jonathan does not improve. Since Mr Hoggart is Master of School House, this is a problem.

'Bridgeman! What, *pray* are *those*?'

'These, sir? Shoes, sir.'

'Shoes, sir? Shoes! No! They are an offence! An infringement!'

'They're patent leather, sir. I bought them in London.'

'School regulations! Clothing! All eccentricities in dress are *forbidden*. They shall disappear, Bridgeman. *Disappear*.'

Jonathan is saved from serious trouble by the fact that, however poor his record, Gertler's is always worse. Though he may have problems with uniform, attitude, commitment, spirit and other important qualities which help School House in its battle with the barbarian hordes besieging the citadel, Gertler is actively plotting to let the barbarians in. He reads Marx in prep, refuses to train with the cadet corps and, although he is excused chapel, still pronounces loudly and frequently on the death of God and the spectre haunting Europe. As a result he is hated by Fender-Greene, and (with the tacit approval of Hoggart) generally persecuted by the rest of the house. Ink is poured on to his books, and his food is spat on before it is served to him in the dining hall. He is tripped up in the corridor, and every so often Fender-Greene finds an excuse to cane him, only to be infuriated beyond reason by Gertler's habit of laughing as the birch whooshes through the air.

Jonathan notes all this down: *nobility of discipline, respect for religion important but belief optional, check your plate first*. His notes spread out into all areas of school life, from the rules of rugby football to the construction of a jam sandwich. Week by week his understanding of this world improves, the white spaces on his map filling up with trails and landmarks.

His place in the history sixth could have been useful, allowing him to add a diachronic understanding of his subject (Englishness) to the synchronic. But in the sleepy classroom of Mr Fox, pipe-smoker and Sunday painter, history is not so much about change as eternal recurrence. The boys are taught to trace the destiny of their island through a series of devotional tableaux, jewel-like moments which reveal essences, principles, axioms drawn out of race and blood. From Drake kneeling before Elizabeth to the gathering in the meadow at Runnymede, from Wolfe at Quebec to Victoria's coronation as Empress of India, the past is depicted as a blur of large and uninteresting forces which only achieves clarity at certain points, when it instantaneously freezes into still compositions of shining faces and rich drapery. In Mr Fox's model of history, even recent events, such as the war which overtook his pupils' uncles and older brothers, have faded into this artificial duality: long misty stretches of vaguely sportsmanlike activity – striving and muddy endurance – throwing up nuggets of transubstantiation. Flesh hardening into oil-and-varnish greatness. Poppies out of Flanders fields.

Like prize day, history is meant to be a spur to future action, for *success in the world after school*. Such success is the birthright of Old Chophamites, who have found it in fields as diverse as merchant banking and ranching in the Argentine. However, the grand tradition of the school, insofar as it has such a thing, lies in preparing young men for the Colonial Service. In his morning addresses, Hoggart likes to list the places where former house members are currently serving. *The Gold Coast. Hong Kong. Bengal. Burma. Cape Town. Bermuda.* There, under foreign stars, the virtues of scholarship, forbearance and prowess at team sports are helping to maintain Britain's pre-eminence in the world. It is for the Empire that one should applaud the new prefects, and do one's best to thrash the boys of Frobisher and Hawkins in the interhouse sevens.

Like Gertler, Bridgeman is a notable absentee on the touchline. As someone who is only at Chopham Hall to prepare for university, he has something of a special status, but neither Hoggart nor Fender-Greene is prepared to let this go to his head. There is, they feel, something dubious about him. His only saving grace is his ability to study, and that in itself is suspect, having something Semitic about it, something try-hard and grasping.

By the start of the winter holidays, a storm is brewing.

Jonathan himself is unaware of this. As he returns to London to spend a cold and boring Christmas under the eye of Mr Spavin, he feels the anxieties of the first few months are behind him. He no longer lives in constant fear of discovery. He is becoming what he pretends to be, realizing that the truth is so unlikely that, despite his occasional oddities and lapses, no one would ever divine it. He is starting to coincide with his shadow.

Spring term starts quietly enough, and for a few weeks Jonathan is pleased, even exhilarated by his progress. Oxford entrance proceeds smoothly. Papers are assigned, written and sent off to Dr Noble's good friend, the admissions tutor of Barabbas College. *Discuss the mistakes, if any, in the handling of the American crisis of the 1770s. Assess the following. 'Bullion, rather than martial prowess, was the foundation of Spanish power in the sixteenth century.'* The matter of Greek (lack of) is raised, discussed and discarded. A short hiatus, then word returns that several of the Doctor's pupils, among them Jonathan Bridgeman, will be expected at Barabbas for the Michaelmas term. The customary case of claret changes hands, and Dr Noble sits down to write congratulatory letters to parents and guardians.

Jonathan's life is lighter than air, his upward trajectory an assured and perfect arc. Then one afternoon a breathless fag knocks on the door of his set.

'Hello, Bridgeman. I've got a message.'

Jonathan, in the role of imperious upper-form boy, puts down his book and sighs with infinite boredom.

'What is it?'

'Headmaster says to say your great-aunt has come to see you and she's waiting in his study.'

He thinks he must have misheard.

'My what?'

'Your great-aunt, Bridgeman. Sorry, did I do something wrong?'

Gertler thrums his balalaika dramatically. 'Anything the matter, Johnny?'

'No.'

'I didn't know you had an aunt.'

Nor did Jonathan. Mr Spavin has never mentioned one. There were, he thought, no living relatives. What was it the other Bridgeman said? *Last of the line, old man.* He emits a low moan. He should have known something like this might happen. He should have been prepared. Fighting to think clearly, he drags the fag out of his set and walks him in the direction of the Headmaster's Lodgings, telling him to repeat exactly what the Headmaster said. Exact words. Exactly. He keeps forgetting to breathe. The fag whimpers nothing Bridgeman nothing honestly, and is more or less getting dragged along, tripping over his shiny black school shoes. Bridgeman I didn't, says the fag; Bridgeman he didn't say anything ow Bridgeman you're hurting me, and so on all the way to the Headmaster's door, where Jonathan finally accepts he really does know nothing and is moreover terrified, perhaps even about to wet himself, so he lets go and the fag pelts off, rubbing his arm and saying ow Bridgeman.

He knocks and immediately wishes he had not, because the Headmaster's housekeeper opens the door and shows him straight into the drawing room, straight away, no waiting at all, and his entire brain and body scream too soon, but there she is, an old lady swathed in pre-war crêpe, a mildewed floral hat on top of her potato-shaped head. It is a head which sports the mulch of features and the tiny shallow eyes that are the unmistakable genetic marks of a Bridgeman. A real one.

'Good afternoon, young Jonathan,' says the aunt.

It has been a long time since the previous Jonathan Bridgeman was clearly present in his mind. It often seems to him that Bridgeman and he have always been the same person. The aunt's presence instantly drains this pretence of all reality and, with it, drains him of personality, anima, of the power of speech and action. He stands at the door, unable to take another pace into the room, opening and closing his mouth in a stillborn attempt at charm. The eyes fasten on him like two black buttons.

'Good afternoon,' he manages eventually. 'Aunt.'

'Aunt Berthilda,' the aunt grunts at him unappealingly. 'You won't remember me. Come and give me a kiss.'

As he bends towards her powdery cheek, he is hit by a sharp musty smell rising up from her clothes. Involuntarily he imagines that she has been gradually mummified in them, a new layer of papery green stuff pasted over the old each time it wears thin.

'Jonathan,' she says wonderingly. 'Well, I have to say you don't take after our side of the family. Strong faces we Bridgemans have, Headmaster. Saxon faces.'

'How fascinating,' says Dr Noble. 'Would you like some tea?'

'Tea? How could you possibly – that's what did for his father. A tragedy. Tea indeed!'

'Absolutely. I do apologize.'

Dr Noble is finding the aunt's visit almost as trying as Jonathan. Apart from the smell, there are her undisciplined vowels, which slide around her palate entirely uncurbed, and her weird habit of making her crusty skirts rustle and crack beneath her haunches by shifting around on her chair. Though female, she is hardly floral, let alone orchidaceous. She is actually rather disturbing.

'You don't take after your mother either,' she says, squinting at the boy in the doorway. 'Sorry little thing she was, judging by the photographs.'

'Photographs?' says Jonathan weakly.

'Yes. There's one of you here.' She starts to rummage in her capacious handbag, removing handkerchiefs, pill bottles, a vicious-looking pair of dressmaker's scissors and various other personal items, and stacking them in an unsavoury pile on Dr Noble's occasional table.

'Ah, here it is.'

She produces a battered family portrait. A chubby potato-faced baby is being dandled on the knee of a sallow young woman, while a potato-faced young man leans unsteadily on the back of her chair. The baby's button eyes stare accusingly out of the frame .

'You were a bonny wee thing,' says Aunt Berthilda.

'Yes,' whispers Jonathan hoarsely.

'You know, I practically brought up your father. His favourite relative – I suppose he told you some of the stories?' When Jonathan does not reply, she tells one herself, recounting how Bridgeman senior would sit on Nana's knee and Nana would give him little nips of her gin, like a big man.

'How charming to see the two of you together,' says Dr Noble. 'A family reunion. I must say, Miss Bridgeman, it is a surprise to me to find that Jonathan has a family. His affairs are administered by a solicitor.'

Aunt Berthilda looks slightly shifty. 'Yes,' she says.

Noble adopts an expression which, were there a Gentleman's Guide to Correct Facial Expressions, would illustrate the entry for 'Askance'. Her skirts crackling significantly, Aunt Berthilda slides back and forth on her chair.

'Do you think there is somewhere young Jonathan and I could speak?'

With visible relief, Dr Noble suggests the two of them take a walk round the grounds. The old lady grips Jonathan's arm, enveloping him in her fug, which seems to persist even outdoors. When they are some distance away from the Hall, and the sound of the housekeeper opening all the windows is barely audible, she reveals the purpose of her visit.

'Your father was very fond of me, Jonathan. So naturally I feel affectionately towards you, even though we've never met. I almost think of you as my own. Blood is thicker than water, eh?'

'Yes, Aunt Berthilda.'

'Nana. Your father called me Nana.'

'Yes. Right. Nana.'

'Good boy. Now your father wouldn't have held with the way they treated me. My brother, your grandfather, was a very cruel man. He thought the worst of people. It was my baby! But that was all over a long time ago, and Mr Cox and I – it's as Mrs Cox most people know me, though we never made it official – we did well with the boarding house until he died, but the truth is, Jonathan, they shouldn't have sent me to such a place. They shouldn't. And you know how hard good boarders are to come by nowadays. Well, here are you turned up from nowhere with all this money left to you by your father and here am I, his favourite relative, not even able to afford to keep the maid on except to come in once a week and do the floors.' She pauses meaningfully. 'We've only got each other in the world, Jonathan.'

He cannot believe his ears.

'You want money?'

'There's no need to be crude about it. Something to set me up again. When I close my eyes I can see a wonderful little terrace on a cliff-top promenade, and me in front of it, cradling my little cherub in my arms – '

'I don't have any money. Mr Spavin has it in trust until I'm twenty-one.'

Aunt Berthilda spits on the path. 'Samuel Spavin. Always Samuel Spavin. That man is not well disposed towards me, Jonathan. He is a cruel man. So he has your money, does he? How about if you were to have a word with him, if you were to tell him how I'm your auntie and your father loved me – how would that be?'

'What do you mean he's not well disposed towards you?'

'It's a silly business, Jonathan. They're all very cruel men.'

'What do you mean?'

'All I did was squeeze her too tight! There was no reason to send me to such a place!'

Then Jonathan realizes, with a joyous flood of relief, that whatever else she is (and several of the possibilities worry him) she is certainly quite mad. Maybe this is the kind of conclusion that inevitably shows on the face of the concluder. Maybe Aunt Berthilda is merely perceptive. Either way, something about Jonathan suddenly reveals itself to her in an unfavourable light.

Even as she is attacking him he cannot quite stop grinning. She is mad and he is safe! Scratch on, Berthilda! Berthilda, wail away! She screeches at him incoherently, bringing masters and boys running over the lawn as her surprisingly strong fingers pluck at his face and her stiff skirts snag on his uniform, making a sound like wireless static. As two of the rugby masters escort her off the premises, she shouts back insults, choosing, in one of those moments of insight which come with being mad, to scream, 'He's no kin to me! He's not my blood!'

Dr Noble asks Jonathan whether he is all right. Jonathan says he is fine, thank you. Dr Noble says it (meaning Aunt Berthilda) is unfortunate. Jonathan agrees that it is. After that, Dr Noble considers his pastoral duty fulfilled and places Aunt Berthilda into the sack of unmentionable things which English people, like postmen, drag around with them. A week later Jonathan receives a letter from Mr Spavin advising him to have no further contact with Aunt Berthilda, something he has done his part to promote by having her admitted to an asylum on the Gower Peninsula. It was an unfortunate business, he writes. Perhaps we ought not to have sent her to such a place.

This is the English way: linear and progressive, rolling forward on castors of tradition and good manners. Follow hints, and you will glide on indefinitely, blessed by a kind of social perpetual motion. Ignore them and you will crash into the walls.

Paul Gertler's Cambridge application is rejected.

He and Jonathan crunch along a frosty path by the river, and Gertler tells him at length how much it does not matter and how the old universities are elitist establishments anyway. Jonathan says he is sorry. Gertler describes how it will be after the Revolution, when every working man will have access to education, and the people will be properly provided for by a caring state. They shake cigarettes out of a pack and stand with shoulders hunched up inside their coats and free hands shoved into their pockets, their breath mingling with the fag smoke in fluffy white plumes. Winter is amazing to Jonathan. The silvered surfaces of the leaves and the whiteness blanketing the flat Norfolk fields make it hard to concentrate on Gertler's utopia. The notebook in his breast pocket contains entries on *Christmas carols* and *ice skating*.

'I have a car,' says Gertler, apropos of nothing. 'It's parked at the Services.'

'You're not serious.'

'I am. It belongs to my father. I doubt he's even noticed it has gone.'

'What're you going to do?'

'How does London sound to you?'

And so, bundled up in scarves and hats, Gertler's woollen-gloved hands slipping on the steering wheel, they head off. The car is a pre-war Wolseley, spacious and grand. Gertler has paid the man at the Services a guinea to garage it, and he stands watching them depart, his arms folded, face inscrutable. The headlights illuminate two wobbling discs on the icy surface of the road. Otherwise darkness. It is an eventful ride. Once they slide off the road altogether, gliding sedately round a corner to nestle in a hedge. Somewhere near Colchester it begins to snow. By the time London starts to assemble itself around them, they are cold and tired, letting the low brick houses pass by without comment. Only when the silhouetted buildings get taller and the streetlights brighter do they pick themselves up and ask each other what they are going to do.

Coffee and sandwiches at a stand somewhere in Islington. Then . . .

THE

WEST

END!

where it doesn't matter what time it is and they park the car near a pub called the Coach and Horses dive in up to the bar carrying two pints overhead the place is so packed and excuse me excuse me crammed against a pillar can I interest you two gents in no thanks suit yourself same again out on the street people in doorways music coming out of basements shuffling syncopating girls who say smiling why not come home with us we share a flat in Shepherd's Market but insist on going somewhere to drink a cocktail first the Egyptian Room you can wait can't you it's very modern very much the American thing oh and what would you know about the American thing then somehow they are outside a place with no sign only a bell called Mother Taylor's the girls are gone Paul's wallet hat and everything else too, the people draining out of the icy streets like blood from a wound.

Gertler is shouting *damn you damn you all!* up at windows in St James's, which is definitely going to get them arrested unless Jonathan, who has been drinking less fiercely, can persuade him that they need to get to school for breakfast, which means they have to go now. *Come on, Paul.* Jonathan has the thought that each minute of delay is storing up bad energy for them, and that later he will look back on this as the moment things started to slip away from his friend. They drift back into Soho, Gertler kicking a rubbish bin which clatters all the way down Beak Street. Then Jonathan forces the keys into his hand and tells him to drive. Which he does.

The journey back to Norfolk is far, far worse than the journey down. Gertler is so drunk that his head keeps nodding down towards the wheel. Every few minutes some crisis – a milk cart, a turning cab – is narrowly avoided. Jonathan is surprised they even make it out of the city.

'They all bloody hate me,' Gertler is saying, somewhere in Essex, when they finally run into a tree. Jonathan thinks he may have been unconscious for a few seconds, or a minute, but when he opens his eyes Gertler is still talking, as if nothing has happened. 'They all – why do you think they do it?' he asks. The windscreen has shattered, and he has a cut on his forehead, a trickle of blood running down into his left eye. The front bumper of the Wolseley is battered, but somehow the engine is still running and they are more or less unhurt. A few minutes later, apart from the wind blowing through the empty windscreen frame and the dried blood on Gertler's face, it might as well have been a dream.

When they arrive at Chopham Constable, the man at the Services, dressed in his church clothes, looks at them astonished. Two smashed-up haggard boys. Walking wounded. They leave the car and skirt the crumbling wall of the school grounds, looking for a place to climb up. Sunday morning in the country. Birds at amplified volume like a very high-pitched jazz band. Jonathan is halfway over the wall when he sees a figure watching them from the trees. The cherubic face is unmistakable. Framed by auburn curls, pricked by sly calculating eyes: Waller, the House Tart.

As Gertler lands beside him, grunting and falling to one side, Jonathan points. Waller sees he has been spotted and dives behind a bush. Flicker of running boy between tree trunks. Gertler starts after him, swearing. Aghast, Jonathan watches as he catches the smaller boy and knocks him down. Bad idea. Such a bad idea. Waller is a special protégé of Fender-Greene and

Gertler is laying into him, really losing control. Waller wriggles about in earth and leaf-muck, spitting, snarling *I'll get you I'll get you*, as Gertler kneels on his chest, punching his face. Jonathan runs up and pulls him away. They watch Waller stumbling towards the school, handkerchief to his bloody nose. Then they turn on one another, each accusing the other of fouling things up. Side by side, not speaking, they trudge through the grounds back to the house.

Sure enough, trouble is not long in coming. At lunch-time a fag appears in their study, summoning them to a meeting with Fender-Greene. He receives them in state, a new waistcoat and an ostentatious gold watch demonstrating the seriousness of the occasion. Fortunately, though he has his suspicions, all he can prove is that they have broken bounds. There is the question of bullying. 'Somehow typical of you, Gertler. Somehow *unchristian.*' Jonathan is apologetic, Paul cold. Loss of privileges, a caning, and the matter appears to have been resolved. That is, however, all on the surface. Jonathan knows they have hurt one of Fender-Greene's special little lushers, the boys who do personal things for him, and do them the way he likes them done. And Waller is no ordinary lusher, being the Theda Bara of School House, a poisonous and exotic plant who has already caused the expulsion of two senior boys, and is only tolerated because of the patronage of Fender-Greene and the existence of the Waller Cup for Services to House Drama, recently (and hurriedly) donated by his father.

Waller is a dangerous enemy and, in conjunction with Fender-Greene, cannot be underestimated. Yet though Jonathan tries to make this clear to Gertler, his warnings are ignored. Paul seems to feel he has nothing left to lose. He stops doing schoolwork, refuses to wear a tie and spends the next few days pacing the study talking about the steppes, vodka and the downfall of the plutocracy, jumbling Russia and Communism together until they merge into one thing, a free country of the mind where he can be away from the frost and school and Fender-Greene. He has never been to Russia. He would go tomorrow, if he could. Jonathan listens quietly, and gradually withdraws into himself. At least one of them ought to be on guard.

Fender-Greene's first move comes a couple of mornings later, as Jonathan shivers in the bathing-house, standing under one of the backbone-building dribbles of cold water that passes for a shower. Thinking himself alone, he is surprised to hear some-one at the next showerhead along. He turns to see Waller, materialized out of nowhere, soaping a large erection and pouting at him lasciviously. As Jonathan blinks water out of his eyes, Waller steps closer, reaching out as if to kiss him. Though he is half asleep, Jonathan moves quickly, pushing the other boy aside and grabbing a towel – just in time to see Hoggart burst in, followed by a pair of prefects. The whole thing has obviously been set up, and Hoggart is clearly disappointed to find Bridge-man and Waller on opposite sides of the room. Still, he delivers a lecture on Immorality! Continence! Sin! wagging a finger in Jonathan's face and blasting him with his rank-smelling breath. 'There is something wrong with you, Bridgeman, whatever Dr Noble says. Something sick.'

Gertler lasts three more days. That Saturday, a few minutes before lunch, Jonathan bowls into the study to find him ashen-faced, kneeling by his trunk, flanked by two of Fender-Greene's lieutenants. He is packing his bust of Lenin on top of a jumble of clothes and papers.

'You should check your stuff, Bridgeman,' says Porter, the taller of the two prefects, who has a waistcoat and moustache modelled on that of his glorious leader, 'in case the bloody yid's made off with it.'

Jonathan looks at Gertler, who shrugs.

'Go on. Check it, if you like.'

'Don't be an idiot.'

Gertler's eyes are red. It looks as if he has been crying.

'Your loss,' butts in Porter. Manning, standing by the window, snorts with laughter.

'They say I stole a five-pound note from Waller's pocket book,' Gertler murmurs.

'We don't *say* anything,' sneers Manning. 'We found the bloody thing on you. Bloody thief.'

'What's going to happen?'

'It's already happened. Briggs is driving me to the station to catch the four o'clock train.'

'I'll help you. I'll go and see Dr Noble.'

Gertler looks infinitely tired. 'It won't do any good,' he says.

Jonathan insists. Full of determination he sets off for Dr Noble's lodgings, but on the way something happens. He finds himself slowing down, hesitating. Perhaps, he thinks, he is being unwise. Perhaps Gertler relishes being an outsider . He certainly wears his Communism like a badge. His family has money. Surely nothing too bad will happen to him. Jonathan does not want to do anything to draw attention to himself. He should be blending in with the background, not sticking his neck out for no reason. After waiting a suitable time, he heads back and tells Gertler that Dr Noble would not change his mind.

'Thanks for trying, Johnny,' says Gertler. 'I won't forget it.' He gives Jonathan his father's address, and Jonathan promises to write, although he already knows (a knowledge growing like a sick feeling in his stomach) that he will not. They are travelling in opposite directions, he and Paul; one breaking out, the other tunnelling in. At half past three they stand by the pony trap, as Briggs harnesses the fractious old horse.

'Goodbye,' says Gertler.

'Look, Paul,' starts Jonathan. He wants to tell him about himself, to give him something true to go away with. But it is too complex even to begin. 'Good luck,' he ends lamely. They shake hands.

'Give my regards to Oxford. Tell them I'm coming to burn it down.'

With that Paul Gertler is driven away. Jonathan goes back to his study and stares at the cleared desk, the half-empty bookshelf. He has rarely felt so lonely.

'The orchidae,' says Dr Noble, 'can take many forms.' A week has elapsed since Gertler's expulsion, and he is twining strands of wire over a wooden block to make a perch for a new epiphyte. 'They can also appear to be many things. Their folk names reflect this, based as they often are on a perceived resemblance, a connection between the flower and some other aspect of nature. I am thinking for example of the Dove Orchid, the Tiger Orchid, the charming Birds-in-Flight orchid, the various Slipper Orchids, and particularly of *Aceras anthropophorum*, the so-called Man Orchid, with its clusters of little yellow blooms that are so unavoidably reminiscent of the human body. Rather like the root of the mandrake, I suppose, though I am not aware of similar superstitions attaching themselves to this species.'

Jonathan passes him a pair of secateurs.

'On the other hand, some orchids are actively deceitful. The Bucket Orchids entice insects with attractive sexual scents, trap them and only release them when they are freighted with pollen. The little fly's desire is cruelly manipulated for the flower's own purposes. Decadent and beautiful. And yet above them all we have you, my dear, so elegant and yet so debauched.'

Jonathan hears a dull shattering sound. Somehow he has knocked a flowerpot on to the wooden floor.

'Clumsy, Bridgeman,' says Noble, shaking his head. Jonathan goes down on his knees to pick up the shards of pot. As he scrabbles about by Noble's worn brown Oxfords, he realizes the speech was addressed to the little terrestrial in the planter in front of them, whose bright petals are variegated yellow and red.

'*Ophrys apifera*, commonly known as the Bee Orchid. Yes, my darling. Of course I mean you. With your exact picture of a receptive female bee, your enticing perfume. Good enough to fool the poor lovelorn worker. Good enough to draw him in.'

Noble bends down from the little flower to watch Jonathan on the floor.

'We are not born, Mr Bridgeman. We are made. I, for example, did not always feel myself possessed of a pedagogical destiny. I was one of the generation of ninety – hothouse flowers all of us. We lived for artificial paradises, the exotic, the bizarre. Yet, when it became clear that my picture of myself as an aesthete would not wash, I entered the classroom. So here I am, Mr Bridgeman. Here I am.'

He turns his attention back to the Bee Orchid, stroking the flower's lush mock-insect lower lip with rapt affection.

'Why strive for naturalism? That was our question. True art should never deny itself. Now, Bridgeman, Mr Hoggart has indicated to me that he is not happy to have you in his house. He believes that you and Paul Gertler exert a debilitating effect. What do you have to say to that?'

'Sir? I haven't done anything. Neither did Paul.'

'*Nor had* Paul. Gertler is gone, Bridgeman. He will perhaps find a more suitable place somewhere else. And as for not doing anything, that may be precisely the problem. Inaction breeds all manner of evils. When we have time to contemplate, we are at our most vulnerable. You are an interesting case, Bridgeman. At least I find you so. Mr Hoggart obviously disagrees. However, you must try to conceal certain things, and work harder at fitting in.'

'I –'

'I suggest cricket. And that is what I shall tell Mr Hoggart.

Now that your university place has been secured, your immediate purpose at Chopham Hall is achieved. None the less, this is not a time for self-congratulation. For your own good, your attention must still be held. Otherwise you run risks, Bridgeman. Terrible risks. Excessive inwardness. Sloth. This, you will understand, is a common problem, and one to which the English public-school system has over several centuries evolved a solution. Cricket is that solution, Bridgeman. You must turn your attention to bat and ball. Every aspect of cricket proves it a marvellous game: its formal rigour; its extended duration; the reduced colour-palette which presents us with a green and white world centred around a darting red dot. A stroke of genius, that, Bridgeman, proof of a higher intelligence! Cricket is a relic of a slower age, an age exquisitely tuned to the vibrations of the higher planes, an age which allowed itself leisure to contemplate the quiddity of time and space. Cricket, in its complexity, in its ornamental quality, might be termed the last flowering of the Baroque. What could be more elevating? A game like – like a perfect automaton, yet an automaton somehow infused with spirit. A game which refers both player and spectator outside themselves, harkening out beyond the veil of gross matter to the music of the spheres. What could be more beautiful? It is life itself!'

He sighs, and falls silent, letting his head rest on his hands. After a while he begins to weep gently on to the workbench. Jonathan watches him, shuffling his feet. Best leave, he thinks, and tiptoes out. Dr Noble obviously has things to consider.

For a game so gentle, cricket has a disastrous effect. As Jonathan walks out on to the field on the first sunny day of term, his eyes stream and his nose leaks a fine colourless mucus. Both are soon red from rubbing, and the sleeves of his white shirt slimy and wet. The whole afternoon is torture. It is impossible to concentrate on the game, which appears to be taking place some miles away through the watery haze. Placed in the outfield he has nothing to do but feel sorry for himself, and when, some hours later, he is called to the crease to bat, the first ball hits his stumps almost without him noticing, so wrapped up is he in his own wretchedness. As he walks back to the pavilion, the opposing team give him a desultory round of applause, kicking their boots together and smirking.

Hayfever is an entirely new experience. It comes as a shock, as if the English countryside is taking revenge, making some point about people who belong, and people who may pretend but whose bodies betray them. As term progresses he starts to dread Saturday games afternoons, reduced to hiding indoors with a book, feigning hand injuries or (India is helpful for this) sudden touches of fever. Naturally his performance on the field is dreadful, and there is never any danger of him being picked for a team.

Cricket is necessary but cricket is impossible. Impasse. The Gordian knot is sliced by Fox the historian.

'A scribe, Bridgeman. A monk in the scriptorium. You shall be the keeper of memory.'

So Jonathan becomes scorer, sitting on the pavilion steps with a log book across his lap and a pile of metal number-plates by his feet. When he is left on his own the allergy mysteriously lessens, and he even starts to enjoy himself. Marking the progress of a game is a kind of meditation. He feels as if he has found his place in the cricketing world. Neither inside nor outside, participant nor uninvolved spectator, he becomes a minor recording god, observing the actions of others with dispassionate concentration, marking them down as dots or little figures in his oblong-gridded book. Not taking sides, he views the affairs of men at a distance, noting the manner of their passing – stumped, run out, caught behind – their victorious sixes and fours, joining the six domino dots of a perfectly bowled over into a single M or W.

Ball by ball, the summer term heads towards a conclusion. Besides the big score book, there is still his own recording. The first pocket book is filled up and a second started, with entries on *Victoria sponge, bumble bee, fair play* and *groundsman*. Sometimes the two marking processes seem to refer to each other, the secret decoding of the world and the distant observation of politely warring cricketers. They combine to suggest a grammar of behaviour, a social language which might be written down and read off again, one day in the far future allowing Chopham Hall to be reconstructed from traced patterns of dots and figures.

Sometimes Jonathan thinks of Paul. He has not written since his expulsion. Jonathan considers asking Dr Noble for his address, but does not. He tells himself that it would reflect badly, which is true, but this is not the real reason. He feels he failed his friend. By not defending him. By not telling him the truth.

This feeling is made worse one night, when Fender-Greene knocks on his study door. Jonathan hears him before he comes. The tell-tale squealings and bangings of a lusher being chased round the junior prep room float up through the floor, followed by a heavy lumbering climb. Fender-Greene is obviously drunk. He lurches into the study like a sleep-walker, one side of his shirt hanging over his trousers in a wrinkled white curtain.

'Johnny? There you are, Johnny.'

'What do you want?'

'Johnny. There you are. No hard feelings Johnny-*boy*. Not between you and me.'

Jonathan says nothing.

'No hard feelings, Johnny-boy. You're a lovely fellow. And you like me, really, don't you? You like me.' He leans heavily on the mantelpiece for support.

'Look here, Bridgeman. Come over here. You're a lovely fellow. You always look so lovely.'

'Stay away from me.'

'You're so lovely.'

'Piss off, Fender-Greene.'

Fender-Greene takes a step forward, then sees the look in Jonathan's eyes. He hesitates for a moment, swaying backwards and forwards on the hearthrug.

'I'll do you yet,' he says. 'I'm going to be up at Christ Church next year.' Then he lurches back out of the door.

On Founders Day, the last day of term, Jonathan walks on the lawn between two and four and is not shouted at. Boys and parents mingle with one another, clinking teacups and mentally ranking each other in order of precedence. Mrs Dodd marshals her girls to and from the kitchen, carrying large plates of cucumber sandwiches, while a fifth-form string quartet saw up Mozart under a striped awning. Since Mr Spavin is not in attendance, Jonathan can wander through the crowd alone, enjoying the feeling of loosening bonds, of Chopham Hall slipping away from him brick by brick. Around him floats a shimmer of barbed conversation, Though Dr Noble stands on a podium and makes a speech about *long roads* and *example*, Jonathan does not feel the need to take notes. These are things he now understands, which have worked underneath his skin. Instead he slips away and stands alone in the hall, hands (defiantly, illegally) in pockets, idly examining the faded photographs lined in rows along the oak-panelled front corridor. Old school teams, their backs straight and arms folded, the chosen ones of rugby, association football, athletics and cricket, stretching back into distant sepia time. Rugby, association football, athletics – *cricket*. There in 1893. There, tall and hulking in his whites, face like a roughly split half brick, is *F.M.V. Bridgeman*. Father of. Hurriedly, he walks away, and so does not see, standing slight and school-uniformed beside eleven white-clad figures, a pale boy with a large leather-bound book. According to the legend he is *R.A. Forrester, scorer.* If you were to look closely, you would see that his eyes are misty with hayfever.

Bridgeman, J. P. (Barab.)

◼ *His father was in the – I think it was the Colonial Service. Wants to follow in his footsteps apparently, although how fooling around with a lot of – well, you know I don't want to speak ill of theatricals, but Midsummer Night's Dream is hardly the stuff that built the Empire, now is it? Oh of course you disagree. How could I have – yes, absolutely, the English character, absolutely – yes, yes I walked straight into it, but all the same I must say it's not as though we sent Shakespeare over to civilize the benighted Hindoo. In a sense, perhaps yes. But no. No! Now really, Willoughby, I think you're being deliberately obtuse . . .*

Harold says he's gorgeous. Yes, in a kind of Italianate way. Sort of marmoreal. Mmmm. Where? Oh, Christ Church meadow. He was leaning out of the window of his set and the fellow came past – sort of floated – practically oneiric, says Harold . . .

Sound? Sound enough, but he comes from nowhere. Who told you that? Beaumont's people are from that part of the world. Your country's near Lechlade, isn't it, Boomer? If he was anyone at all Boomer would know him. And you don't, do you? So I vote no. Just on – on prophylactic grounds. I think that's fair. Speaking honestly, I don't think he's the Satyricon type. After all the dinners do get rather – yes exactly. When one is in one's cups, one doesn't want just anyone – I mean, if things were repeated . . .

If you was to ask me I would have to say as how he was a rather sinful young gentleman – although, and fair's fair – clean enough in his habits. Not like some of them on that staircase – you would have thought they was brought up in a pigsty the way they behave. Couldn't lift a finger by their selves, nor to put a jacket on a hanger nor a cup and saucer on a tray. The mess which that young Honourable makes – not as I'm saying he's not polite, mind you – manners of an angel – but I went in once and – sinful? Well, you don't do for the young gents for as long nor I have without getting to know the signs. I think as you should be asking that little red-haired baggage that helps Mrs Parker in the kitchens – how? You can smell it on the sheets. And once . . .

A good-enough historian. So yes, I think he'll do for Honours. Although I would say rather inclined to romanticize. He has some odd ideas about civilization. Well, Willoughby, racial ideas since you ask – now are you going to pass the Madeira or am I going to have to mount some sort of assault on that decanter? Well, am I?

Actually, FG says he didn't even make the college third eleven. Nor the fifteen. So I can't see that there would be any reason for Jock to bring him into Vincent's. Doesn't even row. Yes, precisely. What would one talk about?

It was too. This big. Shut up, Ethel. It was. Enormous. You don't think I saw it, Ethel Smith, but I did . . .

Yes, dear heart, je vous jure. Cyril and Harold sat up all night writing sestets or something – perhaps it was ottava rima – all about his profile. Yes I have – and I have to say I agree entirely. Delightful. Cyril is going to have him for tea. Mmmm? Oh very droll. And then there's the matter of Harold's new trousers. La-la says they look ridiculous but Harold swears they'll be all the rage by Trinity. Had them run up by the little tailor on the Turl . . .

Sir? Sir?

Shut your eyes. Warm. Try to sink down further.
   Sir?

Sunlight on yellow stone. Watery light filtering through glass. Green angles of a monkey puzzle tree framed in the window.

'Sir? Five and twenty minutes past seven, sir.'

'Oh go away, Willis.'

Musty self-smell rising up from the covers. Faint metallic taste in the mouth. Red wine. Sitting upright will not be pleasant. Willis's disapproval seeps underneath the blanket like a dribble of cold water.

'Might I beg to remind that sir is giving a breakfast this morning? The other young gents will be arriving before long.'

Breakfast?

Hell.

Though it is early summer, Oxford mornings are damp and Mr Bridgeman's tropical upbringing means that he feels the cold. Willis has lit a small fire in the study grate and his charge shuffles over to stand beside it, arms folded bad-temperedly over his dressing gown. The scout makes rattling noises with jugs and bowls of water, and gradually Mr Bridgeman is induced to shave and dress. By five to eight he is seated blearily at the head of a scarred round table that has been covered with a white linen cloth and arrayed with toast racks, teacups and a tall silver pot of coffee.

Ten minutes later the air is blue with pipe smoke and Willis is forking bacon, eggs, breaded lamb chops, sausage and grilled tomatoes on to the plates of a gaggle of young gentlemen, who are engaged in a heated debate about the comparative merits of Middleton and Marlowe as tragedians. These gentlemen are all dressed alike in grey flannel trousers, pale shirts, waistcoats and jackets of light Scottish tweed. Their legs are elegantly crossed. They suck intermittently on their heavy briar pipes, and use them to underscore important points of argument. A casual observer would have some difficulty telling them apart.

The expert, on the other hand, would note certain tell-tale

features that distinguish this group's niche in the ecology of the university. There is the predominance of suede shoes. There is the brightness of the ties, some of which are made of silk. There is also the unusual length of hair, which, in several cases approaches (scandalously, perilously) the collar. Such are the unmistakable marks of the Aesthete. These specimens are not fully fledged, being only first-year students, but later some of the more committed will come into their full plumage, sporting broad-brimmed hats, flowing trousers and jackets of unusual cut and provenance. Statistically at least one is likely to start wearing scent.

Most will, if they persist, have their rooms trashed and their flowing trousers forcibly removed by Athletes. The Athlete is the Aesthete's natural predator. Aestheticism is seen by him as a kind of illness, sign of moral and mental degeneracy. Debagging and room-trashing is a reasonable response to such evidence of decline, a sort of social shot across the bows intended to warn the Aesthete to spend more time on the rugger pitch and less reading Huysmans. Of Bridgeman's friends, only Levine has so far suffered this fate (sketchpad and provocatively yellow socks in Hall), although the crew of the first eight have indicated their willingness to do the same for any Barabbas man who goes too far down the artistic road. It is generally accepted that Extreme Aestheticism, which is to say anything involving black masses, Japanese textiles, pornographic engravings or the bits of Catullus left out of school editions, will inevitably lead to violence. This attitude is covertly encouraged by the senior common room.

Bridgeman knows all this, and is almost paranoid in his care not to lay himself open to trouser-removal. Though his shoes are suede, his hair is short and his silk tie is an acceptably discreet shade of burgundy. These friends, his Aesthete friends, are only one of several groups he cultivates, in a large but highly compart-mentalized range of acquaintance. Today he is giving breakfast

to Levine and the other committee members of the Barabbas
College Players, who have cast him to play Iago in their forthcoming *Othello* – opposite Levine himself, who in black-face will
play the Moor. Tonight, however, he is due to dine at the Union
and tomorrow with some Tory hacks at the Carlton Club.
Yesterday he attended a demonstration of wireless telegraphy,
and last week went along both to Monsieur Émile Coué's lecture
on autosuggestion and Captain McLaglan's ju-jitsu class (as
recommended by the Chief Constable of Oxfordshire) in the
town hall.

Throughout all his varied activities Bridgeman's watchword
is convention. In a place where everyone is clamouring to be
noticed, he is careful to clamour just enough to fit in, but no
more. In this latest version of himself he has been sure to
emphasize everything that is honest, true and English. He is seen
to frown upon novelty, and to deplore the current decline in
social standards. In literature he is a Georgian, and in politics a
Tory. He speaks little of his family, but lets it be known that he
comes of old Gloucestershire farming stock. He is, in every
possible way, the average undergraduate.

Despite this some doors remain closed. Since birth, most of
his peers have been entangled in a web of symbols and relations
so dense and pervasive that they barely notice them. Bridgeman,
on the other hand, knows nobody – and nobody knows him.
This is unusual, even culpable. As the opposite of Being-known,
which (at least in Gloucestershire) is recognized as a kind of
a priori existential condition, Not-being-known implies deceit,
distance and a troubled relationship between self and social
world. There is always the possibility that such a state of Not-
being-known is not necessarily accidental. County folk and their
sons intuitively feel this state as a deep well of trouble, something
obscure and potentially dangerous which exists before language,
and instils in them a kind of primordial dread. So, on the whole,

they prefer to avoid a chap that makes them feel that way. Thus the hunting set of the Bullingdon Club find Bridgeman shifty. He will never wear the pink tails of the Bollinger or the pale blue ones of the Satyricon. His lack of association, his appearance in the world of Oxford so startlingly devoid of connection or anchor, makes a lot of people think twice. Even those who share his colonial background, and understand about India and distance and loneliness, sometimes sense a hidden layer. Worse still, despite a painful summer trying to learn tennis (as well as French, the New Testament, pipe smoking and the names of English birds) Bridgeman arrived at Oxford no Athlete, and has done little about becoming one.

It is a serious omission. Though the university is commonly perceived as an institution dedicated to academic excellence, it is in fact a machine for the formation of character. The difference is subtle. Character is not cleverness. Sports are almost always more effective at forming it than books, and sportsmen (who can do such things as sit a horse, walk slowly towards a machine gun and show a firm hand with natives) have higher status than mere quoters of poetry or enumerators of factors of x. Crumpled behind Bridgeman's sideboard is the current edition of the university magazine, *The Isis*, whose 'Isis Idol' is, as always, a sportsman. 'After spending his formative years climbing trees and rousting poachers in the rolling hills of Shropshire, the irrepressible Gerald Fender-Greene, OUCC, OURFC, OUBC . . . came up from the academic hothouse of Chopham Hall school . . . known to all simply as FG . . . His stylish turn-out . . . prowess instantly recognized . . . plucky innings' etc., etc. This is character writ large. The same issue has a short report of the previous week's Union debate on the motion: This House Believes Americans are Human, which records (passim) the first contribution of J.P. Bridgeman (Barab.) who, 'in responding to Mr Barker's mention of the importance of the League of Nations, treated the House to a long and somewhat otiose statement of the White Man's mission to "farm the world". He should avoid appearing hysterical in the future, and should take care to remain relevant.'

Yes, there is something shrill about Jonathan Bridgeman. Something strained. At the Union, his mouth dry, his fingers unconsciously fluttering around his tight collar, he stood up and began to speak about America, a speech which soon became about the West and then slid into the clash of colour and the tide of racial movement on the shores of humanity and whiteness whiteness whiteness until he realized what he was doing and sat down. Sometimes it just comes out, the guilt. He has to watch for it.

The conversation round his breakfast table slips from drama to the proctor's proposal to ban gramophones on the river, then to the perennial 'Turkish or Virginian?' and the latest rag perpetrated on the undergraduettes, something to do with tying a pig to the back gate of one of the women's colleges. Bridgeman, the host, is included, valued, a part of all these concerns. Yet when the breakfasters drift off, he sits looking at the wreckage of smeared plates and empty cups with a hollow, expressionless face. In the brief minutes before Willis comes in and starts clearing up there is a blankness, a suggestion that Bridgeman, like a forest tree, exists only when being observed. Behind his face, beneath it, there might be something else, but it is inaccessible.

It only lasts a moment.

The figure who appears in the front quad is jaunty and unconcerned. His hands dug deep in his pockets, pipe raffishly slung out of the left-hand corner of his mouth, he saunters over to the Porter's Lodge and leafs through his mail. Nothing important. A reminder of an unpaid battels bill, a notice advertising the formation of a mountaineering society. The only interesting item is a note from the Duce of the Oxford Fascisti, who heard the Union speech and would like to invite the orator to tea. The orator is flattered, and, as he walks down Broad Street on his way to a lecture, he tries to work out whether Fascism is conventional. Some evenings one can see the Oxford group on their way to meetings, showing off their sleek black uniforms. Levine says it is all a conspiracy against laundry. One could make the same collar last for days.

'Look where you're bloody going!'

He has barged into a haggard young man limping out of Trinity, leaning on a walking stick. He mutters an apology and hastens on. Ghost. Oxford has a lot of these characters, the ones who fought the war and came back again. They tend to live as far away from the town centre as the rules allow, and have little to do with the other students, forming a sort of parallel university, brooding and sombre. The two planes intersect, occupy the same space without ever quite touching. Rags and jazz and cocktails. Mud and decayed flesh. Incommensurable.

'Beaver!'

The ghost is dispelled. A fat man with a bushy beard looks round, annoyed. Ragged gowns disappear round the corner, with a faint sound of undergraduate laughter.

He crosses St Giles, smiling. Then, all of a sudden, something rare and significant happens. Like one of those minor celestial bodies whose trajectory requires slide rules and conversion tables to calculate, Jonathan, homeless particle, undergoes a collision. It is an event which changes everything, for ever.

It begins with a bell, and the sound of a chain in need of oil. Turning the corner outside the Ashmolean Museum is a bicycle, and on the bicycle is a girl. Bridgeman steps out of her way, and for a moment she looks him straight in the eye. Blue eyes. His world turns syrupy and slow-flowing. She is wearing a white summer dress, and over it an academic gown. On her head is a wide-brimmed straw hat, with yellow silk flowers around the crown. As she wobbles towards Cornmarket, he confirms that she is beautiful, and a string section materializes in his forebrain, drenching him in grand and stylized emotion. Beneath the hat her cheeks are flushed with the effort of cycling, and as her feet work the pedals the white cotton of her dress stretches with the line of her thighs, taut and slack, taut and slack. Her face is like a doll's face, fine and oval, the features painted on it with immense delicacy. A tress of fine blonde hair tumbles over one eye. Bridgeman stops walking, stares openly. She is Elgar and tea roses. She is rolling green fields with drystone boundary walls, she is willow trees, fruit cup, sunset over – the torrent of metaphor overwhelms him, and he finds himself sucking furiously on his pipe, quite brimming with the aestheticism of it all. The pattern, the type, the very essence of the English girl.

Thoughts of the girl block out the Italian wars. The lecture goes in one ear and out of the other. Alliances are made and broken and cities sacked without leaving a trace on a consciousness entirely devoted to blonde hair and white cotton stretching taut and slack, taut and slack. He considers looking for her. There are only a few women's colleges, and it would not take too long, but the idea brings back bad memories of waiting in the shadows, bowing from behind bushes. He reminds himself that Oxford is a small place, and he is certain to meet her again. Sooner or later.

It happens sooner, on the last night of *Othello*. Every evening for a week, Jonathan has spoken Levine fair and watched him succumb to the green-eyed monster jealousy, before putting out the light of Percy Twigg, a melting, (if broad-shouldered) Desdemona. Though the college authorities denied permission for a real female to take the role, several undergraduettes have managed to sneak into the cast party, giving it a daring, illicit atmosphere. It is held in Levine's set, decorated Venetian-style for the occasion, a look largely created by draping muslin over his battered furniture and placing large bowls of fruit on the sideboard. Levine himself, in order to maximize his tragic effect, is wandering around in costume, slapping his rapier against people's thighs and making them spill their drinks. Full of champagne and artistic triumph, he insists on kissing everyone French-style on both cheeks, leaving large black marks behind him. An owlish boy from Balliol is shouting at Jonathan over the un-Venetian gramophone jazz *you do ha ha do it so well the dissembling part of it quite sent a chill down* – when the door opens and she walks in. As she scans the room, for one illogical, exciting moment Jonathan thinks she is looking for him. Then she rushes forward and throws her arms round Levine.

'Darling!'

'Darling!'

'You were –'

'I know.'

Jonathan disengages himself from the owl and makes his way towards them, intending to force an introduction.

'But really,' the girl is saying, in a loud voice, 'such savage nobility. So visceral.'

Levine simpers, and plays with the pommel of his sword.

'Star, you are too kind.'

Jonathan appears at his friend's shoulder. The girl carries on talking about Levine's performance. She is wearing a pale green gown, and several unusual carved wooden bangles on her arms, which click together when she gestures. Describing Levine's 'generative force' and his 'feel for the Negro soul' she sounds like an abacus, which, to Jonathan, only adds to her charm. Though she is wearing heavy mascara and pistachio eye-shadow, she somehow still manages to look quintessentially English. Beneath a layer of white face-powder, her complexion is pink and healthy. There is nothing washed out about her blonde hair, which pulses with yellow life like a cornfield in September, a rolling, waving field, seen in the warm evening light as the weary harvesters trudge home, their scythes on their backs, whistling, yes, a country air – Jonathan pulls himself out of this mental Wessex and tries to concentrate. Levine, basking in praise, shows no sign of diverting any of it by acknowledging his friend, and finally it becomes apparent that he will have to do the work himself. He sticks out his hand and says hello.

Levine looks annoyed. The girl ticks him off.

'You're very rude, Veenie.'

'Sorry, Star. Jonathan Bridgeman, Astarte Chapel.'

They say how do you do to each other and she smiles encouragingly. Jonathan ventures a question.

'Astarte?'

She sighs, and turns to Levine. 'Why do they always do it?

Levine shakes his head. 'We all have our crosses to bear.'

Jonathan realizes he has done something obscurely wrong.

'Look, Veenie,' she says suddenly, 'got to dash. Flying visit and all – I'm sure the porter will be here in a trice and everyone will end up in frightfully hot water.'

'Absolutely, Star. You must flee, or Jonathan here will start making attempts on your chastity. He's an absolute demon.'

'Is he?'

She arches one eyebrow playfully, kisses Levine goodbye and sweeps out, leaving Jonathan pink-faced, grabbing on to a fading image of pistachio and bootblack smudges on a white cheek.

'That was unfair, Levine.'

'Was it? Sorry.'

'And you never told me you knew anyone like that.'

'Well, I know lots of people. Anyway, you already landed yourself in it. Out for a duck, I'd say.'

'What did I do?'

Levine shrugs. 'She's very sensitive about her name. Everyone asks. Bores her terribly.'

'It is a very strange name.'

'Mmm. Her father's fault. Professor in the anthropology department. Quite mad. The name's the least of it.'

'But what does it mean?'

'Astarte? Oh, something ancient and anthropological. Why don't you look it up?'

Astarte: *Semitic deity. Phoenician goddess of love and fertility. Related to the Babylonian* Ishtar *and the Greek* Aphrodite. *One of a group of ancient mother goddesses notably including* Cybele, Demeter *and* Ceres *(q.v.). In some forms of the cult, a male deity, her lover, is also worshipped. The sacrificial death and resurrection of this masculine partner is taken to symbolize the regenerative cycle of the earth.*

The encyclopedia closes with a thud, and Jonathan replaces it on the library shelf. Just in time for examinations, the sun has come out. The long rows of desks are all occupied, final-year students sweating uncomfortably through their revision. Magnanimously, the librarian has permitted the windows to be opened, and from outside float tantalizing fragments of conversation, each untroubled burst of laughter bringing new pain to the faces of the prisoners inside. Jonathan is relieved that he is free to walk down the stone steps and out into the open air. As he stands in the library quadrangle, clinking his change in his pockets and wondering how to spend the afternoon, a gang of undergraduates runs past him, heading in the direction of the Sheldonian Theatre. On a whim he follows them, and finds himself at the back of a laughing, jostling crowd.

A rag. A lecture has just finished in the Sheldonian, and the attendees have come out to find that someone has carefully picked out all the female students' bicycles and tied wire around the frames, giving each a crude masculine crossbar. The crowd has gathered to watch the spectacle of a dozen embarrassed women trying to untangle the mess and leave as quickly as possible. They whistle and catcall, cheering as one woman gives in and rides off 'as a man'. 'Go on lads!' shout a gaggle of boys in blazers and cricket whites, clinging to each other with the prankish jollity of it all. Jonathan smiles – and, as he does so, realizes that one of the victims is Astarte Chapel. She is kneeling by her bicycle (*the* bicycle), wrestling with it, her face a mask of impotent fury. As if prompted by fate, she looks up and, seeing Jonathan's smirk, gives him a look which suggests that she would be more than happy to kill him and plough his body into the soil to ensure the continuation of the seasons.

Quickly, he tries to marshal his face into a pattern of disapproval, but ends up with an odd twisted rictus, like a snakebite victim whose muscles are in spasm. With hand gestures he tries to show his dissociation from what is happening, making pushing motions to indicate his total rejection of everyone and everything involved in bicycle tampering. With a sinking feeling he realizes he must look deranged, and pushes through the crowd to help her.

'I suppose you think you're terribly amusing,' she spits.

'Honestly,' he splutters, 'I had nothing – I mean it's awful – terrible. Really. It wasn't me –'

'Oh,' she sneers. 'I suppose they made you.'

'But Astarte –'

She is not interested in his explanations. Giving the wire a last tug, she swings a haughty leg over the saddle and wobbles off down the road. Her dress is rucked up over her thighs, and Jonathan watches her depart, his chest a battlefield of mixed emotions. He knows that this spells the end, that she will never forgive him and all his hopes are dashed, but it only makes the sight of her angrily pedalling rear all the more affecting, as if she is receding down Broad Street into another world, lost and for ever out of reach.

Transfixed by these high-flown feelings, he does not notice that a copy of *Les Fleurs du mal* (borrowed from Levine) has fallen out of his jacket pocket.

'What in hell's name do we have here?'

He turns round to find that his bad day is about to get worse. Behind him, at the head of the phalanx of cricketers, is Gerald Fender-Greene. In his hand, pinched between thumb and forefinger like a very smelly rag, is his book.

'Hello FG,' he says warily.

'Foreign muck,' pronounces Fender-Greene. The other cricketers peer to see what he has found.

'Baudelaire,' reads one. There is a pause as the information is processed. Then, the verdict: 'Shirtlifter.'

The gathering takes on a very serious tone. Though Athletes do not take much notice of books, especially the subversive and morally undermining kind favoured by Aesthetes, the name of Baudelaire is infamous enough to have made an impression. Jonathan starts to wish he had chosen another prop for this afternoon's Aesthetic tea.

'And,' says Fender-Greene, as if pronouncing a death sentence, 'you were sucking up.'

'Sucking up?'

'To that – girl.' He says it with all the venom that a manly man, a man whose thighs will always be snugly encased in trousers, can feel for a person around whose bare legs air freely circulates. There is a pause, and suddenly a dozen eyes are fastened on the narrow leather belt which holds Jonathan's own lower garments to his unworthy, poetry-reading, sexually dubious body. The same thought occurs to batsman and bowler alike: if a chap will insist on being effeminate, with his Frenchie books and pretty girlfriends, by what right does he wear such flannel symbols of manhood? There is an imbalance. It must be rectified.

'Debag him!'

Does the shout go up first, or does Jonathan anticipate it? Either way, he makes a sprint start worthy of an athletic blue, tearing off down Broad Street before the first eleven even realize he is gone. They come after him, yelling incoherently, waving bats and pads over their heads like regimental colours. Passers-by duck out of their way, recognizing a war party when they see one. Jonathan heads down the Turl, weaving between startled shoppers, and elbowing a decrepit classics don into a tailor's doorway. The old fellow picks himself up, cursing eloquently in demotic Latin, only to be sent flying by the horde of cricketers, his satchel of unseen translations and bicycle clips exploding messily over the cobbles. Soon two University Bulldogs, ex-army men with bowler hats and evil tempers, are in hot pursuit of the miscreants, puffing red-faced behind them. They are followed by a number of tag-along undergraduates, keen to see blood. Jonathan crosses the high street without breaking stride, narrowly dodging a cab and a milk cart. He snatches a glance behind, and sees that the cricketers, who train hard for just this sort of occasion, are steadily gaining ground. Pink and yelling, they look like a gang of large psychotic babies, the terrifying simplicity of their will-to-debag erasing everything else from their faces. Jonathan realizes they are going to catch him. He is about to endure the ultimate humiliation. He does not stand a chance.

But fate, who is chronically indecisive today, flips things round again. Ahead, like a mirage, her bicycle divested of wire with the help of a passing clergyman, is Astarte Chapel.

'Come on, Johnny-boy! Hop on!'

He cannot believe it, but if his life has taught him one thing, it is that belief is optional. He straddles her back wheel and a moment later is accelerating away from his pursuers, arms round the object of his desire, transported down the high street in a glorious, heavenly backie.

Later, when he is wiser to the ways of Miss Astarte Chapel, he will begin to detect a pattern in the day's events. Outwardly the combination of vitriol and charity defies explanation. Is she angry? Forgiving? Indifferent? These are hard questions to answer – and this difficulty is perhaps the point, at least as far as Astarte herself is concerned. She believes in keeping boys guessing. Relations with her are composed of a series of dyads, positive and negative held together by a strong bond, as if one attracts the other through some yet-to-be-analysed physical force. If she lets you hold her hand, two hours later she will slap your face. If she swears never to talk to you again, she is guaranteed to arrive on your doorstep the next afternoon, dressed for a picnic. Thus, after Jonathan laughed at her, she naturally made up her mind to rescue him, and to allow him to take her to tea.

Like any well-brought-up English girl, Astarte has been taught to rate qualities like asset liquidity and breeding over mere attractiveness. Still, Jonathan's looks are pleasing to her. Also his aestheticism, for Astarte is that quasi-mythical thing, dreamt of by every sleepless undergraduate painter and poet – the artistic beauty. Jonathan discovers this over tea, a ritual in which, like much else about her life, Astarte manages to be both strenuously bohemian and utterly English. She must have the table with the view. She does not take milk. She says in a loud voice that she would much rather be in Paris, drinking a tisane. Then she puts a scone daintily in her mouth, and says, 'Scrumptious,' looking like a little girl in a Pears soap advertisement. She and Jonathan talk about important things, or rather she talks and Jonathan watches her lips move. For most of an hour he rests his chin on his hands and agrees wordlessly with whatever she says, trying not to drift off into violin-section fantasies inspired by her eyes, or hair, or the crumbs caught at the corner of her mouth.

Paris features heavily in Astarte's conversation. Her father is keen for her to be cosmopolitan, a quality neglected in the traditional English system of education. When it comes to cosmo-politanism, Paris is the world centre, and this year she will be spending the entire summer there. She has been before, of course, but not for an entire summer. Paris, Jonathan learns, is a place with élan, ésprit and several other things which have to do with energy and vital force. The key to life is to remain in contact with this force, which is dissipated by contemporary existence. Modern man is degenerate (because of train travel and illustrated papers), and renewing the vital force has taken on a special urgency. Seen in this light, spending the summer in Paris is a particularly worthy thing to do. Astarte calls all this her aesthetic. Jonathan has never met a girl with her own aesthetic before.

Everyone calls her Star. Jonathan calls her Star. She likes to shock, but what shocks him is not the pistachio, or the bangles (from the Fotse people of Africa, a present from her father), but her ideas about European degeneracy. He cannot understand how someone who looks like her could feel that way.

'But aren't you – aren't we a civilizing influence on other races?'

'Oh silly Johnny, civilization is the problem! It's stifling us! We've forgotten how to feel. We've – you know – lost contact with the earth. We should tear it all down and go back to our primitive emotional selves, running naked on the sands of life!'

There turns out to be a place on the Côte d'Azur where one can go to do this. Star has never been to the Côte d'Azur herself, but Edie's older brother Freddie is living in a peasant's hut there. Actually it is several huts converted into a villa, but done in a very rustic and primitive style. Edie went down and ran naked last summer with one of Freddie's friends, and Jonathan has to promise not to tell Edie's parents, who are very stifling when it comes to primitivism. Jonathan promises, which is easy enough, since he does not know any of the people she is talking about.

Then, as suddenly as she arrived in his day, Star leaves. He is trying to say how sorry he is about the bicycles, when she kisses him on both cheeks, says have a nice summer, and sweeps out of the tearoom, the little bell above the door jangling behind her. He wonders if he did something wrong, but cannot think of anything. She did not seem upset. She seemed happy. He walks back to college, feeling dazed but elated. About halfway he remembers the cricketers, and speeds up, not slowing down until he is in his rooms.

The next day he walks over to Star's college to leave her a note. When he hands it to the porter, he is told that Miss Chapel has gone down for the long vacation, and is not expected back in Oxford until September. The news brings on a strange crisis. He stands outside the gate feeling stricken and cheated. Star has given him a glimpse of something, and immediately taken it away again. He trudges back to Barabbas and sits forlornly in the garden, watching the college tortoise make a stately progress across the lawn. That night he has a nightmare about the cricketers. They have multiplied a hundredfold, legions of whiteflannelled men hunting him down through the streets. The vision is extraordinarily clear, and comes back for several nights afterwards, running in his brain like a horrific cinema reel. It lingers during the day, and he finds himself staying in his rooms, afraid of meeting Fender-Greene in the street. Finally, feeling that the old stone walls are about to crush him, he takes the train to London and spends a weekend awake, flitting between pubs and nightclubs in a haze of alcohol. Though he starts off in the West End, he is pulled steadily east and south, and finishes the evening under a table in an establishment called the Fishy Mitten, located in an alley near the East India Docks. There, at last, he experiences a blessed, dreamless sleep.

A week later his trunk is loaded on to a London train, and a boring summer vac begins. Mr Spavin is concerned about

Jonathan's future plans, and thinks it would be best if he had a taste of the world of work. Working in Paris, a suggestion of Jonathan's, is dismissed as impractical. His arguments about combating the degeneracy of European man carry no weight. What is the boy to do? He has announced that he no longer wishes to go into the Colonial Service. He does not appear to be suited to the military. The answer is clearly the law. Legal experience is what he needs, and it so happens that the firm of Spavin & Muskett are in need of clerical assistance. What could be more simple?

Buried alive in ledgers, Jonathan's days pass painfully slowly. As he carries files from one room to another, in his mind he is running naked on the Côte d'Azur. He shudders to think what Star would make of Spavin & Muskett: civilization at its worst. The other juniors are wan shadows who talk about either football or money. With their florid complexions and unvarying routines, the two partners seem devoid of anything resembling a powerful emotion. Jonathan scrutinizes them, hoping to unearth at least one visceral urge: he finds none. Mr Muskett occasionally shouts at the typists, but that seems to be due to rich food and lack of physical exercise, rather than any uprush of Nordic soulfulness. July turns into August. Fat bumble bees knock against the dirty windows, and the law gradually drains him of life, until even his skin seems to be yellowing, turning the colour of land deeds and testaments.

One afternoon, young Muskett floats through the office, dressed, as usual, in tennis clothes. Turning his profile to its best advantage, he rocks on his heels and describes a wonderful motoring holiday. 'Bombing around Cornwall' is how he puts it. Bombing around Cornwall in a friend's Wolseley. He is only passing through London, which is awful in the heat. He doesn't know how Bridgeman stands it. Luckily he is not going to have to stand it long himself, for tomorrow he is on his way to a house party on the Côte d'Azur. Jonathan's tortured expression gives him away. Poor Bridgeman, Muskett laughs. Poor inky-fingered Bridgeman, working for Pater all summer. Better luck next time, old chap.

After that, the offices of Spavin & Muskett feel like a living hell. Jonathan walks around in a cloud of jealousy, tormented by visions of Star and Muskett coming to terms with their primitive selves in the second-most-important part of France. One of the typists tries to help him, taking him to the stationery cupboard and pointing out that there is no evidence the two even know each other. Despite her best efforts, he is inconsolable. By the time term starts again he has developed his suspicions into a three-reel orgy, in which the two are lovers, rolling around on a silver strand in the throes of gymnastic, highly financed passion.

When Jonathan goes back up to Oxford, everything has changed – or stayed the same, it is hard to tell. Rudolph Valentino is still on at the George Street Cinema, but in a different film. The 'beaver' craze is over and bearded men can walk the streets without fear of ridicule. Someone has set a fashion for wearing jumpers. An enterprising self-publicist has hired a bus to drive round the town centre with his name painted on the side. There are new faces, nervous young men who ask directions to places they are standing in front of, but they look exactly like the old faces they have replaced.

Jonathan listens to stories of walking tours in the Bernese Oberland, and visits to churches in Italy. Someone has been sailing in the Caribbean. Someone else has been to New York. He does not admit he has been working in an office, preferring to hint that he has been caught up in a whirl of mysterious and fashionable London parties. He does not think he sounds convincing. On the third day of term, as he is returning from a bookshop with a manual on mah-jong under his arm, he spots Astarte Chapel, cycling down the high street dressed entirely in pale yellow. He calls after her. She turns round, and waves hesitantly.

'Star, you're back!'

'Of course, chéri. As you see.'

Over the summer she has acquired a very odd accent. Her cloud of hair is gone, chopped down into a severe, geometrical bob. She is marvellously coordinated. Even her shoes are pale yellow.

'How wonderful. Did you have a good time?'

She sighs and rolls her eyes, as if to show the impossibility of verbally encompassing the joy of the previous three months. The unwelcome image of young Muskett springs to Jonathan's mind.

'Did you stay in Paris?'

'Oui, chéri.' She laughs musically. 'I'm so sorry. I'm out of the habit of speaking English. Yes, I did. It was divine.'

'You didn't go to the south?'

'Oh, I did – for a couple of weeks. I stayed with Freddie.'

'Oh.' Jonathan's mind renders a quick pastel impression of her in ambulatory seaside nudity, which he instantly smudges out. She looks around impatiently, as if scanning for other people to greet. Then she sighs.

'So, chéri, are you coming?'

'Coming where?'

'To my father's lecture. He's talking about his Africans.'

Of course Jonathan is coming. He walks beside her as she wheels her bike along the pavement. They talk about Professor Chapel's work with the Fotse, who live in a remote and inaccessible part of West Africa

'They must be wonderfully primitive.'

'Yes, it's a shame, the poor dears. Most of them don't even wear clothes, unless they're going out. Just a lot of beads and these rather lovely bangles.' She waves her arms, which make the clicking sound he loves so well.

'But – I thought you were in favour of primitivism.'

'You are a strange boy! The Fotse are savages! I mean, they've never even seen a bath. Daddy has to take a collapsible one whenever he visits them. Of course, they treat him like a great chief. It's very impressive, apparently . . .'

The topic of Professor Chapel's high Fotse social status lasts them until they reach the lecture hall. The Professor is obviously a popular speaker, for the place is packed with serious young anthropologists, jostling each other, squatting in the aisles and perching on the windowsills. Star's entrance is spectacular, unleashing a flurry of greetings and jealous looks directed at Jonathan. He sits down beside her in the front row, in a chair vacated by a ruefully grinning young don, and for a moment feels life is paying him back for his summer of Spavin & Muskett. As settles himself, crossing one leg over the other and straightening the seams of his trousers, he sneaks glances at Star. Her eyes are outlined in heavy Tutankhamun black, and she looks even more aesthetic than he remembered, somehow more sophisticated and knowing. He tries not to think about anywhere in France south of the Midi.

Jonathan is engaged in a painful reverie about the Cap d'Antibes when the door swings open and Professor Chapel strides through the audience to the front of the hall. Star waves and mouths, 'Hello, Daddy.' The Professor is an impressive ox-like man, not tall but heavy, a full chest and belly swelling beneath his rumpled tweed suit. The head on top is a large slab, the features on it solid and defined. He greets his daughter with a paternal smile, and squints fiercely at Jonathan, trying to place him. Then he shuffles around, hunting in his briefcase for his notes and, finding them at last with a loud 'Aha!', takes out a comb, drags a few white-blond hairs over his balding head, drums his fingers on the lectern, and begins.

The social customs of the Fotse, he explains, are both complex and opaque. They herd goats in a dry and mountainous region, and because their lands are located away from traditional trade routes they have largely been left alone by the wider world. They remain, he states with an air of satisfaction, almost pristine. The Fotse live apart from one another in homesteads consisting of conical huts, each main living space surrounded by smaller granaries and storerooms. The clusters of pointed roofs give their dwellings the appearance of mud and thatch Loire chateaux. The Professor has made three tours to the Fotse country, and each time has found these forms very pleasing. Around a Fotse habitation is invariably found an area of cultivated millet, a much larger area of pasturage and a fortified compound into which the goats, the main source of Fotse wealth, are herded at night.

Fotse descent is traced matrilineally, inheritances passing to a young warrior through his mother's brothers. Depending on a kinsman's membership of one of the four men's societies (which play a murky but important role in Fotse culture), land or goats may also be passed between men who are not blood relations. On occasion inheritances may also come through the father's younger sister, though it is not yet known under what circumstances this takes place, and it is possible that the information was an example of Fotse humour, at the expense of the fieldworker who gathered it.

The Professor is at pains to emphasize that his account is a simplification. Despite extensive study, Fotse inheritance practices remain almost impossible to untangle. The problem lies in the concept of 'Fo', which is crucial to any understanding of the Fotse world-picture. Indeed the very word 'Fotse' is a conjunction of 'Fo' and 'Tse', 'the people who speak / make / do Fo'. Though the Fotse also use the word 'Fo' to name their language, it commonly refers to a process of bartering and negotiation which takes place after a death.

By custom the goats, land and possessions of a dead Fotse are divided between as many as twelve near-relatives. The process of division is taken very seriously, and shares (allocated in proportions laid down by the Fotse ancestors) must be exact. This means that beneficiaries often find themselves in possession of abstract quantities, like three-quarters of a bull or a third of a wife. Over the centuries, Fotse land, and especially the land on which homesteads are built, has been subdivided so many times that individual plots may be no more than two or three square feet in size. The same is true of most other goods and services. The custom of Fo involves the aggregation of these tiny amounts into useful quantities – whole wives, ploughable fields and so on – through the practice of barter. Since beneficiaries of a dead Fotse may themselves have an obligation to share Fo proceeds with their own relatives, who themselves have a set of Fo obligations, these negotiations become fiendishly complex, a complexity further increased by the Fotse's love of speculation.

During the time of Fo (which in practice is continuous, since most Fo legacies take more than a year to resolve, and individual Fotse are usually involved in several parallel Fo negotiations) it is permissable to initiate 'Gofo' – 'on' or 'upward' Fo. This is a system of betting on future Fo outcomes, and making promises to swap a certain plot of land or number of goats if a certain Fo bequest takes place. If a Fotse believes that three rainy seasons in the future his neighbour may inherit a plot of land in which he is interested, he may undertake to swap a fixed or variable number of goats (or abstract goat parts, or their equivalent in trade goods) for that plot, perhaps with the proviso that there has been a high (or low) millet yield, or that another Fo trans-action does not obligate him to give up the plot with which he intends to aggregate the plot that is the object of the Gofo transaction.

Gofo promises can themselves be bartered, and it is usually through aggregation of promises, rather than through the goods themselves, that Fotse fortunes are made. In Fotse legend, the trickster-hero Lifi is so clever at manipulating Gofo transactions that he frequently finds himself in possession of the entire Fotse herd and lands, though he usually loses them again through his fondness for millet beer. The substance of a major song cycle (which takes Fotse bards up to three weeks to recite in full) is the enumeration of the canny transactions through which Lifi wins the hand of the sky-princess Neshdaqa by leveraging a minuscule holding in her uncle's favourite speckled heifer. Fo obligations are recorded on beaded necklaces, different colours and types of bead representing different states of affairs, the exact patterns varying subtly from district to district. As a result, the Fotse make a colourful spectacle, especially at funerals.

Professor Chapel believes that Fo is the reason the primitive Fotse have made so little technological and social progress. Fo negotiations are so time-consuming that they push most other considerations out of the way. The complete absence of a concept of utility in Fotse culture means that the tribe's eventual extinction is, in his opinion, unavoidable. He drifts into a description of Fotse marriage ceremonies (marriage being conceptualized by the Fotse as merely a sub-form of Gofo), and Jonathan sneaks a look at Star, who appears to have fallen asleep.

The Professor's mind is elsewhere too. He has given his 'General Introduction to the Social Organization of the Fotse' dozens of times before, and, as he delivers the words written on his yellowing typescript, he is far away, exploring a pleasurable chain of mental associations which stretches back to his days as a young lecturer, heroic times before the discipline of anthropology had fully emerged from its chrysalis. At certain points in his speech, images arise that have nothing to do with the Fotse or their customs. They are memories, sensations triggered by the repetition of the familiar words like stored electric charge released from a battery. They are vivid, immediate and oddly compulsive; when they take place, the Professor has a squirming sensation inside, which he rather likes.

Psychology has never been one of Henry Chapel's interests, but if it were, he might be tempted to look to his childhood for an explanation. The kind of baby who would drop his rattle out of his pram a hundred times in a row, he took the same pleasure each time his nanny picked it up and gave it back. The rattle's return produced a charge of happiness, the thrill of the predictable, the controlled. Later there were sewing boxes tipped out and reorganized, all the blue buttons in one compartment, all the thimbles in another. Later still there were collections – of coins, stamps, butterflies and more unusual things, like ticket stubs and cherry pips. What gave young Henry such pleasure was not, like other children, the completion of a set, the aspiration to totality. It had something to do with action, the gesture of sticking a hinge on the back of a penny red or lifting the silver dollar to make it glint in the light. Each time the pleasure was the same pleasure, the very same pleasure, which brought back with it all the excitement and happiness of the first time the action was performed. Carry the coin-box into the drawing room. Lift up the dollar in the left hand, not the right . . . How beautiful! How kind of Uncle Alfred to bring it back! By the time he reached the age of ten, he had hundreds of these rituals, each designed to deliver a little affective charge, all performed with a singular religious devotion.

Events (chiefly a poor grasp of mathematics) conspired against the adolescent Henry's plan to become a physicist, and he was drawn into the study of cultures and peoples, applying to societies the rigorous classifiying spirit he had hoped to use on stars or elementary particles. He did not mind too much, for the pleasure of fitting the messy shapes of life into the clean outlines of a theory was the same, whatever its object.

Silver dollar . . . Cherry pip . . . Solenoid . . . Andaman Islander . . .

Aha!

Oxford beckoned, and later on Africa, though Africa only really became important when he had exhausted Oxford. To a mind like Professor Chapel's, places quickly take on a cluttered quality. When somewhere reminds one of something, and all it takes is an action, a smell, a word or a snatch of music to bring the old feeling back in full, it is often tempting to perform the action, say the word or keep in your pocket an old handkerchief which has a singular musky scent about it, just to help things along. Should tapping your cane three times on the kerbstone outside Worcester College make you happy because it reminds you of the afternoon you received tenure, the natural tendency is to tap your cane every time you pass. When such associations settle too thickly on any one piece of ground, the journey up Beaumont Street can take hours.

Poetical Frenchmen have been bedridden by similar conditions, but Chapel is made of sterner stuff. He is able to control himself, except in cases of extreme stimulation, and usually the routines are inconspicuous enough to pass without notice. Perhaps a few people have remarked that he invariably whistles the 'Ode to Joy' in the cheese shop (eroticism, the aroma of cheddar, an intimate moment, 1899), or that he always waits for three vehicles to pass before crossing the road outside Christ Church (relief, terrible traffic accident, man not looking, 1908). But not many. There are, however, less discreet landmines of memory buried around town. Whenever he enters the Barabbas College Hall, he has an urge to engage with the nearest dark-haired person in what can only be described as fondling, because it reminds him of something that happened at a college Gaudy in 1902. There is also a spot in the university parks where, in 1897, he stumbled across a courting couple. These days he avoids it entirely, having developed an unhealthy fascination for the place.

That was a black period. When he was almost caught by a policeman before he had time to get his trousers back on, he knew he had to do something. Oxford had become a palimpsest. Each time he walked through its streets, he was forced to read off all the previous walks in tiny rituals, a cascade of tics, mutterings and abrupt gestures which led the gossips in the senior common room to diagnose overwork. Chapel felt trapped, and began to dream of escaping to a blank place, somewhere to which he was perfectly, blessedly indifferent.

Africa!

The idea of actually visiting some of the people he studied had never occurred to him, but fieldwork was coming into fashion, and nowhere seemed blanker than the desert lands north of the Oil Rivers in British West Africa. The Fotse had been briefly described by a French missionary, but were otherwise unknown to science. To his excitement, Chapel found, as he pored over a map, that nothing about their country reminded him of anything at all. Most of the paper was blank white space. As soon as the next long vac came around, he set off.

That was many years ago. Despite the privations of Fotse life, Chapel discovered what he had sought in Africa. Everything was new. Everything was soothingly unfamiliar. The natives gathered to meet him under the big frangipani tree at the centre of their village looked entirely unlike a common room full of dons, or a lecture room full of students, or a tea party, or a congregation, or a theatre crowd. The land went on for ever, a uniform alien red. When he went back to Oxford for Michaelmas term, he felt refreshed – or rather, that Oxford had been refreshed. The cleansing effect lasted several years. When it got bad again, he did more fieldwork. A rhythm was established, only interrupted by the war. Every few years, the Professor would spend the vac in Fotseland, taking notes about the people and trying not to drink unboiled water, which they had an annoying habit of offering him, even after he explained that it would make him ill.

On his fourth visit, he had the insight that made his reputation, confirming him as one of the great Africanists of his generation. It was about the water. The thing had become absurd. Everywhere he went in Fotseland, people would rush out with cups, clamouring for him to take, drink, quench his thirst. On his first tour he had supposed it was simply traditional hospitality, and would decline with elaborate and tiring courtesies. Then, little by little, he discerned that the liquid in the proffered gourds and beakers was even dirtier than most Fotse water. It was as if the villagers went out of their way to make it so. For some time he reined in paranoid thoughts. Only when, on returning for a fourth time, he was presented with a pitcher of green-brown slime with an unidentified brown solid floating on the surface, did he ask, through an interpreter, whether there was any reason for it.

Gofo, was the answer.

It took him hours of interviewing to discover what the word meant. Gradually, week by week, the truth emerged. It seemed that soon after his first arrival and acceptance by the tribe, his chances of survival had been discussed and rated as poor. Fotse elders opined that disease, heat stroke or leopard attack were almost certain to kill the white man within a few weeks. This was not considered a controversial judgement, having always been the case before. On this basis, and on the basis that he was patently a loner with no clan or society ties (having arrived without goats, women or sons, at the head of a column of Hausa porters), they performed a valuation of his clothing and possessions, converting them into nominal quantities of goats, wives and millet. In anticipation of his imminent death these Fo amounts were divided among the more important elders, and immediately became the subject of intense Gofo bargaining.

When Chapel departed alive, there had been great disappointment. The Gofo had, in the way of Gofo, drawn in several huge aggregates of promises, covering a significant proportion of Fotse land and wealth. The amount at stake was now enormous, and because conflicting valuations had been put on a pair of his riding boots by two rival clan heads, the issue had taken on political significance. While he remained alive, nothing could be resolved.

So, when he came back two years later, the welcome was ecstatic. This was not (as he had written in *Some Months in a Hut with No Plumbing*, his popular memoir of the first two tours) 'an outpouring of uncontrolled joy at the return of a great chief', but relief that the controversial transactions, which had become a festering sore on the Fotse body politic, finally stood a chance of completion. Again the Fotse were disappointed, and over the next few years the matter continued to create tension between northern and southern clans. Some disaggregation of the positions took place during this time, along with a corresponding increase in the number of potential beneficiaries, until (the informant sheepishly revealed) almost everyone in Fotseland now stood to receive a small but significant lump sum on Chapel's death. However, the complexity did not end there. Because of the interconnection of a series of transactions concerning riverside pasturage in the south, certain conditions had to be met. Only if Chapel's demise was caused by one of the many waterborne diseases endemic to Fotseland (the pasturage case turning on a recondite issue concerning the rate of death of goats from such diseases, which had become linked to the disputed valuation of the boots, a figure largely derived from the area of leather required to make them, as expressed in sixteenths of a cow) would the Gofo trigger the long-awaited mass distribution of wealth.

The discovery that everyone had been trying to give him bilharzia because of his boots was troubling. The Professor was not sure he had understood correctly. Most of the nuances of Gofo escaped him, and for some time he thought he was in danger of being murdered, sleeping with a revolver under his pillow. He considered leaving, but was persuaded by his interpreter that no one actually bore a grudge against him. The interpreter assured him that he was in fact a popular man, and the desire that he might catch a fever and die was strictly a business matter, not affecting his personal relationships with anyone. The interpreter reminded him that for a Fotse it would be dishonourable to kill him. This put his mind at rest, a little.

Though direct murder was out of the question, the interpreter admitted that giving him dirty water was seen as an acceptable level of gamesmanship. No one seriously expected him to die, since over the years he had consumed great quantities of dirty water without knowing, in his food and so on, and now there were rumours that a profitable position was being built up by some speculators in the Lizard Society around the proposition that he would lead a long and healthy life. He should look for signs. For example, the first time he was offered the minced masculine organs of a camel at dinner, it would be a signifier of positive change. Where once there was water, soon there would be glands, to give him procreative strength. Professor Chapel had always been of a phlegmatic disposition, and he understood about the importance of separating one's business and emotional lives. So he weathered the storm and returned to Oxford at the end of the summer, to ruminate on what he had discovered.

The thing that struck him was not Gofo, which he thought rather a waste of time, but the fact that the Fotse were aware of the waterborne transmission of disease. His subsequent *Magic and Medicine among the Fotse* was to become an early anthropological classic. By the time of his next trip he had become an academic legend, courted by his peers, flocked to by students, awarded the Pargetter Medal for Progress in the Study of Backward Peoples . . .

Thoughts of his glorious career, slightly embroidered, always coincide with the final paragraph of the Social Organization lecture, reminding the Professor that it is time to wind up. He finishes with his usual rhetorical flourish (rising tone, a few daringly southern European hand gestures) and receives polite but enthusiastic applause – what passes for rapture in an audience of anthropologists. Then, as usual, he is surrounded by eager questioning faces, and hugged by his daughter, who specially wants him to meet some young fellow of hers. The fellow in question is reasonably presentable, and at least does not appear to be a Jew or wearing rouge, like most of the highly unsuitable types Astarte trails round after her.

'Daddy,' she gushes. 'This is Jonathan Bridgeman, and he's terribly terribly interested in your work.'

'I am?' says the young fellow, who like most of Astarte's young fellows, appears a little light-headed. 'Yes, absolutely. I am.'

Chapel extends a hand, which receives a firm shake. Taken by a fit of bonhomie, he invites his daughter and her friend to lunch.

Jonathan cannot remember ever being so happy. Star and her father talk to each other, or rather *at* each other, following separate but oddly parallel trains of thought. The restaurant revolves around their conversation, the other tables describing slow arcs about its centre like minor satellites in an orrery. It is full of names: names of cities; names of people she has met and books he has read; a huge apparatus of name-conjuring and name-arranging which awes him with its scope and variety. So much done and visited and known. So much to pass across the table.

The waiter darts forward with rolls and cutlery, and is sent away again without breaking the flow. Jonathan feels he has stumbled into the inner sanctum of things, where the patterns are rational and serene and the inhabitants live far from their acted upon, blown-about neighbours. With the Chapels, every-thing is simple. A wine list is produced. A party is produced. When one wants to go to France a path opens up, equipped with a mechanical moving walkway.

Anthropology, he decides, is the very highest mark of civiliz-ation. Professor Chapel's lecture, with its effortless comparisons between Fotse customs and those of the Trobriand Islanders, the Hopi Indians, the Inuit and the Karen hill tribes of Burma, represents the end of a long journey, a hard climb up to a giddy elevation from which it is finally possible to survey the world and the people in it. All the earth is available. Everything and everyone has a place. What could be better than to stand and look down over these valleys of the past? What better proof of your own place, of having reached the end of your own journey?

As he listens to the Chapels, he fits his body into their confident postures, tastes their ease plum-sweet in his mouth. He hears his English voice ask Star for some horseradish sauce, and with a sort of wonder watches her fingers close on the little bowl and lift it towards him.

Too soon it is over; the plates cleared, a litter of coffee cups and napkins. He says a formal goodbye to Star's father, and a long, lingering one to Star, who kisses him on the cheek and promises to see him in a day or two. He walks back to Barabbas like a conquering prince and celebrates by making Levine drunk in the buttery. Some time in the evening they are asked to leave, on penalty of a fine.

In the morning he settles down with his hangover to wait for the next instalment of his new life. But Star does not call on him. She does not call the next day. She does not call for the rest of the week. Finally he walks over to her college, only to be told that Miss Chapel is no longer in residence. She has decided to discontinue her studies and start an interior design firm in London.

He is aghast. She has done it to him again. Interior design? She said nothing about it over lunch. Such an important decision, to leave university, to leave *him* – a complete change of life. Yet she said nothing. In vain he sifts through his memories of the restaurant for a mention of rugs or heated towel rails, anything which might have foreshadowed this news. She said a lot about smoking, which she had just given up, and about a kind of vibrating slimming belt which a friend wanted her to buy, but about interior design – nothing. He wonders whether the closeness he felt over lunch was an illusion.

He does not see Star again for almost five months. During this time his life feels empty. It follows its usual course, a cycle of lectures, drinking, Union meetings and dinners, but it is weightless, insubstantial. Then one afternoon, as casually as if it had indeed been a day or two, she turns up at his rooms, proffers a cheek for him to kiss, and asks if he is going to stand there all day or put his hat on and take her to tea.

He puts his hat on.

London obviously suits her. She is wearing an ensemble that looks more milled than tailored, all flat planes and acute angles, a piece of precision machinery in stiff grey fabric. Her face hovers bored and exquisite over its collar, wearing a characteristically London expression made entirely with the mouth. It is an expression attempted by most fashionable undergraduates (Jonathan included) but rarely executed as perfectly. He knows instantly that she has been moving in the best circles.

As he feared, the tearoom fails to meet her standards. Though it is the same one she took him to last year and is completely unaltered, it is now seen to be cluttered with vulgar and unnecessary decoration and crammed oppressively full of 'the herd'. The herd is much in Star's conversation, contrasted with 'people', a word standing only for those in her immediate set. People are always mentioned by their first names, especially if they are famous. Jonathan listens appreciatively, marking off David the up-and-coming playwright, John the witty young politician and Pamela the gorgeous musical theatre actress. He does not ask Star why she left Oxford. That much is obvious.

Abruptly she breaks the flow of names. With a peculiar fake casualness, she asks how he is getting on with Daddy. Jonathan wonders if she has paid more attention to his life than it appears, and the thought makes him happy. Deprived of her, he has done the next best thing and attached himself to Professor Chapel. He is a fixture at the Professor's lectures, sitting at the front, asking lengthy questions, materializing afterwards in front of the lectern to check a spelling or query an item in a bibliography. Gradually he has been rewarded with a little conversation, the occasional hands-in-pockets walk along Parks Road.

He has also been spending much of his spare time in the Pitt-Rivers annexe of the university museum, a treasure-house of artefacts collected by previous anthropologists, archaeologists and explorers. Its mahogany cases are crammed with the detritus of world culture, a dizzying array of objects formed for every kind of social use. He has filled a notebook with a single long meandering list, itemizing *magic seed capsules, surgical instruments, Chinese gambling chips, Naga horned skulls, a bull roarer, a jade pendant, a helmet made from the skin of a porcupine fish by natives of the Gilbert Islands, a witch in a bottle from Gloucestershire, an Arapaho bone whistle, a set of steel Sikh chakras, Moroccan tiles, a Norwegian wolf-hunter's spring gun, a seal club carved from the penis bone of a walrus, trade ornaments, weights, bangles, boomerangs, torques, quipos, bismars, bone dice, palm leaf cards, earrings, canoes, a Beninese war flag, an Ashanti stool, a caduceus, a penis gourd, snuff bottles, smudge feathers, teapots, censers, lace bobbins, chopsticks, spoons, fans, mats, masks, mandolins, zithers and axeheads, Azeri kilims, Persian gabbehs, Turkmen boxes, Daghestani samovars, Anatolian pots, Astrakhan hats, a Georgian cross, a Lao Buddha, a lingam, a rosary, thimbles, rings, musket balls and snowshoes, totem poles and astrolabes, a Maori war club and a Siberian shaman's rattle*. To allow comparison, all these things are arranged with others of their kinds, the eye soaring high above the world it surveys, able to view waves of influence, family traits, trade routes and lines of descent. All the earth packed into a single room. All waiting for him to order it, and order himself within it.

'Your father and I are getting on very well,' he says to Star. 'Anthropology is a fascinating subject.'

'I'm glad. You should keep it up. It suits you.'

'Thank you. What do you mean, suits me?'

'Well, Daddy says you're like him, very serious about races and origins and things.'

'He does?'

'Well, you are, aren't you?'

'Yes, I suppose so. I don't have to be.'

'What do you mean?'

'If – I mean, if you don't like it.'

'Of course I like it. Daddy brought me up to like it. Customs and so on – I adore them.'

Jonathan smiles with relief. Something in the exchange leads Star on to the topic of the Empire Exhibition, which is being put on in a part of London called Wembley. She is going to visit it at the weekend, with a poet friend of hers. The herd will be there, and he wants to observe them. Jonathan tries to disguise his jealousy of the poet by talking impressively about the morphology of culture, and the importance of primitive practices in understanding modern civilization. Star describes a flat in Mayfair which she has decorated like an East African game lodge, with bamboo and zebra hides. He describes the importance of heredity in forming national character, then wonders aloud if the Empire Exhibition might be a good opportunity to study the subject further. Which day is she going? She frowns and says she does not know. It is up to Selwyn, the poet. The flat belongs to his mother. That is how she met him. Wembley, she thinks, is an odd place to have something. She has never been there. Nor has anyone she knows. Again he mentions his interest in the Exhibition. Again she does not invite him, and he is reduced to outlining the debate over the evolution of cultural characteristics, whether independently originated or diffused from a single primary source. He has only defined a few initial terms when she remembers an appointment at the dressmaker, and gets up to leave. Seeing his downcast expression, she sighs.

'Oh Jonathan, I do wish you wouldn't be quite so boring. It spoils your prettiness.'

Outside she hails a cab and directs it to the station.

'I'll see you in a day or two,' she says. He nods morosely,

conceding his abject failure. Then, quickly, almost absent-mindedly, she kisses him on the mouth. Before he can say anything or even respond, she is gone. As the cab pulls away he does not know whether to be elated or crushed. She kissed him. That night he cannot sleep. Is he boring, or pretty, or both? Is it a problem? Should he change? On Saturday, still confused, he takes the early-morning train to Paddington, planning, by accident, to bump into her.

Wembley, when he finally reaches it, turns out to be a quiet suburb of low brick houses, strung out along the track of the Metropolitan Railway. A line of visitors trickles out of the station towards the new stadium, a sort of modern Roman arena ready for motorized chariot racing or machine-pistol gladiatorial contests. Around it has been laid out a fantasy land of poured concrete. Families drink tea at concrete refreshment kiosks and sit on concrete benches, while their dogs urinate against concrete lamp-posts arranged along the margins of a wide concrete walkway. The crowd seems cowed by the expanse of rough, featureless grey, uneasy at taking its leisure in such an alien space. Signs point the way to the Palace of Engineering, the Palaces of Arts and Industry and the HM Government Building, vast hangars which dominate the smaller pavilions, one for each colony of the Empire. Jonathan spends the morning wandering through the displays, stopping at roped-off enclosures to look at Chinese women making fans and Canadian Inuit pretending to gut a stuffed deer. Eventually he finds himself leaning over a fence looking at a group of Negroes in khaki shorts, sitting glumly round a fire in front of a conical hut. Their label reads:

Fotse Village
Fotseland
British West Africa

He looks uneasily at the squatting men, with their blank faces and government-issue shorts. These are the subjects of Professor Chapel's study? He has always thought of the Fotse in a very vague way: as a collection of attributes, a set of practices and artefacts only dimly attached to real bodies. Like that they had seemed rather noble; keepers of the past, possessors of ancient wisdom. Yet here, in all its horror, is blackness. One of the men makes – surely against regulations – a sign at him, and the others look round. Their red eyeballs and dull sooty skin, their whispering mouths full of yellow-white teeth, every feature low and disgusting – he spins on his heel and marches off, glad of the tightness of the collar round his neck and the flash-flash of his polished shoes ahead of him on the pavement. He feels angry at Star for making him come here. Tribes and origins? It is like a bad joke. Why, to please her, should he have to spend so much time thinking about savages? It is like staring into the toilet bowl, looking at what he has expelled from himself.

In this mood he joins the crowd filing into the stadium to watch the Pageant of Empire. The pageant is poorly attended. Small clusters of people dot the stands, and he finds that he has been seated entirely on his own, a vast empty curve of concrete separating him from the nearest other person. In the arena a military band plays a march, then a man in black tie speaks into a microphone, his amplified voice echoing around the huge space. 'This,' he says, 'is a family party of the British Empire – the first family party since the Great War, when the world opened astonished eyes to see that an Empire with a hundred languages and races had but one soul and mind. Welcome!' There is scattered applause.

The announcer steps down from the podium. Soldiers and Boy Scouts enact the birth of the Empire, pulling Britannia on a large float into the centre of the space. When they have done this, they perform cameos of the Empire's growth, assisted in each case by real natives of the newly conquered territory. Maori warriors perform a haka, then surrender to Scouts dressed as naval officers. Zulus run on with spears and hide shields, then fall over as they are defeated by Queen Victoria's glorious cavalry. The cavalry ride circuits round the stadium, firing blanks like performers in a Wild West show.

The pageant moves into its final sequence, a procession representing the Empire of Today. His heart beating wildly, Jonathan spots Star. She is sitting in a box some way in front of him. Beside her lounges a thin dark-haired man, one arm hooked casually behind the back of her seat. Jonathan cannot see their faces. As the imperial subjects parade past, waving up at the stands and carrying signs proclaiming their origins, they pass directly beneath the couple. To Jonathan it appears as if the whole spectacle is directed solely at them, a homage which they can accept or reject as they please. His imagination transforms Star's unseen face into a single huge eyeball, greedily sucking in light. When the Indian contingent march past he gets up and leaves.

Back at Oxford he is troubled by the memory of the Fotse villagers. He wants to be rid of them, as if just by entering his thoughts they have cemented some link to his life. Why should they drag at him? He still attends Professor Chapel's lectures, but does so uneasily. As the Professor speaks about taboos or marriage customs, Jonathan looks around the hall, afraid of catching an eye or seeing a smirk on the face of someone who *knows* – who understands that he is called to blackness and savagery by his tainted blood. Star does not visit him, and his only connection to her is through her father. Gradually Chapel is drawing him into the inner circle of his admirers, keen young men who visit his rambling North Oxford house to sit in the garden and argue and drink sherry. Though he participates in these anthropological discussions, he feels he has to compensate for them. It is important to show where his loyalties lie.

Beyond the boundaries of Oxford, Britain is gripped by politics, as the country lives through its first year of socialist government. Jonathan's friends are horrified by it. MacDonald and his gang are already signing treaties with the Soviets. They are obviously tools of Bolshevism, and it is only a matter of time before they attempt to subvert the whole basis of British democracy. Within months, they will dissolve the army, force industry to grant huge wage increases, purge the Civil Service and dismantle the Empire. It is up to right-thinking Englishmen to stop the rot. Jonathan throws himself into the fray, arguing loudly in the junior common room and attending a noisy public meeting in the Oxford Town Hall. The National Citizens Union festoon the place with flags. A gramophone plays 'Jerusalem', drowning out the sound of the stewards fighting with hecklers at the back. Jonathan sings out the words, loud and clear. Surely no one could mistake him for anything but a bona fide Briton.

One morning he hears from the Professor that Star has gone back to Paris. She is thinking of moving there permanently. The news depresses him, and when some of his political acquaintances suggest he travel down to London with them for a rally, he accepts, hoping it will take his mind off her. He crams into a train carriage with a motley collection of students, a wicker hamper of food and a huge Union Jack that someone has borrowed from their college Officer Training Corps. By the time they reach Paddington, the hamper is wrecked and empty champagne bottles are rolling around in the corridor outside their compartment. Some of the party start a medley of boating songs, annoying the ticket collector, who threatens to take their names.

From the station they take a cab to the East End, the mansion blocks of the Marylebone Road and Regent's Park melting into the sooty tenements of Islington. Gradually the houses become meaner, the streets narrower, until they find themselves in

Whitechapel, the Jewish quarter. Opposite the hospital on the Mile End Road a crowd of several hundred has gathered. Flags frame a makeshift platform, from which a snub-nosed woman in quasi-military uniform is haranguing the audience. She holds up a picture of the Prime Minister, denouncing him as a Pied Piper, a tool of the Semitic–Bolshevist conspiracy. Jonathan's friends clap and cheer. Jonathan claps and cheers too. He looks at the names painted over the shops behind the platform: *Silver's Kosher Delicatessen, Bloom's Bakery*, and imagines the Elders of Zion plotting among the sausages and sacks of flour. An older woman appears, wearing the same uniform as the first. She talks about the need to build up the navy, and resist the emasculating influence of international Jewish finance. She shakes her fist. A face appears at one of the upstairs windows, then quickly vanishes. Fascist Party workers hand out flyers advertising a dinner-dance, and members of a group called the British Workers League sell books from a stall. Around the fringes of the crowd, a few policemen half-heartedly attempt to keep the demonstration from blocking the road. By the time the woman comes to a conclusion, they have disappeared altogether.

A third speaker, an old soldier with a row of campaign medals on his chest, is exhorting the crowd to protect the nation from foreign competition, when a sudden surge of people propels Jonathan towards the platform. There is the sound of shouting, and a bottle arcs down over his head. A full-scale fight has erupted at the back of the crowd, and while some people run to escape it, others are pushing against them, trying to force their way through to join in. One of Jonathan's friends tugs at his sleeve, terrified. He is clutching his temple, which has been gashed open. For an instant the two of them are the only still point in a seething mêlée. Jostled by Blackshirts carrying sticks and truncheons, they stumble their way towards the platform. The speakers are surrounded by a phalanx of men, some in uniform, some wearing armbands with 'Defence Force' written on them. He steers away from them and makes it out of the crowd, turning back to see a red flag waving in the thick of the battle. Another group of attackers is running towards them, young men in caps and shirtsleeves with red scarves tied round their necks.

He bolts down a side street, the frightened Oxford boys running after him. The noise and chaos vanish behind them as suddenly as a window slamming shut. They run until the demonstration is far behind. No one follows them.

An hour later they are drinking pints in the snug of a Blooms-bury pub, telling each other tall stories about the riot and the number of agitators they faced down. Slowly they are rewriting their roles, transforming themselves. By the time they get back to college they will be heroes: staunch longbowmen, hearts of oak. Only Jonathan is silent, transfixed by the memory of what he saw as he ducked down the alley. The man leading the charge was Paul Gertler.

What began on the day of Paul's expulsion has been completed: the long, slow process of betrayal. He wants to run back and tell him that he did not mean it, that he does not hate him, or want him to die or disappear. *It was a disguise, Paul, it was only a game.* He cannot rid himself of the memory of his friend's face, the look of horror as he recognized him, the quick sequence of hurt, anger and defiance. Loneliness crushes him like a physical weight.

After the demonstration, Jonathan backs away from politics. It is too confusing. That October, mired in rumours about spies and Moscow gold, the Labour Party loses the General Election. Oxford breathes an institutional sigh of relief. The Conservative landslide has returned God to his heaven, and the cosmic hierarchy is restored. One morning, soon after the start of the new term, Willis props an invitation beside the coffee pot on the breakfast table. Selwyn Tredgold requests the pleasure of Jonathan Bridgeman's company at a cocktail party and poetry reading at Lady Tredgold's Mayfair flat. On the back is scrawled something which looks like 'Do come, darling – A'. Immediately all his resolutions – to forget her, to concentrate on his work – are forgotten.

On the appointed evening, Jonathan arrives at the address on the invitation, and is shown by a butler into a chromium-plated hallway lined with big-game-hunting trophies. Horns, tusks, antlers and entire mounted heads protrude from the shiny walls. A gorilla snarls at him over the doorway to the reception room, which is packed with people. He hands his coat to the servant, and steps into air that is grey with cigarette smoke. Through the haze the animal prints and carved idols of Star's game-lodge decor are dimly visible, like set dressings in a horror film. All the guests are painfully elegant, and many faces are familiar from newsreels and the gossip pages of weekly illustrated papers. The only person he knows personally is Levine, who is sandwiched between a stuffed baby giraffe and an arrangement of dwarf palms, attempting to persuade a famous producer to stage his play. For a while Jonathan hovers at the edge of their conversation. 'Light comedy is the defining mode of our times. What I've written is a sort of jeu d'esprit, set in a ladies' deportment academy. There are two sets of twins . . .' The producer looks impressed. Sensing success, Levine carries on, acknowledging Jonathan with a brief wave.

Suddenly Star comes shooting over, almost knocking over a waiter carrying a tray of empty highball glasses. 'Thank God you've come,' she hisses. 'It's absolutely deathly here. Selwyn is going to read his elegy, and he's invited a lot of critics and editors and people. Or is it a eulogy? Anyway, he's dying to meet you and you have to come with me. Where's your drink?'

Jonathan has no drink, so he is given a cocktail, something new and American with a lot of gin in it. Without asking him anything about himself or offering any information about how she has passed the last six months, she propels him towards Selwyn, who is leaning on a large ebony fetish talking to a group of eminent literati. At their approach, Selwyn assumes a sour expression. He does not look as if he is dying to meet Jonathan. Star introduces them, and Selwyn says a clipped how do you do, softly brushing Jonathan's fingers with his.

'It is important,' he growls, turning back to a hook-nosed woman wearing a mountainous silk turban, 'to lose hope. Unless we do that, we are denying the basic conditions under which we live. We are people of the aftermath. What could hope be to us?' There are murmurs of assent, and he expands on his theme, describing the need for a new kind of man, a new kind of society and a new kind of art, offering himself and his poetry as a 'sort of prototype' for these things. While he speaks, Jonathan has a first chance to examine his rival. Selwyn is short and dark, almost feral looking. As he talks, his thin hands describe sleepy patterns in the air. He makes up for his unappealing features by an air of total confidence. He radiates assurance into the room, toasting his audience in it like muffins. It seems self-evident that he is a great writer.

Star is paying very little attention to Selwyn's speech, sipping her drink and scanning the party distractedly. To Jonathan she looks more beautiful than ever. Her face is powdered, her lips have been rouged into a tiny cupid's bow, and her backless tiger-print gown clashes startlingly with her English-rose looks. The effect is arousing, like a virgin being menaced by wild beasts. After a while she pulls him away from the literary conversation and finally asks him what he has been doing, 'stuck in stuffy old Oxford'. Selwyn does not appear to register they have gone, and Jonathan realizes he said nothing to Star, barely even looking at her as they stood with him. With a rush of encouragement he launches into a string of stories about his college friends. He concentrates on anything amusing or glamorous, copying her habit of using only first names and trying hard to avoid topics which might bore her. It works for a while, but his names do not seem to carry the same weight as hers. She is soon fiddling with her necklace and looking wistfully at her empty glass.

An imposing woman makes her way to the centre of the room and rings a small silver handbell. Lady Tredgold calls her guests to attention, and announces that the main event of the evening is about to commence. Her son will now read from his forthcoming *Crepuscle of a Continent*. Selwyn steps up on a carved wooden footstool. He spends a moment theatrically polishing a pair of steel-rimmed spectacles and fitting them on to his face. Then he takes a notebook from his jacket pocket, clears his throat and starts to declaim in a sonorous, nasal voice:

> 'Eheu!
> Eheu!
> The image of Mars
> Floats o'er
> The face
> Of the gibbous moon
>
> Armoured, cruel
> Let us
> The magnetic men
> Forge our steel
> Anew
>
> Eheu!'

An air of seriousness settles over the party. Several of the younger men adopt agonized postures of concentration, shading their eyes and grinding their knuckles into their temples. As he gets into his stride, Selwyn's voice rises, quivering with suppressed emotion.

> 'Let us too
> The electrical ones
> Les beaux, les dynamistes
> Chide
> Deride
> Those smug-faced
> Traditionalists
> The critics
>
> Let them cry
>
> Eheu!'

At the daring mention of the critics, Selwyn pauses and sweeps the room with his eyes. Star looks unimpressed. 'He always puts them in,' she whispers to Jonathan. 'He says they like to know he's thinking of them.' As Selwyn continues chiding and deriding various groups of people, she begins to fidget. 'You know,' she says loudly, 'his eyesight is perfectly fine. Those glasses are just for effect.' Several people turn round. Jonathan notices that she is slurring her words. Selwyn carries on describing the condition of the anti-poetic classes of society, who are not fit *'To lick the boots / of tomorrow's sons / radium bright / and new'* and she sighs loudly, hoping from one foot to the other. Finally she pushes out of the room, returning with a full bottle of champagne and a waiter hurrying after her trying to open it. As Selwyn declaims the final stanza: *'Though in this European twilight/ we smash our lyres / Eheu!'* she fires the cork, which smacks into the wall by his head. He ducks and loses his footing on the stool, tumbling back against his mother. Lady Tredgold fixes Star with a murderous look, her cheeks and forehead cycling serially and distinctly through every shade of high emotion from puce to magenta.

'Oh dear,' says Star.

The room is completely silent. Some Georgian poets, who were trying to storm out in protest at Selwyn's use of vers libre, come back to see why no one noticed them. Someone starts to applaud, then stops again, cowed by Lady Tredgold's expression. Star hands Jonathan the champagne bottle, and puts her hands behind her back.

'Jonathan,' she says reprovingly, 'you shouldn't give me those things to open. They go off without warning.'

Lady Tredgold shifts her basilisk gaze from Star to Jonathan. Then to Star again. She is not to be diverted so easily. Divining that her ruse has not worked, Star grabs the champagne back. Then she grabs her coat, grabs Jonathan and heads for the door. Were Jonathan a little less confused, they could have made a clean getaway, but he is not sure why they are leaving, and Selwyn appears on the front doorstep while they are still trying to hail a taxi. Star throws her shoe at him.

'Go away,' she shouts.

Selwyn takes a few steps towards her. He looks furious. 'Why in God's name did you do that? I can't believe it. Did you see there were people actually walking out? That was my moment. I was going to have my very own succès de scandale and you went and upstaged me. Now all anyone's talking about is you – you – you – bitch!'

Jonathan steps forward. 'Don't you talk to her like that.'

'I'll talk to her how I like.'

'I demand an apology.'

'Well, I shan't give you one.'

Jonathan sneaks a glance at Star. She is taking no notice of either of them. She is standing in the road and waving her remaining shoe at passing cars. When he turns back, he finds Selwyn sneering at him.

'You'll be disappointed, you know.'

'What do you mean?'

'With her.'

'Shut up, Selwyn,' shouts Star. A taxi pulls over to the kerb. 'You're such a pig,' she says, and gets in. Jonathan makes to follow.

'Go on,' Selwyn calls after him. 'Run after her. She'll make lots of promises, but she won't actually let you touch her.'

'How dare you!' says Star, and gets out of the cab again.

'Don't you talk to her like that,' repeats Jonathan.

'She won't do it with you, Bridgeman. She's frigid. She won't even let you feel her up.'

'Pig!' shouts Star.

'So bloody old-fashioned. Not even a hand on her '

'Pig!'

'Bitch!'

'Pig!'

It takes the appearance of another figure on the doorstep to break things up.

'Selwyn Arthur Tredgold, come inside this instant!'

The shame of arguing in the street like a member of the labouring classes has turned Lady Tredgold's face a shade of violet that edges some way beyond the visible spectrum. She is monumental, terrifying. Selwyn's shoulders droop.

'Yes, Mother.'

Seizing the moment, Star and Jonathan dive into the cab, yelling at the driver to move on as fast as possible. Once they are safely underway, they start laughing with relief. Star kisses him on the cheek.

'Really, Jonathan, I can't take you anywhere.'

His heart flies up through the roof.

After that he sees Star almost every day. She comes to stay with her father in Oxford, saying she has got tired of London. According to Levine, London has also got a little weary of her. The 'Tredgold affair' is only the latest in a series of similar incidents. London art people do not really like bohemianism except to read about, and then only if practised by foreigners. 'You know, Johnny,' Levine tells him, 'I don't think she's the girl for you. She's rather fast. Look what she did to poor Tredders. He's a shadow now, a hopeless shadow. Wracked with longing and entirely unable to work. You're a solid man. Why don't you find yourself a decent sort, someone who rides and can partner you at bridge? Forget about Astarte Chapel. I admit she's rather something, but she'll end up with some foreign chap. You mark my words.' Jonathan tells Levine to mind his own business. They part on bad terms.

As far as Jonathan is concerned, Star is exactly the girl for him. Now it seems that for the first time she feels the same way. He helps her run errands on Cornmarket, and is rewarded by the envious glances of other young men as they pass by. Standing in the queue for the George Street Cinema, she lets him hold her hand. Sitting at the back of the stalls, they kiss. On his birthday, she gives him a pair of enamelled cufflinks in the shape of little Negro jazz musicians, a saxophonist and a trumpeter.

It is a significant birthday. He is twenty-one. He has come of age. Mr Spavin makes a last attempt to persuade him into the law, but is finally forced to admit that the battle is lost. In a sober meeting in his chambers he delivers a homily about prudence, foresight and the good prospects of shares in a certain Canadian logging company. Then he releases to Jonathan the capital of his inheritance, a sum of several hundred pounds. As they shake hands, Jonathan avoids his eyes, feeling suddenly guilty about the other Bridgeman, dead and anonymous in Bombay.

The guilt soon passes. By the time he gets back to Oxford it has vanished completely, and he holds a celebratory dinner in a private room at the Randolph Hotel, at which Astarte is the guest of honour. Surrounded by admiring undergraduates, she sparkles as if the birthday belongs to her. Afterwards Jonathan drunkenly escorts her home, and on the way diverts her into some convenient shadows. At first she resists his kisses, and after a while, panting and blushing, she takes his hand away. There is, however, a stretch of time in between which would make Selwyn Tredgold extremely jealous.

That term Jonathan is a conquering hero, the world laid out before him like a white cloth. He sees his future stretching away into the distance, an infinite golden thread. During long afternoons when he should be revising for his finals, time and space embroider a depiction of admiring faces, interestingly designed interiors and Astarte Chapel, proud yet somehow submissive at his side. He is sleeping better too. When he is invited to spend Christmas with the Chapels, he takes it as a sign.

In the village church he mouths the words of carols, the sweet taste of the Professor's best port on his lips. *We-e three kings* ... Candles and stained glass and outside a crisp Cotswold Christmas Eve. There are three more days of paradise ahead, the snow lying round about deep and crisp and even, the rolling hills faint in the darkness behind the hundredth generation of English men and women to shake hands with their vicar. *O! Star of wonder* ... walking with him along the lane, breath pluming, her hand hot in his through its damp mitten. After the Professor has fallen asleep by the fire, the two of them push open the chill dark of the boathouse and light a brazier, dragging wicker chairs close together and listening to the gurgling of the river outside the door. Coats are pulled open, buttons undone, layers of wool and cotton mined for warm flesh. Her hand worms into his trousers and he tugs her petticoat up round her waist, indiscriminately kissing her jaw, her throat, her ear. Soon she is rubbing hard against him, clenching his thigh with hers, moaning and wriggling. 'Yes,' she sobs, as the tips of Jonathan's fingers slip inside her, 'yes, you big buck – do it to me – make jelly roll with me, baby!' His face is buried in her breasts, and he can hear nothing but the pounding of the blood in his ears. 'Mmm?' he pants, not really understanding. Her rhythm falters. 'Nothing. Don't stop. Just – just a song.' She groans. 'Please don't stop.' He carries on, glancing up at her face, which flickers red and gold in the low light. Her eyes are screwed shut. Disconcertingly shut. As if she is not with him, and is imagining – but he has no time to pursue this line of thought because suddenly the shut eyes open wide and she goes completely rigid in his arms. 'Oh God,' she says, 'that's my father.' And so it is, calling their names down the garden, his voice getting rapidly closer.

They launch themselves into action. A few seconds later, fully clothed, they have made it halfway to the house. Their faces are studies in angelic innocence. The Professor appears to notice nothing out of the ordinary.

'Ah there you are, Astarte. What on earth were you doing in the boathouse? I'm afraid I shall have to borrow Mr Bridgeman from you. There are things we have to discuss.'

'I thought you were asleep, Daddy.'

'So I was. But now it is time for business. Come on, my boy.'

Jonathan is led unwillingly into the study. The Professor paces up and down, wearing a harrowed expression. Even a nap is hard to achieve these days. Recently things have been bad again, the world filling up with analogies, chains of resemblance and signification which make it impossible to do the simplest thing without becoming distracted. Trying to sit down at his desk sends him tumbling into a vortex of associations, forcing him to perform a series of semi-involuntary rituals. Jonathan watches, bemused, as he spins the old wooden globe in the corner, muttering something under his breath. He takes a bound volume of *Punch* off the shelf, reads three political jokes out loud, pokes the fire, makes an embarrassed attempt to touch his toes, spins the globe counter-clockwise and then hurriedly, almost guiltily, flops down in his chair. After another minute or two of rearranging the objects on the desk into rows and then putting them back in their original places, he looks up and presses his fingers to his temples.

'Now, where was I?'

'I don't know, sir.'

He frowns. 'Your fly is open.'

Bright red, Jonathan buttons himself up.

Chapel's frown deepens. 'I've been thinking, Bridgeman. I find you a most intelligent and perceptive young man.'

'Thank you, sir.'

'You are also close to us. I mean, not only to myself, but to my daughter.'

Jonathan's heart starts to pound. Is this about his intentions towards Star?

'I feel you understand my work, and that you would make a congenial companion –'

'Yes, sir?'

'A congenial companion on a long voyage. Bridgeman, the time has come for me to make another journey to Fotseland. I intend to set off next summer, at the end of the Trinity term. It will be a long expedition, lasting into the following year. I would like you to be my assistant.'

'Your assistant, sir?'

'Yes, that's right. If Astarte can spare you, that is.'

The Professor laughs. Jonathan laughs too, covering a wave of apprehension. Fotseland? He remembers the red-eyed men squatting in the compound at the Empire Exhibition. Suddenly the room seems damp and cold.

'Well, my boy, what do you say?'

What does he say? He cannot think of anything.

'Thank you, sir.'

'Well, then, that's settled. Now you can go back to whatever you were doing. Surely the two of you weren't thinking of going boating, were you? Not now? I mean, it's the middle of the night.'

Jonathan leaves the study in a daze. Fotseland? It is as if the earth is tilting, sending him sliding towards a place where he feels he must not go. He looks for Star to tell her what has happened, but she has gone to bed. For an hour or more he sits on his own in the boathouse, listening to the sound of the river running into the blackness.

On New Year's Eve, they are sitting on a bench in the Barabbas gardens, guests at a party held by the Warden. A string quartet plays Haydn. Jonathan smiles and Star taps her foot, the music communicating its clockwork self-assurance to them both. Around them people hold champagne glasses and make optimistic conversation. The Professor is somewhere inside, within range of the buffet table. They wait impatiently for the clock to strike midnight, when the college servants will light the first rockets of the firework display. Nineteen twenty-five is less than a minute away.

'Oh Star,' says Jonathan.

'Oh Johnny,' says Star.

'I'm so happy.'

'Are you?'

'Why, aren't you?'

'Of course I am. Listen – here it comes.'

People take up the chant: *Thirty seconds to go . . . Twenty seconds . . .* The sound swells as guests spill into the garden from the Hall. Stiffy, the head porter sinks down on one knee, shielding a match. As the count reaches zero he lights a fuse, and a rocket shoots upwards, exploding in a big white burst over the chapel. There are cheers and applause. Jonathan takes Star in his arms. All around them, backs are slapped and hands vigorously shaken. She has never looked more beautiful.

'I love you,' he says, and kisses her.

'Darling,' she murmurs. 'How wonderful of you.'

'Is it? Do you really mean that?'

'Of course I do, Johnny. I think it's absolutely wonderful.'

'So – you will?'

'Will what?'

'How silly of me. I'm getting all mixed up. Marry me, I mean. Will you marry me?'

'Oh Johnny, you dear dear thing.'

'So you will?'

Star looks up at the fireworks, which are patriotically studding the sky with rosettes of red, white and blue.

'It does seem rather perfect, doesn't it? Us here in this garden, with all of the fireworks and the party and everything.'

'Say yes, Star. Just say yes.'

'Well, the thing is, Johnny, I'm going away again.'

He is stunned.

'Going away?'

'Don't look like that. I'm going back to Paris. There's a wonderful American lady there, Mrs Amelia DeForrest of Chicago. She and I are going into business. She has lots of money, and she positively adores my designs. I said I'd let her do the fabrics, and I'll do everything else.'

'Business?'

'Yes, that's right, business. Really, Johnny, I do wish you wouldn't say it as if it were something obscene. Lots of girls do it.'

'Sorry. That is – when are you going?'

'Quite soon, I should think. A month or two. You and Daddy can come and see me on your way to the Fotse.'

'But how can you – after we've – I mean, I thought – you said . . .'

'Oh you are so sweet, all pouty and disappointed. Just because I'm over there doesn't mean I'll forget about you. After all, you're awfully pretty. And attentive too.'

'But I want to be with you.'

'You can still be with me, when you come back from Africa. When you've finished looking after Daddy, I think you should come and stay in Paris. It's far better than London. People have exquisite taste, and there are wonderful nightclubs. You don't have to go to bed at all if you don't want to.'

'So – you'll think about it?'

'Of course I will, Johnny. I'm so touched. Now come on, we should go and find Daddy.'

In the morning his head is so fuzzy and his memories of the party such a blur that he cannot remember whether to be pleased or not. She said she loved him, didn't she? At any rate, they have an understanding. He and Astarte Chapel are practically engaged. It is a secret, probably. With understandings, secrecy is a sort of tradition. Still, that does not mean he cannot not tell a friend. A few days after New Year he has lunch with Levine.

By the beginning of term the news is all round the university: Bridgeman is engaged to Miss Chapel, and not only that, he has been picked to accompany her eminent father on his next expedition. A mere undergraduate! Among Chapel's coterie of young scholars it is hard to say which inspires more jealousy, the job or the girl. Acid remarks are passed in the library, and more than once Jonathan is snubbed by people he thought were his friends. 'It's the price of success, old man,' says Levine. 'You can't expect everyone to be happy when something like this happens.' He speaks with the voice of experience. His play is to be produced in London, and the envy sweeping the university dramatic society is violent and consuming.

When a student magazine prints a cartoon of him in a cooking pot, surrounded by grinning cannibals, Jonathan's misgivings disappear. He is a celebrity: 'Beau' Bridgeman of Africa, lover and explorer. He cuts the cartoon out and sends it to Star, who writes back to say they have made his nose too big. Too soon the day comes when he has to see her off at Victoria. They kiss chastely, and he promises to see her in June, when he and her father pass through Paris on their way to meet their ship at Marseilles. He stands on the platform long after her train has departed, feeling windswept and self-important. Surely other people can see that he is in the throes of a grand passion, a great and literary romance? Disappointingly, the passengers looking for their coaches appear oblivious to his emotions.

Once Star has gone, it is time to turn his attention to work. Revising for his finals competes for time with studying Hausa, the trading tongue of the Fotse region. Jonathan picks up some useful basic phrases (*Where is the consulate? I would like the lamb for dinner*), and spends some evenings poring over the only known glossary of the Fotse language, owned by Professor Chapel and compiled by Père Antoine Bertrand, a nineteenth-century French Jesuit who was later beheaded by one of the local emirs. From the look of the manuscript, Bertrand was already preoccupied by his personal safety when he compiled it. His handwriting is almost illegible, and his choice of examples so eccentric that as a way of learning the language the text seems entirely useless. Again and again, phrases occur that refer to chance and possibility. There is also an entire page of terms relating to witchcraft: *I am possessed by a bad spirit / a good spirit / the spirit of an unborn calf / a horsefly / an acacia tree* . . . There is something unnerving about the idea of a country where a person can be taken over by a shrub. Jonathan copies the phrases down in a notebook, the same kind he once used for his observations about the English.

He and Professor Chapel will not be the only members of the expedition. One evening he is invited to dine at Jesus College High Table with his new colleagues, Doctors Morgan and Gittens. His short undergraduate gown makes a poor show among the flowing robes of the senior scholars, their heads bowed as they hear grace. As he dines with the two young dons, Jonathan is nervous, looking down the long refectory tables and catching the eyes of students, who whisper and point him out to each other.

Morgan is affable enough, a big lantern-jawed Welshman who looks more like a farmer than a scholar. This is only natural, his speciality being agriculture. He pours Jonathan glasses of college claret and tells him about the beauties of the Herefordshire cattle he grew up with: their hardiness, their gentle white faces, their marvellous ability to convert grass into lean red meat. This will be his first journey to Africa, where he hopes to see the West African shorthorn up close, and study the practices of the Fotse farmers. Gittens, though also making his first visit, is less pleasant company. A specialist in initiation rituals, he obviously disapproves of Bridgeman's presence on the expedition. 'How old are you?' he asks. 'What have you published?' When Jonathan replies that he has published nothing, Gittens snorts. 'If you don't mind my asking,' he says tartly, 'what will you actually be *doing* in Fotseland?' Jonathan has no ready answer.

Professor Chapel, on the other hand, has a clear idea of his assistant's role. Expeditions serve a valuable function, which is to provide an escape from Oxford. However, their organization is a pain, and should be delegated. It is up to Jonathan to arrange travel and procure equipment and supplies. The Professor sends him to Walters & Co. on the Turl, where he negotiates for hurricane lamps, tents, wicker baskets and X-brand folding washstands. He buys green canvas cots and tin basins, axes and camp stools, laundry soap, a canteen of cutlery, sheath knives and a set of cooking equipment which takes up four steel boxes. There is an open-flap tent for the cooking to take place in, and a waterproof medicine chest full of little glass bottles to treat its after-effects. For himself he buys khaki shirts, shorts and puttees, a pair of mosquito boots, two suits of Jaeger wool underwear of the lightest sort, a cork helmet for wearing in camp and a double-terai hat for hunting. The pile on the counter grows to a mound. Juniors are dispatched to find more brown wrapping paper. The assistant suggests that he has not paid enough attention to questions of personal health, so he buys a flannel cholera belt to protect his abdomen from excessive dampness, and a spine pad which fits inside his shirt and is designed to ward off the sun's harmful actinic rays. Crêpe bandages and a thermometer are added to the medicine chest. Finally he selects a pair of metal-rimmed spectacles with smoked-glass lenses. In the mirror they make him look sinister and inscrutable, like a fly.

On the day before his finals begin, he is down in London, buying sporting guns and ammunition from a dealer in St James's. Watching the shop assistant count out cartridges on to the teak counter, he realizes for the first time what he is undertaking. All he wanted was to come to England and settle into a comfortable life, the life depicted in the postcards pinned above his washstand in Bombay. Now he is leaving it behind. For what? He tells himself again – *for Astarte Chapel*. When he has arranged delivery of the guns, he takes a cab to Regent Street and buys an engagement ring. If he is to go into Africa, at least he will have a reason to come back.

The examinations pass by in a blur. It is impossible to concentrate on the Reconquista or the sack of Rome when Star is only a few days away from him. He scribbles answers on the papers, hardly caring what he argues, whether the dates he attaches to events are real or have migrated from the part of his brain that deals with ticket prices and steamer timetables. Sometimes he drifts away completely, the high ceilings of the examination schools pulling him upwards, dissolving him in imagery he thought he had completely suppressed: murky palace corridors, the smell of gin and lime juice. Oxford seems temporary and fragile. After the last exam, he is carried along in a crowd of undergraduates throwing flour at each other and drinking champagne from the bottle. He clutches his mortarboard in one hand, and runs down cobbled streets, past buildings as insubstantial as a stage set.

The train slides through Kent countryside that is as green and bright as a hymn. The Professor sits with an unopened newspaper on his lap, a schoolboyish grin on his face.

'On our way, eh, Bridgeman? On our way at last!'

Between Victoria and Dover this is all he says, repeating it at intervals throughout the journey. 'On our way, Bridgeman. On our way.' Each time he says it, he rubs his hands together. Eventually, Jonathan feels he should say something. 'You seem very pleased to be leaving, sir.' Chapel gives him a shocked look, mouthing, 'Pleased?' as if the idea is a little indecent.

At Dover they meet Gittens and Morgan, and spend a couple of hours supervising the packing of the expedition equipment into large crates. Morgan has volunteered to accompany it as far as Marseilles, but Gittens is coming with them to Paris. Jonathan is not happy about this. As he runs about the warehouse with inventories and bills of lading, the man's eyes follow him, a patronizing smile playing around the corners of his mouth. On the ferry Gittens makes conversation with Professor Chapel, deliberately cutting through Jonathan whenever he tries to join in. By the time they reach Calais, he has made it clear that he considers him an inferior, more the Professor's batman than an academic colleague.

In port the bored French officials barely inspect their documents, waving them through a high-ceilinged Customs Hall towards the station from which the Paris express is to depart. They find their carriage through a haze of steam, and settle in just as the whistle goes. Soon the rhythm broken by the ferry is resumed, fields unrolling beside the track like great flat carpets. Gittens discourses on the architecture of Notre-Dame, then drops the name of an antiquarian bookseller on the Rue Saint-Jacques. He evidently wishes to show off his knowledge of Paris, a city he has visited 'many, many times'. Chapel listens with interest. Jonathan, irritated, heads for the buffet car.

He sits down and the waiter takes his order, slipping seamlessly into English as soon as Jonathan opens his mouth to speak. A whisky-soda arrives quickly, but something about the man's expression is disconcerting. He swirls the ice-cubes round in his glass, listening to the low murmur of conversation. The fields pass by outside the window. He sips whisky. The passengers talk. Occasionally he sneaks glances at the waiter, who is never doing anything unusual. Even so his discomfort grows. Perhaps it has nothing to do with the waiter. Perhaps it is rooted in something deeper, something about the lilt of spoken French or the unfamiliar typeface of the menu card slotted into the holder on his table. By the time they reach Paris, rattling through suburbs of grey-roofed houses, his unease has grown into a heart-pounding paranoia.

Star has not come to the Gare du Nord to meet them. Jonathan is relieved, too preoccupied by dealing with his panic attack (*breathe iiin, breath out . . .*) to cope with greeting the woman he is going to marry. They take a cab to the Rue du Faubourg Saint-Honoré and check into the Hotel Bristol, which, though expensive, is the Professor's customary base in the city. At reception there is a message saying Star will meet them for breakfast. Leaving Gittens and the Professor admiring the Gobelin tapestries in the entrance hall, Jonathan announces that he feels unwell and will have dinner in his room. He locks the door behind him and throws himself down on the bed.

What he wants is sleep, but it will not come. The room is stuffy. Its ostentatious furniture and richly patterned walls bear down on him oppressively. He splashes his face at the washstand and opens the windows, letting in the sound of traffic from the street below.

A knock. He opens the door to a pair of waiters, who set up a folding table, cover it with a stiff white cloth and lay it for dinner. Once they have gone he sits down to onion soup and a piece of fish with an unfamiliar rich sauce. The food is good, but its very goodness seems to be part of his problem. In desperation he puts on his jacket and heads out into the streets. There he finds bright lights, but no pedestrians. He trudges along the road, heading against a stream of black cars. The Haussmann façades of ministries and company offices are broken by the lighted windows of late-working functionaries, but even this muted kind of life seems to exist at a distance. Cars and buildings seem like carapaces, shields designed to keep him away from human warmth. He drifts, caroming off these impersonal surfaces, meeting no one but a pair of gendarmes, who stare at him so intently that he turns round and goes back to the hotel.

The next morning when he comes down, Star is sitting in the breakfast room. He has spent so long thinking about her that her presence gives him a shock. It is raw, rudely physical, like that of an amputee or someone very famous. Her father sits beside her, absorbed in the morning papers. She offers Jonathan her cheek to kiss. As he expected, she has made herself into a perfect Parisienne, nursing a tiny cup of coffee and smoking a bright green cigarette in a holder. They make stilted small talk, which breaks down altogether when Gittens appears. He pulls up a chair on Star's other side and immediately starts to chat. Wonderful morning. How lucky you are to live here. Within a few moments he is leaning forward and telling her in a confidential tone that since he last saw her she has 'grown into a striking young woman'.

'And when was that?' Jonathan asks, from between gritted

teeth. Gittens adopts a coltish, moustache-twirling manner, like a bad musical hall song-and-dance man. 'Not for a long time. A couple of years at least.' The Professor starts talking about an item in *Le Monde*, which forces Gittens to pay attention to him for a while. However, he keeps shooting little smiles at Star. Why, he suggests, don't they all spend the day sightseeing together? It occurs to him that they could visit the museums. 'A capital idea,' says the Professor.

So begins a morning of explanations. It is as if Gittens has been training for this all his life, has been put on earth for the sole purpose of conducting them around the highlights of the Louvre. He walks from exhibit to exhibit, spouting *Baedeker* prose, his eyes misty with love for the glories of Western civilization. Factual information is interspersed with personal asides, designed to demonstrate that he is not just a scholar but a sensitive soul, a man who in other circumstances might well have been an artist. A Renaissance Madonna is pronounced to have a 'coruscating beauty'. A depiction of the Passion puts him in contact with his 'higher self'.

These pieces of critical appreciation are, of course, all directed at Star. She looks flattered. Jonathan suffers. As they walk through the galleries, the previous night's panic rises up again in his chest. He slopes around behind Gittens and Star, feeling the paintings loom over him, an endless parade of kings and heroes posed in attitudes of serene, self-possessed greatness. He begins to understand what has been preying on him since he first crossed into France. He is foreign here. Even as Jonathan, he is foreign here. And beyond this country is another one, and another capital with a gallery and libraries and boulevards of high-roomed buildings. It is vertiginous, terrifying.

Things are sliding badly. The Professor wanders off to look at the Egyptian rooms. Gittens takes Star by the elbow and steers her towards the nudes. Any will do, it seems. He positions her in front of Venuses, harem girls, nymphs pouring out of classical skies like scoopfuls of airborne marshmallows. He spends a long time before a particularly frothy Fragonard, a group of naked river-bathers, all blonde hair and dimpled pink flesh. Pointing out their 'enchanting pose' and the painter's 'dazzling technique', he stands close to her ear and starts murmuring something about the unbridled sensuality of art. Jonathan, who needs something to take charge of, decides that this might as well be it.

'Look, Gittens, I really don't think this is on.'

'On?' asks Gittens. 'What do you mean, on?'

'I mean – I don't think this is the way a gentleman behaves.'

'Oh Johnny,' says Star, 'don't be so *English*.'

English? *English?* He needs to sit down. The room is spinning, a vortex whirling faster and faster with him at the centre . . .

He wakes up to find his field of vision crowded with heads. Star, Gittens, a uniformed attendant, a man with slick black hair and a waxed moustache. He is lying on the cold marble floor. Someone has loosened his collar. Star is talking rapid French to a person he cannot see. Gittens looks down on him, an expression of genuine concern on his face.

'You all right, old fellow? You had a bit of a turn.'

Jonathan sits on his bed, propped up against the headboard by a pile of bolsters. Yes, he feels much better thank you. This is mainly due to Star, who has come to see him. She is sprawled on a heavy gilt armchair, blowing cigarette smoke out of the open window. It is not so much her presence (nice though it is) that is reviving him, as the way she is talking about Gittens.

'God, Johnny, he's so dull! On and on and on, like a schoolmistress! No wonder you fainted. I was tempted to try it myself. And so convinced that he's the great connoisseur, with his brushstrokes and breathing on my neck. Quelle horreur!'

'You know, for a moment I thought –'

'Oh how could you! He's not my type at all. Look at you! You're smiling. You can't be all that ill. In fact, you seem fine already.'

'Yes, I am. I don't know what happened.'

'Travel, I expect. I hate it too. All the Montparnasse crowd hate it. And the Saint-Germain, though if you're Cole Porter or the Aga Khan or whoever, you probably always go by air. Look, I've told Daddy and Dr Gittens that we absolutely must have this evening together. Dr Gittens looked quite shocked. He started saying he had no idea that you and I were friends, and had he known, and all that sort of thing. I think I actually believe him. Paris takes a lot of people that way when they're not accustomed to it. They find it overstimulating.'

She leaves Jonathan to get dressed. As he is tying his tie, Gittens puts his head round the door and asks after his health. They have a short conversation, by the end of which Jonathan is convinced he has misread Gittens entirely. He is really very decent. Whistling, he brushes his jacket and carefully slips the engagement ring into an inside pocket. The little square box makes a lump against his chest, so he transfers it to the left-hand side pocket. Perfect. He feels calm and refreshed, ready for anything.

Star is waiting in the lobby, dressed in a shimmering grey evening gown. Her Fotse bangles are on her arms. Her hair frames her face with the precision of an advertising illustration. She says, 'Tonight, Johnny-boy, you and I are going to have a marvellous time,' and it sounds like a manufacturer's guarantee. A cab takes them past a line of busy pavement cafés up the hill towards Montmartre. Paris is suddenly full: cigarette-sellers; men on bicycles; elegant women carrying little dogs; citizens of all kinds hurrying along, spilling out of the ornate Métro gates like newly saved Christian souls. This city seems unrelated to the grid of empty streets he walked through last night. It is brimming, boiling with life.

Star tells the driver to drop them off on a corner and leads the way down an alley to a doorway hung with red paper lanterns. They step through a bead curtain into a murky low-ceilinged room. Behind a counter, pigtailed men in high-necked white jackets are chopping vegetables and swirling them about in iron skillets. There is a great deal of steam and a great deal of noise. Tables are crammed together in the gloom. This is the first Chinese restaurant Jonathan has ever been in, and he does not like the look of it one bit.

'Are we really eating here?' he asks. It does not seem like an ideal spot for a romantic dinner.

'Absolutely. And we're both having the chop suey. Isn't this wonderful?'

Jonathan is not so sure. The little room is packed and smoky. Compared to the rest of the clientele, he and Star are wildly overdressed. They are served big blue and white bowls of food which he finds hard to get into his mouth without spattering sauce down his shirt-front. A wizened Chinese man at the next table keeps winking and flashing him the thumbs-up sign. Star, however, seems to be in her element. She eats with her elbows out, grinning at him between mouthfuls. He grins back, fingering the ring box in his pocket. Maybe? No. Best to wait until later.

'Now,' says Star as they swish back through the curtain into the street, 'time for some real fun.' They hail another cab and head up the Rue Pigalle into a zone of low crumbling houses, almost all of which seem to contain a bar or a cabaret. A smell of petrol hangs in the air, and the road is crammed with partygoers. Drunks stumble out into the road and gaudily dressed prostitutes stand around in clusters, their dinner-jacketed pimps sitting in their cars, smoking and preening. The place is shifting, flashy. Unconsciously, Jonathan starts to sink into a younger version of himself, straightening his tie, trying to decipher the chaotic comings and goings. Dotted among the white faces are a disproportionate number of black ones, wailing buskers from some Latin country, pairs of well-dressed Negroes cutting through the crowds like they own the pavement. Jonathan shakes himself, tries to snap out of his moment of regression. He has raised himself above this. The ring in his pocket is about to put the seal on it. So why has Star brought him to such a mongrel place? The black men, with their canes and silk shirts, seem like a bad omen.

The cab drops them outside a little bar called Le Grand Duc. Above the door is a triangular illuminated sign, with the word BRICKTOP! picked out in red.

'I'm very proud of the Duke,' says Star. 'Hardly anyone knows about it yet. And Brick is such a darling.'

A uniformed doorman salutes them as they go inside. The

place is small, only a dozen or so tables arranged around a room, with a bar to one side. In the centre of the space a tall red-haired woman is singing, backed by a drummer and a pianist. Most of the tables are full, but a waiter shows them to a free one, tucked into a corner. Jonathan looks round uneasily. Everyone in Le Grand Duc – singer, musicians, staff and customers – is black.

'Umm – *Star*,' he whispers urgently, 'this seems to be a Negro place.'

'Yes, it is darling. You Oxford boys are so observant. Hullo, Brick? Brick dear?'

She starts waving at the singer, who blows her a kiss back.

'I mean, what are we doing here?'

'Celebrating, Johnny. And don't look like that.'

They order champagne, and Jonathan tries to fight a rising tide of bad feeling. As if mocking him, the singer launches into a mournful song:

> 'Why do people believe in some old sign?
> Why do people believe in some old sign?
> To hear a hoot owl holler, someone is surely dyin''

She has an American accent. Around them, drawled American English mixes with French. Jonathan wonders where all these people have come from, the supercilious manager, the young brown-skinned busboy who keeps peeking through the kitchen door. He feels threatened, hemmed in. It is as if Africa is already reaching out towards him, before he has made sure of his foothold in Europe.

> 'To dream of muddy water, trouble is knockin' at your door
> To dream of muddy water, trouble is knockin' at your door
> Your man is sure to leave you, and never return no more'

A woman at a nearby table whistles her approval. She glances over at Star and says something to her friend, who laughs. Jonathan glares at them, but Star does not seem to have noticed. She is listening to the music, entranced.

'Doesn't it make you feel tingly inside? So sad. You can tell how much they've suffered.'

'Who?'

'Negroes, silly. It's not like you or me. The worst we've ever had to contend with is the bathwater not being heated up in the morning.'

> 'When your man come home evil, tell you you are getting old
> When your man come home evil, tell you you are getting old
> That's a true sign he's got someone else bakin' his jelly roll'

What did she say? Jelly roll? He flashes back to the boathouse, Star's moan as they fumbled about in the darkness. How long has she been coming here? He is wrestling with something, some hidden suspicion, when a well-dressed group of white people comes through the door. Instantly Bricktop switches to a light popular tune, the piano player picking up the pace. The atmosphere brightens. Jonathan watches the white party. They seem to be led by a couple, the woman petite and blonde, her husband older, beaming around at the other tables as if to say *see how I indulge my wife, so charming, so original* . . . They are evidently showing off Le Grand Duc to their friends. Bricktop stands at their table, singing just for them.

'They have something, don't they? Something we've lost.'

Star seems determined to talk about Negroes. Jonathan clutches the ring in his pocket. Now or never.

'Star, darling, I have a question to ask you.'

'Yes, Johnny?'

'The thing is, Star, we've known each other for a while, and you know how I – '

'Hey, sugar! Now how did I guess I was going to find my baby at the Duke?'

In a single movement, lithe as a cat, a man has insinuated himself into the chair next to Star. He slides an arm around her, draws her to him and kisses her full on the lips. Jonathan's jaw sags open. He is kissing her. This man. Kissing. Her. Kissing Star. And he is (this cannot be, this absolutely is not happening) – *black*. Black as night, as tar, coal, pitch, liquorice and the suits of funeral directors. Black as a Bible, his skin shining in the candle-light like something made of polished wood. The palms of his black hands contrastingly pink, his thick lips pressed on hers, kissing her, kissing Star. Kissing. Star. Black man. Star.

'Star?' asks Jonathan. His voice sounds small and far away.

'Sweets,' gulps Star. 'What are you doing here?' She looks flustered, angry.

'Baby,' says Sweets reproachfully. 'I came to see you. Why else would I be wandering around this big old city after dark?'

Jonathan's jaw begins to ache. He realizes he has not closed his mouth. Sweets turns round and extends a pink-palmed hand. He laughs, a big rich laugh full of humour and self-confidence.

'Elvin T. Baker at your service, but most everybody calls me Sweets. You a friend of my little shining Star?'

Jonathan sits there, rooted to the spot. He does not shake the hand. Sweets's good mood seems to fade.

'Sweets,' says Star, 'I thought I told you not to turn up while my father was in town.'

'This your father? He look mighty young to be anyone's daddy.'

'Don't be stupid. This is Jonathan. He's my – my friend.' She looks mortified.

'Star,' says Jonathan. 'Who is this man?'

'Oooh!' cuts in Sweets, raising his voice. 'You want to know who this man is? He's *her* man, that's who he is.'

'Sweets!' Star half screams. The world seems to slow down. Jonathan takes in details: Sweets's narrowed eyes, his diamond cufflinks, the cut of his beautifully tailored suit. Other things: heads craning round to watch the argument, the red-haired singer making a sign at the doorman.

'Johnny,' says Star. 'Listen.'

But Jonathan is halfway out of his chair.

'What are you doing? What are you doing with this – this –'

'Kid, say the N-word and you're dead,' says Sweets icily. 'You ain't at no British tea party now.'

'Sweets!' shouts Star. Then, 'Johnny!'

Jonathan heads for the door, Star following him.

'Johnny, wait!'

He wheels round.

'I meant to tell you, Johnny. I really did. I didn't know he was going to come here.'

'What do you mean, you didn't know? He's – he's a black man, for God's sake. What are you doing with him? You can't be – oh God – you are, aren't you. How – how long?'

'A while.'

'I can't believe it. I mean, what would your father say?'

Star stands her ground. 'Look, I don't care what my father says, and to be honest if you're going to be like that I don't care what you say either. Oh Johnny. I like you, you know I do – it's just – well, Sweets is different. He plays the piano. You should hear him play. He's wonderful. And he's different. Exotic. Strong. I've never met anyone like him.'

'Different? To whom? To me?'

Star looks at him, pityingly. ' Yes, Johnny, to you. Come on. I know you, Johnny. I feel I know all there is about you. Gloucester-shire, Chopham Hall, Oxford, blah blah blah. You're very sweet, but you're exactly like everybody else. You do the same things as everybody else and you say the same things as everybody else. I know if I stayed with you we'd end up getting married and we'd live in the country with horses and a rose garden and moulder away until we were a pair of tweedy old fools smelling of dog hair and making a nuisance of ourselves on the Parish Council.'

'But Star, you're English. I thought that's what you wanted.'

'When did I say that?'

'That you were English? You just *are*, that's all.'

'I mean about the country. I never said that. That's not what I want, it's what *you* want. You're the most conventional person I know, Johnny. I think that's all right, but it's not for me. You like following the rules, having everything just so. I want to get away from it. It's stifling, doing what you were born to do, following it all along from birth to marriage to death like you were on a set of rails. I want passion, primitive emotions. I want to be in contact with the origin of things. Don't you see? Sweets, he's – look Jonathan, he grew up on the streets. He knows about things. He actually shot someone once. And his family were terribly terribly poor. Things like that happen to Negroes. That's why they have soul.'

Jonathan stutters, 'But I've got soul.'

'Not really, Johnny. English people have a soul, which is why we go to church on Sunday, but we haven't got *soul*. Sweets explained it to me. It's about music and suffering. And it's something to do with food as well, but that's slightly different. Anyway, you don't have it and Sweets does.'

'Damn right I have,' says Sweets, who has come up to stand by Star's side. He puts a hand on her bare shoulder. Jonathan stares at it, black skin touching white, half expecting it to burn her.

The manager has arrived too. He looks Jonathan up and down sceptically.

'Everything OK here, Sweets?'

'Sure, Gene. No problem.'

'Good. When you've finished with your um – *personal business*, could you do me a favour and sit in with Brick? Jackson say he gotta make a phone call.'

'Sure, Gene. Sure.'

'Star,' says Jonathan desperately. 'You have to listen to me.' He looks over at Sweets. 'Do you think you could give us a moment alone?'

'Go on, Sweets,' says Star. 'I'll be fine.'

'OK, baby.' He saunters over to the band, and swaps places with the pianist.

'Star, what if I were to tell you that you don't know everything about me.'

'Don't be difficult, Johnny.'

'Star, listen to me. What if I were to tell you I'm not who you think I am. That I grew up on the street too. That I've done all sorts of things.'

'But it wouldn't be true. I know your parents were in the colonies, and while I accept it may have been tough sometimes, it doesn't really count.'

'That's not what I mean. My name isn't really Jonathan Bridgeman. I'm not even – Star, would you love me more if I were like Sweets?'

'But you aren't. Johnny, I don't know what you're talking about.'

'I mean, if I weren't so English. If I weren't so – *white*.'

'But you are, Johnny.'

'Star, I'm not. I love you and though I may not be as black as him, I'm blacker than you think. Honestly. I've got soul, Star. I have.'

'No, you haven't. You're being stupid now. Playing silly games won't make any difference. I'm sorry. I've made my decision. I didn't want to hurt you, but there it is. I think it's best if you go. Sweets has quite a temper.'

'Star –'

'Please, Johnny just go.'

She looks imploringly at him. In a daze, he turns round and walks out. Behind him, drifting through the door comes the sound of a jaunty piano.

When you have organized your whole life as a ladder (with, for example, something shining and white at the top, and sticky blackness at the bottom) there are consequences when someone kicks it away. Jonathan is in a state of collapse. He wanders around Montmartre, oblivious to shouts and offers, barely able to distinguish the pavement from the gutter.

This is what happens. This terrible blurring is what happens when boundaries are breached. Pigment leaks through skin like ink through blotting paper. It becomes impossible to tell what is valuable and what is not.

You're the most English person I know. It's a good one, all right. He can't help laughing, laughing until he is doubled up, bending forward with his hands propped on his knees and his breath coming in gulps. People steer round him, the madman howling in the street for no reason.

When he looks up, a giant is standing there in an astrakhan hat. From the curled toes of his red boots to the sheepskin jerkin belted round his considerable waist, he is an impressive figure.

'Cabaret, monsieur?' he says. 'Cabaret Russe?'

Why not. It makes no difference. Step inside, take a seat at a table in view of a rickety stage, with long silver streamers as a ragged backdrop and a circle of parquet in front where more giants are performing an athletic dance. They sink to their knees and kick their red-booted feet in the air, ethnographically perfect, the Cossack distilled down to an essence easily graspable in thirty seconds by the drunkest or most obtuse tourist. A shot of vodka. A second. One thing smudges into another. What is static is set in motion. What is solid melts, unfolding, birthing itself out of itself . . . And what about Star? He has done everything right, fashioned himself so perfectly. He has made himself into an accurate facsimile of the right man for her, only to find Sweets waiting for him at the end, a black hand on her shoulder. Is it too late to change? Maybe he should revert to an earlier incarnation. Or should he go on? Is Sweets's blackness another kind of skin he could put on and inhabit?

The Cossack dancers stop, and the band strike up a slow waltz. *Voulez-vous danser m'sieu?* She is an artificial blonde, huge sad eyes ringed with black, sunken cheeks hinting that underneath the paper-thin smile it has been a while since she last ate. Her name is Sonya, and you can tip her at the end of each number, if you like. They hold on to each other like drowning people, shuffling in tired figures round the dancefloor. She talks a little, about film stars, about her family who were rich before the Revolution. White Russian. There's another good one. White Russian. You understand? No, of course you don't. She leaves him holding his sides, leaning on a pillar, signs to the bouncers that no, he's not dangerous. Leave him. He will be quiet in a moment.

He goes back to the table. A ripple of applause greets the arrival on stage of a nondescript little man. In his white tie and tails he manages to look neither elegant nor specially scruffy. It is just a costume, a set of work clothes. Illuminated by a wobbly spotlight which casts a washed-out circle on the silver backdrop, he stands very upright and makes a bombastic introduction in a language (Russian?) Jonathan does not understand. There is a pause. He turns away from the audience, then spins back, a false moustache stuck on his top lip. Holding himself as if he is a very important person, a king or a politician, he gives a speech. A little laughter. Some heckling. He spins round again, comes back without the moustache. His voice thin and reedy, he quavers through a few words, his face held in a lopsided rictus.

Jonathan does not understand what he is saying, but he cannot take his eyes away from the man. One after the other, characters appear. One with a deep baritone voice. Another with a little cap and a hectoring way of talking. Each lasts a few seconds, a minute. Each erases the last. The man becomes these other people so completely that nothing of his own is visible. A coldness starts to rise in Jonathan's gut, cutting through the vodka. He watches intently, praying that he is wrong, that he has missed something. There is no escaping it. In between each impression, just at the moment when one person falls away and the next has yet to take possession, the impressionist is completely blank. There is nothing there at all.

The Impressionist

The prow of the liner looms over the port, a stark wedge of black that dwarfs the mud-coloured buildings. Against the ragged line of tin roofs it appears alien, ominous. As it materializes, women make their way towards it, pushing hand-carts, carrying basins of bananas and groundnuts and smoked fish wrapped in palm leaves. Stevedores form a chain, passing sacks and boxes into the company warehouses, and the women set down their loads and squat behind them. By the time the white men step from the launch on to the quayside a market has formed, complete with beggars and dogs and a policeman with a stick clearing a path to the Customs House. The white men shuffle and blink in the sunlight, while the market women pretend not to look at them, taking secret satisfaction in the circles of sweat spreading under the armpits of their fresh shirts, the way they look about nervously, afraid to catch anyone's eye.

Jonathan stares at Africa with uneasy recognition, the visor of his sun helmet taking a black bite out of the scene. All along the quayside, battered cargo vessels are emptying their bellies of canned goods and corrugated-iron siding, and taking on an equal volume in palm oil and bales of cotton and tobacco. They are fed by ant-like lines of men who jog up and down the bucking gang-planks, urged on by foremen with manifests and holstered pistols. In front of one ship a contingent of West Indian troops sit out in the heat, waiting to be told to board. Above them, positioned for enfilading fire, is a whitewashed slave fort, named for Saint James, though it might as well have been George or John; one of the English-sounding saints who would brook no nonsense and give a good account of himself in a fight. From the fort's crumbling parapet, the muzzle of a modern six-inch siege gun pokes out at the sea. The contents of this vista are new to him, but something in its arrangement is familiar. After years in Europe, he is back in a two-speed world, one part digging in its heels as the other part drives it forward. He knows the logic at work here; the system is etched into his skin.

In the Customs House, the anthropologists wait to have their documents processed while officials check a huge consignment of liquor, the smell of gin from accidentally broken bottles pervading the hot, busy hall. Jonathan stands and distractedly watches the bustle. Objects that England made familiar, ledgers and ink pads and uniforms, have been thrown back into strangeness. Umbrellas shield people from sun instead of rain, the faces of their owners black zeroes over their starched collars.

The Professor walks about, tapping crates with his walking stick and getting in the way of the porters. Morgan, sweat running into his eyes from beneath his new cork helmet, leans over to speak to Gittens.

'Look at Bridgeman.'

Gittens looks at Bridgeman. He is wandering around the Customs House, dejected and sullen.

'True, he's not himself.'

'I can see that – but it's been weeks now. Shouldn't we say something?'

'Such as?'

'I don't know. Ask him if something is the matter.'

Gittens stares at him witheringly. Morgan holds up his hands, accepting whatever charge – sentimentality, prying, effeminacy – is being levelled at him. During the voyage from Marseilles, Gittens has made him aware that he lacks certain qualities. Tact, for example. Reserve. It appears that the right thing is not to ask Bridgeman if something is the matter.

A hawker manoeuvres in front of them, holding up a basket of little wooden figures. They wave him away and he goes over to pester Bridgeman.

'Doll, sah?'

Jonathan looks down at the carvings. They are Englishmen, little painted *colons* in white uniforms, with bulbous topis on their heads. Their features stand away from their faces, eyes and mouths and noses sharp and oversized. Their stiff poses give them a formal, hieratic quality.

'How much?'

The man names a price. Jonathan bargains him down, and after a few minutes two of the little carvings are wrapped up in his bag. The hawker goes on his way and he carries on his work, negotiating with the officials and overseeing the unloading of the expedition equipment.

He walks about mechanically, as he has done for weeks, entirely preoccupied with Star. His internal projectionist runs the scene in the bar over and over again: Sweets sitting down, kissing her. Sitting down. Kissing Star. Sitting, kissing, sitting, kissing; a continuous nauseating loop. He cannot contemplate the confusion of that kiss straight on. Hunched into the front stalls of his mind, knees jammed tremulously up against the red plush of the row in front, he has to squint, wishing he could leave the auditorium, but pinned to his seat by this monstrous confusion of bodies.

On board ship he spent most of the voyage on a deckchair, staring at the Atlantic through his dark glasses. Every day he would sit for hours, watching the contrast between sea and sky, until his consciousness erased it and the world became a shifting grey blur. At night he stood at the rail of the ship and watched the water rushing invitingly under the keel below him.

By the same rail, he watched Professor Chapel take the air in the morning. Imposing and proprietorial, he would stick out his paunch and open his nostrils like gates, a munificent landowner permitting the air to frolic in the rolling parkland of his lungs. When he took off his panama to mop his bald patch, the light caught it with a blinding gleam. When the sea wind tugged at a loose strand of grey hair, it floated like a laurel wreath around his head. Faced with this evidence of election, Jonathan took heart. Here was a wise man, a good man. Jonathan was still his assistant, and together they were on their way to extend the boundaries of anthropological science. What higher purpose could one have?

Yet minus Astarte, anthropology seems less enticing than it did. Without Star, his heading is tenuous, his compass needle shivering and spinning around the dial. He tries to remember what he has read, about how explorers find themselves through solitude. Yet she was the final piece of his puzzle; with her, Jonathan Bridgeman would have been entire.

When the formalities are completed, he pockets the forms, now inked with the illegible stamps of a row of officials, and passes through the hall to find the others. They are waiting with a tall barefooted young black man, dressed in white shorts, a fez and a high-collared white housecoat.

'This is Famous,' says the Professor.

'Famous,' affirms the man, smiling. 'Big boy of IRC. Below me three small boy. I come take you there.'

You could say that the Imperial River Club had seen better days, but that would involve deciding when those days were. A bungalow standing at the centre of a baked earth compound, it boasts a driveway marked by a border of whitewashed rocks, a flagpole flying a sun-bleached Union Jack and a pair of miniature cannon mounted on either side of the front porch, their rusting muzzles pointing at the town. Built on what counts as high ground here on the river delta, it is set half a mile or so from the beach, far enough away from the dock to dull the market noise, but not far enough to escape the sewer smell which wafts in through the windows on days when the wind is not blowing off the sea. The stink partly accounts for the desolate aura of the place; that and the fact that the committee has never got round to planting any trees to shade it, so that the heat is stifling, and on days when the wind does blow, it whips fine sand across the floors, silting up the corners and depositing a gritty scum on the surface of the members' drinks.

The members themselves are a dour bunch, who treat new-comers with an unattractive mixture of jealousy and scorn. The scorn is the universal kind visited on first-tour men by old hands across the Empire. The jealousy is a local product. Its precise objects vary: the newcomer's constitution not yet worn down by the heat, or his gut, unpopulated by restive African bacteria. Perhaps it is his looks, or his wife, or simply his ability to take pleasure in life on the coast, the pleasure-taking faculty being particularly atrophied among the members of the Imperial River Club. Whatever its trigger, the jealousy is always there, along with a promise of future pleasure in its removal – after all, the newcomer will one day be an old hand too, and as raddled and bitter as everyone else. This *schadenfreude* is accentuated on funeral-days, of which there are two or three a month. When someone succumbs (they never die on this coast, they *succumb*, which involves a measure of culpability and moral failing, of letting things get on top of you), the members sit around and drink more than usual, itemizing the signs and portents which foretold this latest piece of bad news, and the things the deceased could have done to stay alive. If only he had taken more quinine, or better care, or fewer native girls, or simply switched to lime and soda after the third round . . .

The anthropologists, being boffins, come in for particular criticism. But it is mostly conducted in private, and they are able to settle in to their rooms without too much discomfort. There is much arranging to do. With the expedition equipment stored in a warehouse at the docks, several permits have to be gained, and various government departments liaised with. Soon after arriving they are visited by a political officer, a man calling himself Smith who arrives in a staff car, and introduces himself by showing Jonathan a pass embossed with the seals and signatures of an unnecessarily large number of important people. *The bearer*, says the pass, *is entitled to be in any place and wearing any uniform he chooses. All persons subject to military law are required to give him any assistance he needs.*

'In a way that doesn't apply to you,' says Smith, 'but in a way it does.'

Smith closets himself with the Professor for a while, then comes out and places a file on the smoking-room table.

'All yours, apparently,' he says to Jonathan. 'Have fun in Fotseland. Toodlepip.'

The Professor comes out wearing a grave expression. Jonathan looks up from his examination of a shelf of mildewed thrillers, Gittens and Morgan from their game of billiards. 'It seems,' says the Professor, 'that things have moved on somewhat since I was last in the country. The government has had considerably more contact with the Fotse.'

'Contact?' says Gittens. Both he and Morgan look crestfallen. Contact is one of their bugbears. If people will persist in communicating with natives, how is one expected to study them in their natural state?

'I thought,' says Morgan with his usual ruminative slowness, 'that they were relatively pristine.'

'I think they still are,' says the Professor. 'Relatively. However, the Northern administration feels the time is right for a proper census, prior to the institution of a hut tax. Apparently some steps have already been taken in that direction, but they want us to carry it on.'

Gittens looks outraged. 'That's not our job, surely.'

'That's as may be, but their position is that the patriotic purpose of ethnographic study is to collect information that will allow us to govern more effectively. Hard to argue with, when it's put like that. Apparently finances are tight, or they lack manpower, or something of that kind. So whether or not we like it, they are making it a condition of our permit to travel in Fotseland. Anyway, Gittens, you won't have to worry about it. The census will be Bridgeman's task.'

'Mine?' says Jonathan.

'Oh,' says Gittens. 'That's all right, then.'

'So, Bridgeman. All the paperwork is there, apparently. They have a system. Different coloured slips of paper, or something. All you have to do is fill in the forms.' Seeing Jonathan's appalled expression, he slaps him on the back. 'At least,' he says, looking down at the gin and tonic warming up in his hand, 'there is ice. There is always ice at the IRC.'

Jonathan looks mournfully at the file. Gittens tries to cheer him up. 'I knew there was something rum about that fellow,' he says. 'Did you notice, he was got up as a Belgian naval officer?'

The Professor leans back in one of the creaky cane chairs in the common room. 'By the way,' he adds, 'I have invited the other members of our party to dine with us this evening. I believe they should be arriving soon.'

'Other members, Professor?'

'Yes,' says Chapel, fishing an insect out of his glass. 'Two chaps from the Royal Geographical Society. They're coming with us to do some mapping. Another condition of our permit. The government wants a proper survey of the Fotseland region.'

This is the first the others have heard of it. Gittens raises an eyebrow.

'What sort of survey?'

'I have no idea. I imagine they will be able to enlighten you.'

'I thought,' says Morgan, 'that strictly Fotseland isn't ours to survey.'

'Don't be obtuse,' snaps Gittens. 'Of course it's ours. We just don't administer it directly. We rule through the local emirs, but that doesn't mean we can't make a map of the place.'

'I thought there was some question of the French –'

'Politics, politics,' sighs Chapel. 'Look, they're just coming with us to take a look at things. See how the land lies. Politics has nothing to do with it.'

'Very good, Professor,' says Gittens admiringly. 'How the land lies. Very good.'

The matter seems to be closed, and everyone disperses to change for dinner. At sunset they assemble on the veranda, to listen to the faint crash of waves and wait hungrily for the steward, an ancient man with tribal scars on his cheeks, to finish laying the table. As the light fails, the sound of laughter and yelling comes from inside the club. Famous appears, chased by a wiry European with a ginger moustache, brandishing a tennis racket. 'Famous, are you?' he shouts, whacking the African with the racket. 'What for, eh? What for?'

'Please,' says Famous, edging away from him. 'Please?'

'Don't understand, sambo?' laughs the man. 'I said' – thwack! – 'how' – thwack! – 'did you' – thwack! – 'get so famous?'

The sight of Famous being hit on the bottom with the racket is received with amusement. He hops comically up and down, pleading incoherently. Club members come out to see what the fuss is about and Jonathan finds himself part of a ring of savagely grinning men ranged around the bewildered servant. He steps aside, allowing Famous to make his escape.

'Evening all,' says the ginger man, with a London accent that brings a momentary grimace to the Professor's face. 'You must be the others. Godforsaken spot, isn't it?' He puts out a hand. 'Marchant. George Marchant.'

Introductions are made. Gittens is encouraging the Professor to roll out his 'how the land lies' joke when another figure appears on the veranda. Everyone turns round. It is not only his height, although he has to stoop to come through the doorway. There is something else, something which kills the conversation.

'Good evening, gentlemen,' says the man. His voice is flat and uninflected.

Marchant holds out his hands wide, a ringmaster's gesture. 'May I introduce Captain Gregg.'

'Not Captain any more, Marchant. Just Mister.'

Gregg shakes hands. All eyes are momentarily drawn to his cheek. Just below the bone is a knot of scar tissue, centred on a deep fingertip-sized pit. There is something obscene and fascinating about the little crater. An anus, a star. The man is otherwise unremarkable-looking, but the thing on his cheek gives his face a disturbing movement, as if the other features are about to be sucked into it, and at any moment the whole substantial head might slide away. Gittens, who spent the war at his desk in Oxford, puts on a comradely air.

'Where did you serve?' he asks.

'France. Field Artillery.'

As Gregg steps into the light of the oil lamp Jonathan sees his eyes: calculating, range-finding eyes, used to calibrating their hands and mouth precisely, according to the fall of shot.

At dinner the talk is of maps. Like the anthropologists, Gregg and Marchant have recently arrived in the country. They have come, they say, from Persia, where they were part of a survey team working around the Caspian Sea. What kind of survey, asks Gittens. Much the same as this, says Marchant. Making maps of places where there are none.

During the meal, Gregg hardly speaks. Marchant, on the other hand, never stops. Prompted by Gittens, he keeps up a stream of chatter, about wet heat and dry heat and lions and football and the King and the inconveniences of Persia, which, he has no doubt, will not equal half of what is waiting for them in Fotseland. Latrines, he says darkly. It is all more or less a question of latrines. Once or twice Gregg interrupts him, to correct a fact or damp down some of his more boastful comments.

'Obviously,' sighs Gittens at one point, 'a map of an unmapped place is a useful thing. But I'm still in some doubt about the nature of your work. Why Fotseland?'

Marchant gives him a significant look. 'They say they want a map, so we go and make one for them.'

'Scientific curiosity, Dr Gittens,' says Gregg. 'Could one have any higher purpose?'

'Absolutely not,' says Morgan. 'Isn't that right, Professor?'

Everyone turns to the head of the table, but Chapel does not reply, having fallen asleep. He is lolling forward, his heavy jowls flowing down on either side of his high stiff collar. His face is that of a man who (at last!) no longer has to associate anything with anything, and feels immensely relieved about it.

Another week is spent haggling with merchants and flattering the Governor at his dinner table. In quiet moments, Jonathan gingerly starts to work through his file. The task is daunting. There are three pages simply listing the records he has to produce, one set of documents for a district chief, another for village headmen, a third for the council of village elders, different coloured receipts for various areas, different shapes of chit for men and women . . . All his preparations for Africa, from his studies in the university library to his conversations with Professor Chapel (and further back, through history lessons, head-measuring, poetry-reciting . . .), have shown him the same edifying picture: a lone adventurer, heroically inscribing the English character on a blank land. Instead he is to be some kind of tax inspector. Something seems to have gone wrong.

There is also the question of the Africans themselves. Serving his food, making his bed or driving him around the port, they refuse to remain mere possessors of beliefs or participants in social organizations. Instead they seem irreducibly, disquietingly physical. These abstractions breathe, eat, talk and laugh – laughter that he can kill by walking into a room. Of course, it is what he has strived for; this instant effect is what it means to be the master. So why does he have trouble looking his servants in the eye? Why does he wish he could tell these faces, suddenly grave and inscrutable, *It's all right, I'm only pretending. Carry on, laugh if you like* . . .

On the morning the expedition is ready to depart, he wakes early and picks his way over a litter of coconut shells and driftwood to the beach. Fishermen are propelling long pirogues into the surf, forcing their paddles down into the water, dragging them back with fluid, determined movements. Slowly the boats clear the line of breakers and escape the fiercest pull of the tide. Only when they have reached the limits of vision do they pay out their nets into the water. The wind carries back little shards of sound, disassembled fragments of their work song. He sits on the sand where the beach rakes sharply downwards and spends an hour watching thumb-sized crabs scavenge the margin between land and sea. The beach stretches for miles. The crabs are operating on its entire length, a ribbon of tiny metropolitan bustle bisecting the stillness. There is something comforting about their little liminal world, something he does not want to leave. When he finally gets back to the club, Famous is calling for him in the yard and the anthropologists are standing around impatiently on the veranda.

Their steamer is waiting for them, wallowing at a riverside mooring a couple of miles up from the coast. It is an uninspiring sight: a square flat-bottomed hull with a flimsy roof over the top that was once painted white, but years of service have turned it more or less entirely rust-red. A single large paddle-wheel squats at the rear, its blades patched in several places. Forward, a pair of narrow funnels rise from the boiler, jutting through the roof behind the wheelhouse, which is a kind of knocked-together shed accessible by a ladder. A barely legible sign on its side proclaims this the good ship *Nelly*.

Almost all the deck space is taken up with crates and chop boxes, and the expedition members have to string their hammocks where they can. Jonathan ends up next to the engine. The crew, a silent captain and a trio of grimy deck hands, watch their passengers with somnolent disinterest, the stoker occasionally throwing a shovelful of coal into the boiler and tapping the glass of his gauges.

Several club members have come to see them off, and as the *Nelly* turns its head upriver there are shouts of encouragement and urgent warning gestures made at Jonathan, who has taken off his hat. He waves back, pretending not to understand. He is saluted by Famous, whose own head is adorned with a bulbous pith helmet.

As the sea recedes behind them, the *Nelly* steers through a wide delta, picking its way between shoals and rocks. Gradually the river narrows until it is a single channel, flowing sluggishly between densely forested banks. From time to time they pass villages where excited children paddle out towards them on pirogues, or turn somersaults off the jetty.

'So, we'll be seeing the cannibals soon,' says Marchant, grinning at Jonathan.

'Actually, the Fotse are farmers,' says Morgan.

'They told you that, did they? They're pulling your leg. I bet behind our backs they'll be cooking up their grannies in the pot.'

'No, really . . .' says Morgan, then trails off, seeing that he has missed a joke. Marchant rolls his eyes heavenwards.

The sun rises and falls several times to the sound of this sort of conversation. Marchant tries to start a game of cards, but comes up against Morgan's Nonconformist conscience. The Professor snoozes in a candy-striped deckchair, a piece of equipment whose status he has continually checked and fussed over since Dover. Gregg, who seems unhappy unless he has a distance to stare at, climbs up to the wheelhouse and sits in front of it. He leans his back against the wooden planks and smokes cigarette after cigarette, cupping them inside his closed hand like a sentry on night watch.

'Doesn't say much, does he?' remarks Gittens on the fifth day, jutting his chin at the roof and, by implication, at Gregg. Marchant leans confidentially close.

'Half the time he doesn't hear you. Blew his eardrums out

in the war. At Beaumont-Hamel we once had to fire those eight-inchers for thirty-six hours straight. None of us could hear a bloody thing for a week afterwards, and he stayed like it. Since then he says everything comes to him through a kind of whistling.' Here he adopts an especially significant expression. 'Like the sound of an incoming shell.'

Gittens looks uncomfortable. 'That's rum.'

'Too right it is. Drives him mad.'

'So, you were with him in France?'

'I was his CSM.'

'And you're still together.'

'Well,' says Marchant, allowing his pause to stretch almost to breaking point, 'after you've seen certain things, and done certain things, the only people you can really talk to are – you know . . .'

'Really? That is, yes. Absolutely. Yes.' Gittens contemplates for a moment. 'What kind of things?'

'You know. War. Personally I found it hard, but the Major – let's just say he was in his element.'

'*Really.*' Gittens, alarmed, glances nervously at the roof, as if at any minute Gregg might come crashing through it.

At first the river is busy, dozens of steamers like theirs plough-ing up and down, bulging with goods, or people, one with a Maxim gun mounted on the roof carrying glum khaki-clad soldiers. They halt at trading posts, clusters of huts built round warehouses and company stores, once at a native town, where narrow streets of houses wind round a mud-brick mosque. Gradually the river traffic thins and the journey becomes monot-onous, one bend looking just like the next, the fringe of green trees constant on either shore.

Weed clogs the wheel. The *Nelly* grounds on a bank, and the crew have to lever it off with long wooden poles. For a week or more Jonathan lies in his hammock, listening to the irregular roar of the engine and trying to find out something, anything, about what he thinks and feels. He is utterly unavailable to himself, his motivation for even the simplest thing fleeing before his introspection like a dream figure down a corridor. Not knowing what to do, he does nothing, like the others. Slowly the parade of days falls out of step. Time starts to organize itself in more elusive patterns. Things repeat. Sounds project him forward, or shuffle him back.

Minutes or hours? The Professor sleeps. Gregg smokes. There are no surprises, except from the land. Jonathan is waiting to be swallowed by towering forest trees, to feel he is approaching the primeval heart of a little-known continent: this is what happens when you go up an African river. Yet instead of closing in, the country opens up, the skies widening and the foliage on the banks thinning to tracts of low acacia scrub. Along the banks the settlements are fewer. The European trading posts space themselves further apart and the native villages get smaller, meaner looking. The one positive thing about the tedium of life on the boat is the sense of travelling in a straight line, of sedate movement from a beginning towards some guaranteed end. Little by little this ebbs away, the line of water unfolding another dimension, that of the truly unfamiliar, the unforeseen.

One day they come to a fork in the river, and carry on up a channel that is suddenly narrow, little more than twice the *Nelly's* width. Hour by hour the water gets muddier and shallower, and it becomes obvious that soon it will be unnavigable. After sunset, at the point where the river loses itself in silt, they come upon a crumbling jetty, its wooden pillars splayed out at precarious angles, like buck teeth.

The shore behind the jetty is alive with movement. At the sound of the ship's engine, hundreds of ragged people have come to crowd the bank, holding out their hands and calling to the white men. Behind them, the glow of campfires lights up the darkness, and an acrid smell of woodsmoke and excrement catches in Jonathan's nostrils.

Unnerved, the Professor gives the order to moor on the far bank. This does not deter several men from wading into the river and swimming out to the *Nelly*. They try to drag themselves on board, grappling with the crew, who push them back in, where they bob among the floating rubbish, only swimming off when Gregg fires a pistol round over their heads.

'Where are we?' asks Gittens plaintively.

'The end of the river,' says Morgan.

Marchant spits. 'End of the bloody world, more like.'

No one feels like going ashore, so they arm themselves and pass a tense night, taking turns to go on watch. Twice they are disturbed by sharp cracks, which Gregg says are rifle shots. 'So,' he concludes, 'there are other white men out there.' No one takes much comfort from the news.

Gradually most of the watching people drift away from the shore, and they are left to squint into the darkness, listening to a susurrus of unseen movement. It is impossible to say how many are camped there, and all the Professor remembers from his previous journeys is a little trading post, where the owner once sold him a bad can of Argentine corned beef.

The morning reveals a weird scene. The trading post has gone, if (as Marchant whispers) it was ever there at all. In its place is a mean little village, and the ruins of a large iron-roofed shed, which a wooden cross in front indicates is a church. Parked beside it are two lorries, their flatbeds stacked with giant reels of cable, and all around, for perhaps half a mile in every direction, is a makeshift camp. People swarm about, cooking food, washing, collecting water or simply huddling together in disconsolate groups. For some distance in either direction the river bank has been denuded of vegetation. Everything combustible has been gathered up.

The ethnographers go in search of authority, warily stepping into the confusion, pistols and hunting rifles at the ready. Instantly they gather a huge crowd, which, though not immediately hostile, has an intentness about it, a mute insistence that Jonathan finds terrifying. The others obviously feel the same, gripping their weapons tightly, and looking rapidly from side to side. There seems to be no evidence of order, no sign that the civil power has the situation under control. They are about to lose their nerve completely, when a heavily accented voice hails them from the direction of the trucks.

'Hey! Hey! White men! Come over here!'

There are two of them, and though Eino's hair is white-blond and Martti's dark, both their faces are horribly blistered by sunburn. Their surnames defeat even the hardened ethnolinguists in the party, they have been parked in the middle of the chaos for a week, and more than anything they want to know if the Englishmen have brought their fish.

'Fish?' asks the Professor.

'Herring,' says Martti.

'In cans,' explains Eino. 'We have the akvavit, but we need the herring.'

'Do we have herring?' asks the Professor.

Jonathan checks the provisions list. 'No, sir. No herring.'

'So,' says Martti. 'That is a blow. We thought you had herring.'

'I'm very sorry,' says the Professor.

'So,' says Eino. 'The tyres.'

'For the lorry,' explains Martti. 'You have brought the tyres?'

'No,' says the Professor. 'I don't think so. Come to think of it, I didn't know there were lorries up here. There are no roads.'

'You are wrong,' says Eino. 'There are roads. So, you have something else for us? Some provisions? Some letters?'

'Jonathan, do we?'

Jonathan shakes his head.

'So,' says Eino despondently.

'If you don't mind my asking,' says the Professor, 'what are you doing here?'

Picking a flake of dead skin off his nose, Eino points to the reels of cable. 'Telephone,' he says. 'We make the telephone line. To go along the road.'

The anthropologists are incredulous. Martti and Eino look pleased. They start to tell them how their job is very important because one day the whole world will be connected together, and how it is a hard job because the natives do not understand, and they cut the wire for the copper, or pull down the poles for firewood. Perhaps they will not make money. Perhaps they will find things better back in Finland. And now they have a breakdown in the lorry, and they have to sit here and wait for the steamer to come with the parts, and with their letters and supplies, and they think the Englishmen's steamer is the steamer, but it is not. 'So,' says Martti. 'We have to sit here some more.'

'But all these people,' asks the Professor. 'Where have they come from?'

The Finns shrug their shoulders. 'Some come to build the road. Others come for other reasons, maybe.'

The Professor shakes his head, and turns to the others. 'It wasn't this busy last time,' he says. 'It was really quite peaceful.'

'Do you think it will be like this everywhere?' asks Morgan, who seems upset.

'What about the authorities?' the Professor wants to know. 'Why does no one have this in hand?'

'He is in the church,' says Eino. 'You have to hit him, you know, with your open hand. He wake up after two, maybe three times.'

On closer inspection the church proves to have been converted into a house. Though most of the mud walls have dissolved, the part where the altar once stood has been repaired, and the holes in the roof have been patched with woven straw. The rest of the perimeter has become a yard, with a hearth, numerous pots and a bicycle standing in one corner, its chain rusted into a solid lump.

'Hello?' calls the Professor through the doorway.

From inside comes the sound of coughing, and a disembodied English voice. 'Piss off. Can't you see I'm thinking?'

'I beg your pardon?'

'Look, chum, is your name Johnnie Walker?'

'No, sir, it's Chapel. Professor Henry Chapel of Oxford University.'

'Well, if it's not Johnnie Walker I don't bloody well want to talk to you. So piss off.'

There is a muffled thud – the sound of a heavy object falling to the floor. Then a groan. 'Help!' wails the voice plaintively. 'Help me. I've gone and fallen out of bed.'

His name is Short and he's the bloody government round here and every other thing besides and if they want to give him a hard time about it they might as well come outside and fight. In the yard, after a bucket of river water has been poured over his head, he is a sorry sight, his eyes milky and unfocused, his skin a battlefield of broken veins and insect bites. He is a young man, not much older than Jonathan, but whisky and fever have wrecked him completely. He looks at the circle of anthropologists and cracks a smile over a mouth of black and mossy teeth.

'Jesus,' he says. 'You're real. I thought I'd made you up.'

They help him back to bed and stand in conference in the yard. Short's incapacity is a problem. As District Officer, he would be expected to help them find porters, and brief them about the latest situation in Fotseland. At the coast there was some conversation about an escort, perhaps even a detachment of WAFF or native police, yet Short shows no sign of understanding who they are, and seems incapable of feeding himself, let alone helping them with their expedition. Now Jonathan understands why the census job has fallen to him.

When they get back to the *Nelly*, they discover that someone has broken open one of their crates of provisions. The deck hands have seen nothing. Gregg orders a round-the-clock guard, and they spend the rest of the day arguing about what to do next.

As the sun sets, a high wailing voice calls over the camp. Some of the people gather for evening prayers, laying out mats on the baked earth and facing Mecca. Gittens, standing at the rail, looks at the wrecked church and makes a face.

'Doesn't look like the missionaries made much of a go of things here, does it?'

As the light fails, clouds of mosquitoes rise up off the water, and it becomes apparent who truly owns this district. Each English head is encircled by insects, like tiny Apaches around a wagon train. They settle on exposed arms and crawl into the openings of shorts and shirts, provoking a frenzy of slapping and ineffective applications of lemon-scented ointment. To escape, Jonathan trudges over to the church and sits in with Short, who is lying on his camp bed, mumbling. Intermittently he becomes coherent enough to hold a conversation, though it rarely makes much sense. 'Do you know what?' he says, over and over again. 'I haven't seen a white woman for two years. What do you think of that, Johnny?'

They spend two miserable weeks at 'Short's Landing'. The people follow them round everywhere, begging for food and money. When they first try to recruit porters they almost cause a riot, hundreds of men forming a scrum around the Finns' good truck, which they are using as a sort of stage to speak from. Trapped on the rocking flatbed, Jonathan clings on to the frame and tries unsuccessfully not to panic.

Every evening the flies come, bringing an hour of hell to

anyone not sitting close to a smoky fire. At night the Finns play orchestral music on a gramophone and take potshots at anyone straying too near the trucks. Despite their vigilance, women can already be seen wandering around with anklets made from twisted copper pair, their children with little copper charms tied to their wrists.

Sometimes Jonathan sits in with Short. During a brief interval of lucidity, he is able to make him understand that he is a scientist, headed for Fotseland. 'Bad show up there,' is all he says, and drifts back to Johnnie Walker and the fortunes of the Kent county cricket team, which are much on his mind. Though Short is clearly dying, being with him is restful, or at least better than the part of each night which Jonathan dreads most: when he is on watch. Alone on the deck of the *Nelly*, with the shoreline flickering with silent shuffling Africans, his personal landmarks vanish one by one. After a quarter of an hour he feels uncertain, after half an hour actively fragile. By the time his two-hour stint is over, his boundaries have dissolved altogether and he is lost, or perhaps not so much lost as dispersed through the darkness, his turning world bereft of still points, radically uncertain about who or where or why he is, or even whether he has the right to call himself a he at all. Once he enters this regress there is no turning back and whoever comes to relieve him invariably finds him wild-eyed and moaning, clutching his gun like a talisman. Naturally they are too polite to bring it up, but it is clear his companions think this is a matter for concern.

Finally someone manages to get a message to the local emir. Jonathan is half asleep in the church compound, listening to slurred fragments of pre-war batting averages, when a distant wail of trumpets announces the arrival of El Hajj Idris Abd'Allahi, who, though a slave of God, is hereditary ruler of all the plains to the north and east of the river, for as far as a man can ride in ten days.

The Emir's party is impressive. Outriders swathed in indigo robes are followed by an escort of chainmail-clad guards who surround the Emir and his courtiers, resplendent in fetching white and gold. The Professor, who in the absence of Short is representing both himself and His Majesty's Government, is ready with a feast. Once the greetings and introductions are complete, the anthropologists and the royal household share a meal of roast goat and British canned goods, the tinned peaches in syrup being a particular hit. Presents (more tinned peaches, a tea set and an umbrella) are made. Compliments are exchanged. It is well after midnight when the two sides finally settle down to business.

Despite the peaches, the Emir is in a contrary mood. No, he says, you do not want to go to Fotseland. Yes, insists the Professor, we do. You do not, says the Emir, vigorously backed up by his ministers. The Fotse are very dirty. They are infidels and their women are prostitutes. Nevertheless, affirms the Professor, we want to go to their country, and we will pay. Do not go, says the Emir. They are poor. There is a drought. Fotse women will give you inflammations of the skin and private parts, because their men lie down with livestock. Nevertheless, says the Professor . . .

Trade goods are useless. The Emir wishes to be paid in internationally negotiable currency. The sum the Professor suggests is unacceptable. Even doubled, it is unacceptable. Talks carry on through the night. The fire has burnt to embers and the grey light has started to pick out the shapes of sleeping men, when Gittens unwittingly breaks the deadlock by lighting a cigarette. The Emir indicates that Gittens's silver cigarette case is pleasing to him. Be a sport, whimpers Gittens, it was a present from my mother. Nevertheless, says the Professor . . .

Once the cigarette case is securely in his possession, the Emir agrees that a man called Yusef, one of his headmen, will lead them to Fotseland. The Emir also consents to sell the party some camels at a cut rate, which means that Yusef will have to recruit only eighty or so porters. The Professor is provided with a valet, and a man who once worked for a European household in a neighbouring district is hired as head cook. Finally it is agreed that Yusef's brothers will guard the caravan. At the end of the week, leaving the Finns sitting on their lorries, and Short propped up in bed with a hip flask and some cans of beans, the expedition is able to set off on the last leg of its journey, Professor Chapel swaying precariously on a camel in the midst of a straggling column of men.

Day by day the column advances up a newly laid gravel road, a startling white scar on the red land. The drivers pull at the reins of their bad-tempered camels, while porters balance the lighter loads on their heads, a line of sweating men carrying padlocked chop boxes, tents, the Professor's precious deckchair. At night Jonathan goes to sleep to the sound of the porters singing round the fire. Their songs are mournful, filled with the heaviness of their burdens and the hardship of being away from home. When he wakes again the singers are walking about in the colourless pre-dawn light, kicking their animals and sullenly undertaking the business of striking camp. One morning a broken line is visible on the horizon. Every morning afterwards it is more distinct; the ragged ring of hills which marks the borders of Fotseland.

Finally the road runs out, ending abruptly where a work gang of fifty or so men are breaking up the earth and pounding out a flat surface with hammers and rollers. Near by is a camp of army-issue canvas tents.

'Fotse,' explains Yusef. 'Government bring them to make the road.'

'Those men are Fotse?' asks Morgan, aghast. 'Where are their Fo necklaces? Where are their combs?' The labourers are dressed just like any Hausa peasants, with no Fotse status marks at all. Their foreman confirms that they have been brought down from Fotseland to do compulsory labour. The ethnographers question them for a while, though they seem reluctant to answer even basic questions about their names or their clan affiliations. The foreman, a Yoruba from the coast, is amazed anyone would want to go up to Fotseland. 'Show your guns,' he advises. 'They have respect for that.' The Professor tells him not to be ridiculous, that the Fotse are a very peaceful people, and they will welcome him with great joy because he is a chief in their land. The foreman seems unimpressed, and wants to know if they have any gin, as dash for letting them speak to the men.

The party moves slowly towards the hills, the earth under their feet baked hard, its surface patterned by fine cracks. From his rolling saddle, Jonathan squints through the heat haze at a world which shimmers as if perpetually on the verge of evaporation. Gradually the ground rises, and breaks up into a litter of boulders. They pass through the neck of a valley, following the dried-up course of a river. Sheer cliffs push up on either side, gnarled bushes clinging to the rock faces like ticks on the hide of a cow. The going becomes hard, and they have to scramble up steep slopes, the camels complaining and tugging at their halters. Finally they see their first Fotse homestead, a little knot of conical huts approached by a path dotted with coils of dried human excrement. Built under the shadow of a huge rock, it is surrounded by a patchwork of fields, marked by boundaries of river pebbles. Here and there, signs and charms are tied to stakes: animal skulls wrapped in dried grass to ward off pests; strings of beads and spider-egg sacs marking a plot's position in a Fo negotiation. The anthropologists are thrilled, and then disappointed. The farm is completely deserted.

So is the next farm they come to, and the next. The Professor, who was expecting the customary party of women singing lilting traditional songs of welcome, can think of no explanation for it. That evening they camp deep into Fotseland, without having seen a single live Fotse. They order Yusef to post a double guard. As the sun sets, Jonathan looks back down towards the plains, and wonders when he will see them again.

The next morning they come to the end of their journey. Under the great escarpment which the Fotse call the Lizard's Back is the compound of the Daou, the paramount chief. Around it terraced fields step down to a dry river bed of flat round stones. Behind it the cliff face is honeycombed with the caves where the Fotse lay their dead. Like the other farms, the mud walls of the chief's compound are deserted, and the goat pens empty. The silence in the valley is beginning to beat on the white men's eardrums, when Gregg spots movement up near the escarpment. He hands the binoculars to Chapel.

'They're hiding in the caves,' he says.

'Good God,' breathes the Professor. 'Why would they do that?

They give orders to make camp, while the Professor, Gittens and Gregg climb up to the escarpment, guarded by a dozen of Yusef's men. Jonathan watches them slowly picking their way towards the caves, and later on watches them pick their way back. The Professor looks distinctly unwell.

'Will you credit it,' he fumes, 'they actually asked me to go away. Me! They have no greater champion. My work has made them world-famous.'

'That's probably overstating the case a little, Professor,' smirks Gittens.

'And I'm sick of your sarcasm!' snaps Chapel.

'Go?' asks Morgan carefully.

'They seem,' says Gittens, 'to have a rather jaded view of white men. They think we're going to take more of them for government work.'

'But they were supposed to be *pristine*,' complains Morgan, rounding on the Professor like a man who has been given a dud tip on the stock market. He digs into a pack and brings out a battered book. 'May I quote, from your own description, *"the Fotse are a docile, joyous people, almost untouched by the ills of modernity, their pastoral —"'*

'Yes, yes,' says the Professor. 'Look, how am I supposed to help it if the administration wants to muck around with them? You know how keen they are on getting the natives working. I try to explain, but they haven't a thought for science! All you can ever get them to talk about is their blasted tax base.'

'If they want us to go,' says Jonathan, 'shouldn't we go?'

Everyone stares at him as if he is mad.

'Stop taking pops at each other,' says Marchant, 'and look up there.'

From openings all along the ridge the Fotse are emerging, hundreds of people leading their goats out of the caves, as if, like their ancestors, they are being born out of the rock of the escarpment.

The white men look at the Daou. They see a haggard Fotse sitting on a carved wooden stool. The fine scars on his face are lost in wrinkles. The weight of the multicoloured Fo necklaces looped across his chest appears to drag him down. Behind him his wives kneel in order of precedence, surreptitiously pinching each other, or coaxing termites to run into their neighbour's hair.

The Daou looks back at the white men and sees trouble. Around him his people are whispering, making wagers about the newcomers. Someone has to maintain tradition. Certain things must be done, even if they are distasteful. He signals to the griot, who steps forward and starts to sing the royal ancestry, enumerating his dead father's status and possessions, the number of his children and his most profitable transactions. Then come those of his father's father, and his father's father's father, and so on back into the obscurity of the past. After every few generations, refreshments are served.

Just as Fo necklaces become tangled up in one another, chains of debt and obligation that lose themselves in irresolvable complexity, such are the worries of a Fotse ruler. While the Daou listens to his genealogy, the shadow of the great escarpment gradually lengthens. It crawls over him, and over his people. By the time the griot sings the name of the first ancestor, only the white men and their servants remain in light. His voice shakes a little as he tells the visitors it is their turn. The young one is pushed forward and starts to chant in their language.

Jonathan sings (flat, to the tune of 'Land of Hope and Glory')

Son of Je-re-my Cha-pel, very wi-ise and strong. The Professor has prepared the lyrics on a neatly typed sheet of paper. There are several verses, tracing the story of the Chapels back to misty seventeenth-century obscurity on a Wiltshire smallholding. As the Professor beams with pride, the others look at their feet. When Jonathan's song comes to an end, the assembled Fotse whisper uneasily to each other.

'It was a bit short,' whispers Gittens. 'They probably think we're rather nouveau.'

Though he lets them know he thinks their genealogy despicably brief, the Daou is finally satisfied that they have not come to take more labourers, and grants them leave to camp near the river. They pass some days organizing their living arrangements and paying off the surplus porters. Unfortunately most of the men want to be among those who leave. They do not like the Fotse, who are heathens and eat forbidden food.

One morning Yusef the headman announces that he wants to go with them. This provokes an immense argument, which takes place outside Jonathan's tent, waking him from a troubled dream in which the dark mass of the escarpment tottered precariously over his bed. 'What's the matter?' he asks, pulling open the tent flap and rubbing his eyes. He never gets an answer, because Marchant emerges from his own tent brandishing a pistol.

Yusef starts, thinking he is about to be shot. Other porters rush up with knives and pangas, and during the confusion Marchant discharges the gun into the air. By noon, very few men can be persuaded to stay; they say the others fear pollution, but they do not. They are not superstitious men. They are brave men. They are also poor men, and want more money. The Professor has no choice but to give it to them.

For some hours, snatches of a happy hand-clapping song can

be heard far down in the valley. The sound of Yusef's departing column of porters makes everyone uneasy, and no one will speak to Marchant, who takes a spade and slopes off to dig a first-stab latrine.

For a long time the Fotse avoid the white men completely. There are no curious onlookers around the camp, no passers-by. Their unfriendliness increases the tension among the party, and though the Professor maintains it is unnecessary, Gregg and Marchant decide to post a guard.

One night Jonathan sits up late in front of his tent. He is watching Gregg stalk round the perimeter with a rifle in the crook of his arm, when he notices a group of flickering lights against the silhouette of the escarpment. Gradually they are joined by others, until there are dozens of them, and the cliff face glows like a termite mound. The lights remain there for hours, and for hours he sits and watches, his blank notebook lying untouched on his knee.

The following night the lights appear again, swirling about near the mouths of the caves where the Fotse take their dead. Deep and regular, the sound of drums floats down towards the camp. One by one, the white men hear the drumming and come out to find out what is going on. Peering up at the lights, Professor Chapel appears stricken. 'They never used to do that,' he says. 'It was taboo to go near the caves after dark.'

'Is there actually anything they did before that they still do now?' sneers Marchant. The Professor can barely contain his anger. 'You, sir,' he splutters, 'are an impertinent little man.' Marchant makes an obscene gesture (one Jonathan has seen many times, but which is obviously new to Chapel) and from that moment the expedition splits irrevocably in two, Gregg and Marchant moving their tents to one side of the hearth, and the Professor, Gittens and Morgan moving theirs to the other – or rather, the porters moving all the tents, running back and forth trying to fulfil the conflicting demands of the two groups.

After the initial exchange of insults, the feud is conducted in the traditional British manner. The warring parties simply cease to recognize each other's existence, politely avoiding eye contact, conversation and simultaneous occupancy of the thunderbox, fireside or mess table. An icy silence descends, broken only by the curt issue and receipt of orders. Since nothing is actually said, Jonathan mistakenly assumes the argument is over. Though he is puzzled by the rearrangement of sleeping quarters, he does not move his own tent. Thus he unwittingly makes everybody suspicious. Gittens in particular looks at him very strangely the next day. The following evening when he drags two folding chairs towards the hearth, the Professor refuses to sit with him, pretending he wants to take a walk.

That night Jonathan cannot sleep. Again the lights are clustered up by the caves, and the uneasy throb of the drums is oscillating the airless heat of his tent. Some time after midnight he decides to go and investigate. It is not so much that he wants to see what the Fotse are up to, but that he is afraid of what will happen if he does not. It is like being on watch on the boat. If he does not put a finite, determinate shape to his fears, he could go mad. Reluctantly, he pulls on some clothes and walks in the direction of the escarpment.

As he passes the latrine, a figure stands upright, fumbling with its shorts.

'I say! I say! Where do you think you're off to?'

It is Gittens, who will not be got rid of, firmly believing that he has uncovered some kind of plot. 'You're mad,' he blusters, when Jonathan tells him where he is going, but his suspicion is stronger than his fear. 'I'll come with you,' he decides. 'I suppose it's all right. I've got a gun.' He pats at his belt, swears, and goes to retrieve it from the latrine.

They climb up towards the sound of the drums, picking their way over the terraces by the moonlight. The rhythm tugs at them, speeding up their pace. It is impossible to tell how many drummers there are; when the music reaches one of its periodic crescendos, it sounds as if hundreds are playing. As they get closer, Jonathan and Gittens begin to tread carefully, in silent mutual acknowledgement that they are transgressing. To Gittens, despite his scientific training, the sound of native drums still has *Boy's Journal* associations of the cooking pot, and he looks mournfully down at his legs, wishing them a little less plump and white beneath their baggy shorts. Jonathan's unease has a different source. He is afraid of stepping into the firelight and feeling Fotse eyes upon him. He is afraid of what they might see.

At the base of the cliff, in front of the caves of the dead, a crowd of several hundred Fotse men and women are sitting in a ragged circle, marked out by flaming torches. To one side are the drummers, a mere six of them, beating out clattering sewing-machine rhythms over the regular whoop-whoop of an enormous double-headed drum. Wallowing on its side, each cowhide face as tall as a seated man, this drum seems to be the central focus of the gathering. In the cleared space before it a group of women are dancing, their bare arms and legs glisten-ing with sweat. Charms and bangles strike together on their wrists, the sound reminding Jonathan, with a sudden pang, of Star. The women form up in ranks facing the drummers, and then approach the bass drum in pairs, flapping their arms and kicking up the dust. Jonathan and Gittens, who are hunched behind a rock, are more or less immediately spotted by people near by. Gradually, in a wave of unease, news of their presence is passed around the crowd, but the dance still goes on, and slowly the two of them gain in confidence and inch out of their hiding place to stand, head and shoulders taller than the

Fotse men, like two white flagpoles at the back of the crowd.

The cycle of the dance continues, pair after pair stepping up to the drum, then giving way to the next. The rhythm becomes more intense, patterns doubling, the bass drum grumbling and booming like a discomforted giant. One by one the women fall out of step, spinning around with their arms held out, staggering, their bodies bucking and shuddering in the grip of trance.

Then the music stops.

It is as if something flows into the silence. In an instant, the bodies of the women snap into new forms, and they start to rush from side to side, shouting and moaning. Each one of them is in the grasp of something individual and specific; one hobbles around and wags a finger at the audience, another rubs her haunches lasciviously with the palms of her hands. Some of these personalities are comic, others threatening.

'Ah yes, the ancestors,' begins Gittens, turning to Jonathan authoritatively. 'According to most accounts –'

Jonathan nudges him, pointing to a group of dancers whose movements appear different to the others. 'What about them?'

Everything about these new arrivals is stiff. The women they are inhabiting move with a rigid, pompous gait, swinging their arms swiftly to the side, or holding them behind their backs. One clutches something square in its hand, slapping it and waving it at the audience. Others hold sticks, jamming them against their shoulders and aiming them like rifles.

'My God,' breathes Gittens. 'I think that's us.'

No one in Fotseland can say exactly when the European spirits first arrived. New spirits have come before, out of the desert or up from the coast, but there were never so many of them, and they were never so angry. Some, like Massa-Missi, scold and give orders. Others, like Sahjat, take hold of people and try to carry them off. They are hard and unpredictable, and to many Fotse they are a sign that the old times have gone, and the new ones will be bitter.

In the past nobody left Fotseland, or, if they did, they went down on to the plains and vanished into the villages there, never to be seen again. Now there are Fotse who have gone and come back, with strange stories of travelling over water or digging under the earth. Always the white men are at the root of it. The white men's spirits move them to build huge granaries and slaughter one another like bridegrooms killing goats before a marriage feast. Somehow those spirits must have crawled into Fotse men while they were asleep, and travelled back with them.

Certainly the European spirits have brought changes, unless the changes brought the spirits. That is one of the questions which trouble the Fotse elders, when they discuss the new times in the shade of the fruit trees outside their farmsteads. Which of the two, spirits or changes, came first? Before, no one would have spoken like that, or even spoken of old and new times, because there were no such things. Time was just time. People followed the ways of the ancestors. They ate only the clean parts of their animals and harvested their millet after making the millet sacrifice. They avoided sexual intercourse before their newborn children were weaned, and, when it was right and proper to do so, they made Fo with each other. In return for all of this obedience, the ancestors kept turning the year and bringing forth more harvests, which fed more children, who became adults and then died and became ancestors in their turn, helping to spin the year, the ancestral force always growing stronger, powering the Fotse world through a kind of mythic perpetual motion.

Now the machine has broken. Now there are the old times, and the new.

Maybe the missionary brought the past and future with him

in his saddle bags, when he rode through the land talking about the high god and the dead god and the end of time. He left little else but that: the idea of a beginning, and an imminent end. He told people to think about their own endings, and about where each of them would be when there was no more time. Instead of asking the ancestors, 'What is right for us to do?' people started to say, 'What is right for me? What will happen to me now, in these end times?'

Government white men came and gave the Daou a magic stick with a silver tip, and gave other chiefs sticks tipped with brass. The chiefs were proud, but then in return for the sticks the government took many Fotse men away with them, and some were away for a long time, and they could not harvest their crops, and their wives ran away with other men.

People began to say, 'Life was not like this before.'

The white men warned them about sorcery, which seemed natural: Fotse doctors and rainmakers do the same. No one in Fotseland likes sorcerers, but they are a fact of life. Everyone has jealous neighbours, which is a good reason to live far apart from one another. If spells fly back and forth, that is only to be expected.

If your pregnant goat dies, or your child is bitten by a snake, you can consult oracles to find out the name of the person responsible, and make them pay you restitution. Sorcery can be reversed, or turned back on the sorcerer. Charms can protect you. Only in the most serious cases, when ill-will brings people to the point of death, does magic ever become a public matter.

Yet some people have been asking, what if the new times were brought on by sorcerers? What if upside-down people banded together and changed things for the worse? Would it not be a good idea to eradicate them once and for all, and live in a world free of sorcery? Then maybe there would just be time again, with no old or new.

These are frightening thoughts, full of change and upheaval; they are new-time thoughts. Lately the oracles have been working hard. Fresh sorcerers are discovered every day, and people are dealing with them harshly.

There are some who have another idea about sorcerers. The world beyond the borders of Fotseland is a confused place, where sorcery is ordinary, right is wrong and people walk upside down. The evil of the outer lands has always been known, and the new Fotse travellers confirm that the further away you go, the worse it gets, until you reach freezing places where the living people are crammed together while the dead ones lie out on open fields.

Who comes from the outer lands to take the Fotse men away? Whose troublesome spirits ride the women before the great drum, so that even if, in desperation, they dance in front of the caves of the dead, the ancestors rarely emerge to take them over, and leave them to the stamping and marching possession of Sahjat and Massa-Missi?

Who could be more upside down than white men?

Some time before morning, Jonathan and Gittens walk back down the hill to the camp. They are not sure how to interpret what they have seen. Jonathan is troubled, but Gittens seems relieved. Just a festival, he says. Just their way of celebrating our arrival.

When they tell him, Professor Chapel is not at all pleased. He ignores Gittens's excited description of the possession ceremony and makes a blustering speech, using words like 'escapade', 'flagrant' and 'willy-nilly'. Any interaction with the Fotse should, he says, have been sanctioned by him. He is the leader of the expedition and will not have his authority challenged. From the other side of the hearth comes Marchant's loud, insolent laugh. Impotently furious, Chapel turns on Jonathan.

'As for you, I thought you had a job to do,' he snarls. 'Isn't it time you stopped wandering around camp and went on tour?'

The next day Jonathan sets off, crossing the dried-up creek bed below the Daou's compound with three porters to carry his files and camping equipment. The porters' names are Idris, Ali and Danjuma, and, as he gives them the order to follow on, he realizes he is afraid of them. They speak softly to one another in Hausa and watch him with blank, dispassionate faces. They are the first natives it has been his sole responsibility to command. It is a relief to be leaving the shadow of the escarpment, but quite how he is to go about the census is a mystery to him. Most of the government instructions deal with such matters as village councils, sub-chiefs and Arabic lists, but since the Fotse (being highly decentralized, and more or less deregulated) do not live in villages, have no obvious system of local government and do not write in Arabic, none of this seems relevant. Until Gregg and Marchant finish their work there will be no accurate maps of Fotseland, and the only records the Fotse keep are the necklaces which list Fo transactions, and these are destroyed once a trade is finalized. When asked how many people he rules over, the Daou habitually uses the word a hundred and ten, which is a common Fotse expression for 'quite a lot'. As work on Fotse mathematics (Chapel 1913a) has demonstrated, their system can accommodate very large numbers, as well as abstractions like fractions; Jonathan gets the impression the chief is being uncooperative. The griot puts the figure at 'as many as the wild goats which clamber on the Lizard's Back', which is also not very helpful. When the griot asks rhetorically why anyone would be so foolish as to want to count the number of wild goats on the Lizard's Back, Jonathan has no answer.

So he begins with the first homestead he comes to, and marks it down on his list as number one.

It is not a very good system.

Mostly the residents hide from him, and he has to send his men to look for them in their granaries, or their animal pens, or out in the bush. The porters search half-heartedly, and usually come back alone. Jonathan develops a system of estimating the number of people living in a farmstead by the number of eating bowls. When the owners are found, they are sometimes too scared to speak and huddle together in their yards, pleading forlornly with him to go back to the outer lands. If he can get them to calm down, they often do not understand what he wants, or say obviously ridiculous numbers ('Three? I can see at least ten'), or try to bribe him to leave them alone, offering him goat meat and millet beer, and whispering to their children to clutch on to the fabric of his shorts and sob. It works. If there is one thing he cannot cope with, it is being tugged at by crying children. When it gets to that stage he usually leaves, scribbling down whatever figures seem most likely.

By end of the first week he has covered thirteen farmsteads.

He tries various tactics to make his visits less traumatic. He smiles. He sings. He gives the coloured census chits out to the children to play with, and does not ask for them back. Nothing makes the people less frightened or his job more pleasant. His servants hate the Fotse and dislike touching them, complaining of various kinds of disease and pollution. When they have to drag reluctant farmers out of their hiding places, they show their distaste by handling them roughly. First Jonathan orders, then asks, and finally begs them to be gentle, but they ignore him. When Idris slaps a man round the back of his head in front of his wives and children, Jonathan realizes he cannot go on.

He pitches camp that night under the shade of a large tree. After the porters have gone to sleep, he sits out in his creaking canvas chair and tries to think. He knows that he has come to the end of something. It is a shock, like diving off the high board and touching the bottom of the pool with your hands.

Why should he do this?

As the hours wear on, the heat of the day seeps back out of the earth and out of his limbs, until he is chilled through, and finally faces the possibility that what he has found the bottom of is himself.

Why count the Fotse? Who could be so upside down? Of course he knows why – for God and England and the Empire and Civilization and Progress and Uplift and Morality and Honour. He has it all written down in his notebooks; but though it is in his notebooks, it is not in him. He finds he does not really care about any of those words. He does not feel them, and that lack of feeling marks the tiled bottom of the pool. Jonathan Bridgeman can go so deep but no deeper. If he felt the words, he would have the will to count the people, and the will to transform them according to his counting.

He does not feel the words.

Self-pity sets in with the cold. He starts to mutter to himself. It was supposed to be an adventure. Bridgeman would find it an adventure. By now he would be an imperial hero, dashing and wise: Beau Bridgeman of Fotseland, the most English man in Africa.

What is he doing here?

Since he has been Jonathan, he has tried never to think like this, never to imagine that the fit between the two of them could be anything less than perfect. Whenever there was doubt, he shook it off.

What would he do anywhere else?

The Khwaja-sara, unfurling new selves like conjurer's flags.

Jonathan has learnt the trick. People care about outward forms: the width of a cuff, the sound of the labial-dental fricative 'v'. Becoming someone else is just a question of changing tailor and remembering to touch the bottom lip to the ridge of teeth above. Easy, except when that becoming is involuntary, when fingers lose their grip and the panic sets in that nothing will stop the slide. Then becoming is flight, running knowing that stopping will be worse because then the suspicion will surface again that there *is no one running*. No one running. No one stopping. No one there at all.

The night presses down on him. For a while he considers blowing his brains out with his hunting rifle. At least he could die as Bridgeman. It would be an elegant and English solution, though it would involve taking his shoes and socks off. When he bends down to undo his laces, he discovers that the strength of will to commit suicide was also one of Bridgeman's qualities, not his own. In despair he digs into the breast pocket of his safari shirt and takes Star's engagement ring from its secret place next to his heart. Cursing and howling, he turns it over and throws it into the distance.

He turns round to find three half-asleep porters watching him blearily. Trying to recover his composure, he tells them to go back to bed, and staggers back to his tent.

The next morning he realizes that while he does not want to continue with the census, he also does not want to go back to camp. Instead, he decides to carry on as if nothing has happened, except that instead of actually going into the farmsteads, he will pass them by, and make up the entries in his notebook. When he first does this, going as far as a few hundred yards from a farmstead, then skirting round it, Idris and the others look at him strangely, but say nothing. After a while they accept it as another routine, no more or less crazy than anything else they have been asked to do. In this way he zigzags across the Fotse countryside, gradually losing his sense of direction altogether.

He does not ask the porters for help. They do not offer it. After a while he begins to see landmarks that he recognizes, and it occurs to him that he might be walking in circles. All the farmsteads look the same, a little knot of conical huts round a central yard; and after the thirtieth or so, they begin to blend into one.

The only way to tell them apart is by the shrines. Each farmstead has one, sometimes in the yard, sometimes out in the fields, where it can take care of the crops. The idols, standing under little thatched shelters, take every form: stone, carved wood, painted and unpainted, a shapeless mound of clay with shells pressed into it for eyes and mouth. Embedded in one is a fragment of blue-glazed tile which must have found its way south across the desert. Another consists of a baton of oxidized metal that turns out to be a flint-lock pistol, its stock eaten away by termites. All are coated in libations – a mess of coloured powder, milk and millet beer offered up to the ancestors. He is standing, considering a bulbous figure with a top-knot on its head, trying to decide if he has seen it before, when he hears the distant crackle of a gramophone and realizes he is only a little way from the camp.

While Jonathan is on tour, Marchant's obsession with latrines is vindicated. His original model (a simple trench), is soon superseded by a mark two version, and then a mark three. The MkIII is an elaborate affair, with twin wooden thunderboxes (pilot and gunner) enclosed by wood and canvas housings with lockable doors. Though Marchant's original intention was to enforce a complete separation of toilet facilities, events overtake him. Illness strikes the expedition, and for ten days it is every man for himself.

The illness is characterized by terrible gut-wrenching pain and an alarming sensation of liquefaction, which means that both thunderboxes are in almost constant use. Possession being nine tenths of the law, no occupant is ever keen to vacate for his frantic colleagues. Rattling the door, abuse and even threats become commonplace. The degeneration into savagery is swift, and comes to a head with Gregg blowing the gunner door lock off with his revolver, dragging out a terrified Gittens and then barricading himself inside. Marchant has to coax him out by singing sentimental soldiers' songs through the wall. Afterwards, by common consent, the housings are removed and the latrines declared a neutral zone. Fotse observers report to the Daou that, curiously enough, even at the height of their affliction, none of the white men think of doing their business in the bushes. The spiritual significance of the boxes is, they suggest, penitential.

The illness subsides, leaving the victims thinner, sallower and consumed with dislike for one another. Marchant and Gregg resume surveying, slowly mapping the region around the escarpment, meshing it in their powerful abstraction of triangles. Edgy and irritable, they discover that while they have been occupied, some Fotse have taken to hovering around at the perimeter of the camp. Most are children, but a few insolent young men sometimes join them, strolling about and listlessly examining things.

One morning a boy scoots out of Marchant's tent, followed by Marchant himself, dressed only in a towel. The boy has a head-start of several yards, and after a few paces Marchant gives up the chase. 'Can you believe that?' he pants to Gittens. 'The little wog stole my shaving brush!'

After this they keep a careful eye on their equipment, and resume night-time patrols of the perimeter, but despite their caution a series of personal things goes missing. The Professor loses his shoelaces, and Gittens a penknife and a tin of dubbin. Some of the things the Fotse steal have no obvious value. Morgan finds two men sifting through food waste behind the kitchen tent. He catches another boy on his hands and knees near the latrine, carefully collecting up hair and toenail-clippings.

When Jonathan comes back from census-taking he finds the whole team sitting together round the fire. They are listening to Morgan's scratched record of Welsh hymns, a nagging paranoia overcoming their distaste for each other's company. Most of the expedition's guns are with them, propped up against chairs, casually fondled in laps. It is dusk and everyone is furiously smoking, a habit which started as an insect-repellent, but over the days has taken on an atavistic, slightly hysterical intensity. Jonathan is greeted by grunts and nods. Morgan shuffles his chair sideways to make him a place.

They ask him a few questions. ('Bloody, was it?', 'Run into any bother?') but do not seem interested in the answers, too mired in despondency to care about much outside their own troubles. The conversation, such as it is, concerns the horrors of the climate and the general degeneracy of the Fotse, who are failing to come up to anthropological expectations. To Jonathan their opinions sound as if they are coming from a great distance away; recordings, inscriptions from a place about which he knows something, and to which he once felt connected, but now has trouble recalling, unable to fix it in the turmoil of his memory.

'This,' sighs the Professor, 'is not the Africa I knew. In Fotse-land I used to be able to shake off the cares of modern man.'

'The burdens,' adds Gittens, 'of civilized society.'

'Well, it's fucked now,' says Marchant. 'Fucking hot, full of bloody flies, and as for the wogs, the ones they have here are worse than gyppos.'

The Professor winces. 'I wish . . .' he begins, but trails off. 'Oh, what's the point?'

Gittens steps in. 'I think I see what you mean. Like visiting our own distant past.'

'You mean, fucking *primitive*,' says Marchant.

'Pristine,' corrects Gittens.

'It must have been such an innocent place,' says Morgan wistfully. 'An Eden. And to think that none of it will be here in ten years.'

'Good riddance,' says Marchant.

'It can't be helped,' says Gittens. 'It's the price we pay for progress.'

The others nod philosophically.

'I propose,' says the Professor, 'that our prime concern should be recording. If we salvage what we can in the way of artefacts –'

Gittens and Morgan nod enthusiastically. 'The interviews haven't exactly –'

'Exactly,' agrees the Professor bitterly. 'And they used to be rather talkative.'

Morgan wonders whether they ought not to try again, suggesting it with the air of a man who hopes he will be contradicted.

Gittens, whose pet theories about noble savages have been rather dented in the last few weeks, is in no hurry to talk to any more Fotse at all. He quickly changes the subject. 'Ten years? That's not completely certain, is it?'

'That,' says the Professor, 'is what the man from the Governor's office led me to believe. There are timetables. When the road grid for this district is finished, the plan is to concentrate the Fotse into settlements around the primary junctions. Nothing will happen for five years, but he advised me to take what I could now. I said it was a shame, but he gave me the predictable line – omelettes and breaking eggs and so forth.'

'What if they don't want to go?' asks Jonathan.

'I expect the authorities are prepared for a certain amount of opposition. Some degree of coercion is often necessary in this sort of case.'

Morgan thinks about this for a moment. 'It's in their best interests of course. From an economic point of view, it makes a lot of sense. The yields they get here are terrible. If we show them how to plant properly, and perhaps move them on to some better soil, who knows, perhaps in twenty years they could even be growing cash crops for export. It's not impossible. If their goats were crossbred with European stock it would increase their weight. They would get more milk –'

'Do you have to talk about goats?' sighs Gittens. 'If I never see another goat in my life, that will not be too soon.'

'I happen to find goats quite fascinating,' says Morgan primly.

Jonathan has a question. 'Don't you think they'd rather be left alone?'

'The goats?' scoffs Marchant.

'The Fotse.'

The men look at him incredulously.

'I don't know what you're getting at,' says Gittens in a measured tone, 'but I think it's typical of your attitude, Bridgeman. I know I'm not alone in my opinion.'

The Professor frowns. 'In retrospect, I think it was a mistake inviting you to participate in this expedition. You haven't really pulled your weight. You're unwilling to work. You haven't participated. Your main trouble, Bridgeman, is that you lack team spirit.'

'Team spirit?'

Morgan looks pityingly at him. 'You're not exactly a joiner, are you?'

Jonathan looks at them, and hears around the perimeter of the camp the sound of the wind rustling the grass.

'No,' he says, 'maybe you're right.'

Though it is still early, he makes his excuses and heads off to bed. He spends the night oscillating between two states – a surreal wakefulness in which the silence sings with tension, and something which may or may not be a dream, in which he becomes aware that cables and wires are strung between every object and person in the darkness around him, forming a single interconnected mechanism. Every time he changes position or raises a hand to his face, he also moves other things, a cascade of effects reaching out into the beyond. Sometimes those things act on him, moving his arms, his eyelids. If he could free himself, he might be all right. If, at least, he could discover how the system worked, he might be able to gain some independence from it. He imagines the Fotse as their huts are bulldozed and they are marched towards their new settlements by the side of their new roads. In the small hours, the past is even more confusing than the future. A suppressed thought starts to take form. What if, long ago, he got lost? What if he got lost from himself, and can never get back again?

The next morning he leaves camp, telling Chapel that he

wants to carry on with the census straight away. The Professor tells him that he can take only two porters with him, because several of the boys have run off, and they are short-handed. He readily agrees, and sets off upstream along the dried-up river which runs past the Daou's compound. He does not know where he is headed. He just knows that he cannot stay.

Jonathan follows the course of the river, walking a herder's path between boulders and stands of tough, spiky grass. Though he passes several farmsteads, he does not stop at them. At the first, he takes out his notebook, but cannot bring himself to write anything in it.

As the sun reaches its zenith, the bed of stones turns towards the escarpment, which towers on for miles to north and south. For the rest of the day the narrow river path runs almost at its foot. Jonathan makes camp in a cleft between two giant boulders, and as the night falls, with the clinical swiftness with which night always falls in Fotseland, the curtain of rock which has loomed over him all day starts to oppress his mind. As he watches Idris cook his supper, he fancies that the change is physical and the cliff is somehow growing bigger. By the time he goes to bed he is not so sure. It is more that the escarpment is concentrating its substance, intensifying itself.

On the second day, walking under the eye of the cliff from morning until night, the feeling is worse, and on the second night he cannot sleep. He hears noises near the edge of the camp, first to one side, then another, and becomes convinced that figures are circling around his tent. Instead of pulling open the flap, or going outside with a revolver, he lies very still under his sweat-soaked blanket, his eyes wide open, his arms at his sides, and thinks, *Let them come.*

They do not come, but when he wakes up in the morning the porters have gone. Their blankets are still lying by the embers of the fire. He calls and calls, but there is no sign of them. As he tries to work out what could have happened, the world jumps around a little at the edge of his vision. The flask from which he takes a sip of brackish water is a dead weight, and the light filtering through his sunglasses is unpleasantly bright. Confused, he tries to strike camp, but finds that folding the tent is complicated. He rolls it and tries to push it into its canvas cover, but it will not fit, and the effort exhausts him. He wanders around scattering things over the site, and though he calls for his servants, angrily, fearfully, all he can really think of is how much his head is throbbing. It dawns on him that he is feverish, but it still seems imperative to keep walking, even without someone to follow him.

There is far too much equipment for Jonathan to carry on his own, so he simply abandons most of it, piling a few things under a tree, then giving up altogether, stuffing some canned rations into his pack and picking up a blanket, a gun, essential items. The camp seems to lurch away from him, and with a jolt he is stumbling off up the path, moving on to wherever he was going. Where was he going? He walks on, and the packed mud of the path crumbles into broken ground, stone scree which is hard to walk over. It is getting difficult even to put one foot in front of another. The sun lances down on to his bare head (Where is his hat? Did he drop his hat?), and eventually his vision is so blurred and his head swimming so fast that he sits down for a moment, just to rest, and before he knows it he is lying down, staring up at the sky, a tree branch creeping into his circle of vision, like a crack in a blue pane of glass.

He thinks, Maybe I am dying.

His dusty body is baked dry of sweat. Chills sing through him, sine waves of cold that propagate up his aching arms and legs, heading in a nauseating rush towards his centre. There are hallucinations. High up on the escarpment an old man clings to the cliff face, dressed in red boots and a red hat. Jonathan's vision magnifies, and he sees that the man is crouched like a spider, scuttling headfirst down towards him. Sometimes the man stops scuttling and leans back to apply a white powder to his hands from a pouch on his belt. Sometimes, almost nonchalantly, he hangs from one arm, suspended over a drop of hundreds of feet. He is moving quickly, coming straight down, the red of his cap and boots impossibly rich and bright . . . and the next thing he knows the blue pane is crowded with Fotse faces, liquid-eyed men etched with spirals of fine scars, and many hands hold him up, and the scars swirl, and he tries weakly to sit up, but all that comes out of his body is a shivering vibration. He is given water, and the blue pane of sky jolts left and right, left and right to the sound of men's low voices, singing the same work-song pattern, round and around and around. The sun bakes his skin, tightening and scorching it. The sky jogs and shivers until, in an instant, it disappears entirely, and all is cold and flickering firelight on stone, and he knows – the only clear thing – that he is now under the ground.

His Fotse carriers take him far into the body of the earth and set him down in a place where there is a crunch underfoot, and the ceiling is like a dome. Under the firelight he sees that the cave is decorated with thousands of red handprints, a dome of red hands suddenly obscured by heads which bend down close to him, one in a red cap, the old man who shakes a bone rattle in jerky spider figures and chants low in his ear. Hands lift him and then, slowly, he is stripped, fingers tugging unfamiliarly at his buttons, hands pulling down the waistband of his shorts. He is too weak to resist, as his ankles are gripped and his legs held apart, as fingers rub and pinch every part of his skin, parting his buttocks, lifting his scrotum, opening his mouth, blowing into his nostrils and his ears, peeling back his foreskin, lifting his arms and feeling through his hair. All the time the energetic red-capped face bobs in and out of his vision, the rattle clattering by his ear, the chant circling around, pausing for a second to bring something forth out of itself, cycling on and down and on. The hands cover him from head to toe in mud, which dries, caking him like a new kaolin skin. The hard clay rim of a bowl grates against his teeth; his head is held upright and he is made to drink a bitter liquid, which runs down his chin.

He sinks back against the ground.

Then he rises up towards the ceiling, while his body rolls in the dust, arching its spine, gnashing its uninhabited teeth in unfelt pain, because his spirit is racing out of the uterine darkness of this cave, out of its mouth in the Lizard's Back escarpment, and over the land, far away, the scrub shooting beneath it like stars. Then, as suddenly as it started, this flight is arrested, and he hovers for a second over the expedition camp, looking down at a row of sullen faces staring into the fire, faces which shudder and blur as he is thrown into reverse, sucked back down through the top of his head into his body, now caked in hard mud, a clay mould inside which all is molten, formless and in flux.

He lies there for many hours or days, while torches burn out and are replaced, and the patterns of hand prints move along preordained trajectories, like constellations in a planetarium. Sometimes young novices come to feed him, spooning porridge into his mouth and dosing him with the bitter-tasting medicine. He looks at the dome of hands and feels the rock breathe in and out, and hears the old man chanting, and finds that he can turn his head, and that his hands respond to him. He feels the floor on which he lies, the crunch of it, and with his new searching fingers picks up a white sliver, holding it up to his new eyes to recognize a piece of bone. The strangeness of it; being able to fly, and being encased in clay, and lying on a carpet of bone in the body of a great living rock.

People come and go, but the old man is always there, rattling his rattle, chanting his chant, maintaining a single continuous ritual before a niche in the rock. In the niche is an altar, crammed with objects of all kinds. Gourds hold the sticky remains of libations. There are beaten copper blades, bunches of herbs, a dog's skull wrapped in dried grass. The niche is spattered with chalk and blood and millet beer, which makes it hard at first to see the other things: the penknife, the hand mirror, the empty tins of beans, and the two dolls which he has not thought about since the day he bought them in the port, the little colonists with their long noses and bulbous hats – all stolen from the camp and brought here to the caves of the dead.

Young men come and kneel before the old man, giving and receiving messages or blessings. Jonathan watches and grows to believe that he is in a secret command centre, that the altar is a campaign map of a disputed territory, its motley collection of objects a magic triangulation of Fotseland, of his body, of the caves. The old man realizes he is awake, and casually puts the ritual aside, as if it were some ordinary task he was performing, mending a tool or preparing food. Together they start to communicate, and though it is fragmentary, and there are long pauses and many difficulties of understanding, the old man slowly gives him to understand that all the dead are present at their conversation, and will hear whatever is said.

He sits up and drinks some water, and together they pause and silently listen to the breathing of the rock. Then the old man tells him about the ancestors, and how they no longer come out to ride the women in the ceremony, and how time has fractured into before and now and it is all the fault of sorcerers. He tells him how beautiful the world would be if there were no sorcery in it to disrupt the lives of peaceful people, and how men have imagined this beauty, and incorporated themselves, men from all clans and lineages, across all the age sets and the secret societies, into a new society, the most secret of all, named for the tough flat-bladed grass the Fotse call needle grass. The part of needle grass that is underground has no beginning and no end, a mat of fibres which lies hidden under the earth, but which can shoot forth points sharp enough to cut you if you are so stupid as to walk through a stand of it. Thus it is with the needle-grass society, which has no head, no centre, which runs under the earth of Fotseland, and when the time is right will shoot up and destroy sorcery for ever.

The old man tells him all this, and he drifts in and out of sleep, cold waves of fever stealing him away and bringing him back again. Little by little the old man makes him understand that everything about sorcerers is upside down, that for them good is bad and right is wrong, and that the time for the destruction of sorcery is now and the sorcerers the Fotse are preparing to act against are camped down in the valley. Before the morning, all the white men will be dead.

The old man tells him another thing. Sorcerers have marks on their bodies, which unfailingly reveal their evil nature. He has examined his body for those marks, and found none. Even though he looks like a sorcerer, with his upside-down skin, and his gun that shoots hard witch substance into people from a distance, appearances can be deceptive. It sometimes happens that a person is foolish about his travelling companions, and does not take the right magical care, or falls asleep in a dangerous place. Then spirits can crawl inside their empty bodies and take them over.

Gently, the old man lets him know the worst: that he has been possessed by a European spirit. Soon the needle grass will rise up through the earth and kill the other white men and grind their bones to dust, but the old man does not think death will be necessary in his case. Instead (though it will be painful) he can draw the spirit out.

He becomes very afraid, and begs the old man not to do it. Please, he says, I am not evil. I am not a sorcerer. If you draw out this spirit, there will be nothing left. The old man pats his shoulder reassuringly and hands him a gourd containing a thick, bitter drink.

As soon as he takes a mouthful of the liquid his guts go into spasm and he vomits it back on to the floor. The old man makes him drink again. Again he vomits. The process is repeated until after some time he notices that his spittle-slicked hands seem very far away. The distance increases rapidly, as if he is being stretched up towards the ceiling. After that there is some confusion. Though he remains in the cave, lying down in the centre of the white chalk figure the old man has drawn on the floor, he also travels up, out of the mouth of the cave, and down the hill towards the white men's camp. The land skims beneath him as he rushes over it, white as bone in the moonlight.

On ground covered with ashes, they sit and watch him with their lifeless eyes. They spoon food into their large mouths, scratching themselves with yellow fingernails.

Behind the Professor is a huge pile of crates, a lifeless ark which over the last few weeks he and Gittens have carefully and meticulously filled. They have taken one of everything in Fotseland: water pots, hoes, oracle dice, Fo necklaces . . . They have made photographs of what they cannot take, and packed the plates alongside the artefacts, the light imprisoned in them a final record of a place they have already consigned to history, to the dead.

He hovers overhead, watching. He sees the crawling warriors, rows of undulating black backs converging on the orange point of the fire. He sees the eating white men. Everything about them is upside down.

*

The old man shakes his rattle and chants his chant, and novices hold the patient's arms and legs, anointing his face and shoulders with ashes. The novices heat metal brands in a brazier, because this has to do with skin, and the way it can deceive, unless space and time are fixed in it so its owner will never lose his way. It cannot be done without drums, because spirits communicate through patterns of sound, and so the drums thud and whoop, arcing over each other, filling in those patterns, threading and doubling as a mask is passed over the patient's head to coax the spirit out. One by one the brands are placed on his body: at the small of his back, at the nape of his neck, his thighs, shoulders and chest, orientating him, linking him irrevocably to the time and the place these marks are being made, so that wherever he may drift or fall asleep, he will always be in relation to this instant.

At the touch of the brand he screams, and once again finds himself rushing over the land, which has become a land of horrors. He passes over a place where a wooden frame has been set up, on which the bodies of the porters, Idris, Ali and Danjuma, have been flayed, their stomachs opened and their intestines rolled out on sticks in search of witch-substance. He is sucked down into the valley, where hundreds of figures are now creeping through the darkness, needles rising up through the earth, making their way to the margin of the sorcerers' firelight.

He can feel the spirit begin to loosen its grip. Florid and rapacious, it tugs at his organs, destroying the integrity of his body and sending pieces of it flying in all directions, gobbets of flesh that stream away in bloody rivers. As he is pulled apart, the world is pulled apart with him and he screams again, because without anything to screen it reality is unbearable and he is an abyss, and the thing he thought was himself is plucked out and flung away, leaving only a nightmare, a monstrous disorder.

The warriors rush into the circle of firelight, the white men's bullets turning to water against their magical armour. Their arms rise and fall, chopping and twisting. Blades grate against bone, snapping sinew and spilling guts through khaki shirts on to baggy-shorted laps. Gregg's grinning head lies on its side in the ashes. The Professor feels the thing that reminds him of no other thing as his split skull flowers brains and his face is beaten to an unrecognizable pulp. Gittens begs, Morgan looks quizzical and Marchant swears as they are eviscerated. By the time the sun comes up there is silence in the valley, and in the caves of the dead.

Week by week the Fotse become accustomed to a world without sorcery. People go back to their ordinary ways: the farmers to their fields, the smiths to their forges, the Daou to mediating between his warring wives and the griot to work on a song-cycle telling of the victory of good over evil.

The rains come and the desert blooms with beautiful and short-lived flowers. The Fotse speculate on the duration of the blooming, and about the size of the next season's millet crop. The rains end and the harmattan blows over the land. Fotse men grit their teeth against the dust and Fotse women's backs ache from stooping to sweep it out of their huts. Below the Daou's compound, the sorcerers' camp is a memory, just a hearth-smudge on the ground. Most of the white men's possessions have been burned, but a few things live on: a bleached skull added to the altar in the caves, a tarnished theodolite incorporated into a farmstead shrine.

Though the European spirits have been banished to the outer lands and once again the ancestors come out to ride the women in the dance, it seems that the wound in time has not healed, and there are still the old times and the new. Wise men point out that the sky over the Lizard's Back is still flecked white with clouds and wild dogs still call out to one another in the night. Such things are evidence of continuity. Yet change seems to have pervaded everything, even dogs and clouds. Perhaps time is something which, once broken, cannot be put back together again.

Down in the valley a grid of roads creeps closer, spawning

villages of roofless concrete houses which as yet have no inhabitants.

12 Jan. **Colonial Office to HM Government Oil Coast**
101. Please advise whereabouts Chapel Fotseland expedition.

14 Jan. **HM Government Oil Coast to Colonial Office**
214. Your 101 not understood. Chapel expedition in Fotseland since June last.

16 Jan. **Colonial Offce to HM Government Oil Coast**
105. Your 214. Expedition expected London. Now overdue. Please relay news urgently.

4 Feb. **HM Government Oil Coast to Colonial Office**
245. Your 105. No news Chapel expedition.

5 Feb. **Colonial Office to HM Government Oil Coast**
114. Your 245. Essential find whereabouts of Chapel expedition. Concern at highest level.

1 Mar. **HM Government Oil Coast to Colonial Office**
287. Your 114. Regret to inform Chapel expedition believed murdered Fotseland. Police action in preparation. Please advise other arrangements.

A broken pocketwatch is carefully wrapped in tissue paper and dispatched to Miss A. Chapel, c/o British Embassy, Paris, its arrival disrupting the announcement of her engagement to the new Nawab of Fatehpur, whom she met at a yacht party in Nice. A steamer packed with infantry chugs upriver, its human cargo dozing and listlessly gambling their pay away, until they are disgorged on to the jetty of the township now known as Short's Landing. The place is bustling, filled with new arrivals from the countryside, drawn by bright lights and government pay. On a corner a barber shaves customers, and drunks sit on the steps of a new wooden courthouse.

A line of telegraph poles follows the course of the main road, which stretches away out of town to the north. By its side, a resting road gang watches artillery being moved along it, mules straining at their harnesses, the wheels of the limbers throwing up a cloud of red dust.

His camel casts a jaundiced eye on him, and as he walks beside it he is careful to keep out of the way of its legs. Together they trudge up the gentle windward slopes of the dunes, sliding down each leeward face in an ankle-deep cascade of sand.

Ahead of him plods a long line of camels, each tied to the one in front. Their haunches roll from side to side, the movement obscenely exaggerated by the bundles of trade goods tied to their backs. Their drovers tug on their halters and urge them on with songs and snatches of banter.

Every so often, as he adjusts the hood of his burnous to shield his eyes from the sun, he slips his hand inside it and runs his fingers over the braille of scar tissue on his neck. For now the journey is everything. He has no thoughts of arriving anywhere. Tonight he will sleep under the enormous bowl of the sky. Tomorrow he will travel on.

Acknowledgements

Thanks to my parents Ravi and Hilary Kunzru, Simon Prosser and all at Hamish Hamilton, Jonny Geller, Hannah Griffiths, Carol Jackson and all at Curtis Brown, James Flint, Zadie Smith, Jess Cleverly, Sneha Solanki, the Borg (www.metamute.com), Rosemary Goad, Jon Bradshaw, Penny Warburton, Elaine Pyke, Gaston and François, the staff of the Oriental and India Office collection of the British Library, Google, and everyone else who supplied facts, opinions, money and love during the writing of this novel.

refresh yourself at penguin.co.uk

Visit penguin.co.uk for exclusive information and interviews with
bestselling authors, fantastic give-aways and the
inside track on all our books, from the Penguin Classics
to the latest bestsellers.

BE FIRST

first chapters, first editions, first novels

EXCLUSIVES

author chats, video interviews, biographies, special
features

EVERYONE'S A WINNER

give-aways, competitions, quizzes, ecards

READERS GROUPS

exciting features to support existing groups and
create new ones

NEWS

author events, bestsellers, awards, what's new

EBOOKS

books that click – download an ePenguin today

BROWSE AND BUY

thousands of books to investigate – search, try
and buy the perfect gift online – or treat yourself!

ABOUT US

job vacancies, advice for writers and company
history

Get Closer To Penguin . . . www.penguin.co.uk